# TRIO

# Phyllis Bentley

# TRIO

CEDRIC CHIVERS LTD
PORTWAY
BATH

First Published 1930
By
Victor Gollancz Ltd
This Edition Published
By
Cedric Chivers Ltd
By Arrangement with the Copyright Holder
At the request of the
London & Home Counties Branch of the
Library Association
1970

Reproduced and Printed by
Redwood Press Limited, Trowbridge & London
Bound by Cedric Chivers Ltd, Bath

# CONTENTS

# CHAPTER I

## LENA

The three children were all awake, and lay waiting for the
school dressing-bell to relieve them from their enforced
silence. From their little iron bedsteads, beneath their warm
striped rugs, they all gazed across the room at the painted
washstand on which stood two white ewers and basins.
That there were two instead of three was a source of sardonic amusement to Esmé, of indifference to Rachel, and
of misery to Lena. For when the accident to Rachel's
brother, necessitating her absence from home, had caused
a bed to be placed for her between the beds of Esmé and
Lena at the Hudley Girls' College, Esmé had suggested
that the three should race for first turn at the jugs in the
morning. The tall, quiet Rachel had silently agreed without showing much interest, but anguish had torn afresh
Lena's already lacerated heart—it was another of Esmé's
ways of tormenting her, she felt sure. In spite of herself her
full lips drooped, her throat contracted, her eyes filled
with tears and blurred her glasses, and in a voice which
took a quivering, wailing note she exclaimed :

" You'll always beat me, both on you ! I know you
will."

" ' Both *on* you ! ' " repeated Esmé with a sarcastic titter.
" ' Both *on* you ! ' Is that how they talk at Bierley Hall ? "

" Well, if they do," panted Lena, striving vainly to repress a heavy sob, " You needn't always be mocking me."

Esmé turned to Rachel. " Lena can't talk proper English,"
she explained in her high shallow little tones. " Her mother
was only Mr. Howgate's housekeeper."

Lena, crimsoning, started furiously forward. " Don't

you call my mother ! " she cried loudly, thrusting her dark stormy face into Esmê's small smooth fair one.

" If you shout like that Miss Fielding will hear you," Esmé rebuked her contemptuously ; and this was so true that Lena perforce drew back and dropped her voice.

" I wish I was at bottom of t'cut," she muttered despairingly. " It's best place for me."

" She means canal," said Esmé. . . .

Since then the race for the jugs had always gone as Lena had predicted, and every morning the wretched child, waking with a start to a world where everything had gone wrong the day before, lay quivering and panting in an agony of suspense, her knees drawn up, one hand on the bedclothes, ready to hurl herself to the floor as soon as the bell should sound to action. Her very anxiety, however, made her fearful, nervous, clumsy ; she tripped and stumbled by the bed and staggered across the floor ; and if by chance she reached the stand before the others, Esmé's small neat hand always clutched the ewer first—which in Esmé's jurisdiction constituted a victory. Of course it was foolish to mind so much about being the last to wash and dress, as Lena often told herself ; Miss Fielding was never really angry when she was later than the others. But the sense of defeat, of inferiority, stung the thin-skinned Lena like a lash—and besides, her life lately had been such that the mildest remonstrance now made her shrink and quiver like a blow.

When Alfred Howgate, manufacturer, of Bierley Bottom Mills and Bierley Hall—Bierley was a suburb perched on the extreme edge of one of Hudley's surrounding hills—suddenly, during a severe illness following a fall from his horse, married his housekeeper and took steps to adopt her child, there were not wanting plenty of people to say that the child was his own, and he was doing the woman belated justice. Others on the contrary said that he had found it so intensely dreary being ill alone in that great windy house, and the woman in question had been so extremely kind to

him, that it was all perfectly natural if rather to be deplored.
These partisans quoted the Howgate family history to show
how the desperately unhappy married life of Alfred's late
father and mother had put him against the idea of any
ordinary match ; whereupon their opponents retorted that
that argument was on their side. Whatever the truth of
that matter was, when the new Mrs. Howgate died within
six months of her marriage the event was an amusement to
the neighbourhood, a nuisance to Howgate, and an appalling disaster to Lena. The late Mrs. Howgate had been a
buxom, powerful woman, with a rich complexion and
masses of tangled brown hair. Her dress was usually rather
slatternly, her hair frowsy, her general habits careless and
ill-regulated ; but she was a big-hearted woman, with a
tremendous laugh and a tolerant, cynical view of life. She
was also a superb cook. She loved Lena heartily, but thought
her rather a prodigy and did not pretend to understand
her ; she fed her well though without table-manners, saw
that she had warm if untidy clothes, admired her prowess
at the Bierley Green Elementary School, and for the rest
left her alone. In this warm rich carefree atmosphere Lena
grew and thrived, and when Mrs. Howgate died the world
seemed incredibly bleak and cold. Not that her stepfather
was unkind to her—far from it ; he stood firmly by his decision to adopt her, completed the papers, altered his will
suitably, told her that she would be a rich girl some day
and must make herself equal to her position, and having
consulted his father's friend John Deller—Bierley Bottom
Mills had sent cloth to John Deller to be dyed for many a
long year—placed her at the Hudley Girls' College as a
first step towards her doing so. John Deller's grand-daughter
Esmé was at the College, which took a few weekly boarders ;
some other boarders had left, there was a vacancy for Lena,
the two girls were just of an age ; Esmé could keep an eye
on Lena and help her to improve.

Thus John Deller. Lena, overjoyed at the thought of
having a friend of her own age to live with, at their first

meeting blithely and joyfully told Esmé all about herself
and her mother and the Bierley Hall cook and groom and
housemaid and Mr. Howgate and the garden and the
Bierley Green school ; Esmé at first seemed to listen with
interest ; then, presumably acting on her grandfather's
instructions, she began rather peevishly to correct Lena's
manners and grammar. Lena, at first meek and grateful,
presently began to wince, tried to do as she was told but
found it hard and stumbled, was corrected again with in-
creased severity, remembered that she was motherless and
wept. Then Esmé, speaking in a tone of great irritation,
told her she was silly, and taunted her in the presence of
other girls with the silliness of various particulars which
Lena had confided to her. They sounded silly as Esmé said
them, Lena admitted it despairingly ; she sobbed out a pro-
test, however, against this betrayal of her confidence, wailing " I'll never tell nobody anything again, never ! " But
alas ! her grammar was wrong again, and when she wept
over this at tea Esmé told her it was vulgar to sniff so much :
it was as bad as snoring. Lena, crimsoning, prayed that she
did not snore, but she felt guiltily afraid, from the look in
Esmé's eye, that she did ; and she decided to stay awake
every night until Esmé was asleep, just in case. Then Esmé
objected to Lena's vehement way of turning over in bed ;
it shook the floor and kept her awake, she said. Under this
constant icy douche of criticism the sensitive Lena was
gradually shuddering herself into a mere mass of suffering
nerves. What further maddened the tormented child was
that she felt she knew much better than Esmé, really, what
good grammar was. Had she not devoured shelf after shelf
of the books which stood, musty and damp, round the unused library of Bierley Hall ? Whereas Esmé had not read
one of them ; no, not one. But somehow when Lena spoke
in Esmé's presence it all came out wrong—her voice took
on a Yorkshire accent, and her sentences fell into Yorkshire constructions and included Yorkshire words. Esmé,
however, reflected Lena sadly, hardly knew what a

construction was; her essays were very poor, she always got
even the simplest sums wrong, and never remembered any
fact in history. (At French she *was* rather good; but then
that was because she had been abroad.) But for lessons and
all that kind of thing—and it was this which so terribly dis-
heartened Lena—Esmé did not care a button. Esmé definitely and decidedly considered herself Lena's superior,
and no amount of mental prowess on Lena's part would
ever cause her to change that view. The world seemed
bleaker than ever to the child as this chill fact struck home.
Could it be that Esmé was right about this, and looks were
the only thing people ever admired? Surely, surely that
could not be, thought Lena in an agony of doubt. It seemed
very unfair if it were so; for if Esmé would only admire
Lena the tiniest bit for being clever, Lena was ready—oh,
so ready!—to admire Esmé whole-heartedly for her looks.
Esmé was certainly far Lena's superior in looks, Lena admitted that ungrudgingly. That small neat figure and
small fair face, the fair silken hair, the blue eyes, the pretty
mouth, the straight small nose and regular eyebrows, the
perfect rose-and-milk complexion and the exquisite neatness and freshness which always characterised Esmé's person were certainly far superior to Lena's strong sturdy body,
her sombre brown eyes and rough black hair, the deep
colour of her cheeks, her uneven face marred by old-
fashioned steel spectacles, her pouting crimson lips and
clumsy hands and feet. It had been an intense relief to
Lena to discover when Rachel came that though she was
fair her eyes were not blue but grey. They were beautiful
eyes, clear and fine, with a black iris; and their being grey
established the right of eyes to be other colours besides blue
and yet be beautiful. Rachel was beautiful altogether,
thought Lena warmly, beautiful as a tall golden flower
drooping on a slender stem; her oval face was kindly and
serene and somehow warm; she coloured easily, and her
hair was curly and of a deeper tone than Esmé's; she spoke
seldom, and then in a quiet shy tone. Altogether Lena was

prepared to love Rachel on the smallest hint that her love
would be acceptable ; whereas she hated and feared Esmé
from the bottom of her heart. She stole a furtive glance over
her shoulder now to the farthest bed, but turned her face
hastily back to the wall when she found Esmé's blue eyes
fixed coldly, balefully as the child felt, upon her. Esmé's bed
was the nearest to the window, which was very unfortunate ;
for from the window you could see over the tops of houses,
across the valley to the great gaunt brown bulk of Awe
Hill ; by craning your neck indeed you could just catch a
glimpse of that far corner where it began to turn green,
where Bierley Hall clung to its brow. Perhaps the greatest
fear in Lena's life just now was that Esmé would discover
this ; the very thought of Esmé pointing at her home made
her feel literally sick. Rather than allow Esmé to discover
the situation of Bierley, Lena avoided the window altogether, and kept her eyes turned steadily in another direction.

The bell rang, the three children threw back their cover-
ings and made a hasty scramble for the stand. Lena as usual
was the last, staggering on the slippery mat and jogging
Esmé's elbow.

" You are *clumsy*, Lena," Esmé rebuked her impatiently,
shrugging away from her touch.

At this the dreamy Rachel seemed suddenly to awake.
" Lena," she said. She paused, hesitated, then continued
surprisingly : " You can have my basin if you like."

She put down her sponge and drew back from the stand.
" Oh, no ! " protested Lena, colouring. " Oh, no ! "
She longed passionately, with her whole heart, to accept
Rachel's offer ; but at the same time her pride was wounded
to the core by it. She stepped back. "No," she said finally,
" I won't do that, Rachel." Remembering her new manners,
she added : " Thank you all the same."

With her chin in the air, she moved away to her bed and
sat down. Rachel, after a moment's hesitation, began to
wash. Lena's rejection of her offer had, by asserting her

pride, done the child good ; and she swung her feet in a
bold, determined manner, feeling that all that was needed
in the world after all was a little courage, and everything
went well. But as the minutes passed by, a nervous impatience grew upon her ; she would be late, she would be
late ! Pantingly she visualised all the processes she must go
through before she would be dressed, and planned quick
ways of doing them. She arranged her clothes in order
along the bed, and put her glasses in a prominent position
in the centre of her pillow. Then there was her hair, which
was thick and long and terribly tangled, far more difficult
to deal with than that of either of the other two girls. At
home her mother or one of the maids always combed out
her hair ; there was a general admission that to deal with
it was beyond her powers. Her mother ! Well, best not
think of that. She choked it down. How long Rachel and
Esmé were in finishing ! Almost she exclaimed upon them,
but bit the exclamation back ; for Rachel was by nature
slow and dreamy, and Esmé, she knew, was capable of pro-
tracting the process to annoy her. At last, however, they
had done, and Lena rushed forward eagerly to take her
turn. But now that one anxiety was past another took its
place. She disliked intensely washing with the eyes of spec-
tators fixed upon her shrinking flesh, especially since the
day when Esmé—it was before Rachel came—had explained to her in detail all the functions of a woman's body,
and pointed out the coarseness and generally defective
nature of Lena's body as compared with her own. Certainly
Esmé's body was neat and fine and white, but the sight of it
exposed for Lena's admiration awoke in the child only an
intense disgust for the things of the flesh, since that was the
kind of thing liked by the detested Esmé. Her back was
turned to the two girls now, but she felt as certain that
Esmé was watching and criticising her every movement as
that Rachel's thoughts were not in the room at all. Thankfully she turned at last to her clothes, only to find that her
spectacles were not where she had left them. She groped

carefully about the bed for them, then growing frightened, turned the pillows and the bedclothes upside down, in vain.

" I can't find my glasses," she burst forth wailingly at length. Almost all her clothes had been hidden by Esmé on one morning or another, but she could never see the humour of the jest, and this time she was really frightened, for her glasses were her eyes.

" You're always losing something, Lena," Esmé rebuked her primly. " I can't think what you do with your things."

" *You*'ve taken them ! " challenged Lena, turning on her fiercely.

" I wouldn't *touch* any of your things, I assure you," said Esmé, her nose in the air.

Lena, perplexed by this direct denial, continued her search, but still in vain. " Did she take them, Rachel ? " she appealed at last despairingly.

Rachel, startled from a dream, stammered vaguely : " I don't know." She paused. " If she did," she continued more firmly, " I think it was very mean of her."

At this a delicate colour stole into Esmé's clear cheeks. " Take your old glasses ! " she exclaimed angrily. She snatched them from beneath her own pillow and threw them down on Lena's bed. " I only took them for a joke." Neither of the others saying anything to this, she repeated : " I only took them for a joke, Rachel."

" A funny kind of joke," murmured Rachel, and forthwith relapsed into her usual preoccupation.

The result of all this was naturally that when young Miss Smith came to see if the children were ready, Lena was still struggling into the complicated black which the kindly maids at Bierley Hall had decreed as being the proper mourning for Mrs. Howgate. " Late again, Lena ? " said the mistress in a tone of brisk reproof, shepherding the other two from the room.

Lena gave a heavy gasp of distress, and Rachel stood still abruptly. Raising her head, she began to speak. She paused, stammered, paused again, and finally managed to observe in her quiet shy voice : " I don't think it was Lena's fault, Miss Smith."

An intense and overwhelming gratitude flooded Lena's whole personality. That someone should stand up for her, speak kindly of her, not dislike her—it was music to her soul, balm to her lacerated heart. As she watched Rachel's golden head bobbing down the stairs before her, she loved Rachel passionately, adored her, worshipped her ; and she began at once to imagine all kinds of dangers from which she would rescue Rachel—yes, she herself, Lena Holman or Howgate or whatever her name was since it was changed. Esmé might think her a coward, a silly, a cry-baby, but she, Lena, knew that she was capable of heroic deeds. And they should all be for Rachel, Rachel who was, Lena said to herself, compact of strength and sweetness.

All through the morning she longed to tell Rachel how grateful she was and how much she loved her, but there was breakfast and practising, and then school and dinner, and there was no opportunity until the trio were putting on their shoes for their customary Wednesday afternoon walk. Watching her chance when Esmé was busy with a buttonhook, Lena slipped round the other side of the bed-room boot-stack and whispered in Rachel's ear : " Will you walk with me to-day ? "

" I'm sorry, I can't," said the stooping Rachel, " I've promised Esmé."

" But you will some time, won't you ? " persisted Lena. " Do, Rachel, do ! " Rachel nodded. " To-morrow ? " pursued Lena eagerly. Rachel nodded again. " I like you so much, Rachel," went on Lena overjoyed. " Will you be my friend, Rachel ? Do ! Do ! Will you ? "

Rachel, raising her eyes from her shoes, shook back her hair and looked at her with a pitying disfavour.

" Will you ? " pleaded Lena, fixing her dark fiery eyes hungrily upon her. " Will you ? "

" Yes—I will ; I *am* friends with you," said Rachel jerkily. " I wish you didn't cry so much, that's all."

" I won't—I won't ! " whispered Lena in an ecstasy. " I won't really, Rachel, if you'll be friends with me and not mock me."

" That's all right then," agreed Rachel vaguely, more than half lost again in her own thoughts.

So this was now a happy day for Lena. Under the rays of Rachel's promised friendship she expanded like a flower. She laughed and joked all afternoon, although she had to walk behind with Miss Smith while Esmé walked in front with Rachel ; and felt scarcely at all cast down when Esmé said snubbingly : " I'm tired of hearing your voice to-day, Lena." On Miss Fielding's direction the little party called at Rachel's home in Cambridge Place to enquire after Rachel's brother ; the reports were good, and Rachel's spirits seemed considerably raised. That night as the three were undressing, Miss Fielding came and beckoned Esmé away ; it was Esmé's birthday on the morrow, and there was some question of the secret arrival of a superlative cake. As soon as she had left the room Lena, her heart beating fast, hurried towards the window. (It was one of Esmé's complaints about Lena, of which the child admitted the truth, that she could not walk decently, but always rushed at everything full speed ahead, with her head down like a bull.) She drew aside the curtain. Any sudden view of the interlocking hills and valleys of the West Riding, with the mill chimneys springing up straight and tall and slender towards the grey northern sky, always struck Lena's heart into a sudden deep harmony ; at such times she smiled, and felt that for once she knew why she was born. But at night, when all the gaunt brown patches and the raw new houses and the messy canal docks sank into darkness, at night when the scene became one of diamonds and black velvet, at night when jewelled patterns in curves and lovely straight lines swung up and down, showing the roads and the lanes and the little houses and the big mills and all the brave aspiring human things against the dark background of the powerful, fierce, passionate, unsleeping hills : then

Lena fell into an eager tremulous panting, and hardly knew whether to laugh or cry, or both : it was so beautiful, so beautiful, so *kind* and beautiful !

" Rachel ! " she breathed.

Rachel, who had been much less dreamy since her visit to her home that afternoon, looked up enquiringly, then came to Lena's side. A red glow in the sky to Lena's left betokened the town of Hudley ; directly opposite the window Awe Hill, now softly black, reared its great head against the dark cloudy sky. A long line of bright yellow lights sloping gently down it to the left showed the tram route which led from Bierley Green down into Hudley ; a few yellow points scattered about the black mass came from some Bierley farms ; away to the right a zigzag of sparse, dim, reddish and somehow adventurous gleams showed Bierley Lane, winding abruptly upwards through open fields from Bierley Bottom Mills in the valley to Bierley Edge on the brow. Just where the zigzag cut the sky-line there was a faint yellow blur, which Lena knew of old—and loved to know—as the lights of Bierley Hall.

" Look, Rachel ! " she whispered, clutching Rachel's arm and pointing. " That's where I live."

Rachel, in silence, craned her neck and looked at the blur.

" But you won't tell Esmé ? " cried Lena, stricken with a sudden fear. " She's always mocking me. You won't tell her, will you ? "

" No," said Rachel. She seemed to hesitate, then said quietly : " Rowland once took me up there."

" Did he ? " breathed Lena. She was timid, almost awe-struck, before the joy of this intimate confidence, the first she had ever received from someone of her own age. " That's your brother, isn't it ? " she went on, to show that she had understood.

Rachel nodded. Lena's happiness was complete ; for a perfect moment it was full and round and glowing like a coloured ball. Then Esmé's voice sounded on the threshold,

B†

and the moment, jarred, shivered into a thousand spiky fragments.

" What are you two looking at ? " demanded Esmé sharply.

Lena flung aside the curtain in a panic, rushed vehemently to the dressing-table and took up a comb at random. Rachel followed and silently pulled open a drawer. Esmé looked keenly at them, her slight breast ruffled, her small face cold and angry.

" That's my comb, Lena ; put it down," she said irritably. Lena complied. " What were you looking at ? " repeated Esmé. As neither of the girls replied she went on contemptuously : " It's no use asking *you*, Lena ; you always tell lies."

" I don't ! " cried Lena furiously.

Esmé with a swift movement reached the window and drew the curtain aside. " Rachel, what were you looking at ? " she persisted.

There was a hideous pause. Rachel coloured to the eyes ; Lena felt her knees give beneath her, her heart was like water, her throat dry. In spite of herself she gave a panting sob, and a smile of triumph began to curve Esmé's pretty lips. The next moment the honourable Rachel replied staunchly :

" We were looking at the lights."

As she spoke she raised her head and looked Esmé straight in the eyes, as though defying her to say more ; Esmé's fair lashes drooped on her perfect cheeks, she released the curtain and was silent.

Lena was struck dumb with an admiration so great as to be almost awe. The beauty of truth and steadfastness and loyalty, as just exemplified by Rachel, sobered and steadied her ; she undressed quietly, thinking of many things. The other two also seemed thoughtful, and the trio got into their beds without another word.

The next day seemed to open in an auspicious manner, in spite of the customary result of the morning jug race. It was Esmé's birthday ; she received many rich and handsome presents from her family, and was consequently in good humour. Lena, who was provided by Alfred Howgate with plenty of money and instructions to spend it freely, had at the previous week-end bought for Esmé, with some idea of propitiating her, a colossal box of chocolates, which she now presented. Esmé seemed surprised by the richness of the gift, and spoke to its donor more cordially than before. But the dreamy Rachel, who had not known that Esmé's birthday was imminent, had no present to give ; instead she offered good wishes and apologies and seemed to think nothing further need be done. Esmé was not pleased, and Lena, who since her sojourn at school had become susceptible to the slightest chill in the atmosphere, winced at her coldness and Rachel's unconscious calm. Then in their walk between breakfast and school Rachel walked with Lena, while Esmé, to her fury, had to be content with Miss Smith. Esmé made a scene, stormed, shed a few tears, and pleaded that it was her birthday ; Miss Smith seemed inclined to back her up—Esmé was always so polite, so *convenable* in the presence of her superiors—but Rachel, raising her head in the way that Lena loved, said that she had promised Lena. Nothing could be urged against the sanctity of a promise, and consequently Lena, skipping clumsily about for very joy, had the pleasure of walking beside Rachel round Hudley Moor. But even as she held Rachel's fingers in the prescribed manner and basked in her serene calm, she began to worry about Esmé, walking behind, at first with a cold sulky look on her small face which made Lena feel sorry for her, and then whispering confidentially in her companion's ear. Lena looked round more and more often, and strained her ears to catch what they were saying. Her walk was spoiled by fear, and she was not surprised to find when they reached home that her fears were justified, for Esmé and Miss Smith had decided that it was not nice of Lena to hold Rachel to her promise on Esmé's birthday. On receiving Lena's incoherent

expressions of sorrow Esmé seemed inclined to become tearful. " I didn't think *you* would be so mean to me," she said.
She fetched the box of chocolates from the bedroom and
thrust them into Lena's unwilling hands.

" I don't want it if you don't like me," she said with
tearful dignity. " I don't want a present from anybody who
doesn't like me."

Lena, horrified to find that her tyrant had human feelings which could be hurt, just like her own, tried to press
the chocolates upon her. " Do take them, Esmé," she
pleaded in her thick heavy tones. " Come on. I want you
to have them, Esmé ; I do."

" Well, put them on my bed upstairs," replied Esmé at
last with cold ungraciousness. " I'll decide about them
afterwards."

Lena went into school with a heavy heart.

The latter half of Thursday morning was occupied by a
singing lesson which the school took *en bloc* with a visiting
master. Old Mr. Deller was still, in the distance and when
he stood motionless, a fine figure of a man, with his great
height and his magnificent leonine head framed in crisp
tawny hair and beard ; but when he moved and drew near
it could be seen that his gait was wavering, his shoulders
bent, his complexion like parchment, his blue eyes faded
and sad. In his flowing morning coat he looked very impressive as he sat at the piano and struck a chord or two
before turning to his class, but the coat was almost green
from age and of an old-fashioned cut ; and when he spoke,
his voice, though still deep, was timid and husky. The girls
had long since discovered that he was a gentle and sensitive
soul, easily distressed, and sometimes they put this knowledge to an evil use. On the whole, however, they waited
to be led to this by Esmé, for as Mr. Deller's surname was
the same as hers, it was generally concluded that there was
a relationship between them. Indeed Esmé did not deny
this. " He's my great-uncle," she explained clearly whenever the subject was discussed. " But grandfather and he

quarrelled a long time ago, and he won't get any of grandfather's money." In spite of this contemptuous dismissal
Thomas Deller's name remained the same as Esmé's, and
it was felt to be wiser to treat him with respect except when
Esmé herself gave the signal for attack.

Lena and Esmé were in the same class, Lena occupying
the top and Esmé a position rather below the middle. Nobody quite knew where to put Rachel, who had hitherto
been taught at home by her mother, and consequently was
very good at some things and very backward in others. As
the girls rushed in and settled themselves on the benches,
Rachel hung back uncertainly and coloured ; Esmé, who
usually touched no one if she could help it, laid a hand on
her arm and indicated a place beside her. Rachel took it ;
and Lena, in the seat behind, was consumed with jealousy.
The singing lesson began. Mr. Deller seemed in a cheerful,
smiling humour this morning, and took them through their
scales and exercises briskly. But Lena's heart grew heavier
and heavier, for Rachel had no book and shared with Esmé,
and when Lena caught Esmé's eye and gave a pleading,
timid smile, Esmé stared at her coldly, with no recognition
in her eyes, and then slowly turned her head away. They
were now singing part-songs ; Lena was always a little
nervous in these, for she was not able to sustain a part when
somebody near to her was singing another tune, and her
strong resonant voice made these lapses noticeable. But
there was one song she liked very much ; it was called " Ave
Maria," and was full of appeals for protection, with a solemn
pathetic tune. In one of its statements Lena thought its
psychology incorrect, for it seemed to think the perils of
the night greater than those of the day, whereas she loved
the dark concealing night, when you could slip about un-
observed. But she liked the song in spite of this and hoped
that they would sing it next, for she felt it might comfort
her. She was preparing to shout its name if Mr. Deller asked,
as he so often did, which song the girls would like, when
suddenly Esmé turned round to her with a pleasant smiling

face and meaningly held up a song so that Lena could read
the name on its title page. Esmé never shouted out the
names of songs ; her voice was too small and her sense of
personal dignity too great ; and as the girls were supposed
to maintain silence in class she was, so Lena thought,
obviously indicating that she wanted Lena to shout the
name of this one for her. Lena, with a warm gush of joy
and relief in her heart at this sign of renewed friendliness,
nodded her head vehemently to show that she understood
the signal ; and almost before Mr. Deller had opened his
mild old lips to put the question, shouted " ' Merry June ! ' "

A slight titter went round the class, and a slight frown
creased Mr. Deller's fine old brow. He disliked this song
very much (which Lena had forgotten) ; because most of
it consisted in singing " Hey ho for merry June, hey, ho,
hey," and each hey and ho was allotted two notes, a high
and a low one, and the children could not jump cleanly
from one note to the other, but dragged through all
the intervening scale. Mr. Deller looked at Lena and
seemed to consider, then he arranged the song carefully
on the piano with his once powerful but now uncertain
fingers. After a moment's pause he reminded the children
of the hey-ho difficulty, and struck the opening chords.
Some of the girls sang the notes clearly and accurately,
others conscientiously tried to do so but could not manage
it, a few swooped and dragged on purpose. The result was
rather bad ; at the end of the verse there was a titter, and
a painful colour tinged Mr. Deller's sunken cheeks. Esmé,
turning round, gave Lena a sparkling, mischievous and
encouraging smile, such a smile as Lena had certainly never
had from Esmé before. The excited Lena, laughing happily
and showing her strong white teeth, thereupon threw all
her strength upon the dragging side ; the resultant dishar-
mony was fearful, and the titter became so pronounced as
to be definitely rude. The next verse was impudent, dis-
graceful. Mr. Deller's old hands trembled as he angrily
pushed away the song. " *Oh*, Mr. *Deller* ! " cried Lena at

this in an exaggerated tone of pleading. She was rewarded by another sparkling backward glance from Esmé. " *Oh, Mr. Deller* ! " chorused all the class.

" We shan't never learn it if we don't practise it," observed Lena in a loud sententious tone.

The old singing master shot a perplexed look at her from beneath his thick tawny eyebrows, hesitated, but laid the song down and chose another. Lena thereupon gave a loud sigh, and threw her copy of " Merry June " away from her. The class, enjoying itself, also sighed loudly and tossed their copies of " Merry June " in the air. The magic bonds of discipline, so firm when they are not questioned, so fragile when they are, were now broken ; and the rest of the lesson was a medley of flying sheets of music, wrong notes, laughs, whispers which swelled gradually to loud careless conversations, and rude repartee. Beads of sweat stood on the old singing master's forehead, and his blue eyes had the pathetic look of a hunted animal, as he thumped the piano and vainly tried to make himself heard above the noise. A sharp pang stabbed at Lena's heart from time to time at the sight of him, but she resolutely disregarded it. This was the right sort of thing to do, she thought, laughing and pushing her neighbour about, while the class laughed and admired her daring and wondered how far poor old Mr. Deller would let her go. This was the sort of thing other people did, thought Lena, laughing wildly ; and savoured an intense sweetness in being for once with the majority, with the tide. Who said she was different from these other girls and could not get on with them ? Rachel was her friend, and now Esmé was beginning to like her too. She looked at Rachel and Esmé to see if they were admiring her properly, noticed that they were sitting quiet and still, and was slightly sobered. But it was too late now to turn the singing lesson into anything but a fiasco ; and after a few more tumultuous moments the bell rang, and old Mr. Deller took himself away.

Rachel and Esmé disappeared too, into the house. Lena

was delayed for a while collecting the music, which was one of her prescribed tasks, but she followed them as soon as she could, eager to press the chocolates upon Esmé while she was in this friendly mood. She ran upstairs and entered the bedroom. The first thing she saw was the box of chocolates, lying upon her own bed ; the second was Rachel, standing in the middle of the room with downcast head, obviously in great distress. Esmé had one arm about her waist and was soothing her.

" Rachel ! " exclaimed Lena, bounding forward. " Rachel ! "

" Don't touch her," said Esmé coldly, fending off Lena with one hand.

" But what's the matter with her ? Rachel ! " said Lena anxiously. " What's she crying for ? "

" I'm not crying," said Rachel in a choked voice, turning away her head.

" It would be no wonder if she were," commented Esmé severely, " after the abominable way you behaved to her grandfather."

" Her grandfather ! " cried Lena, horrified. " What do you mean ? I haven't behaved abominably to him. I never saw him. You don't," she suddenly screamed, " mean Mr. Deller ? " She saw from Esmé's face that it was so, and the whole complicated scheme of Esmé's treachery burst upon her. She turned pale. " But you——" she cried. " But I——" It was very difficult to explain. " It was you. I never meant—I didn't know he was anything to do with Rachel," she wailed in anguish. " I thought he was your relation, Esmé, and you didn't mind us being bad to him."

Esmé put aside this last point as being rather an awkward one. " He's Rachel's grandfather," she asserted, " and my grandfather's brother. Unfortunately they quarrelled a long time ago."

Lena waited for the sentence about Mr. Deller never receiving any of Esmé's grandfather's money which always closed this explanation, but it was not forthcoming. Instead, Esmé added : " But that needn't prevent *us* being friends, my brother says. That's why I was glad when Rachel came here, and I could get to know her."

" Rachel," said Lena in a humble, quivering tone, " I didn't know. I wouldn't have hurt anyone belonging to you for anything if I'd known. I'd have cut off my hand sooner, I would that."

But Rachel, wounded in her deepest affections, would not answer, and kept her head averted as Esmé, her arm about her waist, led her gently from the room.

Lena, left alone, stood twisting her fingers in an agony of remorse—remorse that she had hurt that dear old Mr. Deller, whom she now saw as a darling, an old darling, a poor old dear. She had been rude to him, rude and hateful. His fine old face, perplexed and harassed, with quivering mouth and those tiny beads of sweat, rose abruptly before her and accused her of the grossest cruelty. And he was Rachel's grandfather ! The maddening part of it, the part that made her want to scream, was that she had not really wanted to be rude to Mr. Deller ; it was Esmé, Esmé who had egged her on. To please Esmé, whom she hated, she had done something vile which had hurt Rachel, whom she loved ; and to crown all, her vile act had thrown Rachel into Esmé's arms. In a fury of despair at the workings of this wicked world and her own foolishness, she suddenly flung herself beneath her bed, and there in its sheltering darkness, amid the dust and fluff, sobbed out her anguished heart.

She was roused by the sound of a step on the stairs. Pride drew her from her hiding-place, and seated her, with chattering teeth and quivering knees, but without tears, on the edge of her bed just as Miss Fielding opened the door.

" What do you mean by behaving in this silly way, Lena ? " said the headmistress sternly. " Come down at once and eat your dinner with the rest."

" I don't want any dinner," invented Lena. She went

on glibly, speaking the truth though intending a lie : " I feel sick."

Miss Fielding's eyes wandered not unnaturally to the huge chocolate box which lay behind Lena on the bed. Lena, following the direction of her glance, in spite of her misery could not help being amused. She shook her head in vigorous denial, but the headmistress looked unconvinced. " Well, lie down for a while," she exhorted the child at last not unkindly. " I'll bring you some medicine after dinner."

Lena managed to ejaculate " Thank you," and Miss Fielding went downstairs.

As soon as she had gone Lena stood up with an air of decision. She felt quite calm and collected now, for she had decided what to do. All hope of happiness for her here was ruined ; she was hopelessly entangled in the web of Esmé's superior cunning, and would never be able to unravel and explain it all to Rachel ; the only thing to do was to break loose and run away. She put on her outdoor shoes and picked up her school hat, which she could hide behind her till she got outside ; it was a bitterly cold day of early spring, but she dared not risk taking a coat, for fear somebody should meet her in the house and wonder. She then took up her hairbrush and stuffed it down the front of her dress ; this was to make her escape thoroughly respectable and high-class, so that Esmé could not sneer at it, as she had sneered last night at Lena's carelessness over other people's combs. The child longed to do something very dramatic and piercing with the chocolates, but could not think of anything satisfying ; she was revolted at the thought of offering something bought for Esmé to Rachel, and yet hated to leave them to Esmé as though she loved her. " Still," she thought, " I gave them to Esmé. They're really hers." She placed them scrupulously in the middle of Esmé's bed, and crept downstairs.

The moments during which she passed the dining-room, opened and closed the front door, and tiptoed up the drive, were too intense for her to know anything of them ; but when she had closed the gate behind her and was running down the road, she regained consciousness. A few belated boys and masters walking homeward from the Hudley Grammar School, just down the road, were coming towards her ; they looked at her curiously, she thought, but she did not care. She did not know any of them, and they would be out of the way long before dinner was over and her absence was discovered. A tram passed the bottom of the road going towards Hudley, and stopped just round the corner. Should she take it, and go into Hudley, and take a Bierley tram from there, or walk in the opposite direction and climb Bierley Lane ? " I must be *sensible*," she told herself feverishly. Even as she hesitated, the Hudley tram moved on ; in some curious way this decided her to take the Hudley route, and she flew after the tram. It did not stop, and she ran, panting and gasping, the whole way into the town. As she ran she wondered why she felt as though she had done all this before, and decided that it was because she had dreamed so often lately of escaping.

When she at last reached the starting-point of the Bierley trams, one was blessedly standing there ; she climbed in thankfully and sat down, her exhausted legs twitching, her face crimson, her hat clinging anyhow to her roughened hair. It was evidently some time before the tram was due to start, for it was empty save for the driver and conductor, who sat at the far end, on the same side as Lena, exchanging jokes. The time of waiting seemed an eternity, and Lena kept peering anxiously out, in dread of being followed. At length her sudden starts attracted the attention of the conductor, who looked round and at once recognised her. Lena too knew him well, for he was the brother of the Bierley Hall cook.

" Hullo, Lena ! " he greeted her familiarly.

" Hullo," returned Lena faintly.

" What are you coming home from school to-day for instead o' Saturday ? " pursued the conductor with friendly interest.

Lena could find no answer to this but a frightened gulp,
and the driver, his curiosity aroused, leaned forward to take
a look at her, stroking his immense leather gloves the while.
He was evidently a man of some experience, for he said at
once : " Are you running away from school, lovey ? "

The terrified Lena whispered " Yes."

At this both men got up and came nearer and stared at
her. " Aren't they kind to you at school ? " enquired the
conductor in a tone of mild surprise. Lena shook her head.
The conductor, shocked, said it was a shame ; and the
driver opined that she ought to get the Inspector on their
track. Lena listened to this with interest and a kind of hope,
but in her heart she knew that no inspector could cope with
Esmé Deller. The driver now pulled out his watch, which
was attached to him by a leather strap, and announced
that it was time to start ; he went out on to the front platform of the tram and fastened the door behind him, the
conductor pulled the bell cord, and the tram moved off,
crossed the bridge and began its long slow grinding climb
up the steep flank of Awe Hill. Twenty minutes later it
drew up at the Bierley Green terminus ; and Lena, dismounting, rushed across the fields towards her home.

# CHAPTER II

# RACHEL

If Rachel Avery appeared to Lena in the first days of their acquaintance as a rather exceptionally dreamy person, this was partly owing to circumstances, but partly to Rachel's nature. The Avery children were rather odd in the mingling of traits they had received from their father and mother ; for whereas Rowland, who resembled his mother physically, being dark and rather good-looking, with thick eyebrows and strong features, was in character a witty lively fellow with a taste for irony and the arts, like his father : Rachel, who had her father's grey eyes and snub nose and slender frame and fair complexion—Mr. Avery's hair had been silvery ever since Rachel could remember, but it was alleged to have been fair in his youth—had her mother's intense reserve, her quiet voice, her shy movements, her calm which was the calm of latent passion and not mere placidity, and her steadfast preoccupation with the service of those she loved. The household at 7 Cambridge Place was run on the assumption that Will Avery, who was Classics master at the Hudley Grammar School, was the most important figure in it ; but everybody, from old Thomas Deller down to the child Rachel, and not least Will Avery himself, knew that it all rested on Lilias Avery alone ; and they all rejoiced in it, for they all deeply loved her.

As a household they were not too well off. Mr. Avery's salary was not particularly large, and a good deal of money had to be saved for the children's education. Rowland of course must go to the university, and perhaps Rachel as well. Then, old Thomas Deller was gradually losing all his

pupils ; he was old and mild, and there were newer-fash-
ioned masters, and the singing class at the Hudley Girls'
College was now almost his only considerable engagement.
During the last year or two the old man had cut his expenses
on clothes and music and tobacco down to a minimum, and
eaten as little as he could, but at last he was obliged to give
in and go and live with his daughter, who had long been
begging him to do so. His brass plate was transferred to
Cambridge Place, and he lost yet another pupil or so by
the change. Everyone in the house did their best to make
him happy, but he never quite got over the loss of his in-
dependence ; his passion for Lilias and his passion for in-
dependence had been the two big things in his life for a
long time now—he had lost the strength of his passion for
music when he lost his wife ; but his other two passions
were still as fierce as they had been seventeen years ago
when by ordering his nephew Clement, John Deller's son,
out of his house to protect Lilias from the risk of insult—
the lad was drunk—he had brought on a quarrel with his
rich and powerful brother which had never been made up.
Later Clement Deller had taken himself and his sins elsewhere, and Lilias had married the young schoolmaster
from Devonshire, and much water had passed under the
Deller bridge ; but the two families had had no inter-com-
munication whatever until the day when Rowland, in his
first term at the Hudley Grammar School, had brought
home to tea a fair, shy, jerky, slender lad whom he announced as his great friend Deller. The elders of the Avery
household of course knew through Mr. Avery that Arnold
Deller was a pupil at the Hudley Grammar School, and
knew too that he was in Rowland's class, but they were all
considerably disconcerted at first at the thought of any
friendship between the two. Lilias's dark gipsy face wore a
look of icy pride, and her tone was stern, as she administered
tea and jam and cake to Clement Deller's son.

Rachel, however, liked Arnold at once—he was so nervous,
he coloured so easily, he so obviously adored Rowland ;

then too his coat lacked a button, his straight untidy fair hair, which stood up in a childish manner at the back and obviously irritated him immensely, needed cutting, and he ate so much that he surely must have had a very poor lunch. That his clothes were practically new and of excellent material, that his cuff-links were gold and his wrist-watch expensive, Rachel's eyes were incapable of perceiving, for they had never been taught to perceive such things. Lilias however saw them, and she and her father sat hardening their hearts against poor Arnold, who accepted everything to eat which Mr. Avery hospitably pressed upon him, and passed up his cup at Mrs. Avery's cold invitation in a nervous and decidedly dirty but very eager hand. After tea the boys retired to the corner of the cellar where Rowland conducted his photographic experiments, and Rachel as a favour was allowed to come too, provided she would promise to remain on the wooden box where Rowland perched her. The promise was given, and of course faithfully observed ; a broken promise was unheard of in the Avery family. The door was tightly shut, the dark lamp lighted ; immediately everything became very lurid and shadowy and mysterious, and Rachel could see only Arnold's long fair anxious face and Rowland's strong dark one bending together over some weird necromantic liquid in a shallow dish. She was not at all afraid, and remained quietly on her box without saying anything, except when from time to time Rowland addressed some cheering or explanatory remark to her. Arnold was simply astounded by her good behaviour.

" My sister isn't at all like that," he explained in the high astonished tone which seemed natural to him. " But then of course she's older than Rachel."

Meanwhile upstairs, round the drawing-room fire, the fate of the friendship was hotly debated.

" To me it is insufferable," said Mrs. Avery in her quiet slow tones, carefully threading a needle the while, " that my Rowland should be friends with Clement Deller's son."

" But what are we to do, my dear Lilias ? " demanded her husband, speaking in his customary quick, warm, lively tones. " Are you proposing to choose Rowland's friends to suit your own taste ? If so I entirely disagree with you." His wife made a slight protesting movement, which from her meant a strong negative, so he went on : " Then what can we do ? We can do nothing. Rowland must choose his friends for himself. This may be a mere flash in the pan, just a chance liking of an afternoon."

" Or it may not," put in old Thomas Deller heavily. " Rollo never brought any lad home with him before."

Will Avery seemed rather nonplussed. " Well——" he began, throwing out one hand in a characteristic humorous gesture of defeat. " Perhaps so. You may be right, Mr. Deller. But it's rather hard luck to condemn a boy solely on account of his father. It wouldn't do in my profession. He may be a thoroughly good lad."

" He may be a thoroughly bad one," said Mrs. Avery, with a flash of her dark eyes.

" What is he like in school, Will ? " asked old Mr. Deller.

" Well," said Will Avery, considering. " He has ability, I should say, but he scatters it. He doesn't know how to concentrate. His home work is always badly done. Easily led, I should think. Unpractical. But he is a nice lad, never rude or gross. Of course I don't see much of those younger boys. Believe me, Lilias," he added on a soberer note, " if you try to stop it you'll only succeed in making Rowland feel artificial and uncomfortable and thwarted. Far better to let it die a natural death."

This, however, was just what it declined to do. From this day onward Avery and Deller, as they austerely called each other, were inseparable friends. Arnold was never off the Avery doorstep ; he called for Rowland in the morning as he went to school—though as he lived on the other side of Hudley Moor it was a good mile out of his way—and had to be almost driven from Cambridge Place at night. On half holidays they were always together ; they also did their

lessons together, somewhat to Arnold's advantage though
they did not mean to be unfair, for in this as in almost
everything else Rowland always finished first. His strong,
practical mind had seized upon the problem, solved it and
got it half written down before Arnold's dreamy intelligence had succeeded in detaching itself from the fly walking
across the window-pane or the light in Rachel's hair. Arnold
was very fond of Rachel, and once at Christmas brought
her a preposterously expensive doll. He flattered himself
that in spite of what Esmé often said he knew how to look
after a girl very well ; Rachel on the other hand considered
that she looked after him. To her he seemed always hungry,
wistful, nervous and oppressed ; she always thought of him
as being slightly perplexed and in need of guidance.
Whether it was nap or geometry or a puncture in his
bicycle tyre which needed attention, it was always the
same : his hair stuck up at the back, his grey eyes opened
wide in perplexed wonder, and he said in a gentle tone of
trusting reliance :

" Avery ! I say ! What shall I do here ? "

He nearly always lost at cards, when they all sat round
the study table at night playing games with counters just
before Rachel went to bed ; but he was a sweet-tempered
loser, always mildly surprised at his own ill fortune and
wondering at it, but quite admitting that it was his own
fault when Rowland— eager that his friend should learn to
triumph—explained his mistakes to him. If they played
what they called Mr. Avery's game—a form of entertainment introduced by him for educational purposes, in which
one person said a word, the next said the word the first word
suggested to him, and so on, and when a sufficient number
of links of association had thus been forged, the chain was
retraced—if they played that game Arnold's associations
were always pathetically ordinary and uninteresting, not a
bit amusing like Rowland's or learned like Mr. Avery's.
There was only one pursuit in which Arnold excelled. The
Averys were a book-buying family, and Arnold caught this

C T

habit from them. (Sometimes, it was true, Arnold seemed
to have no money at all, but at most times he had an outrageous quantity, and would buy the most preposterously
expensive volumes if Rowland were not at hand to calm
him.) Rowland was also a great patroniser of the Hudley
Municipal Library, which was only five minutes' walk
across the park from Cambridge Place ; he introduced
Arnold to this domain, and both boys became tremendous
readers. Arnold, however, could read much faster than
Rowland and knew almost as much about it at the end as
his friend did. Rachel was just a tiny bit jealous of this accomplishment on Rowland's account ; but Rowland himself always spoke of it with pride. " Deller's a tremendously
fast reader, you know," he would say confidentially to
Rachel in his deep strong tones—his voice broke much
earlier than Arnold's, and he was always a little apt to.
speak as though he had a plum in his mouth. " It's quite
extraordinary." He shook his dark head in a sober emphatic manner, and cocked his left eyebrow thoughtfully
just as Mr. Avery did, and Rachel was tremendously impressed. In Rachel's scale of values Rowland and Mrs.
Avery came first, immeasurably first, miles above everyone
else ; then there were her father and old Thomas Deller,
both darlings, perhaps after all following closely after the
others and struggling in Rachel's mind for pre-eminence ;
then there was poor Arnold ; then Susanna in the kitchen ;
after that everybody was in a different class altogether,
strangers and sojourners, not belonging to 7 Cambridge
Place.

Arnold was poor Arnold to her not only because of his
character but because he seemed to have no real home.
The only day he seemed not to be at liberty to come to
Cambridge Place was Sunday, when it appeared his grandfather was at home all day and required him to be in at-
tendance. He evidently went in awe of his grandfather, and
spoke of him as though he were a tyrant to be resented ; as
for his mother and sister, he scarcely spoke of them at all.

Indeed any mention of West View (John Deller's superlative mansion) or its inhabitants to Arnold was the signal for his fair sensitive face to cloud and his pleasant jerky voice to fall silent. Mrs. Avery said once to Rowland in that quiet way of hers which was so full of suppressed fire :

" Does Deller ever ask you to go to West View, Rowland ? "

" No," replied Rowland in his deep voice frankly, cocking his eyebrow with his man-of-the-world air. " He says there's no fun there. So I think we'll come here to tea this afternoon as usual, mother, if you've no objection."

Mrs. Avery had a quiet smile as she replied : " No objection, Rowland." But at tea that day she said to Arnold : " Do they know at West View that you are here, Arnold ? "

The boy coloured to the roots of his hair, hung his head, and replied in a quick low voice : " I told mother."

" But does your grandfather know ? " persisted Mrs. Avery.

" I don't know," threw out Arnold hurriedly. He looked at her with so much shame and misery in his candid young face that Rachel longed to throw her arms round him and comfort him. She could almost feel the quick frightened beat of his heart as he pushed back his chair and seemed ready to rush from the house immediately if Mrs. Avery commanded him.

" Well," said Lilias with a sigh, " if your mother knows . . ." There was a long pause, during which all three children hung upon her words, for they were all well aware in whose hands the decisions of the household lay. At length Lilias seemed to start, and said in her ordinary tone : " Some more tea, Arnold ? "

Arnold, hardly able to articulate from emotion, clatteringly raised his cup, and the moment passed. After this Mrs. Avery, though always a little cold to Arnold, wearing to him the face she had in her portrait in the drawing-room—which Rowland so disliked and Rachel felt she understood—after this Mrs. Avery was kinder to Arnold. Gradually she began to sew on his buttons and quietly scold him into doing his lessons, and advise him about his handwriting (which being very small and pointed, was a source of great unpleasantness to him at school), and in general treat him as the relation which he in fact was.

It was because of all this Cambridge Place and Rowland and Arnold background, as well as because of her own inclination to reserve, that Rachel was so intensely reserved and dreamy during those days at the Girls' College. For, the Wednesday afternoon of her arrival there, Mr. Avery, who had gone to watch a football match in which both boys were playing, appeared unexpectedly early in Cambridge Place with a very sober look, and announced that Rowland had had an accident. The ambulance, he said, was following. (He had left it round the turn of the Place while he came on to break the news.) At this Arnold, who stood beside him with a face the colour of a sheet, allowed his teeth to chatter ; and Mrs. Avery, breathing rather heavily, begged her husband to tell her the worst *at once*. It seemed that Rowland had broken his leg and got concussion into the bargain. It was a compound fracture. " The children," said Mr. Avery, very quiet and white, " had better go into the study and stay there." Rachel and Arnold were forthwith bundled off upstairs. Hardly had the door of the study closed behind them than Arnold, haggard and despairing, burst out frantically :

" It was my fault, Rachel ! Nobody else knows, but it was my fault."

Rachel started and trembled, and fixing wide eyes upon him, waited in silence for him to speak again. Jerkily and almost weeping, Arnold explained ; it appeared that he had kicked or jumped at the wrong moment or not kicked or jumped at the right moment—he was far too incoherent for Rachel to understand which—but at any rate had done something characteristically well-meaning and impulsive and rather silly, and the result was Rowland's broken leg. After this confession Arnold really did weep, with his head

down on his arms on the study table ; and Rachel stood
silently beside him and stroked his shoulder soothingly from
time to time. Then all of a sudden it seemed to be decided
that Rachel should go to the Girls' College to be out of the
way ; a nurse would be necessary for Rowland, and Mrs.
Avery very decidedly did not want Rachel to see her brother
as he then was. If Arnold's sister were like Arnold it would
do Rachel no harm to be with her. Hastily Susanna packed
for Rachel, hastily Mrs. Avery kissed her little daughter
farewell and begged her to do this for Rowland's sake ;
slowly and reluctantly old Thomas Deller, in terrible distress about his grandson, conveyed her to the College,
Arnold pattering alongside with her rather shabby case.
Outside the gate Arnold handed Rachel the case and
jerkily vanished.

Mr. Deller and his grand-daughter were received with
much sympathy by Miss Fielding, and then old Mr. Deller
went, and Rachel was introduced into the room where
Esmé and Lena were having hot milk and bread and butter
for their supper. Rachel hardly needed to be told that the
fair girl was Arnold's sister, and as she gazed at Esmé she
realised that of course Arnold's sister must never be allowed
to guess Arnold's share in Rowland's accident. No ! She
must never have the slightest inkling of it. Poor Arnold !
He was distracted enough already. The three girls shook
hands. Lena was like a massive and tousled spaniel which
had once followed Rowland home. Esmé said, in her small
light voice which was like Arnold's and yet so different, so
much more cold and smooth and composed :

" I think your brother is a great friend of my brother's."

" Yes," agreed Rachel.

" I'm sorry your brother has had an accident," continued
Esmé politely.

Rachel thought of Rowland, of Mrs. Avery, of Rowland,
of her father, of Rowland, of poor old Mr. Deller, of Rowland, of Arnold and of Rowland. Her whole being seemed
to be filled with a racking, violent and oppressive anxiety

for her brother ; and if for a moment this relaxed its grip, she had time to feel sorry for poor Arnold, and to remember that Esmé must never know about his football blunder. These thoughts filled her mind to the almost complete exclusion of all others, though it was her nature to keep them to herself ; it was only at times that she saw Lena and the other girls, and was never more than half conscious of them until the day before Esmé's birthday, when the news of Rowland was really splendid. Only then, too, did the strain she had put upon herself begin to tell ; she felt weak and tired and apathetic ; and then suddenly the cruel scene between the singing class and her beloved grandfather awoke her to a throbbing consciousness and struck upon her tenderest feelings like a lash. When the lesson was over and Mr. Deller left the room she flew after him, flung herself upon him and, clinging to him passionately, begged to be taken home. All the homesickness, the yearning for Cambridge Place which had lain like a deep still pool at the bottom of her heart, now seemed to come surging over her in great waves. She clung to Mr. Deller's shrunken arm with all her force, burying her face in his sleeve. Her grandfather smoothed her hair with one hand ; she could feel that he was troubled and uncertain. Esmé came up, observed virtuously that it was all Lena Howgate's fault, and tried to draw Rachel away ; but Rachel did not move ; she did not mean to move until the conviction that she must go home to-day had filled Mr. Deller's mind as it filled hers. At last the old man, with a sigh, said that he would tell Mr. and Mrs. Avery that Rachel wanted, that Rachel wanted——

" To go home to-day," prompted Rachel.

" To go home to-day," repeated her grandfather, with a perplexed and timid smile.

Rachel, sure that she would be at Cambridge Place before the end of the afternoon, released his arm and suffered Esmé to lead her away.

There was a clock on the dining-room mantelpiece, and

all through dinner Rachel's eyes strayed constantly to
it from her plate. She calculated how long it would take
Mr. Deller to reach home, how long to tell her father and
mother, how long for Mr. Avery to have his lunch and
walk from Cambridge Place—her mother of course would
not be able to leave Rowland, Rachel quite understood
that. She ate mechanically, and did not notice Lena's absence from the table or hear a word of Esmé's disingenuous
account of the singing-lesson scene. When the meal was
over and the two girls went up to the classroom where the
boarders spent their leisure she crossed straight to the small
side window, which commanded a view of the drive, and
perched herself on the sill. Esmé, after one or two vain at-
tempts to attract her attention by blandishments, asked
her outright :

" What are you looking for ? "

" My father," replied Rachel.

" You don't really think he'll come, do you, Rachel ? "
said Esmé incredulously. " He won't come," she added
with conviction.

Rachel, wounded, turned away and pressed her face
against the glass. But her faith in her family was unshaken,
and sure enough, a few minutes later the big green gate
opened, and Mr. Avery tripped briskly down the drive.
Looking up, he caught sight of his daughter at the window,
smiled all over his pleasant face, and waved boyishly to
her. Rachel's heart leaped, and she suddenly noticed that
the sun was shining. The bell rang, Mr. Avery's genial voice
was heard in the hall, the door of Miss Fielding's private
sitting-room was opened and closed ; soon the headmistress
came upstairs, looking vexed, and told Rachel that her
brother was asking for her : she was to pack and go home
at once. Rachel slipped off the sill with alacrity and made
for the door ; she was astonished to perceive, as in a dream,
Esmé's face looking white and hurt. She went upstairs and
began rapidly to collect her small possessions. Esmé stood
by and watched her. Rachel was not without a feeling that

Esmé was criticising her plain clothes and sturdy shoes as she put them into her little case, but she reflected staunchly that her mother had chosen them, and so they must be all right.

" I wish you weren't going, Rachel," said Esmé suddenly in her cool little voice. " I don't see why you want to go."

Rachel, aching with the desire for Cambridge Place and all it held, was silent.

" I wish you'd let me come to tea sometimes with Arnold," pursued Esmé, her gaze fixed on Rachel's sponge-bag.

" Oh ! Yes ? " stammered Rachel, recalled from a vision of herself running up the stairs to Rowland's room. She paused and considered the suggestion. Esmé of course was Arnold's sister. Poor Arnold ! No doubt he would like to bring his sister to his friend's home. Yes, Esmé was Arnold's sister, and she alone had not been unkind to Rachel's grandfather that morning. " I hope you will come," said Rachel at last with grave formality.

" Thank you," said Esmé in her primmest tone.

Just then Miss Fielding came breathlessly into the room.

" Be quick, Rachel," she commanded, " or you will make your father very late for school. Where is Lena ? "

Rachel, without a backward look, picked up her case and flew downstairs ; in another moment she was on her way to Cambridge Place at Mr. Avery's side.

# CHAPTER III

## ESMÉ

It was natural that homesickness should be incomprehensible to Esmé, for Arnold Deller and his sister were accustomed to date the events of their lives by the different houses where they had occurred. There was the bungalow at St. Annes, the flat in Kensington, the *pension* at Lausanne, the hotel at Brighton ; lastly there was their grandfather's house, West View, in Hudley, where they had lived for the past few years. Esmé, though younger than Arnold, professed to remember the house in Hudley which they had occupied when their father was alive, before their mother began those successive removals which her bright ideas for the children's education were alleged to dictate ; but Arnold did not remember it, and was much irritated by Esmé's pretensions on this score. Neither of the children remembered their father ; and this was perhaps as well, for Clement Deller was not a man to be remembered comfortably by anyone connected with him. Proceedings of a very unpleasant nature were being instituted against him by his wife, with her father-in-law's full sanction and support, when in the nick of time pneumonia, superimposing itself upon a riotous and alcoholic course of life, carried him off and rendered them unnecessary. His wife—a pretty, petulant little shop-girl, out for what she could get but not quite clever enough to get it except in the one fatal instance of her marriage, whom Clement Deller had picked up somewhere and presented to his enraged father after the wedding—utterly crushed and overwhelmed by the magnitude of what Clement Deller's wife had had to bear, thereupon decided that Hudley was odious to her ; and, supported by a generous allowance from her father-in-law which she

habitually exceeded, began that series of aimless wander-
ings which gave her two children their chronology.

But after a while John Deller got tired of seeing nothing
of his grandchildren but their photographs in picturesque
poses, with their heads arranged lovingly on each other's
shoulders, and their fair hair falling softly over their eyes.
John Deller was an obstinate, cunning, vindictive and ruthless man of business ; and like many other such men, he
was immensely tender and emotional in his domestic relations. At first he loved to sentimentalise over the photographs to the business acquaintances he so frequently and
so lavishly entertained. A large cigar in one hand, a photograph in the other, his red face redder from his own excellent wine, his small blue eyes watery with genuine emotion,
he always exclaimed on these occasions : " By Gad, she's
a lovely little kiddy ! " as to Esmé ; and of Arnold : " I tell
you he's a fine clean lad." As John Deller had built up one
of the finest dyeing businesses in the West Riding, and
owned other irons all up and down the district in fires which
his genius for finance kept remarkably hot, his guests always
heartily agreed with him, but they usually added : " I'm
surprised you don't have them up here with you, John."
John Deller, shaking his well-groomed white head, was
wont to reply : " Well, May felt it very much, you know.
Aye ! She felt it, poor girl." The business acquaintances
here felt themselves on very delicate ground, and wisely
contented themselves with mere vague murmurs and vaguer
movements of the head, for John Deller could not endure
anyone to blame Clement except himself. He had been
heard to say himself that his only son was a damned black-
guard, but if anyone else suggested that Clement's behaviour had lacked integrity he flew into a rage and said
the boy was like his poor mother, a delicate soul, not fit
for the hard ways of this wicked world. Besides, Clement
had received such a bad blow from his cousin Lilias, who
after leading him on in the most scandalous manner, refused
to marry him. " He was never the same lad again, never ! "

John Deller would exclaim at this point of the story, almost weeping over his dearly-loved son—and the next moment he would be taking advantage of his companion's natural sympathy to arrange some peculiarly acute inflation of capital or transfer of shares. Be that as it may, his guests made that comment about his grandchildren's photographs once too often ; he suddenly felt that it *was* odd, for them to go wandering about the world like that when they had a fine home waiting for them here with him. It made him look ridiculous. There was Arnold's education, too ; he must be brought up to be fit to manage Adela Mills when his grandfather had gone. Besides, he really wanted them ; he was damned lonely by himself in that barracks of a house. He wrote off immediately to May Deller and brought her to Hudley by the perfectly simple means of declining to give her any more money till she arrived. This was quite the kind of thing his daughter-in-law had been expecting from him, and after a few argumentative and complaining letters—which John Deller shrewdly left un-answered—she came to West View, and having quarrelled with all the maids and changed her bedroom twice, being unable to decide whether the glorious view over the hills was worth the wind it entailed, settled down fairly happily into Hudley life again. Esmé and Arnold became day pupils at suitable Hudley schools ; they had a large nursery and heaps of toys, and were healthy children who were used to amusing themselves ; moreover, they behaved with the discretion they had learned in the lounges of hotels, so that they were really no trouble to anybody.

The relation between Esmé and Arnold was curious. Owing to the circumstances of their errant lives, they had spent more time in each other's company than brothers and sisters usually do. When in the company of their elders they preserved a natural mutual alliance against this alien race, and supported each other's tactics ; when alone they some-times loved each other dearly, and sometimes loathed each other with all their hearts, but they were never just good friends. Whatever they happened to be feeling, however, Esmé was always the stronger. Arnold's happiness always depended on Esmé's mood. Sometimes when she bickered and criticised and sneered and snapped and would not leave him any peace he really hated her, but if she changed her mood and was kind he was at her side in an instant, eager for her approval. Unfortunately this was true of other people as well as Arnold—Esmé was so pretty and so graceful and so elegant and so difficult to please that her approval had a value quite out of proportion to its real worth—and all the people of whom it was true bored Esmé. She respected her grandfather because it was not true of him, and despised her mother because it was true of her. She was perhaps fonder of Arnold than of anybody else except herself, but when he came rushing up, his fair hair sticking up in that childish way at the back, his fair silly face beaming with naïve delight because she had said (simply in order to see what he would say if she did) that the shelves of the book-case he was making were very neat, he exasperated her almost to distraction. All the people like Arnold exasperated Esmé—they inflamed a deep-seated sore in her moral being. Esmé was always wanting something, something, she did not quite know what, but *something* ; and nothing was ever just that something, however hard it tried. She wanted more out of everything than it could give her ; her charming little frocks were never just right in her eyes, though of course she knew they were much nicer than other people's ; her toys were never quite perfect ; if she read a story it always seemed to miss achievement somehow ; meals were never served quite as they should be ; and the weather was *always* just a little wrong. How other people could accept these crudities and imperfections as calmly as they did Esmé could *not* understand ; and as for people like Arnold, whom one could send into the seventh heaven with a word, and who were always making themselves happy with some wood and glue, or a book, or a ball, or some crude trifle of that kind, she simply despised them as grossly uncritical and *silly*, and felt a longing to dispel this happiness which she could not share. She tried every new thing and every new person avidly, in the hope that this time they really would be supreme, but things never were supreme. (The only thing, she flattered herself about the time she first met Rachel, which she had not yet tried was the ultimate experience of sex, and consequently she was immensely interested in it and built all her hopes upon it.) As for people, as soon as she found them answering when she called, she despised them as less than herself. Arnold's affection was old and tried and hers for the whistling, and so, except when she was in disgrace and needed it, she found it merely an exasperation.

But then Arnold met Rowland Avery. The very first day they spoke to each other he was late for tea, and when reprimanded said he had walked home with a boy. Sharply questioned about the boy, he coloured, and turned mulish, and gave monosyllabic answers only. The next day he was just as bad, and the next and the next ; and presently came a day when his new friend invited him to tea.

" What is the boy's name, Arnold ? " enquired his mother when he returned home, late and glowing.

Arnold was obliged to answer sheepishly : " Avery."

To May Deller this name meant nothing, for she had always heard Lilias spoken of as a Deller ; but Esmé, who frequented the West View kitchen, was better informed, and acquainted her mother with the relationship. The look Arnold gave her stung. May Deller, afraid of offending her father-in-law whether she spoke or kept silence, in a rare burst of courage told him that night of this new complication as one of the difficulties of her life in Hudley. John Deller blustered and stormed at first, then gradually became sentimental, almost maudlin, and at last said : " Let him go, May, let him go ! " and drew an emotional picture of the two lads indulging in an undying friendship in spite of the irreconcilable feud of their grandfathers. Fortunately Arnold was asleep upstairs and did not hear this, and John Deller was much too shrewd a judge of character to mention it to him, so the friendship grew. If at times John Deller was rather disconcerted at being thus taken at his word, at other times the sound common sense which lay beneath his surface vagaries urged him to leave it alone and be thankful if Clement's son made no worse friend. A useful fiction was maintained by which grandfather was supposed to look rather askance on Arnold's visits to Cambridge Place—useful because it enabled John Deller to stop the visits, without loss of consistency, at any moment he chose.

This fiction was useful to Esmé as well as to her grandfather, though not so useful as she could have wished. For an intense and overpowering jealousy of the Averys gradually took possession of Esmé's heart. Arnold was always at Cambridge Place ; the most expensive entertainment, the prettiest coaxing, could not keep him away. When at times she used the grandfather threat to force him, or affectionate caresses to persuade him, to accompany her on some expedition or other, he yielded with a bad grace and walked beside her in a moody silence ; as they drew nearer home he became more and more cheerful with each step they took, until when he had at last politely seen her through the great West View front door, he flew off like an arrow in the direction of Cambridge Place, beaming all over his expressive young face. (Esmé was like Rachel in regarding Arnold as very young.) And he always returned so happy, so full of smiles ! He grew more independent, too, and contradicted some of Esmé's most cherished views. " Avery says," he began constantly ; and in defence of what Avery had said was willing to endure scorn and jeers. After a while Esmé abandoned the policy of jeering at the Averys, and, casting her pride to the winds, asked Arnold to make her known to them.

" You wouldn't like them," said Arnold instantly.

" Why not ? " demanded Esmé on a sharp note.

Arnold coloured and repeated sheepishly : " You wouldn't."

" Why not ? " repeated Esmé. After trying many varia-
tions of this query without success, she said suddenly : " I
believe you're ashamed of them."

At this Arnold flew into one of his sudden quick furies.
" More likely I'm ashamed of you ! " he cried.

" Arnold ! " said Esmé, pretending to be shocked.

" Well, it's true," mumbled her brother.

A kind of rage possessed Esmé as the days went on and
she saw her Arnold, her silly easy Arnold, slipping away
from her like this ; and she made an immense, prolonged
and varied effort to retrieve him. If only she could get to
know the Averys she felt sure that she could conquer them—
especially Rowland. Everybody always liked her, reflected
Esmé with a sense of power—especially boys. She even
descended to strategy of the crudest kind to gain her end,
and hung about and waylaid Arnold as he returned from
school. In this way she once or twice gained a sight of the
redoubtable Avery, but no speech with him ; for as soon as
Arnold saw her he left his friend and came to her side, usually
with a cross word. Esmé chafed and fumed, but could
accomplish nothing.

At last there was a crucial scene. Arnold had arranged to
go with the Averys and some other schoolfellows to a
Shakespeare play on a Saturday afternoon. Esmé commanded, begged, implored him to get her a ticket too, but
Arnold would not ; they were going in the cheap seats,
which would not be suitable for Esmé, he said. Up to the
day of the performance Esmé had not succeeded in making
him change his mind, and after lunch she made a last
effort, employing all her arts upon him. She threw her arms
round his neck, put her cheek against his, called him
" Arnie "—" I should so like to go to the theatre with you,
Arnie," she said wistfully—but all in vain.

" I *can't*, Esmé," said Arnold irritably. " I *can't* take you.
There isn't a ticket for you."

" There are sure to be heaps of seats not booked," said
the experienced Esmé. Unfortunately for her effect on

Arnold she added : " For a Shakespeare play," in a tone
which betrayed the contempt she actually felt for the performance, and her brother, making an impatient sound,
freed himself and escaped.

In a few minutes Esmé heard him moving about upstairs ;
after some consideration she went up too, and found him
drying his hands and face in the gleaming bathroom.
Standing in the open doorway, with one hand resting in a
queenly pose on the silvery radiator, she delivered her last
word on the subject : " Arnold," she said, " I *want* you to
take me to the theatre." She then turned on her heel and
left him. Arnold took the towel from his face to say " I
can't " in a tone of intense exasperation—like all weak
natures his was easily exasperated by opposition—but
Esmé did not choose to hear him. She went straight downstairs into the large drawing-room, and began to play the
piano to show Arnold where she was. " If he doesn't come
and say he'll take me," she told herself, banging a ballad
accompaniment out ferociously, " or at any rate if he
doesn't come and say he's *sorry*, I'll never forgive him as
long as I live. Never ! " She heard him come downstairs ;
his footsteps crossed the hall and stumbled as usual at the
skin rug. Her heart leaped—he was coming ! A sneering
look crossed her pretty face—after all why bother so much
about Arnold and his Averys ; they were not worth troubling
about, just ordinary silly boring people like everybody else.
The next moment, with a jangle of the keys, she flew across
the room to the window ; yes, it was really Arnold who had
closed the front door behind him and was running down the
steps. His face, a moment ago so perplexed and cross, was
now blithe and sunny.

" Arnold ! " called Esmé imperiously, knocking at the
window, " Arnold ! "

He did not hear, but ran off out of sight. Esmé, her small
face cold and set, returned to the piano stool and began
to murder another ballad with tremendous force. " I hate
him, I hate the Averys, I hate the theatre, I hate him ! "

she whispered fiercely to herself, playing in the vilest man-
ner possible, with a great deal of " expression," because
Arnold detested it so. Presently her lips quivered. " I really
*wanted* to go ! " she exclaimed aloud pathetically. John
Deller, lighting a cigar in the hall before starting for a football match, was astounded by these rolling chords when
Arnold was out—on a Saturday afternoon too—for usually
Esmé had to be driven to the piano to practise, and many
were the unpleasant little scenes which took place at West
View on this account. He opened the door to say a word of
praise, and found Esmé with tears on her cheeks—dainty
little tears, for everything connected with Esmé was dainty,
but tears all the same. Horrified, he advanced and bent his
big red face yearningly to her level.

" What's the matter, love ? " he asked in a tone of tender
sympathy.

Esmé had learnt by experience that nothing but the
truth would satisfy her grandfather. " I wanted to go to the
theatre with Arnold, but he won't take me," she explained
in her clear little tones.

" Quarrelled with him, eh ? " said John Deller shrewdly.
" Well, never mind, I'll take you myself. Go and get ready.
Be quick now. The car's at the door. We'll get a box."

Esmé saw in a flash of delight the picture of herself in a
box whilst Arnold languished in the cheap seats, but then
with a pang she realised, for she was shrewd enough, that
it would not really be a revenge or a victory ; Arnold would
be with his Averys and she merely with John Deller.

" It's very kind of you, grandfather," she began politely.
Then her grief overwhelmed her. " I wanted to go with
Arnold;" she wept. " He's gone with a lot of his friends and
their sisters—*I* wanted to go too."

The first result of this little scene was that Esmé went to
the football match with John Deller, and afterwards dined
with him at an hotel, in company with two or three of his
friends who admired the pretty little girl—so cool and well-
behaved, it was astonishing—and pleasantly teased her.

D T

The second result was not so pleasing, for it consisted in Esmé's becoming a weekly boarder at the College.

" You don't look after the child, May," John Deller stormed at his daughter-in-law. " She's lonely. It stands to reason she can't always be with Arnold, but she ought to have friends of her own."

May Deller wept, and said that she supposed she was allowed a little pleasure now and then, even if she was a widow ; she couldn't always be dragging the children about. John Deller growled, and after one or two excursions into the children's lives to find out who looked after Esmé, in the course of which he discovered that nobody did, he sent her where he judged she would receive proper attention and yet be within easy reach of home. Esmé, at first furious at this decision, after consideration decided not to oppose it. After all, home was really very boring now that Arnold was no longer any use, and life as a boarder was new and might prove interesting. She tried it, and found it as boring as everything else, but it made the week-ends jollier, because everyone at West View (including Arnold) now found her a rarity and hung round her and petted her, which Esmé liked very well. It was rather fun, too, showing off before Lena and telling her things ; at least it was fun at first ; afterwards Lena's clumsiness and naïveté were fearfully exasperating.

And then, by an almost incredible piece of luck, as it seemed to Esmé, Rachel Avery was dropped from the skies into her hands. In the very first moment she saw Rachel, Esmé admired her intensely. Not that she thought Rachel beautiful. The experienced Esmé was a connoisseur in looks, and she put Rachel's beauty down at once as mere youthful bloom due to health and happiness. No, Rachel was not beautiful, but there was something else about her. She belonged rather to Arnold's class of person, Esmé considered, for she was simple and straightforward and very good and all that sort of thing ; but she was not weak or silly like poor Arnold—oh, no ! Rachel was deep and strong.

Immediately Esmé made up her mind to be so charming and nice and clever and good that Rachel would not be able to help admiring her. And then the very first evening that tiresome Lena went and made it all wrong. She put up her hand in the middle of after-supper preparation and asked leave to speak to Esmé, and then asked Esmé what answer she had got to a certain sum. Esmé, using a kind, superior, encouraging tone of voice in order to impress Rachel, told her, and Lena grunted and put her book away ; and then Miss Smith, who was young and inexperienced and therefore absurdly scrupulous, said to Lena that it was hardly fair to compare notes in that way—it gave the boarders an unfair advantage over the day girls. Lena stared, and Miss Smith, colouring, explained : " You see if your answer had been different you would have wanted to do the sum again." " Oh ! " exclaimed Lena loudly. " But my answer *is* different." Everyone naturally looked at her in astonishment ; and then Lena actually went on in her rough Yorkshire voice (which Esmé loathed) : " But I know mine's right." She spoke without malice but with certainty, and Esmé had never felt so humiliated in her life. This, before Rachel Avery ! Her cheeks burnt, she could not raise her eyes, she imagined how pleasant it would be to stamp on Lena's vivid uneven face. After this she simply could not bring herself to carry out the scheme of self-sacrifice as regards the washing arrangements which she had planned ; and as the children undressed she thought of all sorts of bitter ways in which she could announce that Rachel and she would always use the basins first. But that would never do ; she must not seem selfish to Rachel ; making an immense effort she choked down her anger sufficiently to suggest the race. That gave *everybody* a fair chance, she reflected virtuously as she tucked her striped rug carefully round her. Really it was astonishing how good one could be when there were people like Rachel to be good *for*.

Since then life had been nothing but a series of combats with Lena for Rachel's good will. Esmé fought ruthlessly, incessantly, with all her skill and cunning, to make Rachel her friend and prevent her from becoming Lena's. That anyone could be friends with both of them was quite impossible, she somehow knew that well. And Esmé could *not* let Rachel Avery slip, she *must* secure her. The singing lesson had been her crowning triumph ; for she felt that each moment of that wretched hour, as it went by, lowered Lena in Rachel's estimation. And now everything was ruined ; the detestable, stupid Lena had overdone it as she overdid everything, and Rachel was gone from both of them. She bit her lips in a fury as she thought of Rachel now hurrying away home. Still, Rachel had asked her to tea. Esmé longed ardently for Saturday to come, so that she might visit Cambridge Place. If she became really friendly with Rachel, she must try to persuade her grandfather to let her become a day girl again, so that she could go out to tea whenever she liked.

" Where is Lena ? " repeated Miss Fielding severely.

Esmé did not know ; and it soon became apparent that this ignorance was shared by everybody in the house. There was a flutter, a rushing up and down, an organised search ; the child was definitely not to be found. It was Miss Smith who discovered that Lena's hat was also missing, though her coat still puzzlingly hung on its hook. All at once everybody seemed to turn sharply on Esmé, demanding what she knew about the affair and where she thought Lena had gone. Esmé, blenching, hardly knew whether to simulate interest or the lack of it, but at any rate her real feelings must be concealed ; for at the sight of the forlorn little coat there had suddenly dinned in her ears Lena's : " I wish I was at bottom of t'cut," and Esmé thought it only too probable, considering the incidents of the morning, that Lena had gone there. At any rate, that would explain her leaving her coat behind. But Esmé, unlike the immature Lena and Rachel, was well able to understand Miss Fielding's feelings when one of her boarders was fetched away and another vanished, and it was partly to soothe that lady, as well as to conceal her own real views, that she hazarded the suggestion that Lena had gone home. This being well received, she further explained that Lena had been very homesick. On this Miss Fielding took action with a briskness which Esmé could not but admire. A taxi with a good engine was telephoned for, and Miss Fielding was whirled away in it with the intention of reaching Bierley Hall by the Lane. She left instructions that the bell for afternoon school, already a little late, should be rung at once and lessons conducted as usual, and Esmé and the few other girls who stayed for the midday meal and had been helping to search for Lena were herded into their proper classes immediately.

Esmé was very quiet and white all afternoon. However she tried to dodge the issue in her mind, she could not but see that it looked odd, very odd indeed, almost as though there were something rather horrid about Esmé Deller, that Rachel should go off home like that, and Lena disappear. (Not that *she* had anything to do with Rachel's departure, Esmé told herself, and told herself again with failing conviction.) It did seem a little strange, she reflected as she sat at her desk during a French lesson, neat and quiet and pretty, with her little contemptuous air of knowing much more than the others—yes, it was rather strange ; there was Arnold slipping away from her ; there was Lena who hated her ; and her attractions had not succeeded in keeping Rachel at her side. It seemed odd ; other people would think it was odd. And suppose Lena had really drowned herself ! Esmé's face became colder and her air more haughty than ever. Suppose Lena had drowned herself, and it all came out about the wash-basins and old Mr. Deller and all that. Suppose Lena had left a note behind incriminating her ! Yes, it was odd ; Arnold, and Rachel, and Lena. Could it perhaps really be the case that Esmé Deller was not a nice girl after all ? Sickness clutched her at the thought ; she felt very cold, but at the same time her whole body burned with humiliation. Miss Smith asked her a question ; Esmé's tongue felt swollen and stuck to her mouth ; she was paralysed, could not make her jaws move apart or even lift her eyelids. Miss Smith, seeing no signs of distress on her face, looked vexed and thwarted, but passed on. Esmé would not look at door or window, but she listened intently for the sound of a car. Once she thought she heard something, but Miss Fielding did not appear, and for the rest of the afternoon Esmé revolved the torturing doubt of whether she had or had not returned to the school.

At length it was four o'clock and lessons were over. Esmé dallied over her desk till she had no excuse for dallying any longer, then she marched away into the house, her small face calm, her head held high. As she passed the half-open door of Miss Fielding's private room, the headmistress's voice called seriously : " Esmé ! " Esmé's heart seemed to stop, and then began to beat in great hard throbs. Thinking " Lena has drowned herself," she pushed open the door and went in. All her fears rushed from her at once and became absurd, for Lena was sitting in an armchair by the fire, very clean and tidy, and very white. A liberal tea, arranged on Miss Fielding's best china, was spread on a low table by the hearth, the birthday cake occupying a prominent position.

" Now, Esmé," said Miss Fielding, " Lena quite realises that it was very unkind of her to spoil your birthday by trying to run away, but I want you both to forget all about that now, and have a happy birthday tea together."

She went out and closed the door behind her. The unconscious irony, and the artificial sugariness, of her speech, were so perceptible to Esmé, and so irritating, that for a moment she felt united with Lena in a common exasperation with the silliness of grown-ups. She advanced a step or two into the room.

" Did you go home, Lena ? " she enquired politely.

Lena turned her head and stared at her.

" She caught me in the porch as I was going in," she said at last in thick despairing tones.

This was certainly a very bitter ending to an escapade, and Esmé, advancing to the table, cast about her for some friendly thing to say. At length she found one.

" I expect you'll be glad Rachel has gone," she said kindly. " You'll be able to have a basin of your own again now."

With a loud cry of rage Lena snatched up the heavy knife which lay beside the cake and flew at her. Esmé screamed with terror, backed, and threw up one arm protectingly before her face. The powerful Lena seized it and dragged it fiercely down ; her eyes and teeth flashed ; she raised the knife in her other hand, menacingly. Esmé cowered in her grasp, and sobbed " Lena ! "

" She'll kill me," she thought despairingly. " Arnold ! Oh, Arnie ! "

But now suddenly Lena's hand wavered, her mouth lost its wolfish snarl, her eyes grew dull.

" She won't do it," thought Esmé in a flash. " She daren't." In an instant she recovered all her confidence. She stood upright. " Put that knife down, Lena," she commanded coldly. " And let go my arm. You're hurting me." For a moment Lena stood staring stupidly at her, then suddenly she threw the knife into the corner of the room.

" Really, Lena ! How silly you are ! " said Esmé with contempt. She wrenched her arm from the other's relaxing grasp, and crossing the room, picked up the knife. She returned to the table and replaced it on the cake dish, while Lena still stood and stared at her. " You'd better sit down and have some tea," commanded Esmé, in a tone of contemptuous kindliness. She busied herself with the teapot. When she looked up again Lena was crouched upon the sofa, with her thick fingers tightly pressed against her face.

It was a curious incident ; and when Esmé recounted it to John Deller on her return to West View on Saturday, he was loud in his praises of her courage. He was equally loud in his determination that she should not be exposed to the risk of a repetition of the scene, and it was as a day pupil that she returned to the school on the following Monday. To her surprise Lena was not there, and nobody seemed to know why ; so that when she was summoned to Miss Fielding's room in the middle of the morning she went in apprehensively. The headmistress, looking extremely annoyed, was turning over the pages of a letter written in a large, uneven, not to say schoolboyish, hand. Looking sternly at Esmé, she explained that this letter was from Mr. Howgate, withdrawing Lena from the school, because, he said, they did not treat her well there.

" Did Lena say that ? " said Esmé, really surprised that Lena had had sense and courage enough to complain.

Miss Fielding, crossly turning the thick leaves, said no, it was not Lena, she thought ; but there was something she did not quite understand about the cook's brother.

" Do you understand it, Esmé ? " she demanded sharply.

" I don't understand it at all, Miss Fielding," affirmed Esmé. She felt a tiny twinge of remorse for the way Miss Fielding's boarders had fallen from her, but reassured herself : " Well, she should manage better."

" And you are to be a day girl too, I hear," continued the headmistress, a natural suspicion colouring her tone.

" Oh, that's my grandfather," said Esmé, shaking her head with a deprecatory air. " He arranged that."

She did not, however, consider it necessary to tell John Deller that there was no longer any danger from Lena to be met with at the College ; and when in the course of the next week Rowland Avery was reported to be well enough to see Arnold for a few minutes, Esmé accompanied her brother to Cambridge Place. Arnold protested, but Esmé overbore him ; Rachel, she said, had asked her to go there for tea.

After that the Averys and the Dellers were constantly together. Esmé always kept her sweetest smiles, her kindest tempers, for Arnold's Averys—she always thought of them like that, for at the bottom of her heart she felt that all four of them preferred Arnold to herself, in spite of the skilful little traps she often laid to show up Arnold's silliness (into which he invariably fell). Yes, they all astonishingly enough preferred Arnold ; at least Mr. Avery preferred Arnold, and Mrs. Avery much preferred Arnold, and Rachel of course doted on Arnold ; about Rowland's preference she was not quite sure ; she exercised every charm known to her to get him on her side, but she was not quite sure. Sometimes this Avery assumption that Arnold was so much nicer than his sister irritated Esmé beyond bearing, and she let fly an angry sentence ; but she soon repented and even openly expressed remorse, for she knew that if she quarrelled with the Averys she would lose Arnold's love for ever.

# CHAPTER IV

## RACHEL AND ESMÉ

All of a sudden the lights went out, and the Avery household was plunged into confusion. Mr. Avery, who was reading what he called the local evening rag in the drawing-room, threw it down, dashed out into the hall, and called for his wife in a tone of pleasurable excitement. Rowland, who was tying his white tie in his bedroom at the top of the house, swore mildly and groped his way on to the landing. Lilias said quickly : " The fuse has gone," and laid a soothing hand on her father's arm, for old Thomas Deller was in bed with one of the heart attacks which had begun to trouble him recently, and she rather dreaded the effect of any sudden shock on him. In the next room Rachel gasped and struggled and laughed, for she had just thrown the airy folds of her new primrose dance frock over her head, and she could not free her arms or disentangle herself one way or another. After some calling about the house it was agreed that the lights were out in every room, and Mr. Avery, opening the front door, discovered that there was darkness all over Cambridge Place as well. Soon Rowland found his electric torch ; Thomas Deller's nightlights were not far to seek, and Susanna produced a store of candles. In response to muffled calls and laughter from Rachel's room, Rowland went in and saw his sister's predicament, and having made the time-honoured joke that he hoped there was more of her dress than that, he fetched Mrs. Avery to her assistance, and stayed himself at his grandfather's side. Bending forward and peering into the dressing-table glass he resumed operations on his white tie ; Mr. Deller, watching him with sympathetic interest, had yet a listening air.

" Rachel will come in to see me before you go ? " he said presently in a pleading tone.

" Oh, of course ! " replied Rowland, who, knowing his sister, knew that there was no doubt of that. " She's not quite ready yet, that's all."

But Mr. Deller still listened anxiously, and gave a sigh of relief when a few minutes later his grand-daughter and Lilias entered the room.

" Come here, my dear," he said eagerly, waving her round the bed with one of his frail old hands.

Rachel, smiling, came close to his bedside, so that his old eyes could take in all the details of this much-discussed frock, which was his Christmas gift to her. The old man picked up a yellow fold and felt it, but seemed not quite satisfied somehow, so Mrs. Avery held the nightlight high, and Rowland, never lacking in a sense of drama, snatched up a candle and raised it on the other side. Between the two flickering yellow flames Rachel stood, laughing at her brother but slightly blushing and drooping her fair warm head ; her strong young arms looked very white in the candlelight, and the primrose stuff moulded her young breasts closely. Round her firm throat were what the Averys called the family pearls, a far from costly string which Will Avery had given to Lilias on their wedding day, and which now decked mother or daughter according to requirement. Lilias Avery did not need the pearls to-night, for Rowland and Rachel were going to Esmé Deller's twenty-first birthday dance at West View, and she was not invited. (Not, as everybody complained, that it *was* Esmé's birthday ; that auspicious day was still some weeks distant. But then if Esmé had had her dance on her actual birthday Rowland Avery would have returned to Oxford and could not have been present. Perhaps that was the reason why the date of the Deller dance fell well within his vacation, or perhaps not ; at any rate, everyone knew what great friends young Avery and his cousin Arnold Deller were.) So to-night the pearls were round Rachel's throat, and Lilias would not need to leave her father's side. The old man raised his head from the pillows and smiled with some of his former brightness as he looked at his grand-daughter.

"Very pretty," he murmured. "Very pretty indeed." His faded eyes slightly sparkled. "There'll be some young men there, I suppose? Eh, Rachel?" he said.

Rachel's blush deepened, and Mrs. Avery and Rowland forbore to look at her, for they knew well that there was only one young man who counted with Rachel. Old Thomas Deller knew it too, but he tried to pretend to himself that he did not; for it grieved his old heart, in spite of a long affection for Arnold, that his fine and lovely Rachel should love Clement Deller's son. Cousins, too! Then there was his brother, that harsh-souled old curmudgeon John Deller; what would *he* say? He seemed resigned to his grandchildren's friendship with the Averys, but when it came to marrying it might be a different matter. The old quarrel still rankled, Thomas feared; John never invited Lilias or Thomas to West View, and he did not even come to see his brother now, when he must know that he had not much longer to live. A curmudgeon, a harsh, illiberal soul, thought Thomas Deller, remembering acts and sayings long since past; how such a man would receive Rachel as a grand-daughter-in-law was uncomfortably doubtful. It was all a great pity, a great pity, mused the old singing-master; and as he let his head sink back into his pillows again, he hoped it would all fade away and come to nothing. Nothing had been said on Arnold's side as yet, he thought; and Rachel might perhaps see someone she liked better.

Mr. Avery now came running up to say that the taxi had arrived, and everyone except Thomas Deller went down into the hall to see the brother and sister go. Mrs. Avery helped Rachel into her cloak; Rowland arranged his scarf carefully over his shirt front; and Mr. Avery expressed the opinion that it would be awkward if there was no light at West View.

" Yes—won't Esmé be in a chilly rage ! " said Rowland, groping for his coat.

At the mention of Esmé's name Rachel gave a tiny sigh, and Mrs. Avery quietly said " Esmé ! " with a satirical inflexion.

" Yes, she's a nasty little minx," agreed Rowland, " I know all about that. Are you ready, Rachel ? " He limped —since his football accident he had always slightly limped, but it did not hamper him much in walking or dancing— along the hall, and helped Rachel into the taxi. " West View," he commanded.

" I've seen one or two parties going there, as I come across the Moor just now," observed the taxi-driver sympathetically.

" ' There was a sound of revelry by night,' " said Rowland, putting up the window.

" Enjoy yourselves ! " cried Mr. Avery from the gate.

The taxi drove away. " I hope it goes off well, for poor old Arnold's sake," observed Rowland with sincerity as they turned into the main road.

Rachel did not answer, but after a while she said : " I think it's a nice idea to have the dance in the house."

" Bless you, it's only to show off how big their rooms are, my dear," boomed Rowland cheerfully. " It's Esmé's notion, I'll be bound."

" But, Rowland," began Rachel, " if you have such a low opinion of Esmé, why do you——"

" I haven't a low opinion of her," said Rowland, looking out of the window. " I see her as she is, that's all."

Rachel was silent.

When they reached West View they found that there were no lights, and that Esmé was in as cold a fury as Rowland had predicted. John Deller was in his element improvising paper lanterns to replace the two balls which usually glowed at the bottom of the drive ; but Esmé, standing in candle-light between her mother and Arnold in the West View

ballroom, wore the expression of haughty resignation which
she kept for the many occasions when she considered somebody had failed her. Her frock was primrose-coloured, like
Rachel's, for which Rachel was rather sorry. Mrs. Deller
looked handsome in black lace, but Rachel thought the
rumour that she had been starving herself lately to get down
her weight must be true, for her pretty face looked haggard,
and her high drawl was more than usually peevish as she
greeted them. Arnold was hotly explaining to his sister that
he had already telephoned to the Corporation electricity
works to find out what was wrong ; some mishap to an
engine had plunged the whole of Hudley into darkness, but
the damage was only slight, and in half an hour or so the
lights would come on again.

" But why can't they repair this part *first* ? " demanded
Esmé. " You ought to have been firmer with them, Arnold ; you're always so stupid on the telephone."

A slow deep colour filled Rachel's cheeks as Arnold,
sighing, began to explain more hotly than before.

" I should ring up the Corporation yourself and tell them
what you think of them, Esmé," advised Rowland, teasing
her.

" You're too bad, Rowland," murmured Esmé in a
pathetic little tone, looking up at him. Her lips quivered,
and she was almost in tears. That on this night of all nights
everything should go so terribly wrong ! She had meant
it to be such a triumph for her ; she had meant to show
Arnold's Averys the power and the glory of the Dellers and
the marvels of West View in their utmost splendour, so that
their hearts should be like water within them. And now
the lights were out, so that practically nothing could be
seen ; and what could be seen was a failure, for Rachel
was wearing a slightly brighter shade of primrose than
Esmé, so that Esme's dress was absolutely " killed." Oh, it
was too bad. Esmé's pleasure completely spoiled, as usual.
There were so few times when Esmé was able to enjoy herself that she did really think Rachel might have taken care

not to spoil her birthday dance. " It's not kind of you to tease me, Rowland," she faltered.

" The little mishap with the lights will make the occasion a long-remembered one, you know," said Rowland consolingly. " You're having this first one with me, aren't you ? "

Esmé brightened a little as she moved away with him. Rowland's limp spoiled the perfection of his dancing, but Esmé was such a superb little dancer herself that she flattered herself she could dance well with *anybody*. She liked the feeling of virtue it gave her to adapt her steps to Rowland's slightly uneven ones ; besides, she always felt that the on-lookers must be admiring her for the skilful and kindly way she did it. She moved with her accustomed grace now, and she was rather sorry when the end of the dance came and Rowland, saying briefly " I've something to say to you," steered her away into the outer darkness of the far conservatory. Esmé mildly protested that she was hostess to-night and ought not to vanish away like this, but Rowland said : " Nobody can see whether you're there or not," which was true enough. Esmé had the habit of yielding to Arnold's Averys, so she followed Rowland obediently now, and allowed him to take her hand and guide her to a large settee. This process took time, and in Esmé's opinion was not justified by results.

" It's very dark here, Rowland," she objected.

Rowland produced an electric torch from his pocket, and laid it upon a nearby table. " Few girls," he said, " can have been proposed to by the light of an electric torch, Esmé. Rejoice at your unique distinction in this respect."

An immense and delicious feeling of flattery stole over Esmé's heart. This was the reward of her eight years' goodness ; one of Arnold's Averys was going to ask her to marry him. What a triumph ! Rowland liked her better than he liked Arnold, after all.

" Are you going to propose to me, Rowland ? " she enquired in a light caressing tone, laughing.

"Certainly I am," boomed Rowland. "That's what I've brought you here for. You don't suppose I should have barked my shins on all those chairs for anything less, do you?"

Esmé, rather nervous, gave another little laugh and waited.

"Esmé, will you marry me?" said Rowland seriously.

Esmé waited to feel the thrill which this question ought to cause her, but it did not come. "Well, Rowland, really I've never thought about marrying you," she began at last. "I've always regarded you simply as Arnold's friend."

"The two things are not incompatible, I hope," said Rowland.

"No, but——" murmured Esmé, really at a loss as to her own sensations. Somehow the reception of an offer of marriage from one of Arnold's Averys was not as exciting as she had supposed. "I should like time to think it over," she announced, discovering this expedient with relief.

"How can you want time to discover whether you love me or not after eight years?" protested Rowland with some irritation. "That's absurd, Esmé."

"Well, it's the only answer I can give you," said Esmé rather crossly. "I'm sorry if you think it's absurd, Rowland."

There was a long pause. At length the music for the next dance sounded.

"There's the music," said Rowland in a sombre tone.

"And who are you dancing with, pray, that you're so anxious to join her?" cried Esmé angrily, rising.

"Rachel," replied Rowland.

Esmé felt a pang go through her heart. Yes! Rachel! The Averys! Inseparable! Devoted to each other! They and Arnold made a close companionship; Esmé was allowed only to hover meekly outside. Even after asking her to marry him Rowland wanted to fly off immediately to his sister. Angrily she put aside Rowland's proffered hand, and stumbled through the furniture alone. At length they reached the door of the inner conservatory, which was comparatively light ; Rachel was just passing out at the other end into the ballroom. On a sudden fierce impulse of jealousy Esmé stepped back into the darkness. Rowland, who had been walking in front of her, throwing the light from his torch on to her path, stopped in surprise.

" Rollo ! " murmured Esmé softly. " Shall we sit out this dance and talk ? "

Rowland hesitated and threw a glance in Rachel's direction ; Esmé put out a hand and touched his sleeve. With a quick jerk he threw it off, then, closing the door behind him, came towards her. An exquisite triumph filled Esmé's heart ; she had got the Averys, got them for ever ; she could make Rowland do what she liked , Rachel was devoted to Rowland, and Rowland was devoted to her ; she had got the allegiance of Arnold's Averys for always. And the moment she had it, of course, as usual her triumph turned to dust in her hands ; she did not want it. Who were the Averys, after all ? They were poor and unimportant ; Rowland was going to be a mere schoolmaster. How crude of him to make this scene after the very first dance ! " I don't think I want to talk after all," she said distastefully, retreating a little. " Open the door, Rowland."

" Look here, Esmé," said Rowland, stepping towards her. " Let us have this question settled, please. Are you going to marry me or are you not ? "

" I'm not," cried Esmé with disdain.

" Very good," said Rowland steadily. " Then if you'll excuse me I'll go to Rachel."

With a slight bow he backed away from her, opened the door and was gone.

" Well, really," thought Esmé, ready to weep. " How horrid everyone is to me ! And this is my birthday dance ! Anybody might think it was Rachel's." She followed Rowland to the ballroom, and was rather soothed by the eagerness with which her next partner, one of the Annison boys,

claimed her. Was she glad or sorry she had refused Rowland ? She did not know ; his exit had been rather piquant,
and he was one of Arnold's Averys. But then the Averys had
not the same value to her now that she had even for a
moment held them in her grasp : they had lost their
glamour of the unattainable. She did not know what to
think about it all, she was sure. " In any case," she concluded comfortingly, " Rowland's sure to ask me again."

They had danced perhaps twice more when the light
blinked, went out, blinked again, and then amid applause—
ironic at first but later really admiring—rose to a sym-
metrical brilliance which explained Esmé's wrath when she
had found her carefully designed scheme set at naught by
the Hudley Corporation. The guests began to blow out the
candles which had been fixed here and there about the
walls, and in this pursuit Rachel found John Deller—
stocky, red-faced, very glossy and well-groomed, his sparse
white hair firmly brushed, his bow tied much better than
poor Arnold's—at her elbow. As the arbiter of Arnold's
destiny he was always of consuming interest to her ; she had
turned a laughing look in his direction, not knowing that he
stood there, but when she saw who it was her face grew
sober. She made an effort, and produced a shy smile again.

" Well, Miss Rachel Avery," said John Deller, looking
shrewdly up at her from his small blue eyes, " and how are
you to-night ? "

His voice and look were subtly disparaging, as they always were when he spoke to Rachel ; and Rachel felt, as
she always did when he spoke to her : " He thinks I'm not
pretty enough for Arnold." She blushed deeply, but thought
again : " I don't care. I'm what Arnold wants, I know I
am." She had long since made a calm decision to give
Arnold everything he wanted as far as it lay in her power ;
and the thought of his need of her steadied her now. She
raised her head—though she was taller than John Deller :
perhaps that was one reason why he did not admire her—
and said quietly : " I'm enjoying your dance, Mr. Deller."

John Deller gave a little grunt; perhaps he was rather disconcerted ; Rachel hoped so. " And what is it like at Cambridge Place to-night ? " he went on, still with the same undercurrent of disparaging irony. " Dark ? "

Rachel, thinking of her grandfather as she had last seen him, quietly and mildly suffering in his modest dim room, his eyes, once bright and vital like his brother's, now faded and selfless and pathetic, winced, and blushed again for John Deller's lack of decency and good feeling. She knew nowadays a vague version of the quarrel between the Deller brothers, but she could not feel, as she knew Rowland felt, the pathos of John Deller's rage on that occasion. No ! She supported her grandfather and her mother with all her heart, of course, though their accounts of what had happened did not seem to Rachel quite to agree ; but if there were any sorrow to be felt for the Deller side, it was for Clement that she felt it. She had watched for so many years now John Deller's efforts to spoil Arnold—his caprices with the boy, his sudden absurd gifts of large sums of money, his equally sudden decisions that Arnold must learn to " rough it " ; his " tight hand " over certain innocent pleasures, his encouragement on the other hand to Arnold to " knock about a bit " and " see the world " ; his bursts of rage at the mill over things of which he had not previously explained the importance, and his too early initiation of the boy into some of the less savoury of his business transactions, so that instead of being proud of forming part of one of England's foremost industries, as his natural inclination would have been, Arnold had come to regard Adela Mills as a necessary but very disagreeable duty. Rachel had watched it all from Arnold's side, and she had come to the conclusion that Clement and Arnold were the ones to be sorry for. She was therefore always particularly gentle and loyal towards Mrs. Clement Deller, always defending her when Esmé, as she sometimes did, gave vent to long sarcastic accounts of incidents showing up this lady's indubitable silliness.

" Dark, eh ? " repeated John Deller, in a lively tone, the
jocularity of which was meant to veil the subtle sneer.

Rachel had a desire to say that the darkness of Cambridge Place was neither more nor less than the darkness of
West View ; but she repressed it ; after all, he was her host.
" Yes, it was rather dark," she said simply. Let him think
her a ninny if he would. She saw, as he turned away, that
he did think her so, just as he thought Arnold a noodle.
Well ! Rachel was content to share any place with Arnold.

The hours seemed to pass slowly, slowly by until the
dance arrived which Arnold had considered his duties as a
host might reasonably allow him to have with Rachel.
Arnold never *could* hide his feelings, thought Rachel with
a smile as she watched him on the other side of the room,
shuffling from one foot to the other, on tenterhooks to be
gone, maintaining a painfully forced smile while his partner
finished some lively sentence. The moment she had done
he sprang away from her like a stone released from a sling,
and gazed wildly round the room in search of Rachel. His
expression of harassed bewilderment gave way to eager happiness as his eyes lighted upon her ; he forged across the
room, entirely forgetful of, indeed not seeing at all, the
crowd of his guests through whom he pushed. His arm fell
round Rachel's waist like a bird settling into its nest ; his
hand trembled with eagerness as he clasped hers. Rachel
made herself as small as she could—it was one of Arnold's
fancies that he was slightly taller than Rachel, and she always wore low heeled slippers to encourage it. Arnold was
not as bad a dancer as Esmé pretended, but neither was he
as good as could be desired ; for he was conscientious and
jerky rather than skilful in his actions, and in his steering a
trifle ill-judged. Rachel, who danced quite well herself
though she did not get very many opportunities of showing
it—the Averys had no money for subscription dances, and
there were limits to the treats she would accept from Arnold
—knew Arnold's defects in this art well enough, but did not
care. They moved off together, silent, joyful, tremulous.

After a few moments the first ecstasy of their reunion settled into a steadier happiness ; Arnold's heart ceased to thump so wildly against Rachel's, and the rest of the ballroom became visible to Rachel once more.

" How do you think it's going ? " murmured Arnold anxiously in her ear.

" *Very* well, I think," said Rachel in a soothing tone. As a matter of fact she herself had not, before this dance, been enjoying the affair very much ; there seemed to her to be a worldliness, a feeling that the latest fashionable thing must not be strayed from by a hair's breadth, in the air, which laid a constraint upon her spirits ; but after all that might have been mere imagination, or the effect of her interview with John Deller. She was glad that Arnold, who was usually only too sensitive to shades of that kind, did not seem to perceive it.

" Wasn't it awful about the lights ? " he went on in his surprised boyish tones.

" Yes—but I thought it was rather fun," said Rachel staunchly.

Arnold seemed soothed. He stumbled over one of her feet, and said " Sorry ! " mechanically. Rachel was too used to this to bother to reply.

" I like the new frock," threw out Arnold. (He usually spoke in a series of enthusiastic jerks.) " Does your grandfather approve of it ? I see you've got the family pearls tonight." His face clouded, and Rachel guessed that he had perhaps tried to persuade John Deller to invite her mother, and failed.

" Esmé's frock is very pretty," she said at once, to distract him.

" Yes," agreed Arnold with brotherly indifference. " I suppose it is. She's very cross about it because the buttons aren't right, or something."

" Buttons ! " Rachel teased him, looking over his shoulder at Esmé's smoothly beautiful little gown. " Buttons ! "

" Well, buttons or *something* ! " cried Arnold, suddenly in the best of spirits and laughing heartily. He squeezed her waist, to show that he did not mean to stand any nonsense of that kind, and looked down into her eyes. For once his own eyes had lost their wistful look, and were jolly ; and Rachel felt that the Deller dance was beginning to be livelier.

All too soon their dance together was over, and with the crowd of other dancers they herded out through the door into the conservatory. The chairs were all full, the palms shook as couples brushed past them towards the little conservatory and the stairs.

" Rachel," whispered Arnold, " let's go into the billiard-room. Rachel ! "

There was hunger in his voice, and Rachel nodded. They slipped out at a side door, went down a passage or two, and reached the entrance to the billiard-room. Arnold threw open the door and put on a light, revealing a sheeted table and swathed chairs.

" It looks pretty ghastly, doesn't it ? " he said with satisfaction. " Nobody'll come *here*." He drew the door to behind them, and clumsily took Rachel in his arms. She yielded to his grasp ; he strained her to him, and kissed her flushed cheek eagerly, many times. Rachel's head lay on his shoulder, and for a few ecstatic moments they stood thus, listening to the beating of each other's hearts. Then suddenly music sounded in the distance. " Oh, bother ! " said Arnold irritably, raising his head. Rachel put her arms round his neck and pressed her cheek against his for a moment ; then they drew apart.

" I was talking to grandfather about us this afternoon," observed Arnold, moving towards the door.

" Were you ? " said Rachel eagerly. " What did he say ? "

" Nothing much," replied Arnold with gloom. " He never does."

They both sighed.

" Well," said Arnold in a resigned tone, switching off the

light, " usual time and place to-morrow morning, I suppose ? "

" Yes, I think I can manage it," replied Rachel quietly.

" If I have to go to Bradford I'll telephone," said Arnold, closing the door. His young face had fallen into its usual lines of conscientious strain. He took out his programme as they went along. " Lady Annison," he said. " Good Lord ! "

" Mine's Rowland again," Rachel remembered.

" Oh, well, you're all right then," replied Arnold, seemingly rather soothed.

But he sighed heavily, and for Rachel brightness fell from the air, as they passed together through the ballroom door.

She went steadily through the usual routine of the dance, however ; smiled and talked, and ate her supper with appetite, and even danced with a certain amount of pleasure. When they were all leaving the house her spirits rose to joy again ; for there was much manœuvring of the many cars standing in the drive ; and amid friendly shouts and swerving lights and a chorus of dissonant horns Arnold ran about from one car to the other, flushed and jolly, and gave directions and helped to turn front wheels. Rachel enjoyed his joy ; her eyes were bright, and she smiled, until the press of cars had all moved off in a long string, and the Averys' taxi was chugging soberly across Hudley Moor alone. It then struck her that Rowland was very quiet, and that it was rather odd that he had not been running about between the cars at Arnold's side. As they passed a lamp she glanced at him and thought that he looked pale. She now remembered that he had seemed rather quiet all evening. Perhaps he felt the return of her attention to him, for almost at once he announced briefly :

" I may as well tell you, Raikes, that I've asked Esmé to marry me."

" Oh, Rowland ! " breathed Rachel sadly. She could not pretend that this information was altogether unexpected, but that did not make it any the more welcome. Esmé was always so unkind to Arnold that an indignation against her had lighted itself in Rachel's heart and burned steadily, fed by much fuel, during the last eight years—look at Esmé to-night about the lights, for example—and Rachel knew that her mother held strong views of Esmé's worthlessness. Besides, Rowland was so young ; it would be years before he could earn enough to marry. She sighed.

" I know you aren't pleased," said Rowland, cocking an amused eye at her.

" Well——" sighed Rachel. " Of course if it's what you want, Rowland," she began.

" I *do* want her," said Rowland emphatically. " I know she's a selfish little minx and all that sort of thing, but she's the only girl I shall ever care about."

Rachel was touched, and spoke in a warmer tone. " And is she willing to wait a long time for you ? " she enquired.

" Oh, no ! " replied Rowland. He seemed surprised. " I thought you understood—she's refused me, you know," he said, throwing back his head and gazing at the ceiling of the taxi as though it interested him profoundly.

Rachel did not know whether to be glad or sorry, so she said " Oh ! " in a non-committal tone. Having collected her thoughts a little, she added : " I suppose you mean to ask her again."

" That's what she supposes too, no doubt," said Rowland grimly. " But I shan't." He sat up abruptly and turned towards his sister, and Rachel saw that his dark handsome face was really pale and drawn. " That's the only way to get her," he said, " not to ask her." He flung his arms out along the back of the taxi, and tapped its padded surface restlessly with his fingers. " Yes, that's the only way," he repeated with a frown, " *not* to ask her." He changed his position again with a restless movement very unlike his usual self, and sat with his hands between his knees. " *Why* the Dellers and the Averys should have this profound attraction for each other I'm sure I don't know," he said with a kind of humorous irritation. " Can you account for it, Rachel ? "

" No," said his sister shortly. She was vexed ; partly that he should seem to forget the attraction between Dellers which had existed in the last generation—not that it had anything to do with it, of course, but still—partly because she thought that Esmé had done rather more than her fair share in the creation of this " profound attraction " of Rowland's which she now declined to satisfy, and partly because Rachel always disliked to be reminded that Arnold was Esmé's brother. To think that Esmé, who was so unkind to Arnold, was his sister, bound to him for ever by the tie of blood, always depressed her. For a moment she felt profoundly discouraged by this hint of a new tie which would draw Esmé even closer ; then she rallied, accepted this new fact, put it calmly into its place and decided that though it might mean an added irritation for herself and Arnold, it could not alter their love. She would not allow anything to do that. " I don't know what to say about it all, Rowland," she said quietly. " I want us all to be happy. Do you think you'll be happy married to Esmé ? "

" Yes ! " exclaimed Rowland, striking his hands together. He seemed to muse a little, and added : " She'd be different then."

Rachel thought that this was quite possible. There were times—only one never knew when they were going to occur —when Esmé was simply charming. She could be unselfish, generous, loving, long-suffering—at times ; at other times she was just the reverse. Very likely, if she were removed from the bad example of ruthlessness set her by John Deller, and of petulance set her by her mother, she might be charming all the time.

" Perhaps it will all come out right in the end," she suggested, as they swung into Cambridge Place.

" Ha ! " snorted Rowland, who was always inclined to be sarcastic about undue optimism.

They had a latch-key, and expected to find the house

dark and quiet and sleeping ; but in the hall they met Mr.
Avery, fully dressed ; and their mother's voice sounded
from above, apparently in consultation.

"Don't be uneasy," said Mr. Avery at once. "Your
grandfather has had another of his attacks, that's all. He
was rather uncomfortable with it, so we sent for the doctor."

The brother and sister were not deceived, and looked at
each other soberly.

"Poor grandfather !" murmured Rachel.

Rowland took off his coat and scarf, and hung them up
in silence. Mrs. Avery now appeared round the turn of the
stairs, the doctor beside her. She looked sad ; almost upon
the brink of tears. As she passed Rachel she laid a hand on
her daughter's arm, and urged her quietly : "Go up, dear,
and cheer him a little." Rachel went upstairs sadly, and
entered her grandfather's room. He was lying much as she
had last seen him, but the dark rings round his eyes, the
ghastly pallor of his face, and the beads of sweat on his
forehead made him look much older and much weaker,
while his position amid his pillows was somehow that of a
defeated man. He opened his eyes when he heard her step,
and gave her a dim loving smile.

"I've not been so well, you see," he murmured depre-
catingly.

"Silly old thing !" said Rachel in a soft loving tone. It
struck her suddenly, with a deep pang, how like Arnold
he was as he lay there, with his fine aquiline nose and his
high forehead, and the rather childlike look which he had
now from weakness, but which was always stamped on
Arnold's fair perplexed face. The mouth, too, was very like.

"Well, were there any young men ?" enquired Thomas
Deller with a faintly merry look.

Rachel blushed. "Yes, heaps of them," she replied. She
sat down on the old man's bed, and taking his cold, limp
hand between hers, began to give him an exaggerated and
colourful account of her doings at West View, of course
omitting her interview in the billiard-room with Arnold.

Presently Thomas Deller seemed to doze, and Rachel fell silent. In the distance she could hear a quiet murmur of voices, which she felt sure was Rowland telling his parents about Esmé and himself. She began to marvel at the momentousness of the day. There was her grandfather, who, Rachel was almost sure as she watched him, had to-night taken a big step further away from them, had reached that point of the slope towards death where it becomes precipitous. Then there was Rowland's love for Esmé, which to-night had become definite and declared. And there was Arnold. To-night Rachel was surer of Arnold's love than she had ever been before. At the time when they were there together in the billiard-room it had all seemed so natural that she had not quite realised that it was new for him to kiss her ; but now she saw that their relations had taken a definite step forward. And had he not spoken to John Deller of their love ? Yes, it had been a momentous day.

But as time went on Rachel grew to think of the day of Esmé's dance as not so much momentous as typical. In the months that followed there was always Arnold, growing nearer and dearer to her every day. There was always something new in their relationship which made it closer than it had ever been, always some little detail which made Rachel say : " *Now* he really loves me." There was, too, often and often, an announcement from Arnold that he had been talking to John Deller about Rachel ; but nothing ever came of it, they were no more definitely engaged than they had ever been. John Deller did not forbid the engagement, but neither did he sanction it ; and as Arnold had not a halfpenny of his own and was very young, the lovers did nothing drastic about the matter, but just went on loving and meeting and hoping for the best. What her mother thought about it all was obscure to Rachel ; sometimes she thought one thing, sometimes another. Perhaps Mrs. Avery did the same ; at any rate, she placed no barriers and spoke no restraining word. Rachel could see clearly, however, that her father was not quite satisfied about her

position in the affair ; and at one time he even said that
he thought she ought to attend Leeds University daily and
train for something—domestic science perhaps—with the
obvious motive of getting Rachel out of Arnold's way for
a while. (None of the Averys disguised the fact that Rachel
was not clever, either at domestic science or anything else ;
quickness and accuracy were not in her nature ; but they
never worried about it, because she had other gifts.) Rachel
obediently attended Leeds for a while ; but Arnold dropped
into the habit of calling for her and taking her to the station in his sports car every morning, and bringing her home
from the station when she returned ; at times, too, business
legitimately took him to Leeds and they had lunch together.
This was, in Mr. Avery's eyes, rather worse than before ;
he admitted, amid laughter, that he had been hoist with
his own petard, and it became a family joke which Arnold
shared. (Even Mrs. Avery smiled, though rather sombrely.)
So that the Arnold-Rachel affair went on just the same as
it had done before, maintaining a steady advance.

The day of the Deller dance was typical of many other
days, too, as regarded Esmé and Rowland. As time went
on Rowland finished with Oxford, and took a job in a very
aristocratic preparatory school in Kent—he hated the
aristocratic part, but was a born teacher, like his father,
and after all he had to get experience somewhere, as he
observed. But the four cousins were together as much as
possible during Rowland's holidays, and the procedure was
pretty much the same as on the night of the dance, for an
endless argument seemed always in progress as to whether
Esmé should marry Rowland or not. Esmé (who indulged
in various not very serious flirtations from time to time)
constantly said that she would not marry Rowland, and
Rowland said he had not the slightest intention of asking
her to do so ; but somehow the question was never regarded
as settled. Rowland teased Esmé outrageously and was often
really rude to her ; he told her what he thought of her
artificial complexion, her manners, her mind, her taste in

literature and her behaviour to her mother, but he spoke in such a possessive manner that it was obvious he regarded her as his own and deeply loved her. Once when Rachel was feeling definitely miserable—because they had been invited to Sunday night supper at West View, which really looked as though John Deller were coming round to Arnold's engagement at last, and then over coffee in the great silk-panelled drawing-room he had so snubbed poor Arnold and sneered at the Averys that it seemed obvious that he wasn't and never would—she said to her brother despairingly :

" Do you think we shall *ever* be able to marry, Rowland ? Any of us ? "

" Of course we shall," said Rowland cheerfully. " Old Deller knows well enough he'll have to give in about you and Arnold. He's only waiting for some excuse to turn up so that he can pretend he was forced into it and always go on grumbling."

It was so firmly established in the Avery family that while Rachel and Lilias were not good character-readers, Will Avery and Rowland *were*, that Rachel felt quite cheered. " But what about you and Esmé, Rowland ? " she pursued, rather timidly. (They were walking home together after the dismal supper in question.)

Rowland gave a rather bitter laugh. " If Esmé once decides to marry me she'll marry me, John Deller or no John Deller," he said.

His voice had so much pain in it that Rachel was moved to urge him : " Why not ask her again, Rollo ? "

" Because the only way to get her is not to ask her," said Rowland firmly.

So in this too the night of the dance had been typical ; and unfortunately in its third occurrence it was no less so. As the years went on Thomas Deller's attacks became more and more frequent and more and more severe. Rachel gave up going to Leeds, for she was needed at home ; a nurse was secured and stayed two or three weeks, then the old

man rallied and the nurse left, only to be required again
before the end of the month. When Rowland came home
for his summer holidays, he was much irritated because
nobody could tell him exactly what was the matter with
his grandfather ; the Averys did not know, and the doctor
seemed unwilling to specify. But that he was slipping away
from them was clear ; his body, once so big and firm, was
now emaciated and shrunken ; his crisp tawny hair at last
succumbed to time and became grey and thin ; his voice
dwindled. His nights were times of agony and nightmare,
his days of exhaustion ; he seemed to find Rowland's
vigorous personality and deep voice too much for him,
greatly to Rowland's grief ; he often called Lilias by her
mother's name, and would lie sometimes for minutes together with a smile and a listening expression on his face,
obviously hearing music. This was only for a few minutes,
however, for soon he was wandering again, worrying himself about all sorts of people long since dead and incidents
long since over, perplexed as to where he was and why he
was not in his old room in the house he had lived in when
he married. But his politeness and courtesy never deserted
him.

" I should be very much obliged, Rachel," he would say
in his weak, slurring tones : " *Very* much obliged, if you
would have your lunch up here with me."

At such moments he was so like Arnold that Rachel, who
of course had not the slightest intention of leaving him alone
as he seemed to fear, felt the mingled love and pain in her
heart almost stronger than she could bear. Arnold, distressed doubly, for the old man and for Rachel's sadness,
came to Cambridge Place rather more than ever, and therefore presumably John Deller knew of his brother's condition ; but he never came to see the dying man, or even sent
a friendly message. Esmé too, who shrank from pain and
illness, partly because she knew she was useless in a sick
room, avoided Cambridge Place in this dark hour ; Rowland discovered this, and trounced her soundly for it, but

the question of whether they would ever marry or not seemed just as uncertain as before.

At last there came a certain dark December morning. Rowland was expected home that day, and Rachel, who had been up late the night before, making preparations against his return, was sleeping heavily, when she suddenly started awake to find her mother standing by her bed. She sat up and looked her question, and Mrs. Avery said quietly: " He's dead, Rachel." A rush of memories of the kindly sensitive old man whom she had loved for so many years flooded Rachel's mind—memories of him, of Arnold, of Rollo, of old childish things, all sweetly intermingled. His death seemed to have torn more from her life than just himself. She lay back and put her arm across her eyes, and was silent ; her girlhood seemed over.

# CHAPTER V

# LENA

Lena and Alfred Howgate sat facing each other across the hearth in the Bierley Hall dining-room. Lena was knitting and turning over a volume of poetry ; her stepfather, his old-fashioned pince-nez askew halfway down his big bony nose, was reading the *Hudley News*.

In Lena's opinion Alfred Howgate was not a handsome man. She conceded him a well-formed body, for he had broad shoulders and narrow hips, was above the average height, and kept his weight down by exercise taken for the purpose, so as not to spoil his riding. She conceded also that his hands were well-shaped, white and sinewy ; his clothes and linen always irreproachable, his signet ring good—it had belonged to his grandfather. Though his manners were careless and at times even callous, he was never at a loss in any kind of society ; he spoke in light and not unpleasing tones with only a very slight hint of a Yorkshire accent, and he was not without a rather gross but unmalicious, tolerant, as it were worldly-wise, humour. All this Lena conceded ; but how anyone could consider his long sallow face, his sparse fair hair, his big nose, his light grey eyes, his fair moustache—how anyone could consider all that handsome Lena simply could not imagine. Nevertheless she knew that Alfred Howgate was so considered ; in the many hotels they had visited together, at the seaside or near to race meetings, women always seemed glad to talk to him and flattered by his notice. Often they tried to find out from Lena whether he was a widower or no ; in her earlier days as his daughter Lena always replied with truthful directness, but she found that this in some obscure way was regarded

by her stepfather as spoiling sport, so in a confused and
blushing but loyal manner she began to practise evasions
on the point, for above all things and whatever her private
feelings she wished to do her duty by the man who had
given her his name. As a result of this attitude on Lena's
part the Howgate pair got on pretty well together, their
surface relations being quite remarkably smooth. They
lived, however, poles apart. The only occasion on which
Lena could remember anything approaching intimacy between them was on that Monday morning, now so many
years ago, when the Bierley Hall cook, primed by her
brother the tram-driver as to the cause of the tears which
silently rolled down Lena's cheeks as she stood in the long
arched porch waiting for the car to come and take her back
to the Hudley Girls' College, had indignantly fetched Mr.
Howgate out to look at his stepdaughter's distress. The
cook explained with hearty disgust that they didn't treat
Lena "right" at that fine new school, they were unkind
to her ; and she called on the child to corroborate what she
said.

Lena, thus forced into the open, sobbed : " They keep
on mocking me."

" Why didn't you tell me before, you silly little fool ? "
demanded Alfred Howgate with rough kindliness. " Which
of 'em is it that's unkind to you ? Eh ? "

Lena with a terrific effort hauled up the name from the
depths of her soul, and wailed : " Esmé Deller."

" Aye, I darcsay ; if she's like her grandfather I'll bet
she's as hard as nails," said Howgate with some feeling.
" Well, take your things off. You shan't go back. I'll send a
note instead."

In the ecstasy of her relief Lena had flung herself into his
arms and sobbed out her heart. Her stepfather patted her
shoulder not unkindly at first, but after a minute or two
began to laugh, and cried : " Well, that'll do, that'll do !
That's enough ! Get along into the kitchen now, and have
some cake or something."

Lena explained that she had only just had her breakfast,
at which her stepfather laughed again, and said good-
humouredly : " Well, wipe your nose, anyhow." At this
the cook also laughed, and Lena felt humiliated and rebuffed, the more so when she found that her emotion had
really made her hungry. That night Howgate came late
into her room—she was reading in bed, as usual—and
said, looking at her curiously : " So you went for young
Esmé with a knife, did you ? "

Lena, frozen with horror, gazed up at him feeling that
the hour of judgment was upon her ; of course, she reflected,
he had seen Esmé's grandfather, and heard all about that
fearful moment with the knife from him.

" What did you do it for ? " pursued her stepfather with
some curiosity. " Eh ? "

Lena turned away her eyes in a torment of indecision.
If Howgate or anyone else had asked her a month or two
ago for an account of any incident in which she had taken
part, he would have been overwhelmed by a flood of eager
childish chatter ; but Esmé had taught her how horribly
one could be hurt when one told things about oneself, and
she now felt it an agony to reveal any personal detail. When
one did so people laughed, people despised one, people
jeered, people told bits of it afterwards to other people in a
scornful tone. How could one expose details of washing
basins and chocolates to Howgate ? They were so absurd ;
he would laugh and laugh, and Lena would wince and
wince. She could not explain the singing lesson even to herself, so it was hardly likely she could make him understand
its subtle torture. And then Rachel ! It was impossible to
betray one's deep, obscure feeling for Rachel to be jeered at.
Before she had contrived to plan an explanation of the
knife incident which should reveal as little of all this as
possible, Howgate moved away towards the door.

" Well, never mind," he said. He sounded rather disappointed. " Good night," he added in an artificially cheerful tone.

"Good night," said Lena with relief.

The door closed behind him.

From that day to this no caress had ever passed between them. Lena was sent away to an excellent boarding-school in the south of England, where almost from the first day she was fairly happy. She had expected everyone to behave to her as Esmé had done, and was able to bear smaller cruelties with composure. Moreover, as she made no pretensions to gentility, it was considered a point of honour not to jeer at her blunders. Then she was clever, which here seemed rather to count. As time went on her manners grew more conventional, her taste in dress improved, and her speech became indistinguishable from that of the other girls ; she took examinations, and played games with a fierce enthusiasm which almost atoned for her natural inaptitude. She did not make any very intimate friendships, but had several "friends" with whom she was comfortable enough. During the holidays her stepfather always took her away for a week-end or a fortnight, according to the season of the year ; and it was then that they went to those enormous hotels at large seaside resorts, where the inquisitive ladies attacked Lena. In these hotels Howgate invariably discovered a few bachelor friends ; Lena trailed after these parties of men, or, as she grew older, went off by herself. She thus had rather too much time in which to brood over herself and her life, and in her middle teens a very natural sentimental phase overtook her, in which she dwelt romantically on the subject of her own unknown father. Who was he ? What was he ? Obviously someone belonging to her mother's class, thought Lena, and with flushed cheeks told herself that she was not ashamed of *that*. On behalf of this unknown parent she revolted chivalrously against Howgate's assumption of his privileges, and, greatly daring, showed this revolt by addressing Howgate as "Uncle." The first time he heard this he let it pass, but on the third or fourth repetition he coloured and said uneasily :

"What do you mean—uncle? You're my adopted daughter."

At this Lena, fixing her eyes earnestly on him, blurted out with much feeling : " I wish I knew more about my real father."

Howgate, scowling, enquired : " What did your mother tell you about him ? "

" Nothing," replied Lena with a woebegone expression, " except that he was dead."

" Best let him stay dead, then," said Howgate with a sarcastic smile.

Lena thought this brutal, and put her stepfather down definitely as a person who did not understand the finer shades, and to whom it was useless to confide generous youthful feelings. It was not in her nature to keep up any steady personal animus, for the moment anyone threw her a kindly word her affectionate heart leaped responsively out to them, so she did not dislike her stepfather consistently ; but by this rebuff she was thrown back, as far as he was concerned, into the reserve which Esmé had first taught her, and the two Howgates drew still further apart. From the strain of this kind of intercourse with her stepfather Lena found it a great relief to return to school, especially as she grew older and achieved positions of responsibility, and her qualities of loyalty and simple honesty became recognised. To be elected by vote to any position was an ecstasy to Lena, for she was extremely proud of being thought worthy of anybody's suffrage. She was also proud of being thought reliable, and proud of her examination successes, and she loved her work ; and altogether she felt happy in the essentially decent atmosphere of the school, where all regarded truth and justice as their ideals, even if they did not always manage to live up to them. As the end of her school time drew near, she was seized with an overwhelming desire to put off the evil day of her withdrawal from scholastic life by going to some university ; but Alfred Howgate seemed to think this rather nonsense, and hung back—

probably, as Lena saw now, to see if her wish were really
serious—and as she thought it her duty to remain at home
with him if he wished it, she gave up the idea and settled
down to life at Bierley Hall.

The trouble was that there was not much life at Bierley
Hall. In the morning, if the chauffeur-under-gardener had
some special job on hand, Lena drove her stepfather down
to the mill. Then she went into Hudley and shopped, and
then returned to Bierley and had a mild argument with
the cook. The cook was the same one as in the Hudley
College days ; as she had married Howgate's groom she was
indeed a permanent fixture, though she was growing elderly
now and rather difficult, and her brilliant efforts were apt
to be followed by lapses. At times Howgate, who was particular about his meals, sniffed irritably as he carved—
which he did to admiration—and observed to Lena :
" Nobody can cook like your mother used to ; I don't know
what women are coming to nowadays, I'm sure." (This,
by the way, was the only reference to the late Mrs. Howgate
which he ever made ; Preston, the elderly groom who also
served as a gardener, had orders to place flowers on the
Howgate grave in Bierley Green churchyard at suitable intervals, but Howgate never went there himself, and this
still further enlarged the gulf between himself and Lena.)
At other times also her stepfather enquired : " How often
have you spoken to cook lately, Lena ? " and if the number
sounded rather large, he would say : " I'd better have a go
at her myself." As soon as the meal was over he would
stride off to the kitchen and do so, returning flushed and
laughing, while the cook stormed and wept, and Lena,
who was incapable of saying a word of rebuke to anybody
unless she lost her temper first, marvelled. On the whole,
however, Lena was an efficient housekeeper ; the mistake
she made lay in flattering her stepfather's little prejudices
too anxiously, which by making him appear a tyrant to
himself irritated him. Lena saw that it irritated him, but
the next time she would make the same mistake, putting

all the force of her nature into, for example, the securing of
the proper brand of tea. She had little else to put force into,
for once she had dealt with the cook her duties, except for
being present at Howgate's meals when he was in, were over
for the day. However, she made duties for herself by throwing herself energetically into all the village concerns of
Bierley Green—the bazaars, the dramatic entertainments,
the Women's Institute, the Literary Society, the provision
of a billiard-table for the young men's club. Howgate was
generous to her with money, and also as regarded the
house ; she could buy what books and join what libraries
she liked, provided she was not too immersed in reading
to talk to him when he wanted to be talked to, and she could
have any kind of meeting she liked in Bierley Hall, provided
it did not interfere with meal times and was kept out of his
sight and hearing. With village meetings and reading, then,
she kept herself going ; for there were plenty of days when
her stepfather left the house immediately after breakfast and
did not come back till late at night—he had many clubs and
many invitations—and Lena had only Mr. and Mrs.
Preston and an elderly maid to speak to. As it chanced there
were no old schoolmates of hers within easy reach, and her
own nature, combined as time went on with sheer lack of
use, made it difficult for her to form new friendships un-
aided with the young people of the neighbourhood, of
whom in any case there were not many. Occasionally
Howgate would be smitten with a sense of duty, and would
take her to a subscription dance and try to find some friends
for her. On these occasions Lena's spirits beforehand were
positively wild with expectation, and as she surveyed herself in the mirror before setting out she could not help feeling that really she was not as ugly as she had been wont to
think. Or perhaps it was just that she was improving in appearance as time went on, for her black hair was now short
and showed its unruly masses to advantage, her dark eyes
seemed larger and she had given up wearing spectacles ;
her complexion was clearer ; her vivid lips were fashionable

nowadays, and her figure, though still on the heavy
side, was not so thick as of yore. In a deep rose-coloured
gown she looked almost handsome. But that was at home ;
when she reached the ballroom she was always dumb-
founded, smitten to earth by the beauty and loquacity of
the other girls there. (Just occasionally she saw Esmé in
the distance, brilliant, beautiful, surrounded by hosts of
partners, with her brother and her mother and her grandfather in the rear ; and then Lena's heart sank very low indeed. Howgate never tried to introduce Esmé's brother
to her, although he knew John Deller so well ; Lena
guessed that there had been a slight tiff between them about
the Hudley Girls' College incident, and that though they
did not wish to quarrel because of business, Howgate was
too proud to mention Lena to him again. After all, Howgate
was Alfred Howgate of Bierley Hall ; whereas who was
John Deller ? A rich man, certainly, but a nobody, a self-
made man, and probably of foreign descent. When these
feelings were slightly hinted at in Howgate's conversation,
Lena felt drawn to him for standing by her so loyally and
thinking so little of the Dellers ; but was immediately hotly
ashamed of such snobbish futility—or at any rate tried to
be.) When Lena danced with older men, Howgate's friends,
she found herself able to talk to them—because, as she told
herself frankly, with people of a different generation one
can always " act " a little—but she felt abashed and self-
conscious because all the other girls of her age had younger
partners. But when she danced with young men the results
were disastrous, for she was always attacked by a fit of shy-
ness and self-depreciation, and either could not say a single
word, or in a desperate attempt to be lively welcomed them
with such effusiveness that they were alarmed and snubbed
her. In any case, no young man ever danced twice with
Lena ; so the return from a dance was always Napoleon-
after-Waterloo for her. And so gradually all the building
up, the buttressing and reassuring, which her comparative
success at school had achieved on Lena's personality, began

to crumble away under the disintegrating force of loneliness. She was indeed at times horribly lonely, achingly lonely. Her stepfather gave her a car on her twenty-first birthday, and in this she roamed about the country a good deal, within the limits of his meal times. She passed pairs of friends and lovers and groups of giggling girls, and looked back, and envied them with all her heart. At night sometimes when Howgate was absent she tramped out a long way, until she came to some houses whose inhabitants she did not know ; then she would walk slowly along the row of little yellow lighted squares, and speculate as to what lay within, or peep in and see vignettes of family life. She used to imagine what it would be like to have brothers and sisters, friends, a husband ; and carried on a long winding story in her head about the adventures of a girl rather like Lena Howgate, but intensely popular and admired. She knew that all this was very silly and schoolgirlish, and often scolded herself severely for it. Here she was, she told herself, young, healthy, rich, comparatively free ; she had no right to be unhappy. " When you feel unhappy," she told herself firmly, " go out and do something for somebody else." And out she went and tried to follow this precept, sometimes with success. Of course there were moments of joy in her life ; there were sunny mornings, when the hills stood up all round green and fresh and clear against the bright pale sky, and Hudley, sprawling along the side of the slope across the nearest valley, looked like a toy town with its neat rows of houses and its tiny mill chimneys and its little moor and its pretty curving roads, and a toy church clinging to the end of the bluff just opposite Bierley Hall. Surely there could be no harm or pain or cruelty in a sparkling, brightly coloured world like that. And there were days of wild storm, when the wind howled and dark ragged clouds flew fiercely through the air, the hills grew black and Hudley looked battered and grey but somehow staunch and defiant. And there were clear starry nights when the Hudley lights looked like jewels, and winter afternoons when the setting sun made the sky red and a frosty mist seemed undecided whether to cling to the vague Hudley houses or rise above them into the clear cold air. But however much one revelled in a view of hills and moors, one could not live on that alone, and on the whole—Lena turned a page, and read the words : " All my life is a rehearsal for something which never takes place."

" How true ! " thought Lena. " How absolutely true." And she felt comforted by its truth. At the same time she could not help smiling cynically at her own youthful despair ; it was so exaggerated and unnecessary, she thought, as to be funny.

Alfred Howgate was at home to-night because he had a bad cold, in token of which a large crumpled monogrammed handkerchief lay unconcealed on his knee. It was owing to this cold that they were spending the evening in the diningroom, which he said was warmer than the other rooms ; but then he was rather fond of finding excuses to remain in this room, because he preferred it. Lena shared this preference. The room was long and large, with a fine window (now thickly curtained) at the far end overlooking the magnificent Hudley view ; over the fireplace hung a striking portrait of Alfred Howgate's mother of unhappy memory— in a pink evening dress, with a diamond star in the tremendous plaits of dark lustrous hair which were coiled about her handsome head ; she had grey eyes beneath full lids, like her son's—and other family portraits decked the walls. The furniture was all of the colossal mahogany type, richly carved ; Alfred Howgate occasionally felt the top of the enormous table with one hand, and murmured : " A piece of good wood." When his friends suggested, as they sometimes did, that his furniture was old-fashioned, he simply smiled. The sideboard was crammed with ornate silver dishes and with cups won by Howgate in his early days at steeplechases ; there was also a hoof of one of his past horses, mounted in heavy silver as an inkstand. All this silver and mahogany gleamed in the electric light, which Bierley Hall made from its own battery. Perhaps once a month these lights would suddenly grow dim, and Howgate would start up and rout out Preston from the kitchen to see what was wrong ; usually it was a mere matter of not having run the engine long enough. Lena always felt guilty on these occasions, though her stepfather rarely spoke a word of blame to her. But then he rarely scolded her for anything, and this was one of Lena's silent quarrels with him ; she suspected that he regarded all women as by nature incapable of sense, and treated them with indulgence accordingly. If she forgot to order something for which he had asked, when her forgetfulness came to light he simply said : " Eh, well ! " and rang the bell himself. He seemed simply astounded when he found that she could write his letters for him in a really sensible manner—though, as Lena observed with some cynicism, he did not hesitate to make use of this curious accomplishment on her part. But after all that was only natural, for he loathed writing letters intensely ; his writing sprawled, and his spelling was not too safe—not that he minded that ; if people didn't like Alfred Howgate's spelling they could dislike it, for all he cared. He had finished the *Hudley News* now, Lena saw with a sigh, and would have to be talked to ; he folded up the paper carelessly, and took off his pince-nez and put them in their little case.

" What about tea, Lena ? " he said. (It was one of his little whims to have tea after dinner instead of coffee, and Lena, feeling that it was Trollopean, enjoyed it.) " I think I shall get off to bed pretty early to-night, with this cold."

" I've ordered hot milk for you," observed Lena, closing her book and rolling up her knitting.

" Well, let's have it then," said Howgate with a sniff.

Lena rang the bell.

" Do you want the paper ? " continued her stepfather.

" Well—is there anything in it ? " enquired Lena, looking at the crumpled mass dubiously.

"Nothing to speak of," said Howgate. "Old Deller's dead."

"What! John Deller?" exclaimed Lena, surprised at his taking the loss of a close business associate so calmly.

"No, of course not. His brother," replied Howgate with another sniff. "They're a long time with that milk. He taught music or something of that kind, you know. Thomas Deller."

"Thomas Deller!" repeated Lena. She stretched for the paper.

The maid entered with tea for Lena and a glass of hot milk in a silver holder for Alfred Howgate. He proceeded to sip it, complaining, as he always did, that it was hot.

"That's what it's supposed to be," replied Lena mechanically. She had opened the *Hudley News*, and was scanning its pages for Thomas Deller's name. "Where is it?" she enquired with some impatience. "Is it just in the deaths, or in a column?"

"Oh, there's quite a piece about him," replied her stepfather. "He seems to have been quite a celebrity in his day. It's on an inside sheet."

Lena had now found the notice. It was headed "Death of a Hudley Musician," and had a small square photograph inset. The photograph was a blurred one of ancient date, but Lena knew that crisp hair and fine head well, only too well; they were for ever associated in her mind with her vilest action—the remembrance of it attacked her sometimes suddenly in the middle of the night and made her blush and writhe with shame. Yes, that was Rachel's grandfather, whom she had once jeered at and ill-treated in the way which she despised and detested more than anything else on earth. Whenever Lena saw a child surrounded by a jeering circle of playmates or being excluded from the others' games, or when she saw two or three setting on to another, or one child pushing a weaker one face down into the dust, something seemed to snap in her brain, and from being a timid, irresolute, shrinking girl she suddenly became a whirling fury. There had been several occasions on which she suddenly flew across the road, snatched the children apart, smacked the aggressors hard—she who could go all lengths rather than damage a fly—and poured out a burning torrent of words, the gist of which was that they were cowardly, un-English, despicable, and ought to be deeply ashamed of themselves. When these storms were over she trembled so much that she could hardly stand, her teeth chattered, she felt sick ; she knew that she had a neurosis or whatever they were called about this particular aspect of life—she even used such things as cushions and safety-pins in strict rotation so as not to hurt their possible feelings—and that it was due to Esmé Deller that she felt as she did. (There were other aspects of life too on which her outlook was not healthy, thanks to Esmé ; her idiotic behaviour with young men, for instance, was due to Esmé's expressed conviction that Lena was far too ugly ever to attract the opposite sex.) But to oppress one's fellow-creatures by word or deed, to hurt their feelings by superior social pretensions, to make them wretched by a sneer—that to Lena was the last infamy ; and to know that she had once been guilty of it roused in her an almost savage despair. Every line of old Thomas Deller's harassed face at that horrible singing lesson rose before her now with a fearful clearness ; she saw each tiny bead of sweat on his forehead, the slight trembling of his hands, the timid appealing smile on his bearded lips. Involuntarily she gave an exclamation of distress.

" What's the matter ? " enquired Alfred Howgate, emerging from his glass. " Tea hot ? "

" No," stammered Lena, " no."

" Why, you aren't having any," observed her stepfather. He slightly stroked his left eyebrow with one hand—a habit of his when he was considering anything—and gave her a shrewd look.

Lena hastily poured out a cup of tea, and returned to the

newspaper. There was, as her stepfather had said, quite a
piece about old Thomas Deller—he had won gold medals,
and had dinners given in his honour, and studied abroad
under famous masters, and altogether seemed to have his
foot on the ladder of fame, in his early youth. And then
somehow it had just not come to anything ; whether it was
because he had married too early, or because he had no
money, or because of some lack of persistence in his character, or because his talent was not really great enough, or
just owing to sheer bad luck, did not appear, and indeed
the paper seemed to think that his useful career as a Hudley
singing master had fulfilled all his hopes. But Lena, who
had her own ideas of what a career should be, could not
help feeling the pathos of a decline from the opera house
at Milan to a set of nasty little girls in a private school in
Hudley. And she had jeered at him, mimicked him, thrown
music in the air, egged the other girls on ! How could she !
How could she ! How could she have hurt that poor disappointed old man ! And now he was dead, and she would
never be able to tell him she was sorry ; she would never be
able to make it right with him, never be able to restore his
self-esteem over that detestable incident. Lena was rather
good at restoring people's self-esteem ; she knew so well
just how and where one felt humiliated, that she was able
to apply balm at precisely the right spot. She imagined a
conversation now between Thomas Deller and herself, in
which she would skilfully make it clear that his inability
to control those children was due to his noble and artistic
soul, and not to any defect of character on his part ; one
should not use a razor to cut wood, nor a Thomas Deller to
teach a set of heartless little Philistines, and so on. She
would like to rush out now, this very instant, and make it
all right with him and comfort his bruised old heart. But it
was too late. Why had she never thought of doing it before ?
What an imbecile she was ! She exclaimed again, and
throwing down the paper tapped her foot against the
fender in nervous anger with herself.

" What's the matter with you to-night ? You seem all on edge," said Alfred Howgate rather crossly.

He was not a man who could easily be left unanswered, so Lena, gulping, forced herself to reply : " I'm rather sorry about old Thomas Deller, that's all." He stared at her in such surprise that she added hastily, to tone down this inexplicable sentiment about an unimportant old man : " I liked his grand-daughter, that time I was at the Hudley Girls' College, you know, and she was very fond of him."

" You'd better send him a wreath, then, if you're as sorry as all that," said Howgate with good-humoured sarcasm. " Well, I'm going to bed. Will you lock up, or shall I tell Preston ? "

" I'll tell Preston. I hope your cold will be better in the morning," said Lena dutifully.

Howgate sniffed, threw out a " Good night," and left her.

When the door had closed behind him Lena was so childish as to make a *moue* in his direction and exclaim angrily : " I just *will* send a wreath, then ! " She unfolded the *Hudley News* and read the Deller obituary again, then picked up her knitting. The needles clicked irregularly, Lena's breast heaved, and the tears smarted behind her eyes as she pictured old Thomas Deller lying dead. If only she had known that he was ill ! She could have written to him, then, saying how sorry she was ; such a loving little letter it should have been, and Rachel would have read it to him. Rachel ! Lena sighed ; she regarded Rachel's society as a sort of Paradise from which she was excluded by her own wicked act, and she had no hope of ever regaining it. But how much she wished she had written that letter before Mr. Deller's death, how much she wished she had written it, oh how much, how much ! The thought of lying for her whole life under the self-accusation of this gross cruelty to an old man, and never being able to express contrition for it, never put it right, was suddenly more than

Lena could bear ; it maddened her ; she felt she *must* say she was sorry and explain it all to someone. Suddenly she flew out of the room across the passage to the library, put on the light, opened her bureau, snatched up her pen and a sheet of notepaper, and began to write.

" *Dear Rachel,*"—she scrawled rapidly in her large black characters, " *I have just seen the news of your grandfather's death in the paper. I am very very sorry that he has gone from us, because he was a good, loving old man, and highly talented, and perhaps not appreciated in Hudley quite as much as he ought to have been. His death must leave a great gap in your life. I am especially sad, too, because now I shall never be able to tell him how sorry I am that I was unkind and rude to him in that singing class at the Hudley Girls' College when we were children together a long time ago. Dear Rachel, it was not all quite my fault, and I was only a stupid, frightened little girl then and had just lost my mother. But do not think I mean to excuse myself by saying that ; my conduct on that occasion was quite inexcusable, and it will never cease to trouble me. I wish I could have seen him just once before he died, to make it all right and ask his forgiveness. I wish too that you could forgive me. I am very sorry, Rachel. With love to him and to you from*

" LENA."

Without reading this through she folded it and put it hastily in an envelope, addressed, sealed and stamped it in a frenzy, then ran along the hall to the kitchen, and opening the door, called : " Don't lock me out ; I'm just going to take a letter to the post." She shut the door again quickly so as not to hear any of the protests which she knew would arise, but was not in time to miss Mrs. Preston's : " Take your coat, Miss Lena ! " Exclaiming crossly that they treated her like a baby, she snatched down an old coat from a hook and struggled into it, then, hot and excited, opened the heavy front door and fled along the dark lane to the wall letter-box. As the letter flopped into the box a weight seemed to roll off her heart ; she gave a great sigh of relief, and groped her way back towards the slightly thicker blackness which was Bierley Hall in a more sober but contented mood. She felt she had done something she had been wanting to do for years.

But next morning as soon as awoke she regretted the letter. Unfortunately she could remember every word of it, and by daylight it all sounded fearfully childish and high-flown, not to say silly. Still, after all, she reassured herself, it was quite correct to send Rachel a letter of condolence on her grandfather's death. But she had written " good loving old man " and " dear Rachel "—it was terrible to think of. She blushed and squirmed at her own naïveté, and not for the first time made a resolution never to post a letter written at night until the following morning. But why should she be ashamed, after all, of feelings which were deep and friendly and sincere ? In the next two days she veered thus back and forth, now feeling that she would sell her soul not to have sent the letter, and now that by sending it she had saved her soul alive. The date and hour of the funeral appeared in the paper ; she ordered a wreath for it from a Hudley shop—for after her stepfather's gibe she would not take flowers from the Bierley Hall greenhouses— and rather to her own surprise found herself lurking behind a neighbouring gravestone on the clear cold December morning when Thomas Deller's funeral procession entered the St. Mark's graveyard.

At once she decided that she had certainly made a mis-take in sending that letter to Rachel, and especially in suggesting that Thomas Deller was not appreciated in Hudley as he ought to have been. (*Why* did she keep on making these fearful blunders ?) For there were not only Rachel and her father, and a lady whom she took to be Mrs. Avery leaning on the arm of a young man who limped and was probably Rowland, and Arnold Deller (though not Esmé) and the great John Deller himself, very much upset and mopping his face with a large white silk handkerchief and carrying an extremely glossy silk hat—not only were there these relations of the dead man, but also crowds of other men in silk hats, and heaps and heaps of flowers. Obviously, thought Lena, Thomas Deller was a man of importance in Hudley, and she had merely insulted his memory and offended Rachel more than ever by sending that atrocious letter. If it had been possible she would have fled from the place in shame ; but it was not decently possible, so she remained where she was through the service, and until most of the mourners had left the church-yard. The Averys and Dellers passed quite close to her, but Lena thought it indecent to look upon them in such a sad hour, and kept her eyes lowered. She could not help however, being conscious of John Deller, for he was making himself rather conspicuous ; his red face was very moist, and as he passed her he ejaculated in a thick emotional tone : " He was the best brother that ever lived ! " Lena, who remembered Esmé's account of the quarrel between the Deller brothers as she remembered every word that Esmé had uttered in her hearing, was surprised at this, and con-cluded that perhaps the breach had been healed during the singing master's last illness.

The next time she saw her stepfather, which was at breakfast on the following morning, she put a question on the point.

" Still harping on old Thomas Deller ? " said Howgate good-humouredly. " Nay, I shouldn't think they ever made it up, those two." He went on to give a somewhat cynical account of the origin of the Deller quarrel, to which Lena listened with deep interest.

" All the same, he cried at the funeral," she observed when it was finished.

" It's just like him," said her stepfather. " He can cry when he wants to, can John Deller. But what were you doing at Thomas Deller's funeral ? It's not much of a way for a young girl to spend a morning, going to a funeral."

Lena countered this by another question. " There seemed
to be a great many people there," she said. " Was Thomas
Deller an important man in Hudley ? "

Her stepfather stared. " What, a poor old chap like
that ? " he said. " Use your common sense, Lena. Those
would be representatives of musical societies and such like,
I suppose. You'll learn as you grow older that plenty of
people turn up at a man's funeral who won't lift a finger
to help him when he's alive. What are you going to do this
morning ? Another funeral, eh ? "

" No, not to-day," replied Lena, trying to sound
amused.

" Then you might come down for me about eleven
o'clock and take me along to Adela Mills," said
Howgate. " Joe's helping Preston in the stables this
morning."

Lena was often irritated by Howgate's refusal to learn
to drive, for which she could imagine no possible reason
except sheer laziness. Considering that he still rode daily
during the hour before lunch—an accomplishment which
Lena did not possess, for Howgate disliked the sight of
women on horseback—he could not be suspected of lacking
nerve for the job ; and the amount of inconvenience and
re-arranging which his refusal to drive a car necessitated
was really quite extraordinary. To-day, however, Lena was
so relieved to find that after all she had not insulted Thomas
Deller's memory in her letter to Rachel, but hit the nail
accurately on the head instead, that she agreed with
alacrity, and presented herself at Bierley Bottom on the
stroke of eleven with a cheerful face. They drove along the
valley through the lower parts of Hudley to Adela Mills, and
Lena sat in the car in the big yard and admired the boiler
fires while Howgate transacted business within. She saw,
as she had often seen before on similar occasions, the red-
faced John Deller at the door, and the pale slender Arnold
crossing the yard towards the office, but as usual did not
have speech with either of them. The interview was not,

apparently, altogether a pleasant one, for when Howgate
came out he was particularly dry and sardonic, although
John Deller waved to him and called " Good-bye, Alfred !
Good-bye ! " in a very hearty, not to say flattering, tone as
Lena drove off. Arnold meanwhile, standing by, looked
even more harassed than usual.

" He's a fool, that boy," observed Howgate trenchantly,
pulling up the rug. " What he doesn't know about dyeing
would sink a fleet of ships."

" Really ! " murmured Lena with interest. She hoped he
would say more, for she always felt most drawn to her stepfather when he spoke of textile technicalities ; she understood his point of view there, which she was far from doing
on almost every other topic. But Howgate relapsed into
vague grumblings and then silence, and Lena felt for the
hundredth time the irritation of his attitude towards the
feminine intelligence.

The Howgates went away for Christmas. Lena, who did
not enjoy sitting alone against a wall watching other people
dance and play games, and was far too shy to make friends
for herself—her stepfather naturally spent most of his time
in the smoking-room, and she was too proud to confess
to him that she was lonely—was very thankful when they
returned to Bierley again. She positively bounded out of
the car into the hall, and seized upon the notices for committee meetings and requests for subscriptions which lay
there waiting for her with a pleasurable feeling of being
once more amongst familiar things. There was one envelope,
however, with a Hudley postmark, which was in an un-
familiar hand ; the writing was a delicate tracery, upright,
highly individual. " Pretty ! " commented Lena, glancing
at the envelope. She opened it, and the blood rushed to her
face as she saw that the signature was *Rachel Avery*. Preston
and Joe brought in the luggage ; Mrs. Preston greeted
Mr. Howgate ; rugs and coats were tossed about the hall ;
but Lena, in the midst of all this bustle, saw nothing but
Rachel's brief quiet sentences. Rachel thanked Lena for her

flowers and for her letter ; they all missed Mr. Deller very
much, especially her mother ; it was a kind thought on
Lena's part to attend the funeral. (" They saw me, then ! "
thought Lena, rather alarmed.) It seemed a pity, continued
Rachel, that she and Lena never saw anything of each other
nowadays ; would she not come in and see them some day
soon ? " *Mother and I*," concluded Rachel, " *are almost
always at home in the afternoon*," and she signed herself "*yours
affectionately*." Gasping with joy, Lena turned back to the
first page and saw that the date was that of several days past,
flew at once into a rage and upbraided the cook fiercely for
not having forwarded the letter.

"But you never asked me to," protested Mrs. Preston,
aggrieved.

"Perhaps I didn't," admitted Lena feverishly. "Well—
never mind. I daresay it won't matter. I can go to-
morrow. I daresay it won't matter. Never mind, Mrs.
Preston."

She flew upstairs with the precious letter clasped to her
breast, and was still re-reading it with her hat and coat on
when the gong sounded for tea.

All next morning, and especially at lunch-time, she was
on tenterhooks lest Howgate should say he wanted her to
drive him somewhere that afternoon, but fortunately there
were many things within the mill that required his attention
after his five days' absence, and Lena was free to do as she
would. The time seemed to drag terribly ; she had decided
that she might begin to change at three o'clock in order to
reach the Averys' house at four ; she knew that this was
allowing ample time, but at ten minutes to three she could
hold out no longer, and began to get ready. Consequently
she was at the end of Cambridge Place by shortly after
half-past three, and had to drive round and round the
neighbouring streets in the frosty dark to pass away the
time. In one of these peregrinations she thought she saw
the lame Rowland entering the Place, but she turned away
her head and did not look at him. Suddenly, while she was

at the point of her round furthest from the Averys', a church clock struck four; she drove back to No. 7 in a panic, the car bouncing over the rough stones of the Place. Hastily she got out and rang the bell. There was a long pause. Lena's spirits sank to zero. Now that she looked more carefully, she saw that the house front was all dark ; there were no lights anywhere. She rang again ; nothing happened ; she felt more and more depressed.

" Of course I can come to-morrow instead," she told herself, but the disappointment was severe.

She was just about to turn away when a light sprang up in the hall, and Lena's spirits sprang up with it. She almost danced with glee when she heard footsteps approaching, and turned an eager face to the opener of the door, who unexpectedly proved to be Rowland Avery.

" Oh ! " said Lena, disconcerted. Recovering herself, she put on her formal tone, and enquired politely : " May I see Miss Rachel Avery ? "

" I'm sorry, she isn't in," boomed Rowland. Lena's face fell. " But she's only gone out to fetch a teacake or something," continued Rowland. " She'll be back in a minute. Won't you come in and wait for her ? " Lena hesitated. " I'm sure my mother would be glad to see you," insisted Rowland, holding back the door. " The maid's gone home for a rest, and we don't hear the bell very well in the drawing-room, so I probably kept you waiting. I'm sorry."

Lena was not used to dealing with young men who spoke of teacakes, maids and bells in this offhand manner, or indeed with young men at all ; she felt abashed at the thought of entering the Averys' house, excited, overjoyed and alarmed, all in the same breath. But the open door was irresistible, she stepped in ; Rowland closed it behind her, and limping down the narrow hall, showed her into the drawing-room.

" Miss Howgate, mother," he announced.

Lena, blushing and stuttering and wondering how he

knew her name, shook hands in the wrong order with
Mr. Avery, who had a large book on his knee so that she
wished he would not get up but he did, and Mrs. Avery,
who she noticed was sewing but did not wear mourning.
Mrs. Avery asked her to take off her coat, and as she felt
hotter than she had ever done in her life before, she complied, and Rowland hung it up in the hall. Just at this
moment she heard the front door open.

" Here is Rachel," said Mrs. Avery quietly.

" Raikes, there's Miss Howgate to see you," said Rowland in the hall.

Lena blushed again at the sound of her name, and had
not recovered from this fresh embarrassment when Rachel
entered the room. She too did not wear mourning, and she
looked so tall and fair and kind and so little changed from
those old days that Lena's heart leaped out to her. She
sprang up. " Rachel ! " she exclaimed. Seizing Rachel's
hand in both her own, she gazed up into the other's eyes
with an eager, loving smile. After a moment Rachel smiled
too, very kindly ; and without quite meaning to do so the
two girls kissed.

After this the situation seemed easier. Rachel retired
into the kitchen to get the tea ready, Rowland moved in
and out of the room, helping her ; Lena sat comfortably
on a rather springless settee, answered Mr. Avery's remarks
on the antiquities of Bierley Green church as well as she
was able, and noticed everything—the rather faded chintz,
the bulbs in bowls, the old-fashioned fire-grate, the grand
piano, the print of Hudley from the south-east in 1822,
Mr. Avery's neat silvery hair and lively face, Mrs. Avery's
dark brooding calm, the portrait behind her, of herself
in yellow silk, which somehow explained something which
was in her and in Rachel too, Rowland's dark hair and
eyes, his jolly booming voice, the way he joked with his
father. He was a trifle conceited, thought Lena with a
tolerant smile, as young men so often are ; but in him
somehow it was rather amusing, as though he knew it

himself and made jokes with himself about it. When Mr. Avery had exhausted the Bierley antiquities Lilias said to Lena quietly :

" You wrote very kindly to Rachel about my father."

" Oh ! No ! " protested Lena, embarrassed. " Not at all ! " She wriggled on the settee a little, and then had one of her disconcerting bursts of sincerity. " I meant it ! " she said in a bold full tone, looking seriously at Mrs. Avery.

" We could see that," was the reply.

Lena with a start became aware that Rowland was at her side listening, with an eyebrow cocked at her ; she coloured with embarrassment, but he merely offered her a toasting-fork and a teacake ; the fire in the kitchen, he said, was not suitable for toast.

" Really, Rowland ! " protested Mrs. Avery mildly. " Miss Howgate is our guest."

"Well, make father do it then," said Rowland pleasantly, disappearing.

Mr. Avery seemed inclined to obey this hint, but Lena would not let him ; and sitting on the Avery's drawing-room floor clutching a toasting-fork and scorching first one cheek and then the other, she became completely happy. Then Rachel brought tea, and they were all very jolly together ; Lena could not afterwards remember what they had talked about, but it all seemed very amusing, and at one joke of Rowland's she laughed aloud. The others all looked at her, and Rachel said :

" I don't think I've ever heard you laugh before, Lena."

" Haven't you ? " said Lena, surprised and a little disconcerted, because privately she rather admired her own laugh. There were times when it suddenly vibrated on the air like the deep notes of a harp. At other times, however, it was the merest conventional hiccough. She had no power over it, and could not turn it from one to the other at will, but when it happened to come out right, she was pleased and enjoyed the harmony.

" Do you sing ? " asked Rowland abruptly from his place on the coal-scuttle.

" Me ? No," said Lena.

" Why not ? " demanded Rowland.

" I can't keep in tune," replied Lena simply.

At this the others all smiled at her very kindly, but Rowland said in an exasperated tone : " How do you know you can't if you've never learned ? With a laugh like that you ought to sing."

" I wish you wouldn't bully my guests, Rowland," observed Rachel.

She spoke jokingly, but Rowland with his nose in the air replied : " I'm sure I beg Miss Howgate's pardon."

" No, don't," said Lena hastily, alarmed at the chill in his tone. " Don't ! "

" Don't what ? " demanded Rowland with a smile. " Don't bully you, or don't beg your pardon ? "

" Please say exactly what you think," said Lena. " I shan't mind."

" That's a very rash promise, Miss Howgate," observed Mr. Avery. " If you knew Rowland better you wouldn't dare to make it."

Lena and Rowland looked at each other, and they both laughed. This time too Lena's peal rang out its rich deep notes, and they all looked at her again.

" It doesn't happen often," said Lena apologetically. " Really."

This seemed to amuse the Averys, and by the time tea was over intimacy was so far established that they allowed Lena to carry a plate or two into the kitchen. Presently Mr. and Mrs. Avery withdrew into the other room. Rowland said he ought to be working but wasn't going to do, Rachel began to mend a basketful of stockings, Lena offered to help her, and the three settled down to talk. They talked about books, and about Rowland's work in school, and about the political situation, and about plays ; the silent Lena found herself arguing hotly.

" Good heavens ! " exclaimed Lena, jumping up, crimson with shame. " Look at the time ! I must go ; it's awfully rude of me to have stayed so long."

" You might as well stay to supper now," said Rowland. " Why not ? "

" Yes, do stay, Lena," urged Rachel.

Lena, stuttering, said she feared not—her stepfather——
" Still ! " she added, brightening, " he might have stayed out unexpectedly ; he sometimes does."

" Telephone," Rowland summed up the situation, and led the way into the dining-room, where the instrument hung on the wall. Mr. Avery was sitting at the table in front of a mass of papers ; Mrs. Avery was at the table too, sewing. " Lena's telephoning to see if she can stay to supper," explained Rowland, and withdrew.

" That will be very nice," said Mrs. Avery, looking at her with a smile.

Lena, hot, eager, tremulous with hope and fear, got through to Bierley Hall. Her heart sank at once, for the voice which answered was her stepfather's.

" Oh, is that you, Lena ? " he said. " I wondered what had become of you. Where are you ? "

" I'm at the Averys'," explained Lena in a low polite tone.

" Where ? " demanded Howgate.

" The Averys'," repeated Lena more loudly, crimsoning and looking apologetically towards her hosts. " Rachel Avery's house in Cambridge Place."

" Oh ! Thomas Deller's grand-daughter, eh ? " said Howgate sardonically. " H'm."

" I was wondering if I could stay to supper," pursued Lena in a polite formal tone, trembling at her own audacity.

" Nay, I think you'd better be getting home," said Howgate. " There's a good deal of snow up here."

" Snow ! " exclaimed Lena. " He says it's snowing," she explained to the Averys. Mr. Avery got up and drew back

the curtain, revealing a white landscape and whirling flakes.
" It's snowing here too," she told Howgate. " But not much,
I think," she added hastily.

" I think you'd better be getting home," persisted
Howgate.

" I could leave the car in Hudley and come home by
tram," suggested Lena, unable to bear the thought of leaving the Averys' just yet.

" There's a little garage at the end of the Place,"
said Rowland suddenly, putting his head into the
room.

" There's a garage at the end of the Place," repeated
Lena. Her voice positively quavered with yearning, and
Howgate said shortly :

" Well, stay, then."

A beatific smile spread over Lena's face. " I can stay ! "
she whispered triumphantly to the Averys.

" But don't try to bring your car home," continued Howgate. " The snow's thick up here."

" No, oh, no, I won't," said Lena in an ecstasy of gratitude.
" I'll come by tram."

" You may have to walk," Howgate told her grimly, and
rang off.

Lena went out to take her car to the garage, and Rowland went with her to show her the way. The engine was
cold, and the self-starter useless ; Rowland had to wind
vigorously, for which Lena was very apologetic. He did
not seem to mind, however, but he had evidently taken
note of the car's make and build meanwhile, for as they
tramped back through the white whirling snow along the
Place together he observed :

" Do you know, I think I saw you at the end of Cambridge Place twice this afternoon, once when I went out
to post a letter, and once when I came back."

" I daresay you did," admitted Lena, colouring. " I was
driving round and round, you know, to waste the time because I'd reached here too early."

At this Rowland shouted with laughter.

" I suppose it *is* funny," said Lena meditatively.

" I *beg* your pardon," said Rowland with remorse. " But I didn't know girls did things like that."

It was now Lena's turn to stare. " How do you mean ? " she asked.

" Well, girls always seem so composed and sure of themselves, you know," explained Rowland, still apologetic.

Lena shook her head. " I'm not," she said with conviction.

" No ? I liked what you said about my grandfather, you know," observed Rowland after a pause. " Most people would have forgotten long ago about that singing lesson business."

" I could never forget that, never," cried Lena earnestly, blushing with shame. " I'm too ashamed of it. But truly, truly it wasn't altogether my fault. It's all too complicated and psychological to explain, but truly a lot of it was Esmé Deller."

It was now Rowland's turn to colour.

" Did she make you very unhappy ? " he asked in a strained voice.

" Yes. Oh, *yes*," said Lena.

" She's very well able to do that," said Rowland rather bitterly.

They had now reached No. 7 ; their footsteps of half an hour ago were all filled in and blurred into smooth shallow white craters.

" ' All bloodless lay the untrodden snow,' " said Rowland, opening the gate for her.

" My mother used to say those verses to me while she brushed my hair," observed Lena. " I haven't heard them for years."

" I'm glad you say verses and not poem," said Rowland, opening the door. " It shows an appreciation of fine shades."

" Not very fine in that case, surely," objected Lena, stamping the snow off her shoes on to the mat.

" Perhaps you're right," conceded Rowland meekly.

They found Rachel in the kitchen preparing supper and began to help her, and Lena became acquainted with the Averys' cellars. They then ate what they had prepared with hearty appetites, Lena in especial being ravenous ; and afterwards cleared away and washed up. Rachel washed the china, Lena and Rowland dried it, and Rowland talked enough for all three. He then proceeded to make the coffee, banishing the girls to the drawing-room while he did so. While they waited for him, and Mr. Avery read out the weather report from the *Hudley News* with gusto, Lena thought she heard the bell ring and voices in the hall, and sure enough a moment later Arnold Deller came into the room, looking cold and pinched. He seemed rather cross at finding Lena there, Lena thought ; and when he had shaken hands with her perfunctorily he went right away across the room and sat down on an uncomfortable chair by the window. Rachel, who was beside Lena on the settee, immediately rose, and with her work in her hand silently went and sat beside him. A pang of jealousy stabbed Lena's heart ; with sudden intuition she flashed a look at Mrs. Avery, and saw on her face the reflection of jealousy too. There were a few moments of silence.

" When does Esmé come home, Arnold ? " enquired Mr. Avery then pleasantly. (Lena had already perceived that Mr. Avery was relied on by the family to dash in and make conversation whenever it was required.)

" Friday," replied Arnold gloomily.

" Esmé is in Switzerland with friends, enjoying winter sports," explained Rachel to Lena.

" You know I think it's rather a pity you didn't go, Arnold," continued Mr. Avery. " It would have done you good, been a change for you."

" I didn't want to go," said Arnold still more gloomily. He frowned and fixed an abstracted gaze on Lena, who wondered if he had been doing something foolish at the mill again and incurred the wrath of John Deller. He

cheered up a little with the advent of coffee, but when after
half an hour or so of talk Rowland enquired : " Well, shall
we sing or play cards ? " Arnold replied : " I don't feel
like singing," in a very melancholy tone.

" What's the matter with you to-night, Arnold ? "
enquired Mrs. Avery. " You don't seem very
bright."

" Yes, what's the matter ? " said Rachel seriously.

" Nothing," protested Arnold with petulance. " I've got
a cold coming on, that's all."

In illustration of this he proceeded to sneeze, and was
urged to come nearer the fire. Rowland brought the card-
table to the hearth and they all gathered round it, while
Lena, glancing at Arnold's fair harassed face, thought with
some sympathy that if Esmé had been away and was coming home on Friday, it was enough to make anybody feel
depressed.

They played childish round games with words and cards.
Lena sat between Rowland and Mr. Avery and received
tuition from both of them, with the result that she did so
exceedingly well that at length Rachel was moved to pro-
test.

" If you three act in collusion any more," she said, " we
shall collude here as well."

" That might be rather fun," said Rowland. " Let's try
it."

" You take your mother and I'll go on the other
side," suggested Mr. Avery. " Then it will be fair versus
dark."

" Not on your life ! " said Rowland firmly. " We need
you on Lena's advisory board."

" And we shan't part with Aunt Lilias," said Arnold
staunchly.

This game concluded by Arnold forcing Mr. Avery to
take a trick he emphatically did not want to take. " Foiled,
foiled ! " cried Mr. Avery dramatically, throwing down a
diamond ace. Arnold, highly pleased with his success—

Lena had already perceived that he did not often win—
laughed heartily at Mr. Avery and admitted that his possession of a small diamond was pure chance. The incident
had revived him, however, and for the rest of the evening
he was bright and jolly ; Lena decided that after all he
was a nice boy ; he obviously adored Rachel ; if he was a
little dull at cards and Mr. Avery's game very likely he
was good at something else which Lena was bad at ; and
if he quoted from Lamb and Montague rather too often
and too seriously and at too great length in the course of
the conversation—well, at any rate, it showed that he had
a real love for beautiful prose, and somehow made one
rather like him even if it was a trifle boring. Rowland also
rather threw quotations about, but as they were never
longer than two or three words and were always uttered
satirically, Lena enjoyed them. In fact she was in an ecstasy
of enjoyment all the evening ; catching sight of her reflection once in the glass, she hardly recognised the glowing
vivid creature. But alas ! the time came when she was reluctantly obliged to say :

" I'm afraid I ought to be going home now."

" Oh, don't go, Lena," said Rachel.

Lena sighed and glanced at the clock again. " I'm afraid
I really must," she said. " The last tram . . ."

" I'll drive Miss Howgate down to the Bierley tram,"
offered Arnold formally. " I've got chains on."

Lena was rather sorry about this, because in the depths
of her heart she had dared to hope that Rowland might
walk to the end of the Place with her and put her on a tram
for the centre of the town ; she accepted, however, with a
show of gratitude ; Arnold went along to the little garage at
the end to fetch his car ; everybody stood up, and Rachel
helped her into her coat in the hall ; the evening was over.

" You'll come to see us again, won't you, Lena ? " said
Rachel.

" Yes—oh ! Yes," said Lena fervently, longing for a more
definite invitation.

Rachel did not, however, offer her one, and though the Averys' farewells were all very hearty, Lena climbed into Arnold's car feeling rather chilled and sobered. They drove off through the snowflakes, which were still falling thick and fast ; Arnold was silent, merely sneezing from time to time ; Lena, gazing out through the blurred wind-screen, saw pictures of Rowland—his dark merry eyes, his thick dark hair with the kink in it, his long face with the wide humorous mouth and the thick eyebrows, his limp, his rather shabby suit. She heard his deep voice, joking or saying " Lena." She sighed. Arnold sneezed again.

" I'm *very* sorry to have brought you all this way round, Mr. Deller," apologised Lena.

" Not at all—won't take a minute," replied Arnold mechanically.

They drew up at the town tram terminus, where the last Bierley tram was standing alone. Arnold let down his window and called to the conductor to know what it was like at the top of Awe Hill. The conductor seemed to think it was pretty bad.

" Is it fit to take a car up ? " demanded Arnold.

" Not unless you have to," replied the conductor.

Arnold turned to Lena.

" Oh, I'll go by tram, of *course*," said Lena, beginning to get out. " I never thought of you taking me all the way." She climbed out. " Good night, and thank you so much," she said, closing the door.

Arnold lifted his hat and turned the car. Lena, climbing into the tram, was really glad to see the last of him, because she could live over the evening again so much better when she was alone. As the tram bumped slowly up the hill and when later she fought her way along the road at the top— the fields were impassable to-night—she hardly saw the snow, which usually excited her, or felt the cold ; she was living in a bright, warm, jolly, friendly world, the world of Cambridge Place. By contrast the Hall, when at last she reached it, seemed dark and cold. Her stepfather was sitting in the dining-room, as usual, in front of an enormous fire, with a book of adventure in his hand ; he seemed rather tired of himself and glad to see her.

" So you've been enjoying yourself, have you ? " he observed in a peculiar tone, and Lena perceived that owing to her disregard of snow during their telephone conversation, her infatuation for the Averys was perfectly well known to him. " Who was there ? " he went on.

" Oh, Mr. and Mrs. Avery," said Lena, tapping the table with her finger-tips with assumed nonchalance. " And Rachel, and Rowland, and Arnold Deller."

" And which do you like best, Rowland or Arnold ? " enquired Howgate sardonically, rolling the names on his tongue so that they sounded foolish.

" Oh, Rowland," replied Lena truthfully. " Though I don't think Arnold is as silly as you say," she added.

Howgate looked at her with a cynical but not unkindly smile. " Rowland," he repeated. " That's Thomas Deller's grandson, eh ? " He looked at her thoughtfully, and touched his eyebrow. " Did you ask them to come here ? " he enquired.

" No," said Lena with a start. " I forgot." She blushed, for it was not the first time she had forgotten the principle of social reciprocity. The reason she forgot it was that she could not imagine anyone wishing to come to Bierley Hall.

" You'll forget your head next," Howgate told her amiably. " You'd better ask them up some time—when I'm out, if you like. How's the snow ? "

" Still coming down fast," said Lena.

" You'll have to do without your car for a few days, I reckon," said her stepfather.

This prediction proved correct ; there was thick snow and then a hard frost, and for a few days the roads were not tempting to a nervous driver. Lena had therefore no excuse to go to Cambridge Place, and she felt it was sheer cruelty to ask anyone up to Bierley Hall in the present weather. The days went by for her in a sort of feverish dream ; she wandered restlessly about the house, could not settle down to reading, and spent hours talking to Mrs. Preston, who seemed to wonder at this unusual yearning for company. Early in the next week she went down into Hudley by tram, and as she was wandering disconsolately along the main street in the middle of the morning, she suddenly caught sight of Rachel standing alone at a corner. Without pausing to think—if she had paused she would have been afflicted with her usual self-conscious fear, and hung back altogether—she flew across the road and hailed her joyfully.

"Rachel ! " she cried. " This is nice ! Will you come and have coffee with me ? "

Rachel turned a vague and rather alarmed gaze upon her. " Oh—Lena ? " she said. She paused, hesitated, and added : " I'm afraid I can't just now."

Lena felt cold all over. Rachel obviously did not want her. Was it all to pass away and never happen again, then, that jolly evening at Cambridge Place ? Was she never to breathe that friendly atmosphere again ? Had she perhaps done something awful on that night, which made the Averys dislike her ? She stammered : " I'm sorry," and gazed miserably into Rachel's eyes. Rachel was not looking at her, but at some point beyond her, and just then she gave a warm loving smile. Involuntarily Lena turned and looked behind her, and saw Arnold on the other side of the road. The blood rushed back into her cheeks, she could have shouted her relief. Of course ! Rachel was waiting for Arnold ! She was not annoyed with Lena at all ! Lena smiled all over her face, seized Rachel's hand and gave it a little squeeze. " I understand ! " she said in a low quick tone, her eyes bright and loving. " I won't stay and be in the way, Rachel." She laughed merrily, and bounded off.

"Lena ! " called Rachel. " Come back ! Here ! " She seized Lena's arm as she was about to plunge into the traffic, and drew her back. " Arnold and I are engaged," she explained breathlessly, colouring. " We've been engaged to ourselves, you know, for a long time, but now we are properly. Mr. Deller gave his consent the day of my grandfather's funeral—he was upset about it, you know."

" And what about Mr. Avery ? " queried Lena, thrilled by these confidences.

" Oh ! Father ! " said Rachel. She smiled, and Lena, understanding, smiled too. " My ring has been specially ordered, and now it's come, and we're going to see it," concluded Rachel.

" I see," said Lena, much impressed. " Well, I think Arnold's very lucky, that's all. I wish," she added, mindful of her stepfather's instructions, " that you would all come up and see me at Bierley some time."

" Oh, we will. But come and see us again, Lena," said Rachel hastily, as Arnold approached. " Come to-morrow night. Arnold and Esmé are coming."

" Rachel," began Arnold anxiously.

Lena stepped back, waved a joyful hand, cried : " I'll come, I'll come ! " and plunged into the traffic.

The next evening therefore found her dismounting from a tram at the end of Cambridge Place. The frost still held, and ice crackled beneath her feet as she hurried along. When she reached the turn in the Place, however, and saw the lights of No. 7, a panic suddenly seized her. Suppose Rachel had not really meant that casual invitation seriously ? Suppose Mrs. Avery had not approved ? Suppose they did not want her ? She stepped off the pavement into the softer and deeper snow of the gutter, and trod gently in it, so that her footsteps should not be heard. " After all, Rachel could have rung me up and made an excuse if they didn't want me," she told herself reassuringly. But her heart beat fast as she rang the bell.

The door was opened fairly promptly by a maid, who led her upstairs to take off her coat. This formality depressed

Lena as being unlike her previous visit to Cambridge
Place ; she noticed too a smell of roasting viands in the air,
and surmised that their supper to-night was to be more
formal, too. " It's because Esmé's here," she told herself,
and felt a shiver (of the goose-over-grave variety) go down
her back at the mere sound of Esmé's name. But she had
thought over the problem of Esmé quite carefully, and when
she had followed the maid down into the drawing-room,
and shaken hands with Mrs. Avery—Mr. Avery was in his
study, working ; Lena had seen his light as she came down
the stairs—and kissed Rachel, and smiled at the two boys,
and Rachel had turned her slightly round and observed :
" Well, Lena, you know Esmé," Lena stretched out her
hand to Esmé and said boldly : " If you'll forgive me for
being so fierce and tiresome at the Hudley Girls' College,
Esmé, I'll forgive you." With an effort she managed to raise
her eyes to Esmé's face—it was just the same fair, pretty,
cold little face—and smiled eagerly, with her head on one
side ; the others seemed to be looking on rather aghast.
Esmé turned her eyes away and for a moment said nothing ;
only a slight increase of colour in her smooth delicate cheeks
showed that she had heard Lena's appeal.

" It's a good offer, with a strong element of sound
mutuality, Esmé," said Rowland, who was standing with
his back to the fire. " I think you'd do well to accept
it."

He spoke rather bitterly, and Esmé's pretty lips moved
into a contemptuous smile. " It's such a long time ago," she
said in her shallow little drawl. " I've forgotten all about
it." She put her small cold hand into Lena's for a second,
then withdrew it. " I know we were all very silly then,"
she added disdainfully.

Lena was astounded. " ' We were all very silly then,' "
she thought ; what a simple way of disposing of such details as an attack with a knife and several weeks' systematic
bullying. For a moment she felt disconcerted, shaken, almost frightened ; Esmé's face and voice were so terribly the

same as they had been in those awful Hudley College days.
Then she rallied ; she had all those years of good education
behind her now ; she spoke good English, she had taken
examinations, she could drive a car ; her rose-coloured
frock was every bit as pretty as Esmé's black one, she told
herself staunchly—yes, and cost as much, too ! She at once
rebuked herself for this last vulgar thought, and in order to
atone for it spoke more warmly than she felt. " I'm glad,"
she said, " that Esmé feels no ill-will. I don't either."
" What a lie ! " whispered some inner self. She repressed it
sternly, and took the chair which Arnold, looking distinctly
harassed and uncomfortable, offered her. There was an
awkward pause ; Lena wished heartily that the door would
open and admit Mr. Avery, that conversation-maker. But
nothing of that kind happened, and at length Mrs. Avery
found something to say.

" Rachel," she suggested (and the tone of her voice rejoiced Lena, for it told how little was her love for Esmé),
" show Lena your ring."

Lena's admiration of the fine sapphire set in diamonds
carried them on until the gong sounded.

After the meal, which as Lena had guessed proved much
more elaborate than that of her first visit, it became evident
that the Averys had drawn up an amusing programme of
games for the evening's entertainment ; it also unfortunately
became evident that Esmé for some obscure reason had determined to take them all to Denbridge Vale to skate.
None of the party except Esmé wished to skate ; Arnold's
cold was still uncomfortable, Rowland of course could not
skate, Rachel wished to keep Arnold by the fire, and Lena
was conscious of her thin evening frock and shoes. But as
this was a selfish argument she could not advance it, and
Rowland was silent for a similar cause. Lena did not at
first remember his disability, and wondered that he did not
advance to the others' support as his face showed that he
wished ; but when she remembered that he was lame, she
coloured deeply and detested Esmé rather more than before.

As Arnold had no will where Esmé was concerned, and
Rachel was limited by her position as hostess, the party
shortly found themselves committed to the project.

"We're hardly dressed for it," murmured Rachel with
a sigh, as they all rose.

"You can change here, and we can call at home and I'll
change there," pronounced Esmé, who had evidently
planned out the whole affair.

"And what about Lena?" suggested Rowland in an
acid tone.

"I don't know, I'm sure," said Esmé, looking at Lena
coldly. It was so obvious that she did not want her
to be of the party that Lena winced, and Rachel said
hastily :

"I can lend Lena something."

"Well, it must be something very old," pleaded Lena
seriously as she followed Rachel upstairs. "I shan't have
it unless it's very old, Rachel; I'm so careless with
clothes."

An exasperated sigh came from Esmé a stair or two
below.

The original scheme was that the whole party should
bundle into Arnold's car and drive round to West View and
wait there while Esmé and Arnold gathered their equipment ; but Esmé was so very impatient while Rachel
searched for clothes and skates for Lena, and so obviously
anxious to be at West View, that at length Rachel urged her
to take Arnold and the car and go. "We three can walk,"
she concluded drily. In a trice Esmé was sitting in the car
with the reluctant Arnold at the wheel.

"You'd better come too, Rowland," she called in her
imperious little tones.

"I think not, thank you," said Rowland from the doorstep.

Rachel, Lena at her shoulder, leaned over the banisters.
"Yes, go, Rowland," she urged. "We'll catch you
up."

" I shall not go," thundered Rowland, swinging round in
a towering rage. " Don't waste time arguing, Rachel ; get
dressed."

The two girls, abashed, withdrew, Lena giggling a little
out of sheer nervousness. Arnold drove off ; about ten minutes later the Averys and Lena left the house. The walk was
not a very pleasant one ; Rachel was silent, Rowland
seethed ; Lena had too much sympathy with them to allow
herself to take any pleasure in finding herself less unpopular
than Esmé, though she really enjoyed it immensely. They
calculated that by the time they reached West View Arnold
and Esmé would have been there some twenty-five minutes,
and rather expected to find them waiting impatiently on
the doorstep or even at the foot of the drive, but Arnold's
car was standing silently by the front door, and there was
no sign of either of the Dellers. They tramped up the well-
swept drive, feeling clumsy after their struggles with the
deepish snow of Hudley Moor, and paused by the door. To
Lena's relief Rachel said decidedly :

" I shan't go in."

She climbed into the back of the car, with whose workings
she seemed very familiar, and sat down. Lena followed.
Rowland stood glaring at them for a moment, then walked
up and down in indecision. Lena hoped that Rachel would
urge him to go in, but she was determinedly silent ; after a
while Rowland put his head into the car and said in a
milder tone : " Shall I go in ? "

" Yes, go in," said Rachel shortly.

Rowland handed into the car the skates he was carrying,
and rang the West View bell. The door opened ; light
streamed out ; in the distance Arnold could be seen, very
much wrapped up in a muffler, gesticulating despairingly ;
Rowland went in, the door closed, the light vanished, the
girls were left to themselves. For a long time neither of them
spoke. Several degrees of frost made the night extremely
cold ; stars twinkled in a dark blue sky, the moon shone,
the snow-covered hills sparkled, everything was very still.

At length Rachel sighed, and Lena stirred responsively.

" I hope you are not cold, Lena," said Rachel formally.

" Not at all," lied Lena.

" I feel I ought to apologise to you, really, for dragging you out all this way," continued Rachel.

" Oh, Rachel ! " Lena reproached her. " As though I care when I'm with you ! " She was silent for a moment, struggling hard to keep back a sentence which kept forming itself in her mind ; suddenly it burst out irrepressibly. " I must just say one thing, Rachel ! " she cried all in a breath. " I'm glad for your sake Arnold isn't like Esmé."

Rachel turned to her. " Nobody would think they were brother and sister, would they ? " she asked eagerly.

" Nobody," agreed Lena with emphasis. (A thought arose in her mind that this was not quite true, but in loyalty to Rachel she repressed it sternly.) " Is she always like this ? " she went on.

" Always ! " said Rachel. There was emotion, almost passion, in her voice, and Lena felt that she had touched some secret hurt. Not wishing to force a confidence, she drew back and said nothing ; and after a moment Rachel spoke again, in a lighter tone. " Rowland imagines he's in love with her, you know," she said.

" Does he ? " said Lena. She felt shocked and somehow disappointed, but could not take the attachment very seriously since Rachel spoke of it in such an offhand tone. She considered the Avery-Deller relations carefully. " Yes, I'm glad Arnold's different," she said.

There was a pause. " Lena, I'm freezing," said Rachel suddenly on an intimate note.

" So am I," admitted Lena cheerfully.

" Let's sit closer together," urged Rachel.

Lena, nothing loth, edged up to her, and amid some giggling they entwined each other's waists and drew the rug up about their shoulders. Rachel's good spirits seemed to have returned, they became thoroughly jolly to-gether and played games against each other with the thick

fur tails of Arnold's rug. The other members of the party,
descending the West View steps in an atmosphere of gloom,
and irritation, were astonished to hear Lena's well-known
laugh, as Rowland called it, pealing from the interior of the
deserted car. The two boys seemed rather cheered by it, but
Esmé, who had changed into an exceedingly pretty and
suitable garb—" Can that be why she wanted to skate ? "
Lena asked herself incredulously—was very cross with her
brother because he could not immediately get the engine to
start. " The Annisons *never* have any trouble with *their* car,
and it's *just* like this one," she repeated until at last Rowland said pleasantly : " Oh, damn the Annisons." Lena,
Arnold and Rachel were all grateful to him for this, while
Esmé seemed rather to like it than otherwise, so harmony
was restored until Arnold, having driven carefully down a
slippery hill and along a narrow little lane, again roused
his sister's disapproval by declining to take the car into the
field which now separated them from the flooded mill-dam
they were aiming at.

" But we can't walk through all that *snow*," objected
Esmé, looking with disfavour at the pathless white.

" But don't you see, if I take her in I shall never get her
*out*," protested Arnold.

The argument was ended by Rowland, who explained to
Esmé that she might have to walk all the way home if she
attempted to save herself from walking across the field.
" Don't mention the Annisons in this connection," he concluded as they all climbed out and Arnold draped the
rug over the radiator, " or I shall drown you in yonder
stream."

Esmé smiled a little. " You wouldn't," she said.

Rowland seemed to resent this. " Why wouldn't I ? " he
demanded hotly. " Are you suggesting I haven't got the
guts to do it ? "

" I wish you wouldn't use those gross expressions,
Rowland," Esmé reproved him coldly.

" Well, abdominal viscera, then," cried Rowland

promptly. In spite of himself he sniggered at this euphem-
ism ; the others joined him, and harmony was restored yet
again. " All the same," said Rowland more soberly, as they
ploughed their way along, " I *have* got the guts to do it,
Esmé, so you'd better look out."

" Yes, Esmé, beware," said Lena, trying to be friendly.
" The untrodden snow must be kept bloodless at all
costs."

" Untrodden ! " said Rowland, standing still. " That's
just what it is. Nobody else can be skating here."

Gloom once more fell upon the party. The truth of Rowland's remark was too obvious to be denied, yet they all
hoped ardently that he would be proved wrong, and that
beyond the wooden hut which they could now see there
would be a field-full of lively skaters. They tramped on
without looking at each other, growing more and more
conscious with every step they took of the surrounding
silence ; and when they reached the hut they found that
the untrodden snow was only too true a prophet, for the
wide expanse stretched before them untenanted. Moreover, the field did not gleam as real ice should, and a
solitary boy, wielding a broom, explained to them that a
slight fall of snow occurring in the middle of one night
had frozen before it could be swept away, so that the
ice was unskatable. " It's all right at Ribourne," he
concluded, naming a suburb several miles on the other
side of Hudley.

" Thank you," said Rowland with sardonic politeness as
the party withdrew. " Well, that was rather unfortunate,"
he continued as they crossed the field. He had apparently
remembered that he was the host of the evening, and his
tone was airy.

" I do really think," burst out Esmé in a fury, " that
you two men might have found out that there wasn't
any skating here, instead of letting us come trailing all
this way."

" My good Esmé," boomed Rowland, " it was entirely

your idea to come here, and yours only ; none of us had thought anything about the scheme until you mentioned it."

" Arnold knew I wanted to come," persisted Esmé. " I told him beforehand."

" I don't see why Arnold should be blamed," said Rachel.

She spoke quietly, but Lena heard a danger signal in her tone. Hastily she cried : " What does it matter after all ? We've had a delightful experience : Christmas card scene by moonlight."

" We're not all such philosophers as you, Miss Howgate," said Arnold, still aggrieved but slightly mollified.

" Why can't you call her Lena ? Miss Howgate sounds so *silly*," criticised Esmé.

" If I'd said Lena you'd have said that was silly," objected the goaded Arnold.

Rachel sighed.

" Well, are we for Ribourne ? " enquired Rowland smoothly, when they were once more seated in the car.

" *I* shall go home," announced Esmé with decision.

" Good ; I'll drop you there," snapped Arnold.

To Lena's regret, however, he did not abide by this, for he drove past the gates of West View without attempting to turn through them, and Esmé made no remark. They returned to Cambridge Place and spent the evening in the manner originally arranged by the Averys, singing and playing games. Esmé looked extremely pretty in her neat grey suit ; beside her the other two in their thick old woollens appeared, as Lena thought cheerfully, simply grotesque. Esmé was quiet and amenable at first, but as the evening wore on she became capricious, sneered at poor Arnold for losing and also at Lena for winning until the girl felt positively obliged to lose a trick or two on purpose. Rowland, however, detected her in this and gave her a steady look ; her blush admitted her deception ; he threw

down the cards and changed the game. Later some refresh-
ments were brought in ; so that they might continue
playing Rowland and Arnold moved them to the card-
table.

" Don't put the cake near Lena," observed Esmé with a
little laugh.

" Why not ? " demanded Arnold, rising to her bait as he
always did.

" I shouldn't feel safe with that knife within her reach,"
explained Esmé.

Lena coloured to the eyes ; the others paused in astonishment.

" What do you mean ? Don't talk such rot, Esmé," said
Rowland at last irritably.

" It isn't rot," said Esmé in a good-humoured tone. " Is
it, Lena ? Lena once attacked me with a knife, in the days
of long ago ; didn't you, Lena ? "

" Yes," said Lena thickly. For one long terrible moment
she felt as she used to feel when she washed last at the little
white basin beneath Esmé's coldly searching eyes—exposed,
defenceless, naked, despised, alone. The blood beat thickly
in her ears ; the walls swayed, the floor seemed to sink beneath her feet ; she felt sick, and was conscious of cowering.
Then Rachel's quiet voice sounded :

" I'm not surprised."

" Well, Rachel ! " exclaimed the two young men.
" Really ! "

" Rachel ! " cried Esmé.

Rachel laughed and began to gather up the cards.
" Don't you know a joke when you hear one ? " she said.
Her tone was light, but her hands shook as she shuffled the
pack together, and her breast rose and fell rapidly. Esmé
smiled, reassured ; Arnold poured out lemonade, Rowland
firmly cut the cake, the game proceeded ; but Lena knew
that as regards Esmé she and Rachel were of one mind ;
there was a bond between them.

After that there were many times when Lena went to

Cambridge Place, many mornings, many afternoons, many
nights. The little garage at the end made almost as much
out of her as it did out of Arnold, for she seemed to be of-
ficially recognised as Rachel's friend. Cambridge Place was
slightly raised above the level of the approaching road, and
as her car turned round a certain corner, the lights of the
houses—if it happened to be dark and they happened to be
lighted—shone out ; Lena always looked for this, and if the
lights were there her heart leaped up, it seemed a good
omen. On those nights she walked on the pavement ; but
on other nights and other days she walked in the mud of
the gutter as she had done before, just in case Rachel had
changed her mind and did not really want her.

There were, for instance, those glowing mornings during
Rowland's holidays when she could hardly wait for Howgate to finish his breakfast before rushing off to Hudley in
a panic lest the others should have started on the planned
walk without her. On these occasions she usually arrived
far too early, and found Rowland just lighting a cigarette
amid the débris of the breakfast table, while Rachel in the
kitchen was cutting sandwiches. Lena, in a fever of expectation, longing to start, melted the butter for her, or helped
Mrs. Avery with the beds, or sat about conversing politely
with Mr. Avery, or argued over a map with Rowland ; in
half an hour or so Arnold would drop in, with or without
Esmé, as that young lady's caprice dictated ; in another
twenty minutes, after one or two false starts and a good
deal of calling about the house, the party started, Lena's
whole body tingling with happiness. They took a bus or a
tram, in which they were pleasantly conscious that their
knapsacks and sticks and lively talk were the centre of attraction, and journeyed out to the confines of Hudley ; then
they tramped all day over the moors, the wind in their hair,
the rain (often) in their eyes. When Esmé was not with
them there were long silences between the four ; if they
argued they argued about large questions of which Lena
sometimes suspected they did not know very much, but

about which they all cared a great deal ; they ate their
lunch in odd places, sang a good many of what Rowland
called " ancient ditties," and usually returned in pairs,
Arnold and Rowland in front, and the two girls behind.
When, however, Esmé came with them, the five remained
together all day, and a constant bickering rose and fell, of
which the chief feature was that the ruder Rowland grew,
the more provocative Esmé became. Rowland, however,
always had the situation well in hand ; in spite of her pretence to the contrary it seemed that Esmé cared, as they
all cared, for his good opinion. On the afternoon of one of
the earliest of these walk days, when the rain proved suddenly too heavy to be disregarded, they found themselves
not very far from Bierley Hall, and at Lena's invitation ran
rapidly over fields and walls to its shelter. To Lena's great
relief and joy the Averys, and consequently Arnold, seemed
to like Bierley Hall, though Esmé was a trifle sulky ; they
admired the view, the mahogany, the family portraits, even
the silver-mounted hoof ; fortunately Mrs. Preston was in
a good humour and provided them with an immense tea,
of which they all ate largely. When they were dried and
fed they returned to Hudley by way of Bierley Lane, and
Lena—the rain having ceased and her car being of course
at Cambridge Place—took them by the short cut down the
steps through the mill yard. Here they found something
else to admire, namely two of Howgate's superb brown
draught-horses. Bierley Bottom Mills had been noted for
the fine appearance of its drays for three generations ; and
though Alfred Howgate was much too practical not to use
motor lorries, he kept on a dray or two and a few horses for
the sake of tradition. Rowland was much struck by the
glossy, powerful beasts, and they all watched them with delight as they stamped their great feet and tossed their heads
and jingled their harness, which gleamed in the light from
the mill windows. Or rather, Arnold and the Averys and
Lena watched them with delight ; Esmé seemed to find the
mill yard dirty and plebeian and the horses coarse, and

stood on the pavement by the arched entrance, calling
petulantly to them to come along. Howgate himself now
appeared at the door of the engine-room and crossed the
yard to them.

"Admiring my horses, eh?" he said in a pleased tone,
when Lena had made the party known to him.

Rowland boomed: "They're magnificent."

"Aye, they're not so bad," agreed Howgate with satisfaction, slapping the nearest animal familiarly on its massive
haunch. He explained the horses' good points; Rowland
listened with interest, but Arnold's attention rather too
perceptibly wandered, and Howgate broke off to say
abruptly: "So you're not at the mill to-day, Mr. Deller?"

"No, not to-day," said Arnold.

The tone of Howgate's answering "Ha!" would have
annoyed a saint, and Arnold coloured angrily. "Your sister doesn't like horses, perhaps?" continued Howgate,
his eyes wandering to Esmé's neat little figure beneath the
archway.

"I don't think she knows anything about them," said
Arnold irritably.

They all stood for a moment in an awkward silence, Esmé
scowling at them across the yard. "Well, I must get back
to work," said Howgate at length in an artificially pleasant
tone. "I haven't got a grandfather to do it for me, you
see. Good afternoon, Miss Avery."

He nodded and left them.

The spirits of Arnold and therefore of Rachel were somewhat damped by this interview; but Rowland seemed to
find Howgate interesting, and asked so many questions
about him that Lena was cheered, and began to feel that
a formal dinner invitation to the Averys might not prove
altogether fatal. She consulted her stepfather as to date,
and found, to her surprise, that he thought she should ask
the Dellers too.

"They're engaged, aren't they?" he said, referring to
Rachel and Arnold.

" Oh, yes," said Lena emphatically.

" Well, then," said her stepfather in a final tone.

Esmé, to Lena's great relief, declined the invitation ; presumably on account of the flirtation with one of the Annison boys which she had begun in Switzerland and was now continuing with great gusto. The other three accepted and came, but the evening was not altogether a success. Lena was nervous ; in any case, the Lena of Bierley Hall was not the Lena of Cambridge Place. Then the conversation unfortunately turned upon politics, on which Howgate, Arnold and Rowland all held different views. Rowland was far the ablest debater of the three, and as he was not distressed by anything the others said to him, he imagined that they were similarly unscathed by his avalanche of arguments. This was not the case, and Howgate adopted in his defence the tone of the experienced man of the world talking to a mere boy, which was calculated to irritate all the youthful members of the party ; while poor Arnold was rent by each of the others in turn. After dinner things went better ; for Lena settled the other four down to bridge, at which Howgate and Rachel managed to defeat Rowland and Arnold by the merest neck. When Lena had seen the guests depart she returned to the dining-room, where her stepfather was already settled by the fire reading the evening paper, and plucked up courage to say to him :

" What do you think of them ? "

" Well," drawled Howgate in a tone of kindly condescension, looking at her over the top of his eyeglasses, which as usual sat crookedly on his big nose : " There's more stuff in young Avery than in that Deller boy. But he's young and untried ; he doesn't know what life is. These schoolmaster chaps never do ; it's all theory and lesson-books with them. He'd soon find his level if he were in business."

Lena, furious, demanded sharply : " And Rachel ? "

" She doesn't seem to care for me, your Rachel," grumbled Howgate.

His tone was so aggrieved and astonished that Lena forgot her annoyance and laughed. " Well, father," she said, " you know you weren't very nice to Arnold the other day in the yard, and Rachel has no use for anybody who isn't nice to Arnold."

" Stands by her man, does she ? " said Howgate in a tone of approval. " Well, I don't blame her for that. But she's too good for him."

" Of course she is," agreed Lena heartily. " But all the same I think you're rather too hard on Arnold."

" Ah ! " mused Howgate. " He'll take her through something before she's done with him, will that fellow.

" Don't, don't ! " protested Lena in distress. " Father ! I'm sorry you don't like my friends," she added stiffly.

Howgate laughed. " They're all well enough," he said comfortably, returning to his newspaper. " I'm very glad you've got some nice friends at last, and I don't object to young Avery at all. Not at all," he added emphatically, with a look at Lena. " But to me they're just a couple of young whippersnappers, you know."

As this was not as well concealed in his manner to the Averys and Dellers as it might have been, it was not surprising that visits to Bierley Hall were reduced to the minimum indispensable for courtesy, while Lena went increasingly to Cambridge Place. There were many long quiet afternoons which she spent with Rachel, when Rowland had gone back to school and Arnold was at the mill ; the two girls sewed and talked, and Rachel spoke as frankly as her nature would allow of Esmé and John Deller, and of how much she wanted to take Arnold away from both of them. John Deller had made it plain that Arnold and Rachel were not to be married for two or three years ; there was no reason for this except his caprice, and Rachel deeply resented it. She was busy preparing household linen against her marriage ; Mrs. Avery was an exquisite needlewoman,

Rachel not quite as skilful, Lena frankly no use at all.
Lena's car, however, was useful ; she often took Rachel to
sales at old houses in the neighbourhood, for it was understood that the Arnold-Rachel ménage, when it finally
materialised, was to be set about with fine old furniture.
(John Deller professed to be extremely scornful about this
taste for moth-eaten bric-à-brac, as he described it, but he
was probably proud of it at heart, for he talked much of it,
so that even Howgate had heard of Rachel's preference for
period pieces. He did not, however, intend to pander to it
in his wedding present, and so he told Lena. " We shall have
to give them something handsome," he said, " as he's John
Deller's grandson and she's your friend. But none of that
old-fangled stuff. I don't understand it. A wireless or a
gramophone I wouldn't mind.") During these long quiet
afternoons, too, Rachel played accompaniments for Lena ;
for everything that Rowland suggested was somehow always
done in the Avery-Deller-Howgate circle, and so Lena had
begun to learn to sing. She had lessons with an excellent
master in Leeds, and to her own great astonishment she
proved to have a contralto voice which, though not by any
means marvellous, yet could give quite a lot of pleasure.
Even her stepfather liked to hear her sing, while Mr. Avery
was positively pressing in his requests for a ballad. The other
Averys, who were really musical, viewed her performances
with less enthusiasm, but they took a great deal of matter-
of-fact interest in them ; and Rowland would from time to
time send her some weird modern song, which Lena took
care not to perform when Howgate was within hearing.
More important than other people's ideas about her singing
was Lena's own feeling for it ; it was an outlet, a means of
expression for her, and at the same time something to do
worth doing. She practised regularly and conscientiously ;
then when at night she sang to her stepfather, the music
seemed to roll away the wall of the room and make the
interior of Bierley Hall, instead of being a dismal lonely shut-
off place, somehow part of the rich exciting world outside,

It

the world which held seas and forests and towns and great men and noble thoughts, and Cambridge Place and Rowland's preparatory school. Lena knew quite a lot about the workings of this latter place, for during those long quiet afternoons at Cambridge Place Rachel would tell her some of the most amusing bits out of Rowland's latest letter ; sometimes she read out a paragraph or two, and by degrees it came to be natural that Lena should hear the whole letter. Occasionally, very occasionally, Rowland wrote a note to Lena herself ; he wrote once, for instance, to ask her to choose a scarf to match a particular frock for Rachel's birthday, Mrs. Avery being confined to the house with some slight indisposition at the time ; and he would sometimes put a note in with the weird songs aforesaid. Rowland shared with his father the gift of letter-writing, and his notes were always highly individual and extremely amusing ; Lena read them to Rachel and treasured them. As Rowland's handwriting was as individual as his style, Howgate was usually aware of the arrival of a note from him ; he would then enquire in a mildly sardonic tone: " Well, how's Bystead this morning ? "—Bystead being the village which harboured Rowland's aristocratic school. To this Lena responded by telling him that the floods were in or out, skating on or off, measles predominant or fading, or whatever other fact in the letter seemed likely to interest him ; but she never, in spite of considerable temptation when Rowland was more amusing than usual, betrayed a single phrase or sentence of the younger man's to him.

When Rowland was at home the party sometimes went out at nights together, to the theatre or to dances. One spring evening when Lena arrived at Cambridge Place, hoping to pass the usual nondescript happy hours in the drawing-room, she found Mr. and Mrs. Avery in alone ; the others had all gone off to the local variety theatre.

" Esmé was with them ! " she exclaimed with conviction.

Mrs. Avery, looking at her with interest, admitted that that had been the case. At this Lena, who had been impressed with a sense of disaster all the way from Bierley Hall, had consequently driven carelessly and involved herself in one or two awkward predicaments, and then rushed wildly on foot along Cambridge Place, looked so extremely hot and miserable and like a lost dog that Mr. Avery took compassion on her and suggested that she should follow them—they had booked a box by telephone ; one more or less would not, he thought, matter. Lena's forlorn face brightened, only to fall again.

" But where could I leave the car ? " she demanded, fixing her eyes intently on Mr. Avery's face.

" Well—why not walk ? " he suggested, amused by her earnestness. " It isn't far, you know."

Lena flew from the house like an arrow, and rushed down Prince's Road into Hudley with every ounce of speed she possessed. By the time she reached the theatre she was crimson and panting ; and she could see by the desertion of the foyer that the performance had begun. Rushing breathlessly up to the commissionaire, she almost buttonholed him in her eagerness as she demanded fiercely : " A large party—in a box."

The man, quite overawed by Lena's threatening air, said hastily : " Do you mean a stout gentleman, alone ? "

" No, no ! " cried Lena in disgust. " Several people, four ! " The man's face seeming to show signs of understanding, she added peremptorily : " Take me to them ! "

She quite forgot that she perhaps ought to pay entrance money, and the commissionaire seemed to forget it too, for he hurried off down red velvet corridors, with Lena in his wake. He stopped at a little door in a blank-looking wall. " This is it," he whispered impressively, and threw open the door. The heads of the Averys and Dellers were revealed in silhouette against the lighted stage.

" Yes, this is it ! " exclaimed Lena loudly in an ecstasy

of gratitude. " Oh, bother ! I haven't got a shilling." The
four heads turned towards her with a jerk, as though pulled
by strings. " Arnold, lend me a shilling," begged Lena,
lowering her voice to a sibilant whisper. " For this man,
you know."

Arnold, between astonishment, amusement, and alarm,
rose up, smiling a trifle wanly, and handed the commissionaire the desired shilling. The man closed the door and
vanished, luckily the curtain fell almost at once on the
first turn, and the four in the box demanded Lena's
explanation. She gave it amid a good deal of laughter.
The commissionaire's reply to Lena's demand was, Rowland said, too good to be true.

" It's perfectly true, Rowland," said Lena indignantly.
" What do you mean ? "

" Oh, *Lena* ! " cried Esmé, laughing really heartily for
once. " *Do* you mean you don't see the *joke* ? A stout
gentleman—a large *party* ; don't you *see* ? "

" Alone, too," boomed Rowland. " Don't forget he was
alone. Lena was evidently going to make him happy for
the evening with her charms."

" I think Lena made it up," said Arnold slyly.

" I didn't, Arnold," protested Lena, colouring to an
even deeper shade of crimson, " I didn't really ; I never
saw the joke at all until just now. What worries me," she
added, laughing but confused, " is whether the commissionaire meant it as a joke or not. What do you think ? "

A chorus of laughter greeted this. " Oh, do *hush*," said
Esmé primly. " People are looking at us. The curtain's
going up too."

" Sit here, Lena," urged Rowland.

" Oh no," said Lena, looking about and perceiving that
there were only four chairs. " I'll kneel."

" Don't be silly, Lena," said Esmé good-humouredly.
" Arnold can kneel. It'll do him good."

This question was decided by the appearance of the
commissionaire with a chair.

" Give him a shilling, Arnold," urged Rowland teasingly.

" I haven't got one," said Arnold, colouring. " I've nothing less than half a crown ; besides I think——"

" Oh, do *hush*," commanded Esmé impatiently.

As the evening wore on and Lena grew cooler she realised that she had committed one of her usual indiscretions in forcing herself thus into the company. Having elicited from Rachel that it was Arnold who had paid for the box, she broached the subject with him as they all walked to Cambridge Place together, and requested to be allowed to pay her share.

" No ! " said Arnold, outraged. " Of course not."

" Yes, please do let me," pleaded Lena, " as I was an uninvited guest."

" No," repeated Arnold. " No." He turned his head away and coloured, and seemed undecided whether to be cross or shy. " The anecdote you brought with you more than paid for your accommodation," he said at length.

" Very good, Arnold," approved Rowland. " Neatly turned, my boy."

Lena with a sigh surrendered the point and thanked the party in general, and Arnold in particular, for allowing her to join them. " I'm very sorry I keep doing such idiotic things, but I can't help it," she concluded rather wistfully.

" Don't worry, Lena ; we're used to it," said Rowland with a merry look.

Lena, regarding him with her head on one side, smiled. It was probable that Rowland's remark was quite correct, for Lena certainly gave the company many opportunities of becoming used to her eccentricities. There was, for instance, a dance one night at which she happened to arrive late owing to car trouble ; it then appeared that the dances Rowland and Arnold had kept for her clashed in one or two instances. It seemed to Lena, who was naturally anxious not to miss any dances with anybody and especially not with Rowland, that they were very slow at making the necessary adjustments. She, who knew Rachel's programme as well as her own, had seen at once how it could be done.

"Don't you *see*, Arnold," she said at last in a friendly but pedagogic tone, as though she were speaking to a child, "if you took Rowland's dance with Rachel before supper, and——" His look of stubborn perplexity irritated her, and she took his programme out of his hand. "Like this," she explained, and showed him with a pencil. She was perfectly correct, of course, and the matter was arranged in that way ; but as soon as he had left her she was filled with remorse. "I'm afraid I hurt Arnold's feelings about the dances," she said wistfully to Rowland next time she encountered him.

"Yes, I'm afraid you did," admitted Rowland seriously.

"Dear me ! I'm awfully sorry," sighed Lena. "I didn't mean it. I do *wish* I weren't so naïve," she added in one of her disarming bursts of candour. "You'll hardly believe this, I expect, Rowland, but it's perfectly true ; I'm always trying really *hard* to be like other people, but somehow I can never keep it up."

Rowland, one eyebrow cocked, looked at her with some amusement. "But why try ? " he boomed. "If one must be a fool, and everybody's a fool sometimes, it's better surely to be a fool in one's own way."

"Do you think so ? " asked Lena eagerly.

"Well, there's always a certain satisfaction in taking one's own way, you know," said Rowland. "If you take somebody else's way, you're just as likely to be a fool that way, and then you haven't even that satisfaction. I don't mean you personally, of course," he added hastily.

"Of course not," agreed Lena. She smiled secretly to herself ; she was pleased, remembering one particular matter in which she was a fool very much in her own way.

At the end of those Christmas holidays when Lena first met the Avery household, there was a good deal of discussion in Cambridge Place about the train Rowland should take to London en route for Bystead. Eventually he decided that an early one, leaving shortly after seven, would suit him best ; and for some days before his departure the Avery family drew with delight pictures of their own inefficiency in early rising, and Rowland's habit of beginning to pack as his taxi drew up to the door. Arnold joined in this rather more seriously than Lena thought pleasing ; she had already observed that in small matters Arnold belonged to the punctual and methodical half of humanity, and that Rachel's serene unconsciousness of space and time sometimes rather irritated him. " Last time I went to see you off," he observed a trifle sarcastically to Rowland, " I was on the platform seven minutes before you arrived."

" It wasn't my fault if you were absurdly early," put in Rowland, a little ruffled.

" The guard had blown his whistle before the Averys appeared," continued Arnold.

" Do guards blow whistles ? " enquired Lena in all good faith.

Arnold glared at her. " Waved his flag, then," he substituted crossly. " It's the same thing."

The notion of seeing people off had now been put firmly into Lena's head, and as she happened to wake early on the morning of Rowland's departure—not that it was just " happening," as she shrewdly told herself ; her mind knew well enough that she wanted to wake—she took out her car, to the great astonishment of Joe and Preston, and ran down Bierley Lane and along the valley through the sordid slums which distressed her so much to the station. She was early ; there was not a sign of the Averys ; she drew up rather to one side and remained in her car. Presently Arnold's sports model came flying down the hill ; he got out and stamped impatiently about, often glancing up at the station clock ; he looked cross, and Lena decided not to join him. A few minutes later, when Lena was really beginning to think that Rowland would miss the train, the solitary and rather ancient taxi which belonged to the little garage at the end of Cambridge Place trundled mildly down, and all four Averys fell out in a considerable fluster. Rowland flew to the ticket office, Mr. Avery seized an evidently precious bag, a porter hurried off to the lift with other cases, Rachel and Mrs. Avery went with Arnold hastily down to the platform. Lena followed them, but as she reached the top of the steps one of the pangs of distrust and self-depreciation which Esmé had taught her as a child suddenly struck her to the heart. The same feeling which made her walk in the Cambridge Place gutter and tremble as she rang the No. 7 bell now poured its poison all through her veins, paralysed her, made it a physical impossibility for her to go forward and brave the Averys' glances. Of course they would not want her; she ought to have had the sense to know that. Mr. Avery happened to look casually in her direction; galvanised into life Lena sprang back behind a girder, and remained there out of sight. From there she watched Rowland enter the train and make his farewells; he kissed his mother and Rachel and offered his hand formally to his father and Arnold; the little party laughed and joked, but had a subdued air, and Lena knew well enough how much the happiness of every person to be left behind depended on the one who was leaving them. The guard whistled—Lena made a mental apology to Arnold—and waved his green flag; the engine snorted. "'The deep-panting train,'" murmured Lena to herself, and then was shocked at her own sentimentality in quoting poetry before breakfast. "This is decidedly a shallow panter," she murmured again with a laugh; and indeed the little local train, which was to join a larger one before being whisked to London, was rather amusing than impressive. It performed its function in the scheme of things, however, by bearing Rowland away, puffing off round the curve and leaving a very empty set of rails behind. The desolation which always descends on a platform when a train has gone filled the Hudley station to the brim; Awe Hill, rising up beyond the station roof, seemed

extremely bleak and barren ; Lena found tears in her eyes.
But suddenly she started from her reverie ; the Averys and
Arnold were moving towards the stairs. Lena rushed out of
the station, sprang into her car, started the engine and
drove off furiously without a backward glance.

Subsequently it appeared on careful enquiry that the
Averys had not seen her at the station ; Lena was glad,
and did not reveal that she had been there. But when after
the joyous glittering weeks of Rowland's next holiday it
was again time for him to return to Bystead, Lena bade
him farewell the night before with a little happy smile—
she knew she would see him again before he went. Again
she arrived early, again Arnold—not Esmé ; it was too
early for Esmé to be abroad—soon drew up, got out and
stamped about and looked at the clock ; again the Averys
arrived in the nick of time, again Lena watched from behind
a girder the departure of the snorting little train. Since then
she had not once missed this little ceremony of friendship,
nor had she ever revealed it to a living soul. During the
actual day of Rowland's departure she was always rather
quiet and preoccupied, for she was imagining the little
train, now swollen into a huge one with a powerful short-
funnelled engine, dashing across the map of England to the
south, roaring through stations in large print that were
farther and farther away as the hours went on. But she was
quite content, when the day was over and Rowland really
gone, to settle down into a less exciting life for a while and
take up her domestic and Bierley Green duties with quiet
assiduity ; content because she knew that in a few short
weeks trains large and small would come rushing up the
map bearing him back to Hudley within her reach again.

In this way, between rapturous holidays and contented
terms, months rolled by and became years ; the wedding
of Arnold and Rachel approached, and everything grew
very interesting. To Lena's great delight Rachel asked her
to be one of her bridesmaids ; to her greater, her almost
ecstatic delight, Arnold and Rachel decided to live in an

old-fashioned house not really very far from Bierley Hall. The Averys and the Dellers naturally spent a great deal of time in this house, adjusting it to Rachel's notions, and Lena spent a great deal of time there too, holding hammers and making cups of tea. It was the happiest time Lena had had in her life.

# CHAPTER VI

## RACHEL

For Rachel, on the contrary, the months preceding her marriage were the worst she had experienced since the time when Rowland broke his leg as a boy. She suffered, and she suffered increasingly ; with her serene and quiet spirit she had no idea that anyone *could* suffer as she was suffering now. She suffered because the difference between the Averys and the Dellers emerged more and more and more clearly every time they tried to do anything in common, and unfortunately the marrying of Arnold and Rachel, and the establishing of them in a house of their own, had to be done in common by the two families to a certain extent. All the current of Rachel's nature set towards quietness and simplicity, and she wanted a very quiet and simple wedding. The blessing of the Church did not mean much to her, but the plighting of her troth to Arnold meant everything, and that it should be done in front of a crowd of people who cared little for them, and amid a host of expensive and ostentatious details chosen because they *were* expensive and ostentatious, seemed to her a desecration. Arnold, who dreaded all ceremonies, of course shared this view ; and it never occurred to Rachel that anyone else had any right to dictate the details of this great act of their lives. She was disillusioned on this point, however, one Sunday night at West View. May Deller had invited her to supper, and Rachel and Arnold and his mother and sister were sitting round the fire in the large costly drawing-room, chatting in the desultory and perfunctory but comfortable manner common to family parties waiting for a meal, when John Deller sauntered in. Everyone at once sat up and felt an increase of tension. After a few sharp queries as to what they had all been doing since tea, he observed drily : " I notice none of you've been to church." As John Deller himself went to church perhaps once a year, nobody thought this required an answer, but the mention of church had by a natural association turned his mind to the forthcoming wedding in the family, and he went on : " Well, Rachel, I hear you and Arnold are going to be married in the autumn."

As he had settled this himself, Rachel again thought that his remark required little answer ; she held her head down, blushed and murmured a vague assent.

" And what kind of a wedding are you thinking of having ? " continued John Deller with an air of simplicity.

Rachel hated discussing a subject so near her heart with him, but she felt a kind of relief that this necessary but dreaded moment had come at last, and she replied truthfully : " Something very quiet and simple, Mr. Deller."

To her intense astonishment he at once flew into a violent rage. " What ! " he cried. His cigar nearly fell out of his mouth ; his thick neck turned crimson, the veins on his bald head swelled ; he struck the arm of his chair violently with his clenched fist and shouted : " Not if I know it you won't ! I won't have my grandson married in any hole-and-corner way, I tell you straight. By God, if you can't change your mind Arnold had better change his girl."

" Grandfather ! " cried Arnold, starting up.

Rachel was terrified by the white fury of his face ; for the first time in her life she shouted. " It shall be just as you wish, Mr. Deller," she cried loudly, drowning Arnold's angry stammer. " It shall be just as you wish," she repeated in a quieter tone when she had silenced him, and added with some dignity : " That is, as far as my father's resources permit."

" Oh well, of course," mumbled John Deller, looking down. (Rachel had noticed before how any reference to a

limitation of income embarrassed him.) " Of course, of
course. Well, you've more sense than I thought," he added
on a complimentary note. The gong sounded ; he got up
and offered her his arm with a jocular air, and Rachel,
biting her under-lip, took it. " I daresay we shall get on
well enough when you're my grand-daughter-in-law ! " he
cried with boisterous cheerfulness, leading her towards the
door. " What do you think ? "

Rachel forced herself to smile at him but could not
manage to utter any words. She felt quite sick with hatred
as she sat erect at the supper-table—Arnold had once told
her that John Deller admired her carriage, and she never
allowed herself to forget it—and tried to eat the elaborate
fare always provided at West View, which she privately
disliked. This was the man Arnold had to live and work
with ! She glanced at Arnold ; he was still pale, and like
herself could hardly eat. Rage rose in her throat and nearly
choked her. To humiliate Arnold like that ! In front of her !
" Oh, my poor boy, oh, my poor boy," she thought,
yearning over him so that her whole body ached. " But
I'll take you away from them, yes, I will ; I'll go through
anything, anything to be able to marry you. Yes, *anything*."
Her breast rose and fell with emotion ; she felt that she
would like to sob for hours, but instead she hardened her
heart, set her lips rather firmly, and with a slight inclination of the head accepted a second helping from the dish
the maid was offering her. As soon as she had done so she
remembered that John Deller did not admire young
women with large appetites ; he thought them unfeminine.
Ah, it was all too difficult for her ; she was not clever, like
Lena, at understanding beforehand what people would
feel. The Dellers were too difficult, too complicated—she
would be beaten, she would never be able to marry Arnold.
" Yes, I will, I will ! " She protested to herself in anguish.
" I *will*.   No matter *what* I have to agree to."

She needed all her resolution to carry her through to the
wedding. There were times, it is true, when everything

went swimmingly ; as for instance when John Deller
presented her with the title-deeds of Oddy Hall as a little
wedding present in advance. Oddy Hall was one of the
charming, not-too-large Elizabethan houses with which
the hills round Hudley are strewn ; it had belonged to
Sir George Annison, who very obligingly died about this
time. Lady Annison, who felt that it was just what Arnold
wanted, and who wanted herself to retire to a small house
in York to be near a sister, very tactfully mentioned it to
John Deller first ; he went to see it, and returned genuinely
impressed. It certainly had an air ; it had been a hall for
a very long time. The purchase was soon completed, and
Rachel had no difficulty in being grateful, for she was overjoyed. To her it seemed that the house had every possible
advantage. It was old and beautiful ; lying as it did in a
hollow on the east end of Awe Hill, it was near Adela
Mills without being in the town ; it was not very far, if one
went across the fields, from Bierley Hall ; and it was a quite
considerable distance from West View. This last was such
an immense advantage in Rachel's eyes that whenever she
thought of it her heart sang. But there were other times
when everything went so terribly wrong that it seemed
likely there would never be an Avery-Deller marriage at
all. There were arguments about the church, the officiating
clergy, the service, the invitations, the list of guests, the
eatables and the honeymoon. Lilias and John Deller
resumed all their ancient enmity, until at last Lilias decided to evade, as tactfully as possible, meeting her uncle
any more ; the making of arrangements then devolved
upon Will Avery, who succeeded fairly well because he
politely, affably but firmly talked John Deller down. But
when John Deller was soothed, there was Esmé to contend
with. Esmé of course was to be a bridesmaid ; Rachel asked
her most intimate friend—Lena—as well, and found that
Esmé did not want to share the honour with Lena, would
not, could not, share it with Lena. Here John Deller came
unexpectedly to the rescue, and said that Alfred Howgate's

adopted daughter was not to be sneezed at ; Rachel was to
have her if she chose. Arguments then arose about the
colour and cut of the bridesmaids' frocks ; Esmé could not
fall in with any of Rachel's suggestions ; it appeared that
she disliked blue, hated yellow, and loathed pink. Mauve
was the only possible wear for her, she said crossly, glaring
at Lena in anticipation of her objections. Lena, however,
to Rachel's amusement, though she looked rather surprised, merely said : " Well, let's have mauve, then."
Esmé, disconcerted at thus having the ground cut away
from her feet, fell into angry mutterings ; of course if
Lena *preferred* pink—— " Well, of course I do like it
better," said Lena frankly. " But I'm sure to look a mess in
anything beside you, Esmé, so why bother ? " Esmé sighed,
exasperated ; the dresses were of course ordered in mauve.
Similar one-sided contests arose about Arnold's presents to
Esmé and Lena. Esmé sneered at everything Arnold suggested until Rachel felt that she should scream if he mentioned one article more ; Lena, when consulted, seemed
ignorant of the custom and had to have it explained to
her ; when this was done she exclaimed joyously that it was
delightful.

" But what would you *like*, Lena ? " persisted Esmé.

" Oh, anything ! " cried Lena, smiling. " Anything !
It's more the occasion and the giver than the gift, isn't it ? "

" Lena, you *are* the most *sentimental* creature," complained Esmé in disgust.

Rachel, however, was more than thankful for Lena's
brand of sentimentality than she could well express, for the
constant succession of small hindrances to her marriage
really wore upon her nerves. Nothing kept her, often, from
being thoroughly hysterical but the realisation that it
would give John Deller a really solid ground of criticism
against her. She had restless, tossing nights ; she dreamed of
being separated from Arnold by rushing streams or horrible
doors which would not open ; she awoke in tears. Details
which she had never noticed before began to worry her ;

at times she—she the serene Rachel—was almost snappy
to those she loved ; the pain she felt when John or Esmé
Deller said some curt snubbing thing to Arnold was as
acute as the pain of toothache but more widespread, a
sharp stabbing anguish which coursed like fire through her
whole body, so that even her wrists hurt. Somehow Rachel
could not tell her mother all these things, because she felt
that Mrs. Avery's ancient dislike of all the John Deller
branch of the family, a dislike which dated from that old
courtship by Clement, a dislike which the gentle Arnold
had scotched but by no means killed, was raising its head
again and becoming dangerous ; a very little would have
sufficed, in these days of strain and stress, to turn Mrs.
Avery against Arnold and against Rachel's marriage
altogether. So there could be no complaining to Mrs.
Avery ; and it was therefore an immense relief to Rachel to
have the loyal Lena at hand : Lena, who always said :
" Well, Rachel, I'm not surprised at anything that Esmé
does," or " I think you're wonderful to stand *five minutes*
of Mr. Deller "—for latterly Lena and John Deller had
been made acquainted in the natural course of events, and
equally naturally Lena took Rachel's view of him—but yet
regarded Rachel's marriage as absolutely fixed and desirable. " Of course," Lena would begin in that alarmingly
frank manner of hers, which always caused her friends to
look at her in trepidation as to what on earth she was going
to say next—" of course you can't expect me to think
Arnold *quite* good enough for you, Rachel, because nobody is ; but I think he's well worth rescuing, if you know
what I mean."

" Sometimes I think we shall *never* be married, Lena,"
murmured Rachel one day, when she felt that she would
choke if she kept this fear any longer without expression.

" You mean it's a kind of struggle between you and
John Deller for Arnold's soul," observed Lena thoughtfully,
going to extremes as usual. " Well ! I know who *I'm* backing
to win."

What balm this kind of thing was to her bruised spirit only Rachel knew ; she relied upon it more and more, as suspense and the continual pin-pricks of opposition worked more and more upon her nerves. She at last reached a stage of mind when every time the bell rang she thought it was some message to postpone her marriage ; Arnold was quite as anxious ; and every evening when the door of No. 7 admitted him the engaged couple threw themselves into each other's arms and clung to each other in a manner quite frantic. The bliss of the hours they spent together was made poignant by the sense of impending disaster and separation which hung over them ; they parted as though for ever ; Rachel dreamed and worried through the night; next morning Esmé would come round to say that the mauve shoes they had chosen were *quite* impossible, or there would be a tiresome message of delay from the decorators, or Arnold would ring up and admit that he had a cold, or some other dark worrying thing would occur, and Rachel's spirits sank and sank. Then Lena would suddenly burst into the house, smiling all over her vivid face ; with her arm round Rachel's waist, she inspected the latest presents and enthused over them, laughed, enquired whether Rowland would come to Hudley the night before the wedding or when, and having sung very dramatically songs which observed : " But believe me, love like ours is the power of magic powers," cried fondly : " You and Arnold are *lucky*, Rachel, to care so much ! " Yes, at these times Rachel felt that what Esmé called Lena's sentimentality was extremely precious to her.

At last, however, the tormenting months dragged by ; the banns were put up, the invitations issued, the catering arrangements settled ; so many presents arrived that even Lena's enthusiasm for them waned ; the week preceding the day of the wedding came and passed without catastrophe, then the day before brought Rowland ; at last the actual day itself arrived. Lena, who was to change at Cambridge Place, flew into the house at a very early hour ;

KT

she was as usual in a fever of excitement, and Rachel, who
had previously been feeling numb and rather dreary, for
the day was warm though dull, as usual caught the infection of her manner and began to feel that it really was the
day of her marriage to Arnold. Presently she found herself
actually dressing for her wedding ; Mrs. Avery, pale and
with shaking hands but pretending to be very calm, moved
about her, or unfolded white silken garments from the
heap on the bed. Lena, looking remarkably ugly in her
mauve picture dress, sat on the corner of the bed by the
wall ; Mrs. Avery had yielded to her impassioned pleading
and allowed her to be present at the ceremony of Rachel's
dressing on condition that she sat motionless and silent ; and
she therefore remained motionless and silent with such intensity that her presence filled the room. Even when the
customary lace veil completed Rachel's conventional
bridal attire Lena said nothing, but her dark eyes gleamed
with such admiration that Rachel, amused, turned back
to the glass again to see if there were cause for it. She herself
never saw her clothes as part of herself, but only as pieces of
such and such material, arranged so and so ; but Arnold,
she knew, thought differently, and she was glad for his sake
that she seemed to be looking calm and fair, not untidy or
haggard. Her shoes—what an argument she had had with
Esmé about her low-heeled shoes ! for of course nothing
would induce her to reveal the real reason of her preference
for them—were rather loose because she had been so afraid
of having them too tight ; but she did not mind ; one could
forget too-loose shoes, she decided, but not too-tight ones.
Rowland now poked his head into the room, looked his
sister up and down and said she would do, teased Lena as
he always did so as to make her give her beautiful laugh,
and informed his mother that their car was at the door.
They drove off together side by side, dark, pale, and handsome ; Rachel, who had now conveyed herself and her
train downstairs, watched them fondly from the dining-
room window. It soon became obvious that Lena was on

tenterhooks for the arrival of Esmé, who had characteristically declined to dress in the comparative discomfort of
Cambridge Place, and was merely to call there to pick up
her co-bridesmaid ; an expression of strain appeared on
Lena's face, which always revealed her feelings very clearly,
and she began to answer Mr. Avery's remarks at random.
In spite of herself Rachel caught this infection too ; she
managed to achieve a smile, but she could feel her heart
thumping against her white bodice in great strong hard
beats, and she dared not look at the clock. If something
were to go wrong now ! Oh, Arnold ! Arnold ! Where was
he now ? Surely he would be at the church already, unless
something had happened—at this Rachel's mind flew
through all the gamut of possible accidents. She pulled herself up with a start, ashamed of such sentimentality, and
relieved her feelings by scowling at Lena, whose face at
once took on a timid and unhappy air. Somehow this
made everything seem more like a crisis than ever ; Mr.
Avery positively drew out his watch ; it was unbearable !
Just then one of the Deller cars, containing Esmé, came
bumping backwards along the Place, and Rachel sighed
her relief. Lena flew out to Esmé, who seemed in a quite
extraordinarily perverse mood, even for her, judging from
the tone of her voice ; they drove off, only to draw up
abruptly a few yards away at a scream from Lena, who had
forgotten her bouquet. This indispensable item being
affably handed in through the window by Mr. Avery, the
car at last disappeared round the corner.

"Our turn next, Raikes," observed Mr. Avery cheerfully, returning ; and Rachel gravely nodded.

In a moment, as it seemed, they too were driving away
round the corner and bowling along over the smooth hard
roads. In the distance the tower of the church appeared ; a
radiant happiness filled Rachel's heart ; she threw back her
head and smiled ; soon, soon they would be at the church
gate, soon she would march up the aisle to a pale harassed-
looking Arnold (poor boy) ; soon they would be married ;

soon, quite soon if she could only keep patient, she and
Arnold would have finished with all this silly fuss and be
away off by themselves for always.

The car drew up at the church gate ; Rachel and her
father got out, walked sedately up the flagged path amid
admiring murmurs from the crowd of Deller workpeople
who had assembled to see Arnold " wed," and mounted the
steps to the porch. Lena and Esmé were standing there,
according to schedule ; so also were Rowland and Mrs
Avery. They all seemed to be talking together with great
agitation, and looked flustered and upset ; then Esmé
turned a drawn and tearstained face towards them, and
Rachel knew that something was seriously wrong. She stood
still and drew a deep breath. Mrs. Avery came towards her.

" Arnold ? " murmured Rachel, fixing her eyes in
anguished question on her mother.

" No, it isn't Arnold," Mrs. Avery told her quietly.
" It's poor Mr. Deller. He has had some kind of a seizure,
apoplectic we think. Arnold and Mrs. Deller are in the
vestry with him now. Mr. Howgate has kindly gone for a
doctor." She looked into her daughter's eyes, and added
rather nervously : " Sit down for a moment, Rachel dear,
while we decide what's best to be done."

" I don't want to sit down," said Rachel clearly. Her
chief emotion at the moment was one of hot anger against
John Deller. " He's done everything else he possibly could
to stop our marriage," she thought, " and now, when all
else has failed, this, this ! " Her conscience reproached her :
" He's an old man, and people don't have apoplectic fits
for pleasure." " Don't they ! " said her other self grimly.
" He's done everything else he possibly could, and failed,
and now he's trying this, this ! But he shan't keep me from
Arnold," she thought, " he shan't ; *nothing* shall " ; and all
her anger and her resolution and her love rose up in her,
hot and fierce and strong, and she said aloud in a clear
ringing tone : " The wedding must go on."

The others all looked at her aghast.

" It's impossible," cried Mrs. Avery. Rachel looked at her steadily, and in that moment realised that her mother, though she did not herself know it, would be glad if the wedding were postponed.

" We could hardly have a reception, Rachel, with the bridegroom's grandfather lying at death's door," observed Mr. Avery.

" Then don't have the reception," said Rachel. " Mother and you can decide about that, father ; I don't mind, it's nothing to me. But the wedding must go on. Besides," she added with a kind of contempt, " Mr. Deller won't die. You'll see, he won't."

Her father looked at her in growing dismay, but Rowland said : " I think Rachel's right, father."

" So do I," chimed in the loyal Lena.

Mrs. Avery made a movement of irritation. " It is Arnold's wishes which must be consulted in this matter," she said in her quiet tones.

" And mine, mother," persisted Rachel. " I have a right to be consulted too. Rowland, promise me you'll tell Arnold I say the wedding must go on."

Rowland cocked his eyebrow at her gravely ; after a moment he said : " Very well." He turned on his heel and entered the church. There was a horrible pause ; it was all exactly like one of Rachel's nightmares. She still stood stiffly clutching her bouquet ; she had not moved since she heard the news. Outside the crowd craned and wondered audibly about the delay ; within the church the guests exchanged whispers.

" Esmé of course cannot act as your bridesmaid, Rachel," said Mrs. Avery, looking at the girl, who had sunk down on one of the benches, and looked almost ready to faint. Esmé did not seem to have heard her, and she added : " I can hardly think she will wish to."

" *I* do—*I* will ! " cried Lena hotly.

Mrs. Avery gave her a sombre glance.

After what seemed about half an hour, so that Rachel

wondered that the church clock did not strike, Rowland
returned. As she heard his uneven steps on the tiles Rachel
thought to herself: " Even if Arnold won't be married to-
day—and he may not, because he's so used to doing what
other people want and I can't get to him—I shan't give it
up for long. We'll be married within a week, whether John
Deller dies or not." Rowland appeared, wearing a dubious
look. " Well ? What does Arnold say ? " demanded Rachel
coldly.

" Well, he says—he doesn't quite know what he ought
to do—if you wish it, of course—he's surprised, rather, but
if you wish it," hesitated Rowland, and Rachel perceived
that poor Arnold was indeed perplexed in the extreme
between two duties. She smiled rather sadly. " Mr. Howgate has come back with the doctor, and the ambulance
has been sent for," continued Rowland. At this Esmé gave
a little gasping cry, and Rowland went across the porch
and seated himself beside her. " This is very hard for you,
Esmé," he said sympathetically, and took her hand. Esmé
clung to him, unable to speak ; she seemed genuinely
moved.

And no doubt it *was* all very pathetic, thought Rachel ;
only she could not see it like that. Something of her youthful
softness of heart had been killed during the last three years,
killed by Esmé and John Deller ; and all she could feel
now was that nothing should keep her from Arnold. No !
Nothing ! Not Lilias's sombre jealousy, not her father's
disapproval, not Rowland's concern, not Arnold's weakness, not John Deller's death ; nothing. She raised her head
proudly.

" It must be nearly three," she said. " I think the
ceremony had better begin."

There was a pause. At length Mr. Avery spoke. " If you
are determined, Rachel," he began in a tone of distaste.

" I am," said Rachel.

Mr. Avery shrugged his shoulders. " Then there's nothing
more to be said. Go in, Rowland, and make the necessary

arrangements. Esmé, my dear, you had better go home ;
I'll put you into one of these cars."

Esmé raised her head. " I think I'd rather stay," she
said faintly.

Mrs. Avery said in anger : " Have none of you young
people any heart ? "

" But, Mrs. Avery ! " cried Lena hotly. " Arnold's her
brother, after all ! A brother's more than a grandfather.
At least, I should think so," she added, her voice trailing
away. " I haven't either, of course, so I don't really know."

With an impatient exclamation Mrs. Avery turned and
went away to her place in one of the front pews. She looked
handsome and serene as she walked up the aisle, but
Rachel, watching her, knew that some bond between
herself and her mother, strained this long time, had now
snapped.

After a while Rowland came to say that all was ready ;
they gave him a moment or two to reach his place at
Arnold's side again, and then the wedding procession
entered the church.

# CHAPTER VII

## ESMÉ

Esmé trembled so that the flowers in her bouquet shook. From where she stood behind Rachel she could see into the vestry ; the door had twice been closed from within by her mother, but it sprang slightly open again, whether because it was newly painted or because of May Deller's characteristic inefficiency Esmé in the tumult of her thoughts found time to wonder. She had heard, a moment ago, the noise made by the motor ambulance backing down to the vestry door, and now she could see a confused mass of straining men's arms and a shoulder or two ; they were evidently lifting her grandfather on to the stretcher. Yes ! She caught a glimpse of his face, crimson, the mouth open, the cheeks somehow uneven ; she felt sick and turned her head away, revolted ; but the sight drew her eyes again. An immense feeling of guilt possessed her ; she ought to be at John Deller's side instead of amid flowers and guests and silks watching Arnold's marriage. For to begin with, his illness was very largely her fault, and the rest of it was due to Arnold's marriage. And Esmé understood so well, so very well, what John Deller felt about Arnold's marriage ; she understood it because she felt the same about it herself. Arnold should have made a great, tremendously brilliant marriage with some extremely beautiful and polished woman of a class higher than his own ; he should not just have married Rachel Avery, half a Deller herself and the other half just a mere schoolmaster's daughter. But Arnold could never be made to see that ; he always seemed to think that Rachel was far too good for him ; he adored Rachel, doted on her, thought of nothing else. Esmé knew

that John Deller was fiercely and passionately jealous of
his grandson's love for Rachel ; she knew it because she
was fiercely and passionately jealous herself. For the last
six months Arnold, she felt, had been simply intolerable
at home ; he thought of nothing, nothing but getting
married and leaving West View ; his grandfather, his
mother, his sister were nothing to him. And what would
West View be like without him ? Esmé simply dared not
think of the appalling loneliness which would be hers when
Arnold was married, and lived in that exasperating Oddy
Hall, which was miles and miles away from West View.
*Why* had her grandfather been so silly as to buy it ? Simply
out of sheer pride, simply because he wanted Arnold to
have the best of everything, simply because he wanted
his grandson to live in a Hall. He was always doing things
like that for Arnold ; but did Arnold see it ? Not a bit !
He was not in the least grateful for all that Esmé and his
grandfather did for him, thought Esmé sadly ; all he
thought of was leaving them ; he never even noticed the
tremendous efforts they put forth to make his wedding
what it should be. What hours and hours she had spent
over the bridesmaids' dresses, for example ! Lena had
wanted to have pink, but then pink was so terribly naïve,
especially for autumn wear ; how could Arnold Deller's
elegant autumn wedding have bridesmaids in pink ?
Lena looked well in pink, of course, but pink was too, too
crude ; quite impossible. Rachel had suggested yellow. At
the mere thought of this Esmé's delicate cheek coloured.
How *could* Rachel ? Did she think that Esmé could ever
forget that horrible night of her twenty-first birthday dance,
when all the lights were wrong and Rachel ruined everything by wearing brighter yellow than her hostess ? Esmé
had hated yellow ever since. However, Esmé's efforts
about the dresses had been rewarded, for really the mauve
frocks were charming, she knew she was looking lovely ;
it would have been too absurd to go home without being
seen, as Mr. Avery had seemed to wish. Lena, of course,

looked ugly, but then poor Lena always did look ugly ;
Esmé always felt neater and daintier and more elegant and
successful and popular when Lena was present than at
other times, from sheer force of contrast. But now the sense
of guilt struck her again ; she ought not to be thinking of
clothes when her grandfather was dying. What would life
be like without him, she wondered ? Not so very different,
she supposed ; his death would not make half so much
difference to her as Arnold's marriage would. For not only
would Arnold be miles away instead of coming home twice
every day to Esmé's side, but the Averys would be moved
miles away too. Telephone messages would be exchanged
between Cambridge Place and Oddy Hall in future, no
longer between Cambridge Place and West View. Rowland
would be the friend of Esmé's married brother, which was
so different. But what did she want with Rowland, after
all ? He was nothing to her, nothing ; except that as a
matter of fact he was the only man who had ever definitely
asked her to marry him. Her other admirers somehow just
didn't. Perhaps she was nicer to the Averys than to anyone else, thought Esmé wistfully. She had known them so
long and always loved them. Of course she was jealous of
Arnold's affection for them as well, but somehow it was the
same thing carried a little bit further ; all her feelings
seemed to fall over into the other side, as it were, if she
tried to go on feeling them too long. Her grandfather was
just the same in that way. That morning, for instance, John
Deller had come down to breakfast simply swimming with
sentiment about Arnold's wedding day. Arnold was a little
late, which usually annoyed his grandfather dreadfully,
but that morning he beamed and smiled as the minutes
went by and no Arnold appeared, and said, " Well, well,
my boy," in a fatherly indulgent tone when at last he came
in. He fussed about Arnold's having just the things he liked
to eat and drink, and Arnold coloured and seemed embarrassed and cross, and ate without enjoyment ; and
Esmé could see, yes she could actually *see*, her grandfather's

feeling falling down on the other side, until at last he said
sharply :

" You're coming to the mill this morning, I suppose ? "

Arnold looked simply horrified, and stammered, " No—
I hadn't thought of it."

" Oh, you hadn't thought of it," repeated John Deller
in a peculiar tone, and Esmé knew that he was furious.

" I thought you were giving the workpeople a holiday,
father ? " put in Mrs. Deller, taking Arnold's side as usual.

" I am—after twelve o'clock," snapped John Deller.

" Are you going down, grandfather ? " enquired Arnold
in a surprised tone.

John Deller looked at him. " Yes, I am," he said. " The
world's got to go on, even if you are getting married,
Arnold."

Arnold hesitated and coloured, then blurted out nervously : " You won't be late back, will you ? "

" I'll see what I can do," replied John Deller drily.

He had evidently not been very successful in this, however, for Esmé was already dressed and wandering about
the house in search of admiration when he returned. She
had been admired effusively by May Deller, and perfunctorily by Arnold (who was by now looking as white as
a sheet) and had begun to wish that she had arranged
to go earlier to Cambridge Place ; it was rather dismal here
at West View. (And what would it be like with Arnold
gone !) When she heard the sound of the car she ran forward
quite eagerly, for her grandfather never failed to admire her,
and to admire her in a discriminating way. As he came up
the steps, however, she saw that he was in no mood for
admiration ; he was carrying his hat in his hand, his face
was crimson, and his forehead dripped with sweat. He
seemed to stagger a little as he reached the top, and he
brushed her roughly to one side, and sank at once into the
nearest chair. He held out his hat for her to take, and then
leaned forward with his hands on his knees, breathing
heavily.

"Is it so very hot?" asked Esmé, surprised.

John Deller shook his head, and was a minute or two before replying. "He'll be the death of me yet, will that lad," he gasped at last.

"Who, grandfather?" demanded Esmé, at a loss.

"That Arnold of yours," gasped John Deller. He gave a deep sigh, struck his chest once or twice, and seemed at last to gain control of his breathing. He then raised his head and spoke in a more normal tone. "I've been all this while putting right something the young fool did wrong yesterday," he said. "Aye! And it isn't what you'd call right yet."

"He'll settle down better when he's married," said Esmé soothingly. "He's too excited to work properly just now."

"Well, it's to be hoped so," said John Deller. He leaned back, took a cigar and lighted it; Esmé noticed that his hands shook visibly.

"How do you like my bridesmaid's frock, grandfather?" she enquired, to turn his mind to a pleasanter subject.

"It's well enough," said John Deller wearily. He looked about him. "What's the time? Am I very late?" he asked. Esmé told him that he was. "Fetch my slippers from my dressing-room," he commanded. Esmé, pouting at this menial errand, but really rather glad to have something to do, obeyed. When she returned he was still in the same position; she put the slippers down beside his chair. "There's no flavour in these cigars," he remarked, laying the one he had been smoking carefully aside. He stooped to his boots, but groaned and raised himself again. "You'll have to take them off for me, Esmé," he said in a weak tone.

"Grandfather, I can't," said Esmé sharply. "I'm all dressed, I can't kneel down."

"Oh, you can't!" repeated John Deller sarcastically. "Well, well. I've got some queer grand-children, I reckon. Now Rachel would take her grandfather's boots off if he asked her, I'll be bound."

Esmé coloured. " I'm not Rachel," she threw out.

" I've noticed Arnold doesn't seem to think so," observed John Deller thickly, fumbling with his laces.

It seemed a long time to the watching Esmé before each boot at last clashed to the floor. " It's nearly time for you to start for the church," she urged then, seeing that John Deller made no attempt to move from his chair. " The car will be here for you and mother in a minute."

" Well, it'll have to wait for me then," said her grand-father. He heaved himself slowly up and went off towards the stairs.

They had to wait for him so long that Esmé became positively frenzied with impatience. (Fortunately Arnold had gone off by himself in a separate car.) " Why don't you start, dear ? " queried May Deller. " I don't see why you shouldn't. The other car's here waiting for you, and after all you've to call for Lena."

" And suppose we arrive before you ? " cried Esmé in a fury. " And suppose Rachel starts immediately we've gone, and arrives before you ? It would be *awful*."

She almost wept with rage, and prepared some bitter things to say to her grandfather when he should appear. When at last he came she began to utter them, but soon stopped, for John Deller seemed not to hear ; he looked dazed and fumbling as he clambered into the car. Then at last Esmé had been able to start, and had gone off for Lena, and then the man had been ages turning round in that stupid narrow Place ; and then Lena had forgotten her bouquet, and then when at last they reached the church nobody stepped forward to greet them, there was no Rowland, no Frank Annison, no smiling face of any kind ; there they stood in the porch and nobody took any notice of them at all, and a commotion of some kind seemed to be going on within the church. All of a sudden Mrs. Avery came out to them, more agitated than Esmé ever remem-bered to have seen her, and told them that John Deller had had a seizure ; and Esmé's heart seemed to stop. She

wanted to cry aloud : " It was his boots," but the words
died in her throat. Guilt weighed her down ; she could not
stand upright beneath the awful load. It was all her fault ;
it was because she had been selfish about the boots. Yet
when Mr. Avery asked her kindly, " Would you like to go
to him, Esmé ? " she gasped " Oh, *no* ! " Then she was
more ashamed than ever, but at the same time she knew she
could not, would not, go : she hated illness and accidents.
But she ought to go, she ought ; why was she so selfish and
horrid ? Oh God, why was she ? Nobody had higher ideas
of what was right and proper than she had, she felt sure ;
and yet she was always doing these awful, selfish, mean,
petty things. She had once driven that silly Lena into
attacking her with a knife, so that even now, when Lena
had forgotten all about it, she could not bear to accept her
hospitality ; and now she had killed her grandfather. It
was because she had nothing really to live for, nobody she
really loved. How she envied Rachel, yes, envied her with
all her heart ; Rachel knew what she wanted, Rachel knew
whom she loved ; Rachel was not dismayed or panic-
stricken in a crisis, she just said calmly : " The marriage
must go on." What courage ! And what calm knowledge
of herself ! Rachel knew what would make her life happy,
and went straight for it, quiet, determined, unshakable.
Look at her face now, as Arnold put the wedding ring on
her finger ; it was radiant with something deeper than
happiness. Tears stood in Esmé's eyes ; she saw in a flash
the beauty of marriage, of long lives spent faithfully and
lovingly together. How she wished, how she longed with
her whole heart, that she could feel like that towards some
man, love him enough to want to marry him and have
children by him, and tend him in sickness and keep his
house warm and clean and happy and share his griefs and
joys. The Frank Annison affair had petered out, and Esmé
was glad ; she did not feel like that towards him. If only she
could feel like that towards Rowland ! Perhaps after all she
*did* feel like that towards him ; she liked him and always

sparkled when he was there ; he teased her nicely ; he
understood her likes and dislikes, he had a strong character,
he was a man in a way that somehow poor old Arnold was
not. Rowland loved her, as Esmé knew by a thousand little
signs in spite of his ridiculous determination not to propose
to her again—she smiled caressingly at the thought ; yes, he
loved her steadily. Perhaps one day she would make Rowland happy, marry him and settle down with him, and live
a normal, satisfying life, loved and loving.

The mood did not last—indeed by the time the register
was signed Esmé had decided that the wedding was tedious,
the expression on Rachel's face silly, and Rowland merely
an unimportant schoolmaster—but its occurrence had made
a mark on Esmé's mind, and it came back again rather
often in the next few months. The weeks following Arnold's
marriage were very sad at West View. John Deller hung
between life and death. Specialists were consulted ; nurses
called in ; steps had to be soft and voices low ; his stertorous
breathing filled the house, and death seemed to hover
above it ; the suspense was cruel. Arnold and Rachel were
of course unable to go away for their honeymoon ; they
remained at West View to be near the dying man. It was all
very pathetic, and the three Dellers were drawn together
by their family memories ; Esmé felt very tender and loving
and conscious of family ties, especially as Rachel was rather
unsympathetic about John Deller, and never seemed to
believe that he was dying. Just when she was feeling most
touched by the pathos of her grandfather's condition—that
he, formerly so strong and dominant, should lie there so
helpless and dependent on others struck her forcibly—a
kindly letter came for her from Rowland ; she replied to
it in a warm little note, and after that Rowland wrote to
her rather often. As it turned out, Rachel was in a sense
right, for John Deller began to recover. He did not regain
the " use " in the left side of his body nor the full stretch of
his mental powers, and his speech was slow, rare and
indistinct ; he required the constant attention of a male

servant, never came from his room until eleven or twelve
in the morning, had his meals alone, and out of doors
became a mere heavy muffled-up body slumped at a queer
angle in a bathchair ; still he lived, and the doctors said
that with care he would live several years. Arnold and
Rachel now went away for their delayed honeymoon in
Italy ; before they returned, Esmé and her mother took
John Deller away to the seaside. These were the most
dreary hours of Esmé's life ; pacing up and down a deserted
sea-front in an icy wind, beside a bathchair containing a
diseased old body which she knew she ought to love but
could not, depressed her so intensely that Hudley and its
inhabitants seemed quite brilliant and gay and joyous by
comparison. *Anybody* young and healthy would have been
an absolute godsend : even Lena would have had a hearty
welcome. Postcards showing brilliant blue skies and luxuri-
ant foliage, breathing happiness in every one of the scanty
words with which they were inscribed, came from Arnold
and Rachel. " A. sends love " made Esmé bite her lips and
writhe. She felt deserted, marooned in this miserable
desolate place for ever with old people, people she did not
love, while Arnold, married and rejoicing in Italy, could
not even bother to send her a postcard. (Next day perhaps
one would arrive from him, but it was either cold and
architectural or full of his wife.) In these circumstances
Rowland's letters were an inestimable boon ; and Esmé
had so many long dreary hours with nothing to do that she
replied to him much more often than she really intended.
In the total dearth of young men which a seaside hotel in
early December naturally revealed, Rowland began to seem
more and more desirable. Then the Dellers returned to
Hudley for Christmas, and Esmé had a round of gaieties,
and Rowland's desirability rather dwindled in her consideration. She remembered his position and prospects,
winced, and decided to give herself another chance or so of
meeting the romantic, brilliant, important husband she
really craved. Still Rowland was always there, handy and

devoted and interesting, not by any means a lover to be ashamed of ; and the idea that she might one day fall back on him was since Arnold's wedding always at the back of Esmé's mind. He was leaving Bystead now, and moving on to a much bigger school in Sussex ; perhaps he would one day become quite a personage in a big Public School.

It was not until Rowland had gone to his new school and the dances were over, that Esmé really settled down to life at West View without Arnold. At first Arnold's absence did not seem to matter as much as she had feared. Arnold came in for a few minutes every day to see his grandfather. Esmé dined at her brother's once or twice—Oddy Hall with its old oak and old brass and its polished floors and scanty pictures was really very charming—and she and her mother often called in on their way home from somewhere else, and had tea with Rachel ; the new establishment made somewhere to go and something to talk about, and Esmé thought of heaps of little details in which it might be improved—not that Rachel took much notice of what she said, to be sure ; she was quite as dreamy as she had been before her marriage, if not more so, and she looked preposterously happy. Then there came a night when Esmé rang up the Arnold Dellers to propose the theatre and found that they were out ; and another night when she found that they were in, but expecting guests, and she had not been invited. Yet another day when she had called and found that the maids did not expect them in for dinner, she overtook the newly married Frank Annison on the way home, gave him a lift, and received from him the information that Arnold and Rachel had gone to Leeds in a lively party. This was very bitter : to hear of Arnold's doings from a mere stranger ! She went up early the next afternoon to Oddy Hall by tram—Mrs. Deller required the chauffeur—prepared to upbraid Rachel with tears for not asking her to join them ; but she found the tiresome Lena there before her, obviously come to stay to tea.

" I wish you didn't live such a long way out, Rachel,"
Lt

complained Esmé fretfully, thinking how near they were to
Lena. " The trams are awful."

" I'll run you home, Esmé," volunteered Lena quickly,
" I've got the car."

Esmé, though furious, had to submit ; next morning she
approached her grandfather as he lolled in his chair in a
sunny corner of the West View garden, and told him that
she wanted a car of her own. He seemed to understand, and
his watery blue eyes had something of their old shrewdness
as he said in his faint husky voice : " What make ? " Esmé
was therefore astonished and hurt when next day Arnold
descended on her in a perfect fury and wanted to know
what she had been worrying their grandfather for.

" I wasn't worrying him," protested Esmé. " I only
asked him for a car, that's all."

" He's been wanting to sign cheques and all sorts of
things," said Arnold crossly. " He's been worrying about
it all night. *I* have a power of attorney now, to do all his
affairs for him ; I thought you knew that."

" Do you mean I've to ask *you* for everything I want ? "
demanded Esmé angrily.

Arnold coloured. " Of course not," he muttered. " I
didn't mean that. All the household expenses are arranged
just as before, only I sign instead of grandfather, that's all.
But extra things like that are different. I should have
thought you'd enough cars at West View already."

Esmé thought : " Can't he see that *he* always used to
drive me everywhere, and now I haven't him ? Oh,
Arnold ! " Aloud she said firmly, " I want one of my own,
to drive myself."

Arnold sniffed and cast brotherly doubts on her ability
to manage a car. Whether it was due chiefly to his remarks
on this point or to an irritable jealousy of Lena, that Esmé
persevered in her driving lessons so tenaciously, she did not
know herself ; but her car soon became an accomplished
fact, and she was able to drive herself up to Oddy Hall as
often as she liked. But there was always Lena or somebody

there ; or Mr. and Mrs. Arnold had gone to Bierley Hall,
or Mr. and Mrs. Arnold had gone to Cambridge Place, or
something of that kind. To Cambridge Place ! In the old
days before Arnold's engagement Esmé had often declined
to go to Cambridge Place with him out of sheer caprice, or
to stimulate Rowland ; but not to be invited ! That was
terrible ! When Rowland came home for the Easter holidays things were much better ; he came to see her at West
View, and the Oddy Hall plans seemed to include her more
frequently. But even then, Arnold and Rowland exchanged
views and settled everything by telephone, and it was not
till later in the day, much later usually, that Rachel rang
up to see if Esmé was free and could fall in with their
arrangements. Summer came ; Arnold was not there to
arrange tennis sets for Esmé, and invite men to play at
West View ; Rowland spent his holiday tramping or camp-
ing or something of that kind ; Arnold and Rachel took
theirs at a small place in Cornwall, and did not invite Esmé
to accompany them, so she spent a boring fortnight in a
large hotel with Mrs. Deller. Hotels were very different
without a brother, Esmé found. Autumn came, and John
Deller had a second slight seizure, but recovered. Then it
was winter, and Esmé found that dances and skating and
the number of one's invitations and everything, everything
was different, when one's only brother was married and
swallowed, as she thought angrily, by his wife's relations.
In February, Mr. Avery had a bad bout of pneumonia, but
recovered. Esmé did not know he was ill at all, until one
day, not having seen her brother for some time, she rang
through to Adela Mills and asked him to bring Rachel to
West View to dinner that night.

" I don't think Rachel can come," said Arnold uneasily.
" She's at Cambridge Place ; it's the crisis to-night, you
know."

" What crisis ? " demanded Esmé, and when she had
been told, hung up the receiver with a feeling of bitter
jealousy—it was just like those old childish days when

Arnold first met Rowland Avery ; the Averys had got him, got him completely, taken him quite away.

The maddening part of it was that Arnold looked so extremely, so almost disgustingly happy. The moment he entered Oddy Hall his face brightened, his eyes shone, he gave a positively childish smile of glee, and kissed Rachel as though they had been married for about one day. Whenever Esmé left Oddy Hall she always left Arnold standing on the doorstep with his arm round Rachel's waist, and she could not help feeling that the pair were glad to be left alone. Arnold loved to balance himself on his own hearth and gaze round gloatingly on his possessions ; if he put up a new peg in the bathroom he took you upstairs and expected you to admire it ; he asked Rowland or Esmé quite frankly what they thought of Rachel's new frock or the old dessert service he had picked up in a back street, and announced that they always had fruit to breakfast at Oddy Hall as if that were quite a marvellous piece of contrivance on Rachel's part. Privately Esmé thought that Rachel's housekeeping was a little vague—it was a good thing, she sometimes reflected darkly, that Rachel's husband had plenty of money—but she admitted that the atmosphere of Oddy Hall was one of rich deep happiness ; it met you on the threshold and pervaded the house like the glow of firelight or the scent of hyacinths. Privately also—or perhaps not quite privately, for Esmé rather enjoyed discussing this with Mrs. Deller—Esmé thought that Rachel, deep down in the innermost recesses of her heart, was disappointed that she was not with child ; but in the second spring after their marriage even this dissatisfaction, if it were one, was removed ; Arnold stuttered out hints, and Rachel quietly and serenely told Mrs. Deller that if all went well her child would be born in August. A dark and bitter flood of feeling filled Esmé's heart when she heard this. Was Rachel to have everything her own way ? When Rachel had no hopes of a child, Esmé had felt able to sympathise with her ; now she felt—she did not know

what she felt. Suddenly she threw out a bitter sentence to
the effect that Rachel and Arnold were cousins : one could
not but feel anxious about the health of their child. The
moment she had said this she regretted it, and she at once
took pains to calm Mrs. Deller's outcry by pointing out that
it was not true : Rachel and Arnold were really only half-
cousins. May Deller was not, however, so easily soothed ;
and though Esmé compelled her to refrain from mentioning
the matter to Rachel or Arnold, her obscure hints and dark
sayings drove her son nearly frantic—till he returned to
Rachel and was calmed. Arnold took great pains, colouring
and stuttering in a manner quite absurd, to make his
grandfather understand Rachel's hopes ; John Deller was
enormously pleased, and announced constantly in his
blurred speech his wish to live until his great-grandchild
was born. Esmé was perfectly sick, as she told herself
angrily, of the atmosphere of sex and sentimentality which
seemed to surround her ; it was almost thicker at West
View than at Oddy Hall, for there at least, especially when
Rowland arrived to stay there for part of the Easter holidays—Mr. and Mrs. Avery were in the middle of a long
stay on behalf of Mr. Avery's convalescence at Bournemouth
—the expected child was talked about frankly and joked
about.

It was really this which, as Esmé phrased it to herself,
led on to everything. On Rowland's last night at Oddy
Hall—he was leaving for Bournemouth next day—Esmé
was invited there for dinner ; later they played bridge as
this four usually did, and Rowland, dealing after a disastrous game, boomed cheerfully :

" Well, Arnold, all I can say is, that I hope Deller
Junior won't inherit your propensity for under-calling."

From force of habit Esmé said, " Don't be coarse, Rowland," while Arnold cried, " I hope he does ! " with a
pleased smile—merely to mention the child was to flatter
him. " Caution is a fine thing, Avery, as the marker shows,"
he added. " But of course," he concluded with a naïve air

of disappointment, " he may not be like either of us much."

" True," agreed Rowland with mock solemnity. " Most true. Who would ever think, for instance, that Alfred Howgate was Lena's parent ? "

" Oh, I don't know," began Arnold, but Esmé, really astonished, cried : " Why, is he ? "

Rachel made an abrupt movement. Rowland looked rather uncomfortable, and dropping his bantering tone said seriously : " It's only a supposition, of course. In confidence and among friends," he added, looking at Esmé rather sternly.

" In confidence, of course," said Esmé, nettled. " What sort of a person do you imagine I am ? But what makes you think it is so ? Does Lena think so ? "

She looked from one to the other in eager curiosity, and Rachel said shortly, " Your grandfather told Arnold that it was probably so."

" Really ! " exclaimed Esmé on a long-drawn-out note of interest.

" Esmé," said Rowland, " don't be coarse."

" I'm not being coarse," objected Esmé indignantly. " Anyway, it was you who began it."

" Anyway," repeated Rowland, underlining this expression, which he much disliked, " I'm sure that Arnold, as the owner of this historic mansion and our host, will now declare the subject closed."

" Closed it is," said Arnold briefly. " Esmé, your call."

But the subject was not closed in Esmé's mind ; as she sat watching Rowland play her hand, she pondered it. Lena an illegitimate child ! More sex, more sentiment, she thought angrily ; everyone has these adventures except me. She began to feel really quite low-spirited about it all ; her twenties were rolling on rapidly, and nobody had fallen seriously in love with her except Rowland, and really if one were to judge by his manner to her, one would think— oh, no, no ! She caught herself up ; of course Rowland

loved her ; he always had and always would ; it was only
the coming of spring which was making her so nervous and
distrustful. She always felt morbid and hysterical and irritable in the spring, always had done, even as a child ; very
likely, if one came to think about it, that had had a great
deal to do with the knife incident with poor Lena. Yes,
spring always upset her ; the afternoons had a weird wan
light, the weather ought to be warm but was not—there
was some nasty half-thawed snow on the ground at this
very minute—there were spring flowers in the windows and
spring clothes in the shops, but if one bought the flowers they
wilted, and if one wore the clothes one caught cold. Esmé
loved summer, and thin neat clothes ; she went out in thin
suits too soon every year, and every year was ill after it.
No doubt she was working up for a cold now, and that was
why she felt so depressed and as if she wanted to sob. Lena
illegitimate ! She thought vaguely but with interest of
Alfred Howgate ; really she had taken hardly any notice
of him on the few occasions when she had seen him. Did
she think better or worse of Lena for knowing her birth?
Really Esmé could hardly say ; it was very unsatisfactory
either way. In any case, Lena was a bounding, tactless,
stupid creature, warm-hearted and well-meaning of course,
but terribly crude. But how Rowland had, as it were,
defended her ! It was a nuisance that Lena belonged to
their circle at all ; when just the four of them were alone
together it was so much nicer. To-night, for instance, it was
delightful. Rowland and she had gone down rather badly
in the last game, it was true, but then how well she had taken
it ! She was really a good loser, much better than Arnold,
who was apt to be a little peevish nowadays. Rachel was a
good loser too, but that was because she did not really care
enough about the game. But here they all were playing
happily together : Esmé wished heartily that they could go
on playing and stay at Oddy Hall for ever, she wanted to
forget that she had to return to lonely West View, and a
foolish mother and a pathetic, difficult grandfather. John

Deller had been rather awkward lately ; he took fits of
obstinacy, and within the limits of his power was querulous
and exacting. His attendant came to the two women and
told long complaining physical anecdotes, which made
Esmé feel sick ; privately she rather felt that they ought to
change the attendant, for she suspected him of slight un-
kindnesses to· his patient, but she dared not tell Arnold
this, for fear he should fly off in a fury to West View and
discharge the man before they had time to find another,
which would be really disastrous. To be away from all that,
to be with young, lively, eager people, one of whom was in
love with her—ah, that was delightful ! But unfortunately
in an hour or so it would come to an end. And to-morrow
Rowland was going away, and Oddy Hall would at once
become less hospitable to her, thought Esmé bitterly. If
she were married to Rowland now ! If she were married to
Rowland the atmosphere of sex and sentimentality would
belong to her as well ; and she would be able to like it and
enjoy it, and not have to pretend to herself to disapprove of
it as she was doing now. If she married Rowland, she would
have a life of her own, and not have to live at West View ;
if she were having a child herself she would be able to
enjoy Arnold's child. She began to consider marrying
Rowland rather seriously.

While she was thinking all this the game was proceeding ;
Rowland triumphantly won the rubber ; Arnold began his
customary half irritable, half jesting analysis of his own
mistakes ; Rachel asked him to ring the bell, and he did so ;
after a pause the maid came in, not with the expected
drinks, but with Lena in a rather elaborate frock of the
rose-colour she affected. She looked hot and rather sheepish,
but pleased ; she kissed Rachel—they always did this at
meeting and parting, and the crudity of it invariably
irritated Esmé—and the two men began to tease her about
a concert in which she had apparently just taken part.

" How many encores did you get, Lena ? " enquired
Arnold.

" Was the organ in good form ? " demanded Rowland.

" How many words did you forget ? "

" Did you and the accompanist reach the last bar together ? "

" Did anyone go out in the middle ? "

Lena laughed and blushed, and opening her eyes wide in a look of glee, informed them that the hall had been quite full.

" But what hall ? " demanded Esmé, astonished and amused at the stupid Lena suddenly turning into a swan of song like this. " Where ? "

" Oh, only at Bierley Green," said Lena humbly.

" Oh ! " exclaimed Esmé.

Her tone was disillusioned, and Rowland rather scowled at her, while Arnold, offering Lena the cigarettes, brought out promptly, " It's very condescending of you to quit the scene of your triumphs to come to see us, Lena ; we're honoured."

" I just came to say good-bye to Rowland," said Lena simply, looking at him. Catching Esmé's eye, she then blushed and added hurriedly, " I've brought one of cook's seed-cakes for Mr. Avery ; I know he likes them ; it's in the hall." Rowland thanked her. " Of course, if you haven't room," added Lena with that constant need of hers for reassurance which was so exasperating because it was so exacting—though after all, remembering her birth, one understood it, thought Esmé charitably—" I can easily post it instead."

" If it won't go in his case he can wear it suspended by a loop of string as a breast-plate," suggested Arnold, indicating the position of the cake on his own chest.

" There wouldn't be much cake left by the time I reached Bournemouth, if I hung it there," objected Rowland, keeping up the joke.

" Why not ? " asked Lena, seeming really puzzled.

The others laughed, and Esmé as usual undertook the necessary explanation.

"Really, Lena," she said kindly, " don't be so silly. Of
course, he means he'd *eat* it."

"Oh, I see," said Lena, enlightened. After a moment
she added on a puzzled note : " But he doesn't like seed-
cake."

Esmé joined in the others' laughter, but she felt a chill.
She had known Rowland a long time—twelve years ?
fourteen ? perhaps even more than that—on the most
intimate terms, but she had not the vaguest notion about
his taste in cakes ; and here was Lena, who had known him
perhaps four years, talking about his dislikes of this and that,
and announcing openly that she had come to say good-bye
to him. Of course, Lena's gaucherie was a by-word, but
still ! Was Lena in love with Rowland ? " If she is she
doesn't know it," thought Esmé contemptuously, glancing
at Lena's strongly marked but somehow utterly unsophis-
ticated and childish face. But the way they all joked together ! Somehow she had not quite realised that Lena's
footing at Oddy Hall was as intimate as all that. Was
Rowland transferring his allegiance from her to Lena ?
Her feeling of chill grew ; very slowly and carefully, so as
not to be observed, she turned her head so that she could
see him. He was smiling, his left eyebrow cocked sardonically at the idiotic Lena, who was describing the
humours—so stale, so crude—of the Bierley Green entertainment. Was he in love with Lena ? It was impossible to tell
from his face. Anger filled Esmé's heart ; that Lena should
dare even to have pretensions to him was disgusting.
Remembering that Lena did not play, she said coldly :
" Are we to have any more bridge ? "

"Oh, don't let me interrupt your game," cried Lena at
once in distress, " Please don't. Please go on. Rachel,
please go on."

" I think not," said Rachel quietly.

" I wish you would," murmured Lena. " Arnold, I wish
you would." She fixed her large dark eyes appealingly on
Arnold, who said : " No, of course not, no," testily.

The entrance of the maid with a tray put an end to the discussion, and Arnold evidently did not mean it to be resumed, for as soon as they were all provided with full glasses and plates, he said, " Let's play Uncle Will's game." Esmé had always thought this a silly form of entertainment, much too educational to be amusing—where was the fun in simply saying words which other words reminded you of, and then retracing the steps later ? It was a silly game ; besides, the words Esmé said were always dull somehow, and she knew it. The Averys and Lena were good at this particular game, and Esmé knew that Arnold had suggested it to atone to Lena for his sister's rudeness about bridge—that kind of obvious tactfulness, which to Esmé always seemed worse than the rudest remark, was rather typical of Arnold. She felt angry and perverse, and would not begin the game when urged to do so. Rowland, therefore, began instead with " cat," and Arnold followed promptly with " Lady Annison," at which the naïve Lena, who was drinking at the time, almost choked. When she recovered, by an obvious association she said " Oddy Hall," and Esmé continued with " Arnold." The transition was a natural one, but her tone of cold defiance was a challenge to the Averys, and Rachel, lowering her eyes, said quietly, " Myself."

" Well, really," objected Rowland, " what am I to say to that ? If I say ' Arnold ' we shall go round in circles. I shall say Deller Junior."

" My grandfather," said Arnold at once.

" Mr. Thomas Deller," cried Lena with a quick look at Rachel.

" Singing lessons," said Esmé promptly. She caught Lena's hurt glance, and turned away with a little secret feeling of triumph.

" Lena," said Rachel.

" Seed-cake," boomed Rowland. " Do let us keep away from persons."

" Bierley Hall," said Arnold.

" That's very poor, Arnold," objected his friend. " It

really connects with the one before the last. I think you ought to say another."

"Well, the Bierley Hall cook, then," amended Arnold.

"Do let us keep away from *persons*," repeated Rowland emphatically. "Come along, Lena."

Lena hesitated. "I'm sorry, I can't think of anything but my mother," she said. "I can't really."

"But, Lena——" began Rowland.

Esmé interrupted him by saying coldly, "Mr. Howgate."

Seeing that Alfred Howgate was presumably the second husband of Lena's mother, the transition was again a perfectly natural one, but Esmé's tone was again not natural, and three of her hearers seemed to become at once conscious of their conversation before Lena's arrival. Arnold's fair face grew crimson to the brow, Rachel's followed suit ; even Rowland coloured and did not know where to look. Lena stared at them each in turn with her mouth open ; and then turned very pale. Rachel was the first to recover ; she threw up her head and said abruptly : "Horses."

"Horses, oh, ah, yes, horses," boomed Roland incoherently. "Horses, very natural. I shall say cows."

At any other time there would have been an outcry about the association of horses with cows ; but now nobody made any objection. Arnold meekly murmured "milk," Lena said sharply "butter," Esmé managed to ejaculate "toast," and the game went off into a round of domestic articles.

Esmé's heart beat fast. "Why did I say that ? " she asked herself in an agony. "How *could* I say it ? How could I be so crude and so cruel ? How *could* I ? It's all because I'm so unhappy and lonely," she told herself. "I shouldn't be like that if I were happy. Oh, I do hope Rowland or somebody has the sense to stop the game before we begin to go back over the words. It will be too awful for Lena to have to hear it again."

Evidently Lena herself felt this, for when the game had

resumed something of its former briskness, she suddenly
sprang up and, throwing her cigarette into the fire, announced, " I think I must go now."

Everybody at once rose, and even Rachel made no pro-
test against her departure.

" Have you the car, Lena ? " she asked, leading the way
into the hall.

" No," said Lena gruffly, " I shall go back across the
fields."

" I'll come with you, Lena," said Rowland.

" You needn't," threw out Lena.

" Just hold on while I get my shoes," said Rowland. He
bounded away up the stairs.

Lena silently began to put on wraps and heavy boots ;
Rachel helped her ; Arnold opened the front door and
decided that it was freezing in spite of being April ; nobody
took any notice of Esmé, who stood by the drawing-room
door with her hands behind her back and suffered. Rowland
came down, buttoning his coat ; Rachel and Lena kissed
farewell, and settled their next meeting for the day but one
following ; Lena passed Arnold without seeming to notice
his outstretched hand, then exclaiming " Oh," turned back
and shook it ; Rowland said, " Don't sit up for me," and
the two passed out of Oddy Hall into the cold spring night.
Esmé advanced a few steps to bid them farewell, and
shrank back into the room again. Arnold and Rachel were
thus left in the hall alone ; Esmé heard a murmur of
voices, and then Arnold's distinct and angry :

" I wish I'd never suggested the confounded game."

" I shouldn't trouble about that, Arnold," came Rachel's
quiet reply. " If it had not happened in that way, it would
have done so in another. Esmé meant to say it."

" Oh, no, I didn't, Rachel; no, I didn't," clamoured
Esmé—mutely, for she could not force her lips to move. She
felt cold and numb, as she had done on that day when Lena
had run away from school. Arnold and Rachel despised
her ; and Rowland preferred Lena, for he had gone with

Lena and left her without a word of farewell. That was why
she was invited so little to Oddy Hall ; they all despised
and disliked her, not without cause. Why was she made like
that, she asked the Fates ; was it her fault that she was easily
irritated ? Had she asked to be made with this little demon
of perversity within her, which lashed out when things were
stupid, and always saw what was wrong with things
instead of what was right, and always craved for something
better, something *more* ? How much she would have preferred to be gentle and simple and loving and easily contented and uncritical ! Well, her demon had done for her
now, at any rate ; she had alienated all the people she cared
for most, made the only man who had ever loved her
despise her ; she was doomed to live a lonely, deserted,
embittered life, with her foolish mother, and her pathetic,
difficult grandfather. At this thought Esmé could have
screamed with pain, but instead she said sullenly as Rachel
and her brother entered the room :

"I suppose I had better go too."

"Just as you like, Esmé," said Rachel quietly.

"Next time you come, I hope you'll be more civil to my
guests," threw out Arnold, in a gust of temper, colouring.

"Arnold ! " breathed Rachel.

"I'm sure I'm very sorry if I hurt Lena's feelings," said
Esmé crossly. "I didn't mean to ; it was quite accidental."
She saw that they did not believe her ; indeed she was not
quite sure whether she believed it herself. "I'd better go,"
she went on in a fretful tone. "Perhaps you'll back my
car out for me, Arnold ; the entrance to your garage is so
difficult."

Arnold, sniffing angrily at this insult to his garage, went
off to do her bidding. He was rather longer than usual in
getting the car to the door—probably, as Esmé surmised
shrewdly, because he was trying to show her how simple
and quick a process it was—and she was dressed and
standing with Rachel waiting for him quite a time before
he actually arrived. The sisters-in-law had not spoken since

he left them, and Esmé was becoming more and more unhappy every minute.

" Go in, Rachel," exclaimed Arnold crossly as soon as he drew up. " You'll catch cold standing there. It's an awfully cold night."

Rachel, saying briefly, " Good night, Esmé," immediately went in. Esmé admired her for it ; she herself, had she been Rachel and known the ascendancy she had over Arnold, as Rachel must have known it, would have argued the point and remained on the threshold till she was frozen rather than give in. Yes, if only she had a deep, still, loving character like Rachel's, how easy and pleasant a thing life would be.

" Good night, Arnie," she said wistfully as he closed the car door.

" Good night," said Arnold crossly. " Mind the turn out of the drive."

The turn out of the drive, and the steep lane up the hill, were distinctly awkward ; Esmé negotiated them with mechanical care, then when she reached the main road she drew up, and looked down to where the Elizabethan chimneys of Oddy Hall appeared among the trees. " Good-bye, Oddy Hall," she thought. " Good-bye my childhood, and all the pleasant happy times we four have had together. It's all spoilt now ; Rowland means to marry Lena, and none of them want me any more." She sobbed ; a few tears rolled down her face, she took out her handkerchief to wipe them away, and her thoughts were recalled to her personal appearance. " How *can* he love Lena ? " she pondered. " She's so clumsy and so *silly*. I don't see how he *can*." She examined herself in the mirror of her handbag. " I have a sweet little face," she thought, " if only I could live up to it." Suddenly she started the car again, and swinging it round drove off towards Bierley Hall. Fortunately there was a full moon, so driving was not difficult, and Esme's spirits soared as the car sped swiftly over the silvered road. The blood seemed to rush swiftly and

hopefully through her veins ; she was making a last desperate bid, she told herself, for youth and life and love and
goodness ; if she failed she was done for, and then let
everybody look out ! But surely she would not fail. As she
drew near to Bierley Hall she put the brakes on suddenly ;
for she saw two dark figures emerge from the fields by the
stile and cross the road towards the Hall. She hoped with
all her heart that Rowland would not go in with Lena ;
unfortunately he did go in, however, and Esmé had fifteen
minutes to wait in the cold just beyond the Bierley Hall
entrance. It seemed hours ; she let down the window to be
ready for him, put it up again because it was so cold, let it
down again ; by the time the door slammed and he came
out she was wound up to a terrific pitch of nervous excitement.

"Rowland !" she cried, leaning out to him.

"Good heavens !" said Rowland on an uncompli-
mentary note. "Esmé ! What are you doing here ?"

"I only came to tell you," said Esmé, vexed by his tone,
"that I did *not* say that to Lena intentionally. I shouldn't
like you to think that I did it intentionally, and as you're
going away to-morrow morning I thought I'd come round
and explain. It was quite an accident."

"I don't believe you," said Rowland bluntly.

Esmé burst into tears. "Oh, Rowland, how can you be so
cruel ?" she sobbed, her face working. "Do you suppose I
say these horrible things because I like them ? It's because
I'm so wretchedly lonely and unhappy myself, that's why ;
and I've nobody to guide me or tell me what I ought to do."

"But surely——" began Rowland.

"Oh, do get *in*," urged Esmé impatiently. "It's too
absurd, arguing like this through the window."

Rowland, with an exasperated sigh, opened the door and
sat down beside her. "In any case, what's the use of telling
all this to me ?" he asked, his voice rough with pain. "What
do you care what I think about you ? Damned little,
Esmé. You've shown me that, often enough."

"Oh, Rowland," protested Esmé tearfully.

"Well, you have," said Rowland doggedly.

"What have you and Lena been talking about?" enquired Esmé in a disagreeable tone.

"Never mind," said Rowland shortly.

"Are you going to marry Lena, Rollo?" demanded Esmé with a sob.

"Of course I'm not going to marry Lena!" shouted Rowland, intensely exasperated. "What a mind you have, Esmé! Can't you think of anything but sex? Lena and I are good friends, that's all; and you behaved abominably to her to-night. Somebody had to do something to atone for your disgusting rudeness."

"I'm sorry you think I'm disgusting," cried Esmé in a fury. "You've changed your mind these last few years, evidently."

"I always have thought much of your behaviour disgusting," retorted Rowland. "But I'm in love with you all the same, and you know it."

"Well, Rowland," said Esmé, suddenly feeling quite calm, "you have a very odd way of making love, I must say; but I suppose I must put up with it."

"I don't know what you mean," cried Rowland roughly. "Do you mean you're willing to marry me? Say what you mean for once, for God's sake."

"If you still wish it," said Esmé primly, fingering the wheel, "I will marry you at once."

Rowland seized her in his arms and kissed her lips, her cheeks, her throat, hungrily and passionately. An exquisite satisfaction flooded Esmé's every nerve—for a moment; then she knew that Rowland's embraces were not really the ones she wanted. She struggled to release herself, but he held her more closely. She liked that; he was stronger than she had thought. But the way he breathed, his hand upon her arm—no; she did not really love him. She made another movement of withdrawal; this time Rowland relaxed his grasp at once and set her free.

MT

" Really I must go home," observed Esmé in an artificial
tone. " It must be terribly late."

" It is," agreed Rowland, looking at his watch in the
light of the Bierley Hall entrance lamp. " I'll come with
you to West View and walk back."

Esmé started the car and drove carefully down the badly
lighted Bierley Lane. She had noticed when Rowland
looked at his watch that his hands were shaking ; but she
herself felt calm, and her hands were perfectly steady. " I
don't love him as he loves me," she thought mournfully as
she drew back the brake. " But perhaps I shall when we're
married. I hope so."

She rather wished that Rowland would kiss her again,
but he did not.

# CHAPTER VIII

## LENA

"Why didn't you come straight home after the concert? Mrs. Preston's been in an hour or more," said Alfred Howgate in a tone of displeasure, appearing at the dining-room door with the newspaper in his hand. "You've been to Rachel's, I suppose? Understand me once and for all, Lena, I won't have you careering across the fields at night alone, to Rachel's or anywhere else."

"I went by the road," said Lena rebelliously; she felt too excited to accept rebuke meekly just then.

"And how did you come back?" enquired her step-father. "Eh?"

"I came across the fields," replied Lena in a loud aggrieved tone. "Rowland came with me."

Her stepfather's face changed. "Oh, well, of course," he said, "that's quite a different matter. Why didn't you bring him in for a bit?"

"I did," replied Lena. "He's just gone; that was Rowland going out you heard, not me coming in. He stayed about a quarter of an hour."

"Well!" exclaimed Howgate. "You might have brought him in to see me, I think."

"We were talking about something," said Lena mutinously.

"You're a funny girl, Lena," observed her stepfather with his usual careless calm. "I can't make head or tail of you at times, or of your Rowland either. I wish to God you'd get on with it and marry him; I'm tired of this hanging about."

"I'm not thinking of marrying anyone," cried Lena, crimson.

"Oh, bosh!" said Howgate. He laughed. "Go and get those boots or whatever you call them off," he went on in a tone of good-humoured command, "or we shall be having you down with a cold to-morrow. You'd better have some hot lemon-water or something, and go straight to bed." He went back into the dining-room and shut the door.

"*I* wish to God you'd leave me alone!" muttered Lena fiercely as she stumped up the stairs. But before she reached her room she laughed; she had never "answered back" so pertly to Howgate before, and she could not help being rather pleased with her own courage. "How can you congratulate yourself on being rude!" she reproached herself immediately, opening her door and finding with pleasure that Mrs. Preston had lighted a fire for her. "You're as bad as Esmé." At the thought of Esmé her face clouded again; then as she sat down and began obediently to remove her boots she gave a doubtful smile; at last, exclaiming: "I don't know, I'm sure!" she tossed back her hair, and with one boot on and the other off limped over to her dressing-table mirror and subjected herself to a careful scrutiny.

During that evening she had experienced both hurt and joy, but the joy had far surpassed the hurt, far, very far. She had suffered keenly when Esmé had revived her old sneer at the inferior social position of Lena's mother. Not that Lena minded that her mother had been a housekeeper or whatever it was; she had far too many democratic ideas (mostly Rowland's) about the rights of man and all that kind of thing for that. No! It was not the fact which hurt; what Lena minded was that Esmé should wish to hurt her with the fact. That Esmé should hate her enough to wish to humiliate her, that was really sad. And the other three had seen clearly that Esmé wished to humiliate her, thought Lena; they had looked embarrassed, distressed. At first she had not quite understood what Esmé intended when she said : " Mr. Howgate " in that odd sneering tone ; there seemed no reason why it should *be* a sneer ; but then Lena had glanced quickly round and seen that the others were embarrassed, and then she had pondered it as the game went on, and suddenly she heard Esmé's childish voice saying, twelve years ago : " Her mother's only Mr. Howgate's housekeeper," and she had understood the sneer, and jumped up, and said she must come home. She had felt miserable and embarrassed while she was dressing out there in the hall under Esmé's cold stare ; but Rachel's kiss, and Arnold's kindly handshake, had seemed to show that they were on her side, and she was comforted. And then Rowland had taken the trouble to walk all the way to Bierley Hall with her. This was the joy, the joy that so far surpassed the hurt. The fields were exceedingly muddy, and the progress of the pair was consequently slow. And all the time Rowland had talked, saying the kindest things —how much they all liked Lena, how fond Mr. and Mrs. Avery were of her, how right she was to do the work which was nearest her hand at Bierley Green. Lena, quite astonished and fluttered, made deprecating murmurs, whereupon Rowland said sternly :

"You think too little of yourself, Lena ; it's quite absurd. You ought to get out of it ; it's just a bad habit. Really you ought to make the effort to remember that you're as good as most other people, and a great deal better than some."

"You overwhelm me by these kind words," said Lena, using one of his own phrases. She spoke jokingly, but it was true. A full moon was riding a flock of little grey clouds ; the scattered patches of snow gleamed whitely against the dark fields ; the hills around were a study in black and silver, the whole scene was coldly, weirdly splendid. Lena drew in great breaths of the crisp, sweet night air ; her heart beat fast with a troubling joy, a kind of painful ecstasy—Rowland had left Esmé on his last night to walk across the fields with her. The mud around the stiles was

thick and slippery ; Rowland steadied her across it, taking
both her hands and instructing her which way to stride.
He said it was kind of her to send the seed-cake.

" I didn't make it, you know," disclaimed Lena hastily.

" You thought of it," said Rowland ; it was those little
thoughtful things which pleased ailing people.

" Is Mr. Avery still ailing, Rowland ? " asked Lena, very
sorry to hear this.

" Well, he's had a nasty turn, you know," said Rowland.
After a pause he added abruptly : " Yes, he is still ailing—
but don't let Rachel think so."

Lena promised to deceive Rachel, and expressed the
hope that it would not be necessary for long. " And how is
Mrs. Avery ? " she continued. " She looked very worn and
ill, I thought, when I last saw her."

Rowland muttered an exclamation, and kicked crossly
at a patch of snow. " She feels Rachel's absence a good
deal," he said at last.

" Rachel," hazarded Lena timidly, " is very deeply
absorbed in Arnold, isn't she ? "

Rowland gave her a quick appreciative glance. " That's
it exactly," he admitted. " Mother feels it. I believe I ought
to have spent all this holiday at Bournemouth with them,
you know."

" Well, you're going to-morrow," said Lena consolingly.
" What time do you leave ? "

She learned, to her disappointment, that Arnold was
going to drive Rowland over to Bradford to catch an early
" through " train, so for once her little silent ceremony of
leave-taking would have to be omitted. But after to-night
that did not seem to matter quite so much.

" Lena," began Rowland suddenly as they crossed the
road to Bierley Hall, " do you think you could persuade
Rachel to write more often to Bournemouth ? "

" Well," said Lena dubiously, ringing the bell, " I'll
try. But couldn't you do it better yourself ? You've more
influence with her, surely."

" I don't know that I have," threw out Rowland with an air of gloom.

" Rachel——" began Lena. The housemaid here opened the door. " Oh, bother ! " exclaimed Lena. " Good night, Rowland."

" I'll come in with you for a minute, if I may," said Rowland hastily.

" Oh, do," said Lena. She stepped in, and looked about the hall rather helplessly.

" Mr. Howgate's in the dining-room, Miss Lena," said the maid, retiring.

" Where shall we go, Rowland?" said Lena timidly. She was conscious of a reluctance to break off the conversation by joining her stepfather, but did not quite know how to manage not to do so.

" Let's stay here," suggested Rowland, lowering his voice as if he perfectly understood her difficulty. " I mustn't stay more than a minute, I mustn't deprive Arnold of his beauty sleep. You were saying about Rachel ? "

" Rachel," repeated Lena, " is *not* a great letter-writer, not like you and Mr. Avery, I mean. She doesn't find it easy, I think."

" But why not ? " demanded Rowland. " To her own family, surely there should be no difficulty."

" Her letters say little, but they mean a lot, just as her speech does," explained Lena, embarrassed but eager. " She can't just flow on over pages without meaning anything very much, like you can." At this Rowland laughed. " Well, you know what I mean," said Lena, repressing her own laugh for fear it should turn into her well-known one and attract her stepfather's attention.

They talked on for a few minutes more, about Oddy Hall, the Averys, Rachel, and the condition of John Deller.

" Well, good-bye, Lena," said Rowland at last, stretching out his hand. Lena, smiling, gave him hers, and Rowland retained it while he spoke again. " Thank you for the

seed-cake and the sympathy," he said. " And look after
Rachel while we're all away, won't you ? "

" Oh, *yes*," promised Lena emphatically. He released
her hand ; she opened the door for him, and sighed a little
to think that he must go. " Every good wish for the new
term, Rowland," she said as he went down into the porch.

" Thank you," said Rowland, turning. " And mind
*you* remember what I say about not depreciating yourself,
and also practise hard. Those are my instructions for the
term's work, madam."

" They shall be carried out," said Lena, sketching a
curtsey.

Rowland laughed. " Good-bye, Lena," he said again on
a kindly affectionate note, and limped off round the porch.

Lena sighed and swung to the door. It slipped from her
fingers and closed with a considerable crash. She turned
round and leaned against it, musing, and it was then that
her stepfather appeared and that conversation took place in
which he made the outrageous suggestion that she should
marry Rowland rapidly.

" I don't know, I'm sure ! " repeated Lena, carefully
examining her face, which was warm and eager, if rather
shiny. Could it possibly be the case that Rowland was fond
of her in that way ? Of course he was always supposed to
be in love with Esmé, but really one had heard so little of
it lately, and seen so little of it lately, that one might be
forgiven for supposing that it was " off." To-night was his
last night, he was leaving Hudley and Esmé early in the
morning, yet he had parted from Esmé without a word to
come across the fields with Lena. And then how kind he
had been ! What kind, affectionate—dared one call them
loving ?—things he had said. Could it possibly be that
Rowland loved her ?

Lena had always regarded herself, since the days of
the Hudley Girls' College, as set apart from the ordinary
woman's hope of love and marriage. Esmé had made it so
perfectly clear to her, and emphasised it with such a wealth

of detail, that her body was coarse and lumpish and ugly, her face too large and dark, her hair messy, her eyes not what men admired, that she had gone on believing it ever since. She thought sometimes in a superficial way that she was looking rather jolly, that her hair was curling well or her dress suiting her, but at the bottom of her heart she always knew quite certainly that she was only looking jolly according to women's ideas, not according to men's ; there was something wrong about her somewhere, it was not her fault and she was not going to be morbid about it, but for some reason understood only by people like Esmé men never thought of loving her ; they didn't regard her as a woman somehow, perhaps because Lena did not often remember that she was a woman herself. But to-night she remembered it ; she was deeply conscious of it through the whole of her being. Something seemed to melt in her, something seemed to flame ; music sounded in her ears, and the colour of all the things in her rather dreary old-fashioned bedroom seemed suddenly to brighten and glow. She had felt like this before, once or twice—oh, more often than that—about Rowland, for the sight of Arnold and Rachel's happiness made one think of these things ; but she had always suppressed the feeling sternly, for no man would ever want her, and in any case Rowland was in love with Esmé. But now Rowland had left Esmé to walk across the muddy fields with her, and that cynical and experienced man of the world Alfred Howgate seemed to regard it as a perfectly natural and reasonable thing that she and Rowland should marry. Kicking off her other boot, Lena sprang back on to the bed, and tucking her feet up beneath her, leant her head against the polished mahogany bedpost and went off into a long delicious dream. Oh, if it should be true ! If it could possibly ever happen that Rowland should love her and want to marry her ! How different the world would be ! Everything seemed to flower about her ; it was the same as when she was singing, only much, much more so ; the walls of dull Bierley Hall sank down and she could

see out all over the world, mountains and seas and proud
cities and sunshine and storms, a whole rich colourful world
of life to which she belonged, of which she was a part, instead of being a silly little ugly person stuffed away in a
nineteenth-century Hall in the suburb of a provincial town.
She gave a sigh of ecstasy. She would not visualise details
of her life with Rowland ; that was a mistake, she had found
that out about other anticipated treats, for then when the
reality came the details turned out differently, and one was
not quite sure whether one was disappointed or not. No !
She would leave it all vague ; anything that Rowland chose
would be right for her. As for the possibility of her having
children, she would not look at it, dared not look at it ;
for she knew that she had a deep, clamorous desire for them
which was difficult to still once it awoke. Oh ! She had
been through it all before, as she supposed all unmarried
women went through it ; she had felt it, and had repressed
it because it was useless ; now perhaps she need not repress
it any longer. She went and looked at herself again in the
glass ; her face already seemed softer, more feminine, more
the kind of face which men could love.

A thundering knock on the door startled her from this
occupation. " Lights out ! " cried Alfred Howgate on his
way to bed.

" Confound the man ! " thought Lena, flying to the
switch. " What a tyrant he is ! " She then remembered
that he had told her to get on and marry that Rowland of
hers quickly, and added forgivingly : " I daresay it's very
late, and he thinks I'm reading in bed." She turned out
the light and undressed by the glow of the fire, and wondered pleasurably what Alfred Howgate would do if she
married and left him. " Marry again himself, I suppose,"
thought Lena, " and a very good thing too."

She awoke next morning to the delightful sensation that
for some reason she was very happy, and in a moment she
would know what the reason was. She blinked a little and
vaguely wondered, and then she remembered that Rowland

was perhaps in love with her, and her whole being
was suffused with a warm steady glow. She sat up and
reached for her watch ; Rowland would be just breakfast-
ing, she thought. Of course her happiness was rather a sad
kind of happiness, reflected Lena, for Rowland was leaving her that very day, leaving her for nearly three months ;
but still she was content, she would not be impatient, she
would ask no more of the fates than just the beginning of
his love, she would not allow herself to hope that he would
not go to Bournemouth after all, she would not wish that
his love for her would speedily reach its consummation ;
she was content to love him, to hope, and to wait. Now he
would be leaving Oddy Hall with Arnold for Bradford ;
she followed them up and down the route she knew so well,
imagined their arrival at the station, the porter coming
forward and taking out his cases—had the seed-cake found
a corner in one of them or not, she wondered with a smile
—Rowland buying his ticket and climbing into a train, a
red-painted, thick-cushioned, elegant, long-distance train
with a long white board at the top of each carriage saying
it was going to Bournemouth, while Arnold stood about,
rather flat because his friend was going but pretending to
be very competent and knowing. Other passengers, poor
dull things because nobody was in love with them, or perhaps excited like Lena because somebody *was* in love with
them, came up and wanted to enter Rowland's compartment ; he stood back politely from the window and perhaps helped them in—he was so different in these matters
from Alfred Howgate, who always behaved on a railway
journey as though every single human soul was his bitterest
enemy. Rowland always admitted that a person who had
bought a ticket had as much right in his compartment as
he had himself, a contention which never failed, by the
way, to irritate Esmé. Now Rowland was leaning out of
the window again, talking to Arnold, perhaps emphasising
his points with a folded-up newspaper which he had just
bought. He sent his love to Rachel, Arnold sent his to Mr.

and Mrs. Avery, perhaps they joked about the seed-cake.
Now, alas, the train was moving ; Lena looked at her watch
again ; yes, it was time ; the long elegant red train would
be gliding out of the platform at this very moment. Lena
sighed ; then awoke with a start to the realisation that she
ought to have got up half an hour ago.

All through the day her thoughts followed the elegant
train down the map, but this did not make her cross or
preoccupied. On the contrary, she was very gentle and
considerate. Life seemed to have more meaning in it somehow, or perhaps it was just that she understood it better ;
she felt that for once she was flowing with the main stream
instead of battling and beating against it. Her day followed
its normal course ; she rushed down just in time for breakfast and made suitable comments on the items her stepfather read from the morning newspaper at that meal,
steered Mrs. Preston's complicated meditations about the
menus for the day to some sort of decision, shopped in
Hudley, practised, lunched alone—Howgate had gone to
Leeds—wrote a few letters—it occurred to her that she
would write at intervals to Mrs. Avery, giving her the latest
news of Rachel, as long as they remained away ; she owed
the Averys all the consideration she could give them—went
to a rather boring committee meeting held in a private
house and talked there affably over tea. But all the time
Rowland, the fields as they had looked last night, the
elegant red train, Rowland, shimmered at the back of her
mind—" It would look well on a film," thought Lena,
amused : " heroine at a tea-party, and then railway wheels
revolving about her head, and a gradual fade-out or whatever they call it into a scene in the train with the hero jolt-
ing along." She felt rather a pang at the word " hero."
" Yes, he's the hero of my little tale," she decided. She
sighed and wished people would begin to make their fare
wells, this affair was really very tedious. To-morrow afternoon she was going to Rachel's, she reflected with pleasure ; but somehow that prospect was not quite as brillian

and thrilling as it had always been before. What a *pity*
Rowland had to go to Bournemouth ! If only the Averys
had been at home !

She returned to Bierley Hall, dined with Howgate, tried
to read but found all the books she opened thin and flat
and boring ; they were not half as thrilling as life itself just
now.

" You're very restless to-night," commented Howgate.

" I think I shall go into the drawing-room and sing,"
said Lena.

" All right—I'll come when I've finished the paper,"
replied her stepfather.

But singing seemed just as stupid as reading. Rowland
would have arrived in Bournemouth now, was sitting talking to his parents or perhaps escorting Mrs. Avery in a
slow walk along the sea-front, if Bournemouth had a sea-
front. The waves would roll and crash, the lights of the
promenade would be reflected in the dark sea ; Rowland
would be booming out descriptions of life at Oddy Hall ;
the seed-cake would have been unpacked, thought Lena
with a smile. She left the piano and wandered restlessly
about the room.

" What, finished already ? " said her stepfather, appearing at the door. " I was just coming."

" I can't settle to it to-night," said Lena apologetically.

" We may as well go back to the dining-room, then,"
said Howgate, turning back.

Lena followed him and took out her knitting. " Have
you ever been to Bournemouth, father ? " she enquired.

" Bournemouth ? " said Howgate. " Oh, yes."

" What is it like ? " demanded Lena.

Howgate described Bournemouth. " Are the Averys still
there ? " he concluded. Lena nodded. " Avery didn't get
over his pneumonia as well as Rachel makes out, I think,"
observed Howgate shrewdly.

" I'm afraid you're right," agreed Lena with a sigh.

"Rowland's a good son to them, though, I reckon," went on Howgate, flicking his eyebrow.

Lena, in spite of herself, blushed and murmured that she thought he was.

The evening wore on, and bedtime came at last. Lena sighed as she thought of the many days like this one which stretched between now and Rowland's return. She hoped with all her heart that he would write to her soon ; she longed for the sight of his writing—very black, rather small, and extremely decided—and for the ring of his amusing, mock-dogmatic sentences. As she undressed she felt as though she had been in love with Rowland, and known it, for years ; a gap as of centuries divided to-night from the moment of her leaving the Bierley Green concert the night before. And she was already more in love with Rowland than she had been the previous night, or even the morning of that day itself. " ' Absence makes the heart grow fonder,' " she mused with a smile. " How true platitudes are ! " She began to long for a sight of Rachel, not so much for her own sake as because she was such an intimate part of her brother.

Next morning life followed a normal course ; there was no letter from Rowland, Lena got up rather late, rushed down to breakfast just in time, made suitable comments on the items her stepfather read out from the newspaper, received his announcement that he was lunching with a Denbridge Vale customer with suppressed glee, drove him down to Bierley Bottom, shopped in Hudley, returned and delivered some committee notices by hand for the sake of the exercise. All this time her meeting with Rachel was drawing nearer and nearer, and she grew happier and happier. Might she not perhaps carefully and skilfully try to find out whether Rachel thought the same about Rowland's intentions as Howgate did ?

" My dear," Lena admonished herself, " you're not either careful or skilful, so you'd better leave it alone."

She lingered over lunch with a book as she often did,

until at length the maid in despair came to clear away
without being rung for. " There's a note from Mrs.
Deller, Miss Lena," she said, and proffered it on the silver
tray.

" Oh ! " cried Lena in acute distress. " *Can* it be to say
I'm not to go this afternoon ? " She was so deeply chagrined
at the mere idea of this disappointment that tears stood in
her eyes. " Surely it can't be ! Oh, I do hope it isn't ! "
she said, tearing open the thick envelope.

Rachel's notes were usually so brief, and her writing,
though upright and decided, was so small and widely spaced,
that there always seemed a great deal more white paper
about her communications than anything else. This one
was no exception to the rule. " *Dear Lena*," it began, " *Don't
come to tea this afternoon*." " Oh ! " exclaimed Lena in a tone
of heartfelt grief. " How disappointing ! "

" Aren't you to go, Miss Lena ? " asked the maid sympathetically.

" *Rowland wants me to go to West View with him*," continued the letter. Rowland ! He hadn't gone back then !
Her heart began to beat hard and fast ; what did this
mean ? Could it possibly mean that he had stayed for her ?
" No, no," she told herself, afraid to hope it, though she
knew she did hope it : " Don't be absurd, of course he
wouldn't, of course not ! " She bent her eyes to the paper
again and read : " *Rowland is engaged to Esmé at last*." There
was a moment when everything stood still, then Lena read
on to the end of the letter. " *But I will tell you all about it to-
morrow, if you will come to tea then. Come early. Ring up if you
can't. Yours with love, Rachel*."

" Leave the table a minute, Mary," commanded Lena
faintly.

She sat down on the nearest chair ; the maid, after an
astonished glance at her, put down the crumb-brush she
was wielding, and left the room. Lena folded Rachel's
fashionably thick notepaper into two, into four, into eight,
into sixteen ; she tried to fold it into thirty-two, but it was

too thick and sprang from beneath her fingers; she burst into tears and threw it into the fire. Immediately she knelt down on the hearth, and snatching up the long brass tongs, bent over and tried to rescue the note from the flames. But it had caught fire and was blazing. In this position she was discovered by Mrs. Preston, who had evidently been alarmed by the maid's account, and come to see what was wrong, for she asked anxiously : " Is anything the matter, Miss Lena ? "

" The matter ? " shrilled Lena on an exaggeratedly sarcastic note. " How do you mean, the matter ? " She felt it was dangerous to end on this question, even though it was an oratorical one, but she could not manage to utter another word.

" Mary thought you seemed upset," said Mrs. Preston apologetically, putting a kindly hand on her shoulder and stooping over her to look into her face.

" Nothing of the kind ! " cried Lena savagely. She jerked her shoulder and threw off Mrs. Preston's hand. " I wish Mary would mind her own business." As Mrs. Preston continued to look at her with a dissatisfied air, however, she reflected that she had after all told Mary to leave the table and go away, and that this certainly required an explanation. " I'm disappointed because I can't go to Mrs. Deller's this afternoon," she said shortly.

" Well, you can go another day, lovey," said Mrs. Preston soothingly. " I should go to the pictures or something instead, if I were you. It would brighten you up a bit."

Lena smiled at the idea of a cinema brightening her up either a bit or a lot ; she thought that a long walk would probably be the best thing for her. She went upstairs, put on her hat and coat mechanically, left Bierley Hall and began to walk up the Lane towards Bierley Green ; but she had not gone many yards before she felt that her legs simply could not be made to move any farther ; she felt as though somebody had dropped a ton weight on her, and she was only just not crushed out of existence. She crawled back to

the Hall, went up to her room and sat on her bed ; but good
heavens ! there was Mrs. Preston coming up the stairs to
her *again*, they would never leave her in peace if she stayed
in, she would not be able to cry her heart out alone till she
was in bed at night and the house was still, so she might as
well put a good face on it and go out—in the car if she
could not walk. A cinema was not such a bad idea after all ;
she was due at a meeting in Hudley at half-past five, and
she could go straight there from a Hudley picture palace.
She gathered herself together, marched down the stairs,
opened the kitchen door and threw in a " I shan't be in to
tea," closed it at once and made for the garage. When she
was driving down Bierley Lane she thought for the first
time : " Rowland ! " " Oh, no, oh, no ! " she whispered to
herself. " Shut up ! I can't bear that part of it yet."

She reached Hudley, put up her car and entered the
cinema. It was not very full, and Lena went away to a far
corner which she thought to be completely empty. The first
time the lights came on, however, there was revealed a
solitary young man sitting only a few rows away from Lena.
He was slouching in his chair in an attitude of profound
dejection. " He's in trouble too," thought Lena, surveying
him. " I wonder what's the matter with *him*. Is it love ? Is
it money ? Or is it a family quarrel ? " She watched his
motionless huddled figure, his fixed gaze, his sullen jaw, for
a long time. " He looks as I feel," thought Lena sardonically. " I think he's got a broken heart, like me."

Somehow, watching this young man had done her good,
and she found that she had made her decision as to how
to take her blow without being conscious of doing so. This
decision was to stand up to it, to take it quietly and with
dignity, to conceal her wound but not be ashamed of it, to
make no fuss, to keep her back straight and her chin well up.
She summoned an attendant and ordered tea at the proper
time, and deliberately forced herself to eat and drink. She
knew that she had an evening with Howgate to face, and
she could not afford to let down her strength by being silly

N⊤

about meals. Occasionally wild thoughts of suicide and running away presented themselves, but she drove them away firmly, curiously enough because of Esmé. " She made me bitterly unhappy once," said Lena to herself, " and I cried and ran away and made a fool of myself with a knife ; and now she's made me bitterly unhappy again, she's taken away my only chance of happiness, the only man I could ever love. But she needn't think I shall cry or run away or make a public fool of myself this time. No ! By God I won't, I won't give her that satisfaction." She reminded herself that perhaps after all she was being unfair ; Rowland had perhaps taken Esmé rather than the other way round. " Oh, bosh ! " said Lena. " You know it isn't so." Still the doubt was there, and it brought another wretched thought in its train : how could Lena have been such a fool as to imagine that Rowland was in love with her, at the very moment when affairs were finally settling between himself and Esmé ? This shook Lena so that she felt it impossible to endure such torment ; it was then that the wild ideas of suicide and America recurred. " I can't have been such a fool as all that," Lena told herself staunchly, " because father thought so too, and he's by no means a fool in such matters." It struck her as strange that it should be her step-father who brought her the greatest comfort in her misery, and her heart softened towards him. A pathetic bit appeared on the screen : it seemed that some couple or other were being parted after two or three weeks' happiness only. " *I've* had only one day's happiness," Lena told herself grimly. " Or shall we say a day and a half ? And that was a fool's paradise." A little voice within her whispered : " It's just like you, it's just like the silly, futile things you always do." " Very well," replied Lena after arguing this point for some time without success. " I admit it ; it *is* like me ; it's thoroughly characteristic. That doesn't make my suffering silly, all the same."

It was now time for her to go to her meeting. While they were waiting for the chairwoman to arrive, the members already present clustered into groups and began to talk. Lena, whose ears were sensitive to the names, heard the Avery-Deller engagement mentioned once or twice in other groups ; at length somebody in her own group, who knew of her friendship with Rachel, observed : " I hear Mrs. Arnold Deller's brother is engaged ; is it true, Miss Howgate ? "

" Yes," said Lena pleasantly. " To Mr. Arnold Deller's sister, Esmé."

A youthful member of the group here blurted out : " When we first heard we thought it was to you."

Lena achieved a creditable laugh. " My dear child ! " she said in well-simulated amusement. " Poor Mr. Avery ! And poor me ! Oh, no ; this affair's been going on a long time, years."

" Some difficulty on Miss Deller's side, perhaps," suggested the first speaker.

Lena raised her eyebrows and smiled condescendingly, as though she knew everything about the affair but thought it bad taste to discuss it, and the subject dropped, not without embarrassed blushes from the girl who had made the gauche remark. She began to be particularly lively with Lena, to cover up her *gaffe*, and Lena amiably seconded her efforts. " How young and naïve you are ! " she thought. " I was like that once."

The meeting went on for a considerable time, and Lena reached Bierley Hall with only a few minutes in which to change. She rushed into the dining-room as the soup came to the table.

" You're always in a hurry nowadays," said Howgate rather crossly. " You'll knock yourself up ; you look tired out as it is."

" I think I've got a cold coming on," lied Lena.

" I thought you would have, tearing across those muddy fields two nights ago," said her stepfather.

Lena winced, and for one moment thought she was going to expose herself by bursting into tears. She kept them back, however, and began to talk feverishly about the meeting, heightening her anecdotes of people's silliness to make her stepfather laugh, which he did heartily.

"You're like your mother sometimes," he threw out at length with a sniff.

Lena was astonished at this unwonted reference, and Howgate seemed a trifle astonished and embarrassed himself, for he fell silent and moody, and required no more entertaining for a while. When the meal was over Lena tried reading, but could not fix her mind on the words, and knitting, but that left her mind too free ; singing was out of the question, so she finally took out the patience cards and played the most complicated varieties she knew. Unfortunately most of these had been taught her by Mr. Avery, but she contrived to pretend that she had forgotten that.

At last the long dreary evening was over, the house was locked up, the maids had gone to bed, the lights were turned out, Lena from her room heard Howgate's door close behind him.

"Now," she said, throwing herself into bed. "Let's tackle it. The part that really matters. Rowland."

She tackled it by living through all the episodes of her life she could remember in which Rowland figured. She lived through again the time when he first opened the Cambridge Place door to her, the time when she rushed down to the variety theatre and found them all there, the walks, the dances, the happy meals at Cambridge Place, the songs, the games. She saw that in all their intercourse together she had always been naïve, foolish, and rather tiresome, at the same time as she had honestly striven to be unselfish and sincere. " I don't blame him for preferring Esmé," she thought. " I'm not really fit to be any man's wife. I've been childish and silly. I don't suppose he ever thought of me in that way at all ; he always was in love with Esmé—I may as well be honest and admit it. Still," reflected Lena, " I believe from the bottom of my heart that

if Esmé hadn't been there he would have loved me ; I believe that, and I believe that he genuinely likes me. And
I've got to resign myself to living with that." She wondered
how Esmé had liked Rowland's leaving her to cross the
fields with Lena. Not much, thought Lena. " Perhaps she
was jealous of me," she mused, " and that brought it all
on." She threw her arms above her head, stretched out her
body to its full length and thought : Rowland, Rowland, Rowland. She saw his thick dark hair, his dark merry eyes beneath thick eyebrows, his large jolly mouth and perfect
teeth, his strong hands, his long thin body—though he was
getting a little stouter since he went to Sussex, and Rachel
and Arnold teased him about it—the way he limped. "Why
insist upon all this ? " Lena asked herself sarcastically.
" Aren't you sufficiently convinced already that you love
him ? " She imagined the future ; presumably Esmé and
Rowland would marry soon, and have a house in Sussex,
and come home to Hudley only occasionally to see their
parents. " I shall scarcely ever see him," decided Lena.
She had an emotional song downstairs—one of a suite with
good music which Rowland had given her—the words of
which ran :

> " *Never on earth again*
> *Shall I before her stand,*
> *Touch lip or hand.*
> *Never on earth again.*
> *But while my darling lives*——"

" Tum tum tum *tumty* tum," said Lena, forgetting the
next line and jeering at her own misery :

> " *Not quite alooone,*
> *Not while my darling lives,*
> *My darling lives.*"

" There is a note of triumph about the music of the conclusion which is quite unwarranted by the real feelings of a person in that situation," decided Lena. Then she began to weep and writhe.

Next morning she had, naturally enough, a bad headache, and at breakfast excused herself from driving her stepfather down to the mill on the grounds of her alleged cold.

" I was going to take Joe, anyhow," said he. " I'm thinking of going to Adela Mills later in the morning."

Life followed a normal course ; Lena listened to the items which her stepfather read from the morning newspaper, then discussed the meals with Mrs. Preston, then drove into Hudley to shop. She did not practise when she came home, however, and she rang up Rachel at a time when she was sure to be out, and left a message with the maid that she was sorry she could not come to Oddy Hall that afternoon. Rachel might wonder, but she must have a day or two before she faced her, if her secret were to be kept as it must be kept. To keep up the fiction of her cold, she then took one or two of Mrs. Preston's remedies and went and lay on a sofa in the library ; and certainly she felt tired and in need of rest. She had gone upstairs to tidy herself for lunch when her stepfather arrived ; she heard him looking for her from room to room on the ground floor, then asking the maids where she was.

" Lena ! Lena ! " he called urgently.

" Oh, God," thought Lena in despair. " He's been to Adela Mills and Arnold's told him." She felt heartsick, but after all, this particular interview had to be gone through some time, so she collected her courage and went downstairs.

Howgate was in the library, standing with his back to the fire. He looked perplexed and uneasy.

" Did you want me, father ? " enquired Lena.

" What's all this about Esmé Deller and young Avery ? " demanded Howgate, going to the point at once.

"They're engaged," said Lena briefly.

"You knew, then?" said her stepfather. "Deller said you did, but I didn't believe him."

"Yes, Rachel told me," replied Lena steadily.

"Well!" said Howgate. "Nay! I don't know what to say to you, Lena, I'm sure. I always thought you were going to marry young Avery."

Lena looked at him. "Perhaps I hoped so too," she said.

There was a pause. "After all, it may not come to anything," suggested Howgate uncomfortably. "It may not last, eh?"

"In my opinion," said Lena, "they'll be married quickly, almost at once."

Howgate's sallow face flushed. He looked down. After a minute he mumbled: "Would you like to go away or anything?"

"No, thank you," replied Lena quietly.

No! she would not run away this time; she would stick it out; she would buy a new car and some new spring clothes, and persuade Howgate to make a tennis court down in the far corner of the garden, and be very bright and lively all summer; she would stick it out; she would not run away this time; she was not a child now.

The gong sounded for luncheon, and ordinary life had to be resumed.

Lena's prophecy as to Esmé and Rowland was speedily fulfilled, for they were married in a few weeks in the Hudley Registrar's office, Rowland obtaining special leave from school for the ceremony. Esmé gave out as the reason for this haste and obscurity her grandfather's precarious condition—the least excitement would be fatal for him. Rachel passed this on to Lena in such a bitter tone that Lena was surprised, and looked interrogative, whereupon Rachel explained that consideration for her grandfather was certainly not Esmé's motive, for Mr. Deller as a matter of fact did not approve of the match at all.

"As far as he can manage to say anything he's said

that," stated Rachel. " He thinks Esmé's throwing herself away." In spite of herself Lena gave a short sigh at this. " He told Arnold so," continued Rachel, " and they had quite a row about it." Lena in her new-found discretion said nothing, and bent closely over the wool bonnet she was making for Rachel's child. " So why she should be so determined to have the wedding at a Registrar's I can't make out," went on Rachel. " Of course Rowland's glad, but that's not why she does it ; I don't understand her idea at all."

" Oh, I think I do," said Lena calmly. " No wedding could be *grander* than yours was, Rachel ; so to excel it Esmé has to have a different kind."

Rachel laughed. " We don't like Esmé, Lena, do we ? " she said rather remorsefully.

" No," agreed Lena on the same half-joking, half-repentant note, " I'm afraid we don't."

" Of course," said Rachel, " if they're not married soon they'll never be married at all ; I see that."

Lena gave an acquiescent murmur, and the subject dropped.

A few days later, however, it was opened again between them, for Lena remarked to Rachel that Arnold was not looking very well. Rachel's cheeks at once flamed.

" How can he look well," she burst out, " with Esmé making all this fuss ? "

" What fuss ? " said Lena, disturbed.

" About her money," cried Rachel. " Arnold has to fix it all up, you know, as Mr. Deller is incapable. If I were to tell you the extent of that girl's demands, Lena, you wouldn't believe it."

Lena thought she probably would be able to believe it with slight difficulty, but she said quietly that she had always understood that legal arrangements, settlements and so on, were very trying.

" Oh ! it's trying beyond belief," exclaimed Rachel in a tone of disgust. " What makes it worse is that Mr. Deller had kept everything in his own hands, everything. It's terribly difficult for Arnold. However," she concluded bitterly, " Esmé will be married by this time next week, and then Rowland can look after her damned money for her if he likes."

" Rachel ! " exclaimed Lena, shocked at her tone.

" Well, it gets on my nerves," replied Rachel, and to Lena's distress she burst into tears. " If only they'd go away and leave us *alone*," she sobbed when Lena offered soothing words and caresses. She soon regained her usual composure, however, agreed that she was not feeling very well that afternoon, allowed Lena to arrange her on a settee, and at length observed in a cheerful if grim tone : " Well, never marry a man with a sister, Lena, that's my advice."

" I probably shan't," said Lena.

The Averys had returned to Hudley shortly after beginning the summer term, as Mr. Avery was eager to resume work after his long absence. Lena did not go to Cambridge Place before Rowland's marriage ; she thought his parents would be too busy to have time for her, and also she was not particularly anxious to come beneath Mrs. Avery's eyes : she was not sure that she could sustain that glance and keep her secret unknown. The wedding itself, of course, was quite private, so she had not that ordeal to suffer, but when Esmé was Rowland's wife, and the pair had left for Sussex, where they were to live in an hotel till more permanent arrangements could be made, Lena went down to Hudley one afternoon about half-past five, thinking that Mr. Avery would have returned from school by that time, and she would not have to face Mrs. Avery alone. She found Lilias sitting in the dining-room by herself, however, embroidering a pram-cover for Rachel's child. The tea-things were laid out for two beside her, but there was no sign of her husband. After a moment or two Lena enquired for him—rather nervously, for Lilias's once handsome face was ravaged, her fine black hair grey, her dark eyes sunken, and Lena was not quite sure why.

" He has to come home by two trams now, and it takes longer," explained Mrs. Avery shortly. " He can't manage the hill."

" Really ! " said Lena, very sorry indeed to hear this. " The summer is coming soon now, with blue skies and sunshine," she went on soothingly, " and then he will be better."

" Probably," said Mrs. Avery.

Lena was quite taken aback by her tone. Anyone who did not know that the Averys were a most devoted couple would have imagined that Lilias cared next to nothing about her husband's health. With her instinct to defend the one in disfavour Lena at once said staunchly : " The boys are glad to have him back, I'm sure."

Mrs. Avery said abruptly : " That card on the mantel-piece is a picture of Rowland's hotel."

Lena, feeling that there was nothing else to be done, got up and looked at it. " Charming," she said in her newly acquired society tone. " With a sea view, I suppose."

Mrs. Avery tightened her lips and was silent. Suddenly she broke into a passionate reproach : " Lena, what have you been doing to let Esmé carry off Rowland like this ? " she cried. " I counted on you so ! "

Lena's heart turned over. " But, Mrs. Avery," she stammered in anguish. " I didn't know you . . ."

" Do you suppose I like having both my children married to Clement Deller's children ? " demanded Lilias Avery fiercely. " I don't ; I can't bear it ; it seems to make all my life nothing, writ in water, as they say. If I'd had my way those Dellers would never have entered my house."

" Then you'd have been very wrong, and deprived Rachel of a great happiness," said Lena firmly.

" Do you think so ? " threw out Lilias in a tone of contempt. " I've no faith in Arnold."

" Then you're very wrong," said Lena, her heart beating fast at having to speak thus openly of her deepest loyalties.

"Arnold might make mistakes about money and do foolish things in business and that sort of thing, but as to his ever being anything but devoted to Rachel, it's impossible."

"I wish I could believe it," said Lilias in a sombre tone.

"But it's so obvious!" cried Lena, exasperated.

"You didn't know his father," murmured Lilias from quivering lips.

"Mrs. Avery," observed Lena with sudden conviction, "I think you were fonder of Arnold's father than you admit."

"How dare you say that, Lena?" demanded Lilias in anger. She raised her head proudly; her dark cheeks were flushed, her nostrils dilated; for a moment she looked beautiful as of yore. "How dare you?"

"I was joking, of course," lied Lena with a sad look at her.

"The joke was not in good taste," observed Lilias in her coldest tone.

"I beg your pardon," said Lena proudly. She hesitated; "To return to Arnold for a moment," she went on. "If you will just consider how seriously he has been handicapped by his father, mother, sister and grandfather, you cannot but admit that he has turned out remarkably well; and personally I consider that to turn out even decent when you have lived at West View for twenty years is quite an achievement. And look how he stuck to Rachel! In the face of quite considerable discouragement, and probably ridicule (which is worse) he never wavered in his love for her."

"Oh, he can be obstinate, no doubt," murmured Mrs. Avery. "But how you're changed, Lena!"

"What do you mean?" said Lena, colouring.

"How much older you are, my dear," said Mrs. Avery softly. "Oh, why did you let Esmé defeat you like that?"

"Rowland never cared for me," said Lena angrily. "He

loved Esmé always, and I'm sure they will be very happy
together. Please," she went on, " don't let us discuss this
again."

"Just as you wish," murmured Lilias.

They were talking of the proposed Bierley Hall tennis
court when Mr. Avery came in. Lena was shocked by his
appearance ; not that there was any very definite change
anywhere in him, but he looked white and pinched and
shrunken, and wore a painful expression of anxiety, the
more painful because, as Lena perceived, he was unconscious of it. He seemed short of breath, too, and Lena felt the
blood pulsing irregularly in the hand he offered her. He
seemed glad to see her ; Lena for her part was so intensely
sorry for him—for she had not by any means been joking
in her allusion to Lilias's fondness for Clement Deller—
that she bestowed all the petting upon him that her affection could devise : propped him up with cushions, urged
him to eat more cake, laughed heartily at his jokes, ran-
sacked her own brain for amusing anecdotes to tell, and
finally entered the marks for three sets of Latin exercises he
had brought home with him in his large worn mark-book.
When she was about to leave Lilias said she had some things
for the baby which she wished to show to Lena, and took
her upstairs. When they were safely in the spare room with
the door shut, Mrs. Avery said in her usual quiet tones :

"It was not true, Lena—what you suggested about
Clement Deller just now. But you know I did not refuse
him, as Mr. John Deller thinks ; he never asked me t
marry him ; he came to the house drunk, and my father
reproved him ; and then he just dropped us out of his life.
My pride was wounded ; then Will came and it was al'
right."

"I'm glad it was all right," murmured Lena, not sure
whether she was convinced or not.

"That is why it's so painful to me that my childre
should marry Clement Deller's," went on Mrs. Avery.

"Yes, I see that," admitted Lena. "Oh, yes, I see that

But you seem to think it's Mr. Avery's fault that they've married them, and I think that's nonsense." She looked at Lilias and smiled frankly. " I do really," she said.

" Well, perhaps you're right," said Lilias. Her tone was not convinced, but when a few minutes later she let Lena out of the front door she said : " Come again soon and cheer us up." Mr. Avery too came to the dining-room window and when Lena started her car, waved and smiled and seemed to be inviting her to return.

Lena drove away feeling very sad. To think that this sombre and pathetic household was No. 7, Cambridge Place ! A house which had always seemed so jolly, so full of life and laughter, so full of people ; a house where she had spent the happiest moments of her life ! It did not bear thinking of. She resolved to call there at least once a week, and to poke up Rachel into going more often. Rachel was not really fit for much just now, but Lena decided to run her down to Cambridge Place the next day ; they could call at the Hudley Grammar School and pick up Mr. Avery on their way there, and so be useful twice over.

This afternoon programme was carried out rather often in the next few months, for Rachel did not want to go away for a summer holiday till her child was born, and the Averys—or at least so Lena suspected—could not afford another holiday after the expenses of Mr. Avery's illness and convalescence. Then Howgate took Lena on a trip to Norway, the duration of which overlapped the brief space spent by Rowland Avery and his wife in Hudley on their way to Scotland. Lena enjoyed herself quite considerably on this trip ; she was becoming quite clever at social inter-course, and was amused by this growing skill. There were many times, of course, when she thought : " What's the use of it all ? It's all no use. How weary I am, how weary of everything ! " But she usually shrugged her shoulders and went on ; one had to live and keep one's end up ; one could not give Esmé or fate or whatever it was the triumph

of having made one into a broken reed. She was sufficiently
ashamed of having allowed Esmé to do that once to intend
never to repeat the weakness. But for the last few days of
the trip Lena was on tenterhooks lest Rachel should be
confined before she returned, and she breathed a sigh of
relief when in answer to her first question Mrs. Preston told
her that nothing of that kind had yet occurred. Another
event had, however, happened in the Deller family ; John
Deller had had another stroke, and was not expected to
live the week out.

" Pity if he dies before his great-grandchild is born,"
commented Howgate.

The next morning Rachel rang up to ask Lena to spend
the afternoon with her ; her nurse, who had been with her
already for a day or two, and whom she seemed to dislike
heartily, wished to go out to tea to some Hudley relatives, so
the friends could be alone. Lena, of course, went across to
Oddy Hall very gladly, taking with her the photographs
and postcards of her Norwegian trip. She had not been
there very long when the telephone bell rang ; the maid
who answered it brought a message from Adela Mills that
Mr. Deller was worse, and Arnold had been summoned
to West View. Rachel received this in silence, though with
an ironic look ; Lena could think of nothing suitable to say,
so John Deller's name was not mentioned between them.
Lena had caught from Rowland the habit of making neat
photographic records of her holidays, and she had brought
the apparatus with her with the idea of amusing Rachel ;
she went on gumming and printing and describing with
gusto until all at once Rachel said faintly : " Lena, I think
you'd better telephone for nurse." Lena gave her a startled
look, saw that she was extremely pale, and flew to the
telephone ; having warned the nurse, the doctor and Mrs.
Avery, and left a message at West View for Arnold, she
returned to the dining-room to find Rachel gone, and
followed her upstairs. Rachel was in the room which had
been prepared for the event, drooping wearily in an armchair

and tugging her clothes off with nervous impatience.
She was obviously suffering and looked very miserable ;
and Lena, as she began to help her, reproached herself
bitterly for not having seen her distress before. " To think
that I never noticed it ! " she wondered. "*I* didn't notice
that Rachel was in pain. So much for human perception."
Aloud she said affectionately : " Raikes, why did you let
me go maundering on like that ? You arc an old noodle ! "

" I was trying to pretend it wasn't anything," said Rachel
wearily. " I wanted to put it off for a few days." Seeing
Lena's surprised look—for Rachel had often previously
expressed the hope that she would not have to endure many
days of suspense—Rachel continued in a sombre tone :
" I'm not very anxious for my child to have a great-grandfather, you know."

" Rachel ! " exclaimed Lena. In spite of her dislike for
Mr. Deller she was really shocked at such a vengeful
attitude towards a dying man, but she realised that it was
not a suitable moment to let Rachel see this ; besides,
perhaps it was only one of the obsessions natural to her
condition. She therefore said on a joking note : " Don't be
so morbid, my dear."

" I feel morbid," replied Rachel grimly.

Lena sighed as she assisted her into bed.

A few minutes later, to her great relief, the nurse arrived,
and shortly afterwards Mrs. Avery. Before Rowland's
marriage Lena would have stayed in the house at all costs,
but now she had the sense to see that she was not wanted
and would only be in the way, so she went soberly home,
and though she had little sleep that night, she curbed her
impatience till a reasonable hour on the following morning.
She then rang up Oddy Hall, and with intense thankfulness
learned from the maid that Rachel had given birth to a
fine boy, and that mother and child were both doing well.
This stereotyped reply received corroboration and enlarge-
ment from Howgate when he came in at lunch time. He
had rung up Adela Mills, and heard some details of the

night. It appeared that the unfortunate Arnold had been
nearly distracted between his wife's bedside and his grandfather's ; eventually John Deller had died at half-past two
in the morning, and Arnold had no sooner returned home
from the deathbed than his son had been born.

" Pity ! " said Howgate at this point.

Lena was silent ; she too thought it a pity, but she knew
that Rachel would be glad. " Probably Mr. Deller would
not have been sufficiently conscious to have understood, in
any case," she suggested at last.

" Perhaps not," agreed Howgate. He went on to say that
if Arnold were to be believed, the baby was the finest ever
born ; he had blue eyes and fair hair, fingers and toes ; he
weighed a lot ; they thought of calling him Charles or
Francis. Howgate was certain that Rachel must really be
doing well, for Arnold was so jubilant that his efforts to make
his voice sound decently sad when he spoke of his grandfather were really funny.

In due course John Deller was buried with befitting
pomp ; Howgate attended the ceremony and sent an
enormous wreath, and vexed Lena by attaching to it a card
bearing both his name and hers.

" I didn't *want* to send a wreath to John Deller," she
objected when she read their names in the long list of
flower-senders given by the *Hudley News*.

" You must do what's decent," contended Howgate
with some irritation.

" I'd rather be sincere," said Lena proudly.

Howgate snorted. " I thought you'd grown out of all
those silly notions," he grumbled. " If you haven't, it's
time you did."

Rowland and Esmé returned from Scotland for Mr.
Deller's funeral and remained at West View for a week or
two, during which period their nephew—owing to quite
unnecessary alarms about his health on the part of Mrs.
Deller, who had never recovered from Esmé's hint about
Arnold and Rachel being cousins—was christened. Lena,

who had contrived to avoid them before, saw them at
Oddy Hall, where the party all collected on their way to the
christening. She had thought that she was now fairly well
steeled against the encounter, but found that she was not
in the least. Rowland, who looked older and thinner and
rather as though he were working too hard (though as it
was holiday time that could hardly be the case), met her
in the hall, shook her hand heartily and said : " Well, this
*is* jolly ; it seems ages since we saw you, Lena." He then
took a step towards the drawing-room, and called :
" Esmé ! " Lena's heart was wrung, for his tone was
definitely the ordinary everyday one of a husband ; if he
had called his wife in an eager, lover-like fashion she would
not have felt the barrier between them so great : but Esmé
and he now had the habit of life together ; he was lost
irrevocably. " Here's Lena," said Rowland cheerfully when
Esmé appeared. Esmé gave her a weary little smile and
shook hands dumbly ; she looked beautiful in her delicate
black, but rather ill, Lena thought, with those violet
shadows beneath her eyes, and also decidedly cross. The
one, however, might have been due to grief and anxiety
about her grandfather, and the other to vexation at not
being asked to act as Charles Thomas Deller's godmother ;
Lena filled this office and Rowland and—to Lena's great
surprise—Alfred Howgate were to be his godfathers. Lena
could not imagine why either Rachel or Arnold should want
Howgate to have anything to do with their son ; but her
stepfather himself seemed to have no such perplexity ; he
had made the child a handsome present, and seemed pleased
to be asked, but regarded the affair as a commonplace.
The afternoon was a torment to Lena ; Rowland naturally
helped his wife in and out of cars, bent his head to listen to
her remarks, put his hand on her arm to steer her past a
projecting pew, and so on.

" Yes, and so on and so on," thought Lena in a deep, aching
sadness. " And so on for all their lives. They're always together ; she's always with him." She felt shut out, apart ; and

gradually (Rachel being still upstairs in bed and so not at
hand to cheer her) the feeling extended itself. What was she,
after all, to these Averys and Dellers, who were all connected by blood ? She was quite glad when she and Howgate at last drove off together to Bierley Hall. " Not that I
am connected with him either, of course," thought Lena.
" I'm all alone, I don't belong to anybody."

This sombre mood lasted as long as Rowland and Esmé
remained in Hudley, for as long as they were in the neighbourhood she would not risk meeting them at Oddy Hall.
But soon Rowland had to get back to school, and life grew
brighter. Rachel made a good recovery from her confine-
ment, and was feeding her baby, who was certainly a
beautiful boy, and justified his father's fondness for having
him photographed. Fair and placid, with a clear skin and
round rosy cheeks and an absurd look of Arnold, he ate and
slept at the prescribed hours and thrived as a baby should ;
Lena saw a great deal of him and grew to love him. Rachel
had an expensive and highly trained nurse, who constantly
drew Lena aside and confided indignantly to her that Mrs.
Deller usurped her duties and left her nothing to do. Lena
soothed her as tactfully as she could ; she already saw in
Rachel that passionate, rather sombre and jealous affection
for her child which Mrs. Avery had for Rachel, and knew
it was useless to remonstrate with her. Once she did jokingly
repeat Howgate's remark on the situation, namely that it
was foolish to keep a dog and bark yourself ; but Rachel
merely gave her serene, beautiful smile, and without raising
her eyes from Charles's face replied : " Not if you like
barking as much as I do." The villagers around Bierley
Green therefore continued to see Mrs. Arnold Deller
pushing her baby in a pram, accompanied by her mother
or Miss Lena Howgate ; or alternatively Miss Howgate in
her new car running Mrs. Arnold Deller and her baby down
to Hudley to see her mother. On these occasions Lena was
increasingly struck by Mr. Avery's frail and overburdened
look ; though the house in Cambridge Place, when occupied

by Charles Thomas and his varied equipment, did not seem as pathetic as before his grandparents had him to adore.

Christmas approached : Rowland and Esmé were to be in Hudley for the whole of Rowland's holiday, part of the time at Cambridge Place, part at West View. Howgate decreed that he and Lena should spend Christmas at a large seaside hotel with a programme full of gaieties. Lena was grimly amused by his obvious determination to give her as little chance as possible of being in love with a married man, but she agreed that his policy was a wise one ; her experience at the christening had taught her that the less she saw of Rowland the better for her peace of mind.

Unfortunately she was not able to act upon this maxim as fully as she could have wished. In January Mr. Avery caught a severe cold which developed into a touch of pleurisy ; he was laid up for a fortnight, avoided pneumonia by the merest squeak, and when he did recover, had to go to school in a taxi. It was obvious that this sort of thing could not go on. One spring afternoon when Lena entered Oddy Hall she found Mrs. Avery and Rachel sitting together with such serious faces that she knew at once they were discussing Mr. Avery's health. When she had greeted them she said lightly : " Don't let me interrupt the family conclave ; I'll go upstairs to Charles until you've finished."

" It doesn't matter, Lena," said Mrs. Avery quietly. " There's no secret about it. The doctor says that Mr. Avery definitely must not spend another winter in Hudley, so we shall have to go and live in the south."

" And leave Rachel ! " exclaimed Lena, aghast. She thought a minute, and added : " But of course you can choose a place near Rowland."

There was a pause. Rachel looked at her mother, but Mrs. Avery did not seem inclined to speak, and Lena felt that something was wrong.

" The idea is," explained Rachel at length, " that Rowland shall come to the Hudley Grammar School next term, work for a term under father, and then take father's place."

" I see," said Lena thoughtfully, forbearing to look at Mrs. Avery.

" It would be a very good post for a man as young as Rowland," went on Rachel in dry tones. " Rowland would like it, and we think Esmé would like it too. They would live at West View, you see," she concluded.

Lena bit back her exclamation at the incongruity of Rowland being in West View, and concealed her dismay at the prospect of having to meet him regularly. She turned instead to Mrs. Avery and said warmly : " We *shall* miss you ; Hudley won't seem the same at all without you both."

" Thank you, Lena," said Mrs. Avery quietly.

A moment later she rose, and moved swiftly out of the room, alleging that Charles, who was supposed to be asleep upstairs, was crying. Lena looked at Rachel, expecting her to follow, but Rachel remained seated.

" He isn't crying," she said briefly. " If anyone's crying it's mother," she added in a softer tone. " She feels it very much, having to leave both Rowland and me."

Lena, remembering her first interview with Mrs. Avery after Rowland's marriage, had no difficulty in believing this. " It certainly seems a pity," she said. Rachel sighed. " Need Rowland come ? " murmured Lena timidly. " Even if it is a good post ? "

" Esmé wants to come," said Rachel shortly.

" Mrs. Deller, of course, will be delighted," observed Lena in her society tone.

" There ! Now he *is* crying ! " exclaimed Rachel, and dropping her sewing she flew towards her son.

When Lena reported the proposed arrangements to Howgate, he seemed rather dismayed, and asked her, as he had done when Rowland was engaged, if she would like to go away for a while, not just go away for a holiday, but leave Bierley Hall and live somewhere else. Lena considered it rather seriously. But to leave Rachel, to leave Charles, to leave the West Riding hills—no ! she would not be driven away from everything she cared for by Esmé. She must harden herself to meeting Rowland and his wife ; she must get accustomed to it ; after all West View was a long way from Bierley Hall ; and in any case she was not going to run away. She told her stepfather this ; he muttered : " Well, if they're going to live here always I suppose it's the best way ; you'll have to get used to it some time. But, Lena," he added, raising his voice : " don't let us have any nonsense, you know."

" What do you mean, father ? " cried Lena in a fury. " Do you suppose I don't know how to play a straight game ? Esmé's happiness is perfectly safe as far as I am concerned."

" Well, all right, all right," mumbled Howgate, looking at her quizzically. " Don't get so hot, Lena ; you fly up so. This fowl's had to walk a long way to get its living, I reckon ; where did you get it ? "

Lena coldly told him the name of the farm. This casual and jocular treatment of somebody else's deepest problems was characteristic of Howgate, she reflected ; it always wounded her and set them apart.

The weeks went on, the end of the term came ; Lena found that the extra end-of-term work was trying Mr. Avery severely, so she went down to Cambridge Place every afternoon, hectographed his examination papers, added up his marks, helped him in the hundred and one details which he used to enjoy but which were now so wearying to him. Meanwhile Rachel was upstairs with her mother, counting linen and turning out drawers ready for the Averys' removal ; they had arranged to store their furniture for a while, until they decided where they wanted to settle down —and, Lena privately thought, until they had succeeded in selling the Cambridge Place house. " I wonder Arnold doesn't buy it from them," she speculated one evening at Bierley Hall. " He could sell it again or let it ; it would be an investment for him and help them."

" He'd have to find the purchase money," observed Howgate.

" Well, surely he's got plenty of money now Mr. Deller's dead," said Lena carelessly.

" Very few people in business have got plenty of ready money," Howgate told her with some irritation. " It's all tied up in machinery. And business is bad just now, especially for young fools like Arnold. It's a marvel to me he keeps any customers at all."

" Don't you still send cloth to him, father ? " said Lena, shocked by his tone.

Howgate gave her a shrewd glance. " Has Rachel been talking to you about it ? " he demanded.

" Rachel ! " exclaimed Lena. " Of course not ! What do you mean ? "

" Well, don't let's have business to dinner," said Howgate roughly. " I get enough at the mill ; I don't want it at home as well. You'd best leave the Dellers to manage their own affairs, Lena. They get through a good deal of money at Oddy Hall, I don't doubt ; then there's West View to keep up, and Mrs. Rowland's dividends. Young Arnold's got as much on hand as he can manage at the moment, I reckon, without buying houses."

Howgate and Lena went away for Easter ; when they returned Rowland and Esmé were already settled at West View. They heard this even before they reached home, for they saw Rachel (wheeling the pram, as usual) as they were passing through Bierley Green, and Joe drew up for her to have a word with Lena. Rachel explained that she was just on her way to Bierley Hall to leave a note.

" We're having a family dinner-party next Tuesday," she said, " in honour of Rowland's arrival ; and we hope," she continued, looking, to Lena's surprise, at Howgate instead of at her friend, " that you and Lena will join us, Mr. Howgate."

The invitation was of course accepted, though Lena continued to wonder why her stepfather should be included

with such *empressement* ; then Charles took it into his head
that he was being neglected, wept a little, and was drawn
into view.

" That nurse of yours having a holiday again, Mrs.
Deller ? " said Howgate, teasingly.

To Lena's surprise, Rachel coloured and said, " No,"
rather abruptly. " We'll see you on Tuesday, then," she
added after a moment in her usual serene tones ; then
nodded and wheeled the pram away.

The dinner on Tuesday proved to be a very impressive
affair. Rachel had evidently made up her mind to show
the family what she could do when she tried, for she used
her best silver and linen and glass, and had some very
charming flowers. All the women wore their best frocks.
Esmé was in white, and looked extremely beautiful ; her
slender arms, her pretty little face, her fair silky hair, her
blue eyes, her slightly reddened lips, her tiny breasts beneath the tight-fitting bodice of her gown, made a picture
of exquisite neatness and freshness and delicacy ; she was
talking to Howgate with a great air of maturity and worldliness, and Lena could see from his expression of sleepy
good-humour that he was amused by her. Mrs. Deller was
very resplendent in grey and pearls ; Rachel had a bloom-
ing but not very fashionable air in a remodelled gown of
her favourite primrose ; Lena as usual was in rose-colour,
and Mrs. Avery, also as usual, looked handsome in well-
worn black. Mr. Avery's dress suit was also well worn, but
Howgate and Arnold were of course glossily new, and Lena
was rather surprised to find that Rowland looked glossy
too. " I suppose Esmé makes him," she thought, as she
took her seat between Rowland and Mr. Avery. The older
man seemed in good spirits, and looked in better health
than he had done for a long time ; he and Lena were never
in want of something to say to each other, and they laughed
and joked pleasantly together. Rowland, on the other hand,
seemed quiet and rather tired ; he looked, decided Lena,
as she felt—that is to say, as though he had been through

some great and sorrowful experience, which had sobered
and matured him. The lines running from nose to mouth
and mouth to chin were now deeply marked on his face ;
his dark eyes were still bright but no longer merry ; to
Lena's distress she saw threads of grey here and there in
his dark hair. Nor did he take the lead in the conversation
as he had been wont to do ; he listened with attention but
said little, coming out only when appealed to, but then
with some clinching and sensible observation.

"He's a man now, not a young man any more," thought
Lena sadly.

By contrast the fair Arnold, although he was the father
of that fine child upstairs, looked a mere boy ; agreeably
excited by the occasion, he smiled and talked and coloured
and told boastful anecdotes of Charles in his light jerky
tones, and seemed not a day older than when Lena first
knew him. All the Dellers (by birth) were good talkers,
and Mr. Avery was a superlative one, so the dinner went
very well.

"Nobody would think I had a broken heart," thought
Lena, laughing heartily at one of Mr. Avery's tales. "But
I have, all the same."

When they were all collected in the drawing-room Arnold put on the gramophone and suggested dancing. Now
that Rachel was able to go out with him again his interest
in this pursuit had revived, and he had been to as many
dances as he could find in the past few months. Rachel
accompanied him to them serenely, but the moment she
reached Oddy Hall again she flew upstairs to her son's cot
—or so Arnold alleged. Arnold told anecdotes of this now,
so that Rachel, who had protested that they were too few
to dance, was laughed down ; Arnold and the maid rolled
up the rugs, and dancing began. Presently the elders of
the party dropped out and sat down, and Arnold began to
instruct the others in a new step he had recently acquired.
When he thought they knew it sufficiently well, he put on
the gramophone again and commanded them to practise

it in pairs ; he took Lena himself, Rachel slipped upstairs
to have a look at Charles, and Esmé of course danced with
Rowland.

" No, that's all *wrong*, Lena," said Arnold reproachfully ;
and at the same moment Esmé's voice was heard exclaiming : " Rowland, you're treading on my *toes* ! "

The two exclamations, similar in matter, were so different
in tone and manner that Lena winced and started, for Arnold's was affectionate and jocular, while Esmé's was peevish,
fretful, and meant to be taken seriously. To Arnold's Lena
replied " Sorry, sorry ! " and laughed. To Esmé's Rowland said gently in his deep voice : " I'm sorry, dear." And
suddenly the lights and the flowers and the pretty frocks
vanished for Lena, and nothing was there but human be-
ings, people who got hurt. Nothing seemed to matter except what Esmé would say next to Rowland. The smile
died from Lena's face, she attended soberly to what Arnold was trying to tell her, and presently succeeded in master-
ing the rather complicated turns. " Oh, well done, well
done, Lena ! Bravo ! You've got it right now," came from
the Averys and Howgate, and Mrs. Deller murmured
plaintively : " What a *pretty* step ! I wish you'd teach me
afterwards, Arnold." Arnold expressed his willingness, and
Lena thought : " So they are all watching. I do hope Esmé
won't say anything more that's unkind. I *do* hope Esmé
won't say anything more that's unkind." She was just re-
flecting that Rowland's limp must make this particular
step very awkward for him when Esmé exclaimed :

" You are *clumsy*, Rowland ! "

Her voice quite rang through the room, and both couples
fell apart. A dark colour rose into Rowland's sallow cheeks.
" I'm sorry," he said stiffly, releasing Esmé's hand. (" Oh,
God, he's afraid of her," thought Lena with a pang. " She's
got him too.") He stepped back. " You'd better try with
Arnold," he continued pleasantly. (But Lena, who was
skilled in such matters by dint of experience, knew what
the pleasant tone was costing him.) " I'm afraid I'm no

good at this job." He drew back and leaned against a book-case beside his father.

Thus deserted, Esmé turned her petulant, dissatisfied, pretty little face towards Arnold interrogatively. Arnold began to prepare to look uncomfortable, whereat Lena exclaimed with great heartiness : " Oh, yes ! Try with Arnold ! Do ! He's an awfully good teacher ; try with him." She laughingly pushed Arnold towards Esmé, and as he somewhat unwillingly put his arm round his sister's waist, added more quietly : " I'll just go and detach Rachel from Charles—if that's possible," and fled from the room.

As she rushed up the stairs she thought : " She must have forgotten that he's lame. But how could she forget ? How could a *wife* forget that about her husband ? I wonder he doesn't kill her when she nags him like that. *I* should." She remembered that she had once tried to kill Esmé with a knife, and thought fiercely : " I wish I'd finished the job. Oh, Rowland, my poor, poor boy ; no wonder you look old if that's what you have to live with all the time. Don't I know what it feels like ? Oh, my poor boy ! "

At the top of the stairs she met Rachel, who looked surprised to see her. " Handkerchief," lied Lena tersely, plunging into the room where they had left their wraps— she did not feel equal to going downstairs again just yet. Rachel followed, and stood silently by while Lena fumbled about and pretended to find the article in question, and really recovered her composure. When they left the room and crossed towards the stairs Rachel stepped lightly to the door of her own room, and bending her head, listened intently.

" Is he asleep ? " whispered Lena. Rachel nodded. " But what is he doing in there ? " asked Lena as they went down the stairs with their arms round each other's waists. " Is nurse away ? "

" I've sent her away altogether," said Rachel. " I gave her notice last month."

" Rachel ! " began Lena in a tone of fond reproof.

" She cost such a lot of money," concluded Rachel.

Lena stared. " But, Rachel," she objected. " Surely that doesn't matter to you."

" As a matter of fact it does," breathed Rachel, gently kissing her ear. " We're rather hard up just now. But don't tell anyone, and especially not your father."

" You can rely on me not to speak of it at all," said Lena, feeling in deep waters. " But are you really hard up, Rachel ? "

" Well, not really," smiled Rachel. " But it's best to take these things in time, isn't it ? "

There was a note in her voice which belied what she said, and Lena was not altogether reassured. " Don't let us dance any more, Rachel," she begged as they neared the drawing-room door. She expected that Rachel would at once say loyally : " We won't," but instead Rachel gave a vague smile and was silent. When they entered the room, how-ever, they found that the dancing had already been aban-doned, and Arnold was replacing the rugs on the floor. Rowland was not helping him ; he was still leaning against his bookcase and watching the process moodily ; Howgate was standing by his side.

" Rowland, don't slouch so," complained Esmé fretfully. " You look less than Mr. Howgate the way you're standing now."

Rowland roused himself and stood up. " I can't add a cubit to my stature by taking thought, even to please you, Esmé," he said. " If I am less than Mr. Howgate I shall have to remain so."

" We're about the same, I think," put in Howgate casually.

" It's just the way you're standing," persisted Esmé. She went up to her husband, and putting her hands on the upper parts of his arms, tried to adjust his shoulders to her liking. For a moment Rowland started, flushed, and bit his lip ; then he removed her hands with exaggerated gentle-ness, and gave her a forced smile.

" Speaking of heights, Rachel," said Lena in a cool easy tone, " how tall is the infant Charles now ? "

This subject carried them safely along for a few minutes, but it was impossible to keep Esmé " off " Rowland for long. She was always *at* him, thought Lena in despair ; if she were not criticising the way he stood, or objecting to his play in the two tables of bridge which they shortly began, or telling the company what a small sitting-room they had had in Sussex and how bad the garage was there, she was trying to attract his notice and exacting small attentions from him. In fact she was so intensely exasperating that it was almost incredible, and Lena was beginning to think that she was being morbid and imagining the whole thing when Mr. Avery exclaimed in a joking tone :

" You're very perverse to-night, Esmé ! "

" Oh, Will ! " chimed Mrs. Deller at this, " she's a very naughty girl, she is indeed."

To Lena's astonishment Esmé's eyes at once filled with tears, and she exclaimed fretfully : " You're very unkind, mother."

" Is someone attacking my wife ? " boomed Rowland from the other table. " If so let them beware ! "

He spoke cheerfully ; and it struck Lena all of a sudden that perhaps Esmé's vagaries might have a justifiable cause ; she was perhaps pregnant, and her nagging was but the temporary caprice of her condition. Lena sighed with relief at this so probable explanation ; it would explain, too, Rowland's weak handling of the situation, which had so much distressed her. She reproached herself for not having thought of something so obvious before, and was shocked at her wicked thoughts about knives. Both for the rest of that evening and for the several other meetings with Rowland and Esmé which took place within the next month or so she found herself able to view Esmé's behaviour with the indulgence which it certainly required.

But towards the end of June the Howgates gave a garden-party. Lena was rather astonished when she found herself

committed to this, and did not quite know how it had come
about ; on reflection she decided that it was mostly due to
her stepfather. There was to be tennis, there was to be
music ; the catering arrangements were on a large scale.
A year or two ago Lena would not have slept for a week
before such an affair, but now she took it calmly ; since her
great disaster smaller things, and especially what other
people thought of her, had ceased to count ; her preoccupation with her tragedy set her free of them, and consequently she was able to behave with the cool indifference
demanded by society. Just as she was beginning to receive
her guests—luckily the day was fine—a message was brought
from Arnold that Charles was having a screaming fit and
consequently he and Rachel would be late. It was indeed
at least an hour later when they arrived ; Lena took Rachel
at once into the house to change her shoes for tennis, and
Rachel offered apologies for their delay.

" Is everybody else here ? I suppose so," she observed.

Lena told her that her father had not come and was not
coming, for he had a slight chill, so Mrs. Avery said ; also
Rowland and Esmé and Mrs. Deller had not yet come and
had sent no message ; at this Rachel stared, surprised.

" Rowland can't leave school till half-past four, I
imagine," she said. " But I don't understand about Esmé
and her mother."

" Perhaps," suggested Lena, eager to excuse her enemy,
" Esmé doesn't want to play tennis this summer, and is
coming later on purpose."

" Why shouldn't she play ? There's no reason why she
shouldn't," threw out Rachel. Her tone was dry and hard,
and Lena felt that she spoke from certainty and had not
mistaken Lena's meaning. Her heart sank. There was no
excuse for Esmé's peevish handling of her husband, then,
and it was not temporary but habitual. " It's simply rudeness on Esmé's part to be so late," continued Rachel, " I
hope Mr. Howgate isn't annoyed."

" They may have had a puncture on the way," suggested

Lena mildly, leading the way out through the side door to
the lawn.

It was nearly five o'clock, and the other guests had all
had tea, when Mrs. Deller, Esmé and Rowland appeared
together. Lena, advancing towards them with a welcoming smile, saw that all was not smooth between them, for
Rowland looked pale, and Mrs. Deller harassed, while
Esmé's cold little face wore an expression of anger, and her
mouth quivered as she spoke as though she might be going
to cry at any moment.

" I am *exceedingly* sorry that we're so late, Lena," she
began in her high fretful tone. " Please accept my apologies. It's entirely Rowland's fault."

" Oh, come, Esmé ! " protested Rowland with a wry
face, " I told you that I couldn't get off till half-past four."

" You never told me anything of the sort," cried Esmé,
almost weeping. " You said you *might* not be able to get off,
and of course I waited and waited, and you never came.
Mother kept wanting me to start, and I kept *waiting* for
you. I'm so *sorry*, Lena."

Several people were beginning to look at Esmé rather
curiously, and Rowland said with an air of finality : " Well,
after all, the loss is more ours than Lena's. *We've* missed
part of a very pleasant afternoon ; I'm sure Lena will
understand and forgive us for being late."

" That's all you think about, your own pleasure," persisted Esmé angrily. " I wouldn't have been late at Lena's
garden-party for anything. I respect Lena far too much to
be late at her party."

Her emphasis in this sentence sounded rather as though
she respected Lena at the expense of Rowland, and her
husband flushed darkly. Throughout the conversation Lena
had been making deprecating murmurs and begging
Esmé not to trouble herself, and she now made her voice
heard.

" It doesn't matter in the least," she said in a soothing
tone. " Pray don't trouble about it, Esmé ; we're so glad to

see you now. You'll have some tea, won't you?" She
seated Mrs. Deller and looked about for a waitress and a
tray, but found that they had all withdrawn into the house,
whence the tea had been served. Seeing that Howgate was
advancing to greet the late arrivals, she murmured an
excuse and went off into the house by the dining-room
window. To her surprise and irritation Esmé, still uttering
apologies in a tearful tone, trailed after her.

"Rowland's so *selfish*," wailed Esmé. "He never *thinks*."

She was not out of the hearing of her husband when she
made this remark, and Lena, involuntarily glancing backward, saw Rowland wince. He looked old and tired and
hunted, a weary and unhappy man ; and all Lena's feeling
for him suddenly flamed. She put her hand beneath Esmé's
elbow and smiled down at her as they walked along together. "Never mind, never mind !" she urged coaxingly.
"What does it matter, Esmé ? You'll feel better about it
when you've had some tea." To herself she thought in a
fierce enduring rage : "Knives are too good for you, Esmé
Deller. If ever I get the chance to do it without harming
Rowland, I'll pay you back for that in words that *hurt*. Yes,
by God, I will !"

When they reached the dining-room Esmé sank down on
a chair and said in a piteous tone : "Couldn't we have tea
here, Lena, just you and I ?"

"Oh, certainly," agreed Lena glibly. She instructed a
maid to attend to Mrs. Deller and Rowland, dismissed the
others and poured Esmé's tea herself. After a moment or
two Esmé seemed to recover her composure, sat up and
began to look about her.

"I don't think I've been in this room before, have I,
Lena ?" she said.

"Once, I think," said Lena. "We all had tea here, one
wet day."

"I don't remember noticing," began Esmé, and paused.

"Noticing what ?" said Lena with an artificially
encouraging smile.

" Well, that portrait over the mantelpiece," said Esmé, colouring a little. " What a beautiful woman ! Who is she ? "

" That's Mrs. Josiah Howgate, poor dear," replied Lena.

" Mr. Howgate's mother ? Why ' poor dear ' ? " queried Esmé with interest.

" Oh, she ran away with the artist who painted it, and her husband fetched her back, and they lived a perfectly miserable life, wouldn't speak to each other and all that sort of thing—at least, so Mrs. Preston says," explained Lena uncomfortably, feeling that this conversation beneath Howgate's roof was not in the best of taste.

Esmé sighed, and continued to look at the portrait. " Yes, there's something wild in her," she murmured thoughtfully, " like there is in you, Lena." She glanced at Lena, and then back at the portrait. " Yes, you're quite like her," she said.

Her tone added : " Except that you're not beautiful," and Lena laughed. She was just beginning to utter her customary disclaimer of all connection with Howgate's relations, just beginning to remind Esmé that Howgate was only her adopted father and not her real one, when suddenly the whole thing burst upon her. One minute she did not know, had not an inkling of Howgate's probable relationship to herself ; the next she knew, and could not imagine how she could have been such an idiot as not to see it before. Hosts of tiny incidents, acts, looks, words, rushed into her mind, making a tremendous total in its support ; hosts of incidents in which she had betrayed her own ignorance for other people to laugh at filled her thoughts, and overwhelmed her with shame. She recognised for what they were Esmé's previous innuendoes on this subject, and even credited her with having known the fact at the Hudley Girls' College. She felt herself blushing from head to foot ; she stood absolutely still and could not say a single word.

The silence was at length broken by Esmé, who proceeded

musingly : " I wonder what sort of a man Josiah Howgate
was."

" I've no idea," replied Lena shortly. She made a great
effort to command herself, and went on : " Will you have
some more tea ? " Esmé shook her head. " Then what
about some tennis ? "

Esmé's face brightened. " Yes ! Rowland has my racquet
somewhere," she said.

They went out together, then Esmé moved away in
search of Rowland. Lena, seeing Mrs. Deller and Mrs.
Avery standing together with their backs to her, went towards them ; and she involuntarily overheard Esmé's
mother saying : " She's such a *naughty* girl, Lilias."
(" Esmé again," thought Lena grimly.) Mrs. Deller continued : " But if you'll talk to Rowland about it, I'll talk to
Esmé." Mrs. Avery turned, and revealed to Lena a face
expressing intense repugnance. Lena spoke a lively word or
two to them, and passed on to some of her other guests ; but
she could not help thinking of what she had heard, nor
could she help thinking that Rachel's dry certainty earlier
in the afternoon, Mrs. Deller's plaints and Mrs. Avery's
repugnance, might all be referred to the same cause. She
reproached herself for this. " It may just as well have been
extravagance or something of that kind which the mothers-
in-law were discussing," she told herself. " Why *does* one's
mind always fly to thoughts of sex on the slightest provocation ? But after all," she reminded herself grimly, " you've
had a good deal of provocation to thoughts of that kind this
afternoon."

At last the guests had all gone—Esmé amid a final salvo
of apologies—and Lena and Howgate sat down to a scratch
supper in the library, the dining-room not being available.
Howgate seemed moody and preoccupied, and replied
shortly to all Lena's remarks : no doubt he was experiencing
a reaction from his four hours' amiability of the afternoon.
After supper they sat facing each other across the library
hearth in silence ; Howgate read the newspaper ; Lena

knitted, and turned over many rather bitter thoughts. She was revolted by Howgate's light and careless treatment of her mother if what she suspected was true ; and such behaviour was so like his character as she knew it that its very casualness seemed additional proof that it was true. She also thought that if she had known all these years that he owed her something instead of imagining that she owed him everything, her life might have been very different : her approach to life certainly would. Then she decided that that was a mean and unworthy thought, and tried to put it from her. Was this perhaps the reason, she wondered again, why she always felt apart from other people, different ? Her common sense rejected that idea ; besides, she vaguely remembered reading of some new law that legitimised—yes, that was the word—such offspring as herself if the parents married after their birth, so that even in law she was probably not regarded as different from anybody else. But the rub was that she had read all that in the papers without any idea of its applying to herself ; other people had guessed her origin, known it, perhaps, for years ; and she had exposed her ignorance for them to laugh at— for Esmé to laugh at. She winced, and experienced a profound humiliation ; everyone had known, and had laughed at her for not knowing. At any rate, she resolved, calling her pride to her aid, she would not continue in this naïve ignorance another hour ; when the clock struck ten she would ask Howgate about it, father or no father, whichever he might be. Having vowed this to herself she would not go back from it, though the blood drummed in her ears as the hour began to sound. She stood up, rolled up her knitting and placed it in its bag, then turned to face Howgate ; and with her hands behind her back blurted out : " Father ! " The moment she had uttered this word she was so struck with its irony and her own ineptitude that she could not go on, and there was a long silence.

" Well, what is it ? " demanded Howgate testily at length, turning over a sheet.

His tone irritated Lena, and she regained her self-command. " Is it true what people sometimes hint to me," she demanded coolly ; " that I'm your real daughter, and not just your adopted one ? "

Howgate, startled—" As well he might be," thought Lena sardonically—sat up abruptly, coloured, took off his glasses, and looked angrily at her. " Aye, it's true," he replied at length in a vexed tone. " I should have told you before, only you seemed so young and silly. But who's been hinting to you about it, pray ? "

His tone was so imperious that Lena felt constrained to mutter : " Esmé Deller."

" Damned interfering little baggage ! " exclaimed Howgate roughly. " What does she know about it ? " His colour deepened, and he looked away. Presently his glance returned to Lena. " Well, it makes no difference to us that I can see," he said with an air of finality. " Don't go getting any silly notions in your head about it now, Lena. You're old enough to know better."

He sniffed, put on his glasses and took up the paper again.

Lena, hopelessly bewildered by this extraordinary (as she thought) manner of acknowledging a daughter, and feeling as much rebuffed by Howgate as if he had physically thrust her from the room, was torn between disgust, perplexity and humiliation. She hung her head to hide the tears which suddenly streamed from her eyes, and turned away, over-whelmed.

" Where are you going ? " demanded Howgate sharply as she opened the door.

" To bed," muttered the wretched Lena.

" Well, you can say good night, can't you ? " demanded Howgate.

He sounded aggrieved, and Lena suddenly lost her temper. Turning to him, she threw up her head, and ex-claimed loudly : " Good night ! " articulating each word separately in a clear, emphatic, absolutely expressionlesss and so highly insulting tone.

Her father coloured and for the first time seemed a little uneasy. " The garden-party went off very well, I reckon," he observed with a conciliatory air, rustling the folds of the newspaper.

" I'm not likely to forget it, if that's what you mean," threw out Lena fiercely.

She jerked open the door and left him.

# CHAPTER IX

# RACHEL

Rachel, slowly undressing that night—she was always slow at this process ; Arnold read vast quantities of books, or so he alleged, while waiting till she should be ready to turn out the light—felt that she would never in her life forget Lena's garden-party, because it had first clearly shown her how greatly she had changed from the serene loving Rachel of old. For the first time in her life she had been glad, yes, glad, not to see her father : she had been glad to hear that he was at home with a chill. She was glad because he was one of the people who had the right to know all the circumstances of her life and ask her questions about it, with whom therefore she had to exercise care in every word she said, lest she should betray the secret she must keep, the secret of Arnold's increasing financial difficulties. There was still her mother and Mrs. Deller and Rowland and Esmé with whom she had to be on her guard, but to be able to cross off even one person for one afternoon was an immense relief. For Rachel was tired, tired, *tired* of hedging and evading when Mrs. Avery murmured about her lack of a nurse, and Mr. Avery told her they ought to have Oddy Hall re-painted. She was tired of smiling vaguely and explaining to Mrs. Deller that Arnold was feeling the heat—or the cold, whichever happened to be in season—when he came in looking absolutely exhausted from a harassing interview at the bank. She was tired of pretending that she liked old clothes best when Esmé hinted that Arnold might prefer her in new ones. She was tired of replying that she couldn't leave Charles behind when Rowland asked why she and Arnold didn't decide to

go abroad for their holiday. Arnold of course thought her
economies silly, and perhaps they were ; he said she might
just as well have a nurse and new frocks and a good holiday
as not, and he would buy the Cambridge Place house from
her father in a minute if she gave the word, for all those
things were mere drops in the ocean of his responsibilities ;
the whole boiling did not amount to one week's wages bill
at Adela Mills. But Rachel, who had been brought up as a
poor man's daughter, could not believe this to be true, for
the sums seemed large in her eyes. In any case, her economies might have the effect of stimulating Arnold to further
efforts—not that he needed stimulating, poor boy ; he
worried himself nearly to death as it was—and it made her
feel that she was being helpful, which was a relief.

Exactly how Arnold stood, and why things had got into
their present condition, Rachel did not know ; when Arnold
began to explain it to her she could not understand it, and
whether this was due to her inability or to Arnold's she was
not as sure as she would have liked to be. Her head was a
perfect jumble of death duties, the clauses of John Deller's
will and his habit of arranging his affairs as though he were
going to live for ever, Esmé's dividends, Mrs. Deller's
allowance, the rates of West View, insurance policies as
securities, bad trade and the iniquities of foremen dyers, and
she could not arrange them in an orderly sequence try as
she would ; she was, however, perfectly clear on the cardinal facts of the situation, namely that Adela Mills was an
enormous concern, that without Alfred Howgate's business
it could scarcely keep open to-day, and that they were deep
" in " with the bank as it was, while Howgate was not too
satisfied, in fact constantly on the grumble ; and though
Arnold slaved from morning to night, week in, week out,
the situation seemed to get no better, but rather worse.
Before John Deller's death, in the spring of the preceding
year, two days after Rowland became engaged to Esmé
in fact, Alfred Howgate had half made a proposal to
Arnold which would have solved all their difficulties ; he

suggested, as far as Rachel could make out (Arnold was so complicated in his explanations), an agreement by which he should send all his cloth to be dyed at Adela Mills, and at the same time in some way or other exercise a certain control in its management. The details were in Rachel's mind hopelessly vague, but again she was perfectly clear about the cardinal facts of the agreement ; namely that it would give Arnold the support of Alfred Howgate's experience and Adela Mills the support of his credit to some extent and his business for certain—all three consummations devoutly to be desired. The moment Arnold told her of the proposal she urged him to accept it and clinch the agreement properly.

" But I must go over it with a solicitor first," argued Arnold " I don't want Howgate to get control of Adela Mills, you know. I told him I should have to go over it very carefully.'"

" And what did he say to that ? " demanded Rachel in alarm.

" Oh, he was very decent about it," admitted Arnold jerkily. " He said of course he had expected me to take all proper precautions, should think me a fool if I didn't. He asked if grandfather couldn't be made to understand it ; and when I told him I thought not, he said it was a pity."

" Well, I should get it drawn up and signed as soon as I could," persisted Rachel. A thought struck her ; she added : " Did you tell him about Rowland's engagement to Esmé ? "

" Yes," said Arnold. " Just as he was going, I told him."

" And what did he say to that ? " asked Rachel in still deeper alarm.

" Nothing," said Arnold in surprise. " Why should he ? " After a moment he added : " He seemed to think Lena didn't know. But surely you told her in your note, didn't you ? "

Rachel replied to this only by urging him to make haste and get the agreement drawn and signed.

That was more than a year ago now, and the agreement, though duly drawn, was not signed yet. Not that this long delay was caused by Arnold ; he had very soon declared himself perfectly satisfied with the proposed terms, and had later risked an explanation of them to his grandfather which Rachel in the secrecy of her heart always believed to have caused John Deller's final stroke. No ; Arnold was only too ready to sign, and became increasingly anxious to do so as the months went by and his situation grew increasingly difficult ; it was Howgate who now hung back, objected to details, laughed the affair off and treated his proposal merely as a joke, and when Arnold persisted showed signs of offence. Arnold at first simply could not imagine any reason for this change of front ; having worried himself sleepless over it, he at length decided that it was an unworthy manœuvre on Howgate's part to depreciate the value of what Arnold had to barter by making Arnold appear eager to barter it. But at the bottom of his heart Arnold, though Howgate seemed a harsh taskmaster to him, could not believe him capable of such a manœuvre towards a young and inexperienced man, the husband of his daughter's friend and the grandson of his father's. Then, if not some such manœuvre, it must be because his dissatisfaction with the work which Adela Mills turned out was becoming extreme—an awful possibility. So Arnold worried and argued with himself, while Rachel tried to soothe him by every means in her power except what she believed to be the truth, for she thought that too dangerous. Rachel was convinced that Howgate, dissatisfied with the present dyeing of his pieces, had chosen this method of improving matters, partly, of course, for business reasons and because he did not want to abandon an arrangement which on the whole suited him well enough (Adela Mills and Bierley Bottom were fairly near, for example), but partly because he thought her brother was going to marry Lena, and so it would be a pleasant family concern controlled by cousins in the next generation ; he had decided to with-draw, postpone, the moment he heard that Rowland was to marry Esmé. He might yet sign the agreement, or he might continue to send his cloth to Adela Mills on the old terms and wait to see what Lena did about marrying, or he might decide to send it elsewhere ; it was this last alter-native which kept Rachel as well as Arnold awake at nights. For if Howgate chose it, Adela Mills were pretty well done for, and though Rachel would have accepted poverty cheerfully for herself, that Arnold should have to suffer the reproaches of Esmé and Mrs. Deller for having lost their money was not to be thought of. Imagine Esmé without money ! Intolerable ! (Rowland too would suffer—but why, oh, why, had he gone and ruined every-thing by marrying her ?) And there was Charles. When Rachel thought of Charles something fierce and ruthless rose up in her and declared that Howgate *must* sign the agreement ; he must be made to sign that agreement, Arnold must make him sign that agreement. A hundred times she debated whether to tell Arnold what she thought of Howgate's motive for evading and postponing ; but always she decided against it : it could do no good, and in the hands of the boyish and too candid Arnold might even do much harm. He was capable of saying something snappish to Howgate about it, and Howgate, Rachel judged—especially considering the unusual nature of his relation to Lena—would not stand that kind of remark for a moment. So she kept it to herself, and kept Arnold's difficulties from the family circle—since John Deller's death the difficulties seemed to have grown progressively worse—and entertained Howgate to dinner, and tried to please him without being subservient or gushing. The sickening thing was—or rather, one of the sickening things : there were a good many—that Rachel, truly and really loving Lena, dared not confide in her about the situation ; for Lena might mention it to her father, who

would be furiously angry at such female interference in his
business, or conversely she might brood upon it and discover the reason for her father's change of front. Rachel
was not quite sure enough of Lena's feelings about Rowland
to know how much of a tragedy such a discovery might or
might not be, but she dared not risk it—Lena was too
candid, too apt to burst out with things at awkward moments. One of these days, too, Lena might find out why
Rachel and Arnold cultivated Howgate so assiduously ;
and then, if she had been anybody else but Lena, she
might suspect Rachel of cultivating *her* friendship for that
reason too. The mere thought of that made Rachel shudder
with disgust ; but no ! she was safe there, surely ; Lena
surely could not entertain so base a notion. In any case,
Rachel here felt the support given by a clear conscience ;
for she knew she would see more of Lena, yes, ever so much
more, and love her far more freely, if she were not Alfred
Howgate's daughter.

Sometimes Rachel grew so sick of all these complications
and secrets and bothers that her courage almost failed her,
she almost gave up Alfred Howgate as a bad job and let
the whole thing slide ; but there was one small person who
always brought her back to the fight again : Charles. When
Rachel bathed Charles or dressed him or fed him or washed
his clothes or squeezed out his orange-juice or brushed his
hair or attended to his nose or persuaded him to wave his
hand to Arnold or did any of the thousand and one things
which he required to keep him alive and well and happy,
then her courage rose again and stood up firmly, and
she felt strong and fierce and unafraid ; strong enough to
protect Charles at any cost, fierce enough to compel
Alfred Howgate to her bidding, not afraid to go through
any anguish, any humiliation, to secure the future of her
child. At this period of his life Charles was quite absurdly
like his father, and he had already some of those slight but
unmistakable gestures which almost more than looks reveal
the power of heredity ; Arnold and Charles, Charles and

Arnold—they were Rachel's life-blood, and she would fight for them remorselessly. She tiptoed over to Charles's cot now ; he was beautifully asleep, his long fair eyelashes exquisitely curved upon his flushed and downy cheek. Immediately her courage was renewed. If she had been glad not to see her father, and ashamed of her gladness— well ! that was just one of the wounds she was bound to receive in this fight for Arnold and Charles ; she must just endure it and fight on. She remembered the phrase in the psalm : *instead of thy fathers thou shalt have children.* Well, it was very true. Rachel set her teeth, and bade Arnold invite Mr. Howgate to drive to the Lakes with them next week ; an agreeable picnic could be planned.

" Did he seem pleasant to you this afternoon ? " she asked.

" Not very," replied Arnold gloomily. " He was sarcastic about my being there so early."

" Early ! " exclaimed Rachel. " But we were late."

" I know," said Arnold. He sighed. " I can't say I enjoyed it very much," he said.

" Nor I," thought Rachel, but she did not sap her husband's courage by saying so. Instead she observed : " He was rather nice to me, about my tennis."

Arnold brightened.

# CHAPTER X

## ESMÉ

Esmé too felt that she was not likely to forget the Bierley Hall garden-party. It marked a period in her life.

There were always being periods in Esmé's life ; she was always beginning another period, making a fresh start, turning over a new leaf, inaugurating a special effort to live up to her ideals ; but nobody appreciated these efforts, nobody helped her to live up to anything ; on the contrary, they seemed to take a perverse delight in thwarting her, in just doing the one thing which brought her low and made her efforts of no avail. She had begun fresh periods in her childhood whenever May Deller moved to a fresh place, and especially when they all came to Hudley ; and when Esmé had first seen Rowland Avery, and when she had first gone to the Hudley Girls' College, and when she had first seen Rachel Avery, and when she thought Lena had drowned herself, and then later when she had put her hair up, and when she had cut it off, and on her twenty-first birthday, and when Arnold was engaged, and when he was married, and when she was engaged to Rowland—oh, a hundred times Esmé had made a fresh start, but always, always somebody had spoiled it. Especially had she made a fresh start, of course, when she was married ; yielding sweetly and graciously to Rowland's plea for an early and quiet wedding, and allowing him to carry her off away with him to that awful Sussex village, where there was nothing on earth to do, and nothing to see except tall depressing trees which rustled at night and kept Esmé awake, and no society to speak of except other schoolmasters' wives, who regarded Esmé not as the rich and fashionable Esmé Deller, but as

the wife of an unimportant junior master. Of course Esmé
was sufficiently clever to catch their tone at once and
imitate it with success, but it was a strain ; and she had
never been away from her mother, and never *far* away from
Arnold, before, and that was a strain ; everything was new
and strange and difficult, everything was a strain ; and
then Rowland, instead of being a very present help in
trouble, as he always had been before, spoiled all Esmé's
good resolutions by becoming a strain too.

To begin with, he put a slight but incessant strain upon
her by being very tiresome about money. Esmé had a very
good idea of the value of money, and knew well the prestige
its possession conferred ; she would have objected vigorously if Rowland had shown any disposition to take the
control of her money out of her hands, and would perhaps
have felt inclined to sneer at him if he had assumed the
right to spend it too soon and too freely ; but there was
reason in all things, and Rowland's attitude to her money
was in Esmé's opinion most unreasonable. He would
insist on paying their hotel bill from his own absurd salary,
and then looking worried because it was so large. He constantly told Esmé that she was now a poor man's wife—
which was ridiculous. He wore shabby suits, and seemed
hurt and surprised when his wife criticised them ; and when
he discovered that Esmé, unknown to him, had ordered a
set of evening clothes from his Hudley tailor for a birthday
present for him, he was not pleased, though he tried to pretend he was : he coloured and thanked her stiffly, and had
to be persuaded to try them on. But though Rowland's
unreasonableness about money made constant slight
friction between them, Esmé could not but admire him for
it, and rather enjoyed circumventing it ; it was not that
which strained her patience almost to snapping-point, but
something far more serious, indeed fundamental. Esmé,
who had studied the matter of sex relationship as widely as
her clashing ideas of what was *convenable* and what was
modern permitted, and knew all the words, very early in

her married life decided that Rowland was a clumsy and
fumbling lover. At first she resigned herself, partly in the
hope that things would mend, partly in the determination
that *her* marriage should not be a failure, partly because she
had always been a little afraid of Rowland and still was so,
partly in a really genuine and wistful " new-leaf " wish to
love her husband and be a good wife to him. But she did not
love Rowland and could not love him, and that Rowland
unfortunately continued to love her fretted her nerves
more every day. It was not only physically that he was a
clumsy and too eager lover ; every evening he came rushing
back from school to her with love glowing in his eyes, and
kissed her eagerly, and expected her to take an interest in
the silly things his boys said—not that he *said* he expected
her to take an interest in them, of course, but he was hurt
and chilled when she did not, which exasperated Esmé
intensely—and smiled fatuously when his hand touched
hers as she made tea, and bent over her caressingly, and
was interested in what she had been doing, and altogether,
by the mere fact of loving her, made constant, incessant,
exacting demands upon her which Esmé knew she ought to
meet, but could not because she had no love for him in
return. At times she forced herself to do her duty, and pretended to meet these demands, till her soul sickened and
revolted, and, unused to self-discipline as she was, she
could sustain the pretence no longer ; then she met Rowland
with coldness and evasion, and he was deeply hurt, so
deeply that Esmé sickened at that too, and, pitying him with
a pity akin to contempt and not to love, began to pretend
again. Then they had their first quarrel. It was on a subject which arose in this form because of the suddenness of
their marriage, namely : where they should live. Esmé
from the first day of her abode there had complained
bitterly, and according to Deller standards justly, of the
local hotel, but when Rowland brought her the keys of
house after house among the neighbouring villages, she
always found some insuperable defect in each, for the

thought of settling down in a house *here*, where the horizon
consisted entirely of trees and Rowland, made her feel
positively ill. If she had loved him, she told herself, she
would have been happy in a desert ; but she did not, and
she must live somewhere where she could find an escape
from him in agreeable society. Rowland at first laughed
and called her a capricious little devil, but presently seemed
to weary of her objections, and one day in the course of an
argument told her with some irritation that she was difficult
to please. Difficult to please ! Esmé thought of all she
suffered from her marriage to him, and burst into tears.
Rowland at once became tenderly remorseful, which exasperated Esmé almost to hysteria ; she almost screamed at
him that he was to go away, go away at once. Rowland,
looking very white, took her at her word and left her, went
out presumably for some long walk or other, and returned
as tender and remorseful as before, and naturally much
more diffident ; meanwhile Esmé had sobbed her exasperation out, turned over yet another new leaf, begun
another period, and managed to receive him on his return
kindly and dutifully, as became such a wife as Esmé Deller
ought to be. But this was the beginning of a series of
quarrels on this subject ; and each time they quarrelled
Esmé's store of dutifulness, and Rowland's prestige as a
husband, decreased. For as Rowland loved his wife and she
did not love him, he dreaded a quarrel, and longed for a
reconciliation, far more than she did ; Esmé could pain
him by quarrelling and by refusing to be reconciled, and
she knew it, and he knew it ; it was worth more to Rowland
to keep Esmé friendly than it was to Esmé to keep him
friendly, and consequently Esmé became the one to be
considered and propitiated.   And the more lovingly Rowland tried to propitiate her, the more exasperated Esmé
felt, and the more difficult she found it to control herself
into a semblance of love for him. When she felt exasperated
she simply could not *help* saying cutting things ; then
Rowland became more loving than before ; and so they

went on, in a vicious circle, all through that first long hot
summer term.

And then at last it was the holidays, and they went north
to Hudley, and saw her mother, and Arnold, and Rachel,
and Mr. and Mrs. Avery, and West View and Cambridge
Place and Oddy Hall, and all the old jolly people and
things, again ; and Esmé felt as though she had just woken
from a nightmare : everything was perfectly all right, and of
course Rowland was a delightful husband. A fresh period of
her married life, a happy period, she felt sure, was just
beginning. Then they went to Scotland. Unfortunately it
was not a very happy tour ; for Esmé's views on trains, cars,
hotels, meals, scenery and fellow-travellers were so different from her husband's, she had so much higher (as she
thought) standards than his in every way, that they could
hardly help but disagree and quarrel. They did quarrel,
with results as before. Then they were recalled to Hudley
for John Deller's funeral. Esmé, who had never seen death
before, was shocked and moved ; she remembered old kindnesses of her grandfather to her when she was a little girl ;
he had always understood her, and she had always understood him ; she was not really a hard, horrid, unsympathetic,
selfish creature, as she had begun to imagine lately, for here
she was weeping beside her grandfather's body, weeping
seriously and sincerely, really sorry that the poor old thing
was dead, even if it did mean trebling her income. Not, of
course, that she was quite sure about that, for Arnold was
such a noodle about business ; Rowland far surpassed him in
all such affairs. In the Hudley family circle everybody
knew Rowland's capacity, and admired him ; and Esmé
was able to admire him too. A new period of her married
life was beginning, a happy period, she felt sure ; and she
was so glad to be able to feel soft and sweet and good about
it once more. Rachel's baby seemed a dear little thing, as
babies went ; and after her first hot anger that she was not
asked to be his godmother, she decided to be magnani-
mous and forgive Rachel, and heap coals of fire on her head

by giving the child colossal presents every year, just as though she had been asked. She was affected by the drama of his birth so shortly after his great-grandfather's death, and savoured to the full the excitement of his christening— it was all so " family " and traditional, and seemed like old times, though why the Howgates should have been pushed into the ceremony like that really defeated her understanding ; she decided to take as little notice of them as possible, so as to be able to keep on feeling good, feeling that the new period was still a bright and hopeful one.

But, alas ! holidays come to an end ; Rowland's profession necessitated his return to Sussex, and Esmé felt that if the new period was to maintain its brightness she ought to return with him. She suffered acutely and bitterly from homesickness—she who had never known what it was before she married Rowland ! How these Averys made her suffer ! —as she unpacked in their hotel bedroom that night, and could not help complaining about the deficiencies of the room as compared with their luxurious apartment in West View. Rowland at once brought up the house question with a hopeful air, and they quarrelled as usual. Indeed the usual term-time régime was in full force, and Esmé's feeling for her husband was at its lowest ebb, when, five or six weeks later, an incident occurred which began another new period in Esmé's married life, and this time not a desirable one. It all arose from some photographs which Arnold sent of Baby Charles, showing him lying about among pillows in various stages of chubby undress. Esmé thought them rather absurd, but when Rowland came home from school he seemed to admire them immensely. He kept picking them up, holding them at arm's length, then drawing them close and peering over them ; discovering new beauties in the child, on whom he obviously doted, to the refrain of : " Fancy old Arnold having a boy like that ! "

" Yes ! he's a dear little fellow," agreed Esmé, bored. " Take your tea, Rowland."

" He's a grand little chap," boomed Rowland admiringly.

" He really is a fine little fellow. Hasn't he grown since we saw him ? Look at his knees ! Fancy Arnold with a son like that ! If I thought *we* could have a fine little lad like that, I *should* be proud."

Even as he spoke Esmé felt an awful repugnance rising within her ; awful because it was so strong, and (she felt) so wrong. She did not *want* to bear a child to Rowland ; her heart seemed to turn over within her at the thought ; she was intensely thankful that she had so far escaped doing so, and she felt she would defend herself tooth and nail, ruthlessly, at all costs, from ever having to do so. At that moment her repugnance to the idea of Rowland as the father of her child was so strong that she absolutely loathed him, and she struck out wildly in her defence with the first thing that came into her mind.

" You don't think he would be lame, then ? " she said.

Rowland started so that the photographs fell from his hand. He looked at his wife, then stooped down, picked them up and put them on the table one by one, then gazed at her again. " What do you mean, Esmé ? " he demanded at length in a strange voice. " Surely you're not so silly, so ignorant, as to think that an accident which occurred in a man's teens could be hereditary ? "

" Wouldn't it ? " said Esmé, not looking at him.

" Of course it wouldn't ! " replied Rowland roughly. " I must really borrow your own phrase, Esmé, and say : Don't be so silly."

This so infuriated Esmé that she cried out in swift anger, hardly knowing what she was saying : " Well, I don't think we ought to risk it ! "

The moment she had said this she was horrified, but she could not utter another word ; she sat with averted head through the long silence which followed. At length she could bear it no more ; finding that she could not see Rowland even out of the corner of her eyes in her present position, she gradually moved her head round, and at last faced her husband with a defiant look. He was leaning forward and gazing at her steadily, his hands clasped between his knees, his eyes black and burning, his face very white.

" Well ? " said he grimly. " What now ? What is the latest word of wisdom from Esmé ? "

" Well, Rowland," repeated Esmé pettishly, " I really *don't* think we ought."

Rowland, still gazing at her, seemed to consider this.

" Perhaps," he said presently in a quiet cool tone, " this is your way of saying that my lameness is repugnant to you, Esmé ? " Esmé, frightened and ashamed, yet suddenly wondering whether perhaps this was at the root of her unhappiness, turned away her head. Rowland sprang up. " Is it ? " he said. " Is it ? You *shall* tell me." He seized her wrists.

" Rowland, you're hurting me ! " wept Esmé.

" You *shall* tell me ! " cried Rowland, turning her bodily towards him. " You *shall* tell me, Esmé ! " His voice was terrible, and Esmé, weeping wildly, cried : " No, no ! " " You mean ' yes,' don't you ? " demanded Rowland in his booming tones. " Tell the truth for once, if you can."

This last clause maddened Esmé—why should people always assume that her moral standards were low ?—and she suddenly screamed : " Yes, it is, yes, it is ! Let me go ! "

Rowland almost threw her from him and stood upright. " Well, if it is, it was Arnold's fault," he said soberly. " The Dellers are well paid."

" What do you mean ? " wept Esmé, feeling her wrists. " How is it Arnold's fault ? " Rowland was hunting about the room and did not answer ; really curious, Esmé repeated : " How do you mean it's Arnold's fault ? "

" I didn't say anything about anything being Arnold's fault," exclaimed Rowland, turning.

" Yes, you *did*," persisted Esmé.

" No, I did *not*," shouted Rowland, glaring down at her. " You misunderstood what I said ; you're talking rubbish ; I simply meant it was a pity you didn't discover your

repugnance before you married me ; I've been Arnold's
friend long enough for you to know. Where's my hat ? "

"By the door," whispered Esmé. "Where are you
going ? "

"Don't be alarmed," said Rowland with sarcastic
courtesy, from the door. " I shall be back in time for dinner ;
but I think we're best apart just now."

Esmé, trembling and exhausted, was left alone to wonder
whether she had committed an act of determined courage
or one of baseness, and to hope that she would not have to
go through another scene that night. If she expected a scene
of pleading, she was spared her expectation, for when
Rowland returned, looking white and utterly wretched,
he terrified her by asking in a subdued but perfectly clear
manner whether she would like their marriage to end in a
legal separation. Esmé was horrified ; what an idea ! That
Esmé Deller's marriage should be exhibited to the world as
such a failure ! After a mere seven months ! Another
Deller scandal ! Everyone would say, like father like
daughter ! And what a position she would be in ! Her
negative was emphatic ; and when Rowland seemed
inclined to insist that it was the only possible course for her
happiness, she withdrew all she had previously said, and
put it down to mere temporary irritation arising from
continual sleeplessness.

"Well," said Rowland sadly at length, disregarding this,
" If you don't wish it of course we won't have a separation,
Esmé. I suppose your idea is that if we can't be lovers we
can at least be friends."

"Yes, yes ! " agreed Esmé in haste, overjoyed by this
solution. " I was only bad-tempered because I haven't
been sleeping, Rowland," she repeated pathetically. " I
never *can* sleep here. If only we could live in Hudley !
We're always ever so much happier there, aren't we ? "

Rowland gave her no cause to repeat this particular
quarrel, but thenceforward whatever the argument her
conclusion was the same, and the Christmas holidays

seemed to support it ; so that when Mr. Avery's illness opened the path for a return to Hudley by way of the Grammar School, Rowland needed very little persuasion to accept. Mrs. Avery, to Esmé's regret, opposed the scheme until Esmé wrote her a pathetic little letter, explaining that she was sure it would be for Rowland's real happiness to come to Hudley, because they were always so much happier together there. Mrs. Avery then wrote to Esmé to say that she would oppose nothing that made for Rowland's real happiness, and to Rowland to urge him to accept the Grammar School offer. The offer was accepted and the move accomplished ; after one really fearful scene with Rowland, who lost his temper and asked if he were never to have a house of his own, they settled down very comfortably indeed at West View. Rowland's opposition on this occasion was vanquished by Arnold, who seemed really anxious for them to live at West View (at any rate, until he could find the purchaser he was looking for), positively pressed it upon them and almost hinted that it was Esmé's duty to live with her mother.

A new period of Esmé's married life now began, and that it would be a happy period she felt sure ; it was delightful to be back in Hudley, where one was John Deller's rich grand-daughter, delightful to be only a short half-hour's drive from Arnold and Rachel and Oddy Hall, delightful to have her mother beside her once more. The people in the shops all knew Esmé, and she knew them, and all the streets and the roads, and everybody's family history ; and it was open and windy and without trees ; and Rowland liked working with his father and being near his relations, and so was much more cheerful, especially when their financial arrangements were put on a definite basis by the Dellers' solicitor, so that they did not have those tiresome arguments about money any more. Of course there were still a few tiresome features in the situation ; Rowland was stupidly obstinate in declaring that he could not afford to keep a car of his own, and Mrs. Deller was shocked when she discovered that her daughter and her son-in-law occupied separate rooms ; she scolded Esmé about it and dismissed her plea that it was due to her insomnia as the lie it was. But Esmé persuaded her, and almost persuaded herself, that it would all come right in time ; time could do wonders, and everything seemed most hopeful, most promising. Oh, yes ! She had been absolutely right to persuade Rowland to return to Hudley, and it was very natural that Rachel should give a dinner in their honour.

"Just the family, I suppose ? " she said when Rachel proffered the invitation at West View the week before.

" And the Howgates," said Rachel.

Esmé pouted—but good-humouredly ; she was too glad to be back in Hudley again to be anything but expansive and good-humoured. " Always the Howgates ! " she protested laughingly. Seeing Arnold's brow darken, she added in haste : " Of course I know Lena is Rachel's friend—I'm very fond of Lena too."

" It isn't only Lena," explained Arnold, dropping his voice to a conspiratorial level. " Mr. Howgate's our biggest customer, you know."

" Well, Arnold ! " said Esmé, smiling. " I'm surprised to find you've so much common sense ; I am really."

" Don't misunderstand Arnold, Esmé," put in Rachel at this, colouring a little and lifting her head. " Lena is my greatest friend ; it's only chance that Arnold's biggest customer is her father."

" And suppose he weren't Lena's father ? " said Esmé teasingly.

" Then I should have to write two invitations instead of one," said Rachel.

" And suppose the interests of Arnold's biggest customer clash with those of Lena's father ? " enquired Rowland, as usual nowadays a little grim.

" I don't see how that could be, seeing that they're the same person," said Rachel quietly after a pause.

" Ha ! Don't you ? " observed her brother. " Poor Lena ! "

" You needn't pity Lena," said Arnold. " She has a very good time of it nowadays, I can tell you." He described some of Lena's holiday jaunts, and her new car.

" I wish you hadn't said that about the wealthy Howgate, all the same, Arnold," said Rowland. " I was interested in him before as a type ; now I shall always think of him as a customer."

Arnold seemed a trifle abashed, and coloured ; and Esmé in her happiness said kindly : " Well, *I*'m more interested in him *now*, Arnie ; I never noticed him before."

" You shall sit next to him at dinner, Esmé," promised Rachel drily.

" Thank you for nothing," replied Esmé with spirit. She was really, however, quite pleased to be trusted with Arnold's biggest customer, and looked forward to the meeting with interest.

The night of the dinner came. After the usual flutter at West View—somehow there was always a flutter when one set off from West View—Rowland and Esmé and Mrs. Deller managed to leave, a little behind time. Esmé and her mother had a slight argument in the car as to whether Esmé's frock were not rather too grand for the occasion ; Rowland, to Esmé's pleasure, supported his wife on this point and said he thought they ought to do Arnold's party proud as it was in their honour ; but he spoiled the effect of this by objecting to her lips, which she had reddened. Mrs. Deller, however, thought there was no great harm in reddened lips, and urged Rowland not to be too severe ; they were not in a Sussex backwater now.

" Does geography make so much difference to morals ? I suppose it may," mused Rowland.

This reflection (so typical of all that Esmé found " silly " in her husband) seemed to console him, and they all arrived in fairly good spirits, which on Esmé's part positively soared when she discovered, by a casual glance as they

passed the drawing-room on their way upstairs, that the
party was to be a very grand one, that each of the women had
on her best frock, and that they were the last arrivals and
could make an effective entrance. She entered Rachel's
drawing-room with her customary cool grace, and thought
pleasurably that her fair little face and slender figure and
the gleaming white of her new frock must be making a
charming picture against the dark panelling of Oddy Hall.
She smiled and made pretty little speeches to her relations,
observing Alfred Howgate meanwhile out of the tail of her
eye. Presently she found herself near him and in Rachel's
company ; Rachel murmured that she supposed Esmé
remembered Mr. Howgate, and she believed Mr. Howgate
had met her sister-in-law.

" I don't know that I've ever actually met her," observed
Howgate calmly, taking Esmé's beautiful little hand into
his cold dry one. " I saw you at the christening, I believe,
Mrs. Rowland."

" Oh, yes ! You're Charles's godfather, aren't you ? "
said Esmé with one of her prettiest smiles, as Rachel left
them. " One of them, I mean."

" So it seems," said Howgate carelessly. This left Esmé
no opening to continue the subject, and for a moment she
could think of nothing to say. Howgate seemed to realise
this, for he presently went on, turning his eyes on her :
" And your husband's the other."

Something in his tone made her cheeks burn ; and
suddenly Esmé felt her heart leap up in a true and anxious
affection for her husband. For she had only to look at
Alfred Howgate—his erect " set " figure, so different from
the weedy slenderness of Esmé's generation ; his experienced
sallow face with its look of cool detachment, the cynical
smile on the full lips beneath his fair moustache, the disillusioned grey eyes beneath full lids—she had only to hear
his light drawl, which he could not be bothered to make
anything but Yorkshire in tone, his casual laugh : she had
only to look at him and hear him for one moment to feel

that she understood his point of view and was on the defensive against it. She knew at once that to this man who was Arnold's biggest customer, this wealthy man who was the son and grandson and great-grandson of wealthy men, this man who had an illegitimate daughter and adopted her and took her about with him in society without a tremor, this man who rode horses and managed Bierley Bottom Mills and Lena's destiny with the same ease and assurance —to this man Rowland and Arnold were mere schoolboys to whom one " talked down," and for whom one restricted one's conversation to subjects they could understand. At once Esmé was intensely anxious to impress him ; she wanted to show him that, though he might think Rowland a schoolboy, Rowland at any rate had a beautiful wife, which was more than *he* had managed to find for himself. She was glad she was wearing her new and exquisitely cut white gown, and that nobody else was in white ; she was glad she had reddened her lips ; she wanted to show Alfred Howgate that she was an accomplished, tasteful and elegant woman of the world, who could fascinate even *him*, and who yet belonged to Rowland Avery. She also wanted— oh, how much she wanted—that Rowland should shine ; that he should show himself to be taller and handsomer and better dressed and cleverer than Alfred Howgate, a better dancer, a more skilful bridge-player, a brighter conversationalist. With all the earnest loyalty of which her heart was capable, Esmé inwardly urged Rowland to excel at these things to-night, and all through dinner, all through the hours afterwards, she kept setting skilful little traps to enable him to show off his good qualities. But he was stupid, stupid ; he would insist on slouching so that he looked smaller than Mr. Howgate, he made a clumsy mess of dancing—with Mr. Howgate looking on—he said the oddest things about politics and finance, showing himself to be what Esmé stigmatised as " schoolmastery," meaning pedantic and narrow-minded and not a man of the world, not like other people. He had not put enough brilliantine

on his hair, thought Esmé with a frown ; he looked bushy
and uncouth beside the sparse fair well-groomed Alfred
Howgate. And then of all things, Rachel, on some ridiculous
notion of separating husbands and wives—not that she
separated herself from Arnold ! No fear !—set Esmé down
to play bridge at a table with Mr. Avery, her mother and
Alfred Howgate, and by a piece of bad luck Esmé and
Alfred Howgate cut together at once. Esmé, unlike Arnold,
was apt to overcall, Rowland after the manner of husbands
being wont to remind her of its bad results before beginning
play. His warnings were usually quite useless ; but to-night
she somehow felt that she dared not play her usual too bold
game. But why should she not, she asked herself, rallying ;
why should she mind what Alfred Howgate thought ? She
overcalled, and went down ; if any one else in the room had
been her partner, they would have teased her about it—
they would have teased her mildly, of course, but they
would certainly have teased her. Howgate, however, merely
gave a lazy smile and made no remark ; he did not even
trouble to raise his eyebrows, did not even look at her.
He despised her too much to bother ; he despised them
all, considered them all school-children, thought Esmé
angrily. She quite panted with her efforts to show
him what a brilliant young piece of modernity she was,
and how devoted to her husband. And then, in the
very midst of these sparkling improvisations, Mr. Avery
exclaimed :

" You're very perverse to-night, Esmé ! "

" Oh, Will ! " said Mrs. Deller at once, " she's a very
naughty girl, she is indeed."

Perverse ! Naughty ! This was all the thanks she got for
supporting them all against Alfred Howgate's superior
worldliness ! Her mother's phrase, too, had been used so
often lately in connection with Esmé's relations with
Rowland that to Esmé it *meant* those aspects of her married
life which were not what they ought to be. She winced at
this public exposure, and faltering : " You're very unkind,

mother," hung her head to hide the tears which sprang into
her eyes.

" Is someone attacking my wife ? " boomed Rowland at
this from the other table. " If so, let them beware ! "

" Thank you, Rowland," said Esmé, really grateful.
Yes, Rowland was solid, Rowland was reliable, Rowland
was kind ; Rowland was her husband, and she was prepared to be a good wife to him to the limits of her endurance ;
nobody should say that Esmé Deller was not a good wife.
If he should attempt a reconciliation that night she would
not repulse him ; she shot a defiant glance at Alfred
Howgate from beneath her quivering lids, and began to
talk, to laugh, to make any serious play impossible.

Unfortunately Rowland did not attempt what his wife
defined as a reconciliation that night, though he gave
Esmé hopes that he would do so by following her to her
room. Instead he said quietly :

" I think in future we'd better consider that I don't
dance, Esmé."

Esmé, astonished and aghast, said : " Why ? "

" You don't enjoy dancing with me," explained Rowland,
his face very white. " And I don't enjoy dancing with
anybody else. So there we are. It's silly of me to attempt it
in any case."

" Oh, Rowland ! " said Esmé sorrowfully. " I didn't
mean to hurt your feelings with what I said about the
dancing."

" I don't suppose you did," replied her husband in a
tired voice, his hands hanging straight down by his side so
that he looked somehow hopeless. " But it's always the
same thing, isn't it ? I won't dance any more."

" I didn't mean to hurt you ; I only wanted you to do it
specially well before—everybody," explained Esmé, winc-
ing with remorse at his reference to his lameness, but somehow unable to make her explanation complete by bringing
out Alfred Howgate's name. She went up to her husband,
put her arms round his neck, kissed him, and ran one hand

caressingly over his hair. " I wish you'd put more brilliantine on, Rowland," she said, remembering her earlier
impression. " I bought you a new bottle last week ; it's in
your bathroom ; do use it more. You'd look so much nicer
if you would. Really your hair's getting quite grey."

Rowland took this very badly ; he disengaged himself
roughly from her embrace and left her. Esmé wept and was
very miserable as she undressed ; the passionate impulse
of loyalty which had driven her on all the evening seemed
only to have widened the breach between herself and her
husband. Things so often seemed to happen like that with
her. She slept badly, dreaming fitfully of Rowland, Arnold
and Alfred Howgate opposing each other in impossible
dramas, and awoke with a bad headache and a feeling of
wretchedness.

The weeks between Rachel's dinner and the Howgates'
garden-party somehow seemed to Esmé to have slipped by
while she was not looking. It was not that they were a blank
—oh, no ! they were full of incidents and feelings—but that
when she came to look back on them she could not remember just how and when everything happened ; they were a
confused, chaotic jumble. She had stood there and thought
thus and thus ; now she stood here and thought, oh ! so
differently ; but how she had reached this position from
that, how and when she had crossed the tremendous gulf
which she undoubtedly had crossed, Esmé did not know
had not the slightest notion ; she could not rescue that
fatal moment from her confused recollection. There was a
morning—perhaps the morning after Rachel's dinner—a
close, dull, misty morning when the sky looked like grey
wool and seemed to weigh down upon Esmé's head and
make everything terribly hopeless and boring, when Esmé
and Mrs. Deller, moving down a Hudley street on their
everlasting shopping, had seen Alfred Howgate standing on
the steps of the Hudley Club, talking to Arnold, who had
his back to the street. Howgate was wearing one of the dark
grey suits he affected—but how did Esmé know he affected

them ? Perhaps after all this was later than the day after Rachel's dinner—and an old-fashioned cravat of stiff silk which somehow gave him a sporting appearance, Esmé did not know why ; he was carrying his gloves in one hand, and leaning on his stick in a jocular fashion ; Arnold was speaking eagerly, while Howgate listened in silence ; presently he put up his other hand and touched his eyebrow in a reflective fashion with his glove. Now he saw them, raised his hat and gave that cool polite smile which Esmé found so scornful ; Arnold turned and saw them too, and came down the steps towards them ; Howgate, however, with another polite smile went away into the inaccessible male precincts of the Club. Esmé perhaps remembered this incident because it seemed to brighten the day, or perhaps because it was so typical of Alfred Howgate—he always seemed to be moving away into something inaccessibly male. Then there was the morning when Esmé and her mother, just as they were entering the café for their usual cup of coffee, saw Howgate pass by up the hill in his large closed car beside his chauffeur. He was past in a moment, and had barely time to show that he saw them ; nevertheless Esmé felt that his light grey eyes had taken in her, her mother, the café and all the other adjuncts of the scene, and she was not really surprised when a few days later she saw him there, having coffee with Arnold, who as usual was talking eagerly. As Howgate was facing the door, it was natural that he should see them first, but if he saw them—and Esmé thought that he did—he concealed it ; his face remained calm and expressionless, with no trace of recognition, until they passed into Arnold's line of sight and he exclaimed and rose to attract his mother's attention. After that these morning meetings took place rather often. But that too must have been later ; surely that came later than the morning when Esmé and Mrs. Deller, driving back from a visit to Oddy Hall to inspect Charles, who was said to be not so well, saw Alfred Howgate galloping across a Bierley field. Esmé slightly slowed the car so that they should meet him at

the corner ; Alfred Howgate merely bowed, smiled, raised
his hat, and galloped away. Esmé for some obscure reason
felt piqued ; he looked extremely well on horseback ; Esmé
supposed that he had a good seat or however one described
it, and riding clothes suited him. The next day was wet, but
on the next she found herself driving to Oddy Hall about
the same time to enquire again about Charles. Rachel was
astonished to see her, for Charles was again enjoying his
normal superb health. Esmé decided not to return by the
tram route down Awe Hill, which after all led one into such
a busy part of the town ; she turned to the right and went
round by Bierley Hall and Bierley Lane instead. As she
turned down the Lane she saw Alfred Howgate at a distance, attended by a mounted groom. On the following
Sunday, after church, Mrs. Deller and Esmé called in at
Oddy Hall ; they found the Howgates already there, drinking cocktails and admiring Charles, who was just beginning
to discover the charms of crawling. The talk was lively and
general ; beneath its cover Esmé observed to her neighbour :
    " Do you ride every morning, Mr. Howgate ? "
    Howgate, without moving from his lounging position in
one of Arnold's uncomfortable chairs, glanced at her and
replied carelessly : " It depends."
    Esmé, feeling rebuffed but determined not to show it,
went on brightly : " I saw you trotting along on Thursday
morning."
    " Trotting ! " exclaimed Howgate. " Trotting ! "
    " Isn't that the right word ? " demanded Esmé, angry.
" I'm sorry."
    " Oh, well ! " said Howgate in a lenient and forgiving
tone, " it's near enough for a young woman, I daresay.
Lena's just as bad."
    " If you'd explain the difference to me, I've no doubt I
should understand," said Esmé haughtily, vexed at being
put on a level with Lena.
    " Not you," replied Howgate on a teasing note. " You've
got a head like a sieve for everything but frills and

furbelows, I don't doubt." He laughed a little as he spoke, and gave Esmé a half-contemptuous, half-admiring look from beneath his heavy lids.

" I haven't ! " exclaimed Esmé, colouring, but not altogether with displeasure. " Why should you have such a low opinion of me, Mr. Howgate ? "

" *I* haven't a low opinion of you, Mrs. Rowland," replied Howgate with exaggerated deference. " I never hinted at such a thing."

" You did ! " cried Esmé, smiling. " You said I had a head like a sieve."

" Only for the difference between a trot and a canter," said Howgate, smiling back.

" Well, explain the difference to me now," commanded Esmé, with her prettiest queenly air. " And then we'll see."

" I can't without a horse," protested Howgate, laughing.

" I don't believe you," said Esmé superbly. " You won't explain because you don't think I'm worth explaining to, that's what it is. And I think it's very unkind of you, very."

She gave him a sparkling glance and turned away.

" Bless me ! What a storm in a teacup ! " murmured Howgate with amusement.

" Well, it was you who began it," cried Esmé, turning on him. Feeling that this was a little undignified, she changed her tone and said seriously : " I suppose you occasionally ride on Hudley Moor as well as up here at Bierley, Mr. Howgate ? "

" No, I can't say I do," replied Howgate, bending down to rescue Charles's ball, which had rolled beneath his chair.

" But why don't you ? A lot of other people do ; I often see them," persisted Esmé.

" I daresay," said Howgate indifferently. He rolled the ball to the eager Charles, and said : " Catch it, boy," to him in an encouraging tone.

Esmé, who was used to ending conversations when she wished and not before, felt rebuffed and irritated. " Rowland, do mind your foot against Charles's arm," she called.

Rowland, startled, moved abruptly, and the child received
a slight knock. " There ! I knew he'd cry," said Esmé.

That this Sunday must have occurred shortly after
Rachel's dinner Esmé knew, for there seemed to have been
so many of these Oddy Hall Sundays between it and the
garden-party. There was the Sunday when they were all
out in the Oddy Hall garden admiring the roses, and Lena,
turning her car in the drive after putting down her father,
nearly ran over Esmé's foot. Howgate seized her arm and
jerked her vigorously backward just in time. Esmé felt very
much shaken—more so perhaps than her danger warranted
—and said fretfully : " Lena, you *should* be more careful ! "
Rowland (who would stand up for anyone sooner than his
wife, thought Esmé irritably) thereupon exclaimed :
" Esmé, it was your own fault entirely."

" It was *not* my fault ! " objected Esmé, almost in tears.
Lena, greatly agitated, flew out of the car and seemed to
wish to feel Esmé's foot to assure herself that it was still
whole. " It's perfectly all right, Lena," said Esmé, much
irritated. " Please leave me alone." Howgate who still held
Esmé's arm in a firm grip, steered her away towards the
house. The others had begun to talk about the roses again
and did not notice, and he steered her away into the drawing-room, plumped her down into the most comfortable
chair, and fetched her some wine from one of the decanters
which were waiting till the guests should tire of the flowers.
Esmé found that her hands shook, and sipped the wine
thankfully.

" Better now, eh ? " said Howgate in his light careless
tones, looking down at her.

Esmé said yes, she was quite all right now, and ready to
go out into the garden again. Howgate, however, did not
move from his position by the empty hearth, in front of
which stood one of Rachel's tallest brass vases with sprays
of delphinium. He put his hand behind the tip of one of the
sprays, and without touching it moved his hand about so
as to show up its blooms one by one. This occupation

seemed to engross him, and he was silent; Esmé tried to
command herself sufficiently to rise and cross the room to
the door, but she could not manage it; her eyes followed
Howgate's signet-ring as it gleamed among the flowers.
The silence somehow grew tense; Esmé moistened her lips
and tried to speak but could not; she hardly knew whether
to be glad or sorry when Mr. Avery suddenly blundered in.
He was dazzled by the change into shadow from the sunshine without, and did not at first see the two occupants of
the room; when he did perceive them he looked rather surprised, for he had not been a witness of Lena's carelessness
with the car.

"Mrs. Rowland nearly had her ankle run over," explained Howgate at once genially, "and she felt a bit dazed
by the shock."

"Really!" said Mr. Avery, concerned. "I've come for
my grandson's ball," he added with a smile, looking round.

Esmé rose and found it for him, then putting her arm
affectionately through his, went out with him into the
garden.

Yes, that Sunday too must have been not very long after
Rachel's dinner-party, for there seemed to have been many
many Sundays since then. It was now quite the established
thing for the Averys and Dellers to run up to Oddy Hall on
Sunday morning—Esmé drove Rowland, while Mrs. Deller
in the large car called for Mr. and Mrs. Avery—and as
often as not the Howgates were already there, Lena looking
hot and untidy, sprawling about on the floor with Charles,
Alfred Howgate calm and spruce, sitting in a chair with his
legs crossed and a cocktail or a cigar in one hand, surveying
the scene with an amused smile and calling her Mrs.
Rowland. (Somehow Esmé detested that name from him.)
There was not enough level ground at Oddy Hall to make
a tennis court, but Arnold in a burst of enthusiasm caused
by the fine weather laid out a putting course, and all his
guests except Alfred Howgate and Esmé made good use of
it. These two non-players—Esmé protested she could not,

RT

and Howgate observed pleasantly that he would not, play
—spent quite a lot of minutes sitting in Arnold's new swing
deck-chairs side by side, with an array of gaudy cushions
about them. At first on these occasions they chatted quite a
lot—Esmé of course making the pace—and presently became sufficiently friendly to warrant Esmé's asking him to
call her by her first name.

"Why should I?" demanded Howgate in his light
jocular tones. "We're no relation that I know of."

"You call Rachel by her first name," objected Esmé,
pouting.

"Rachel's Lena's friend," replied Howgate shortly.

"Am I not Lena's friend too?" demanded Esmé.

Howgate looked at her. "Nay, I reckon there's no love
lost between you and Lena," he said.

"Well, it's not *my* fault," protested Esmé virtuously.

Howgate looked at her again and laughed. Esmé waited
for him to speak, but he said nothing, devoting himself to
his cigar.

"Mr. Howgate," she said at length in a prettily peremp-
tory tone, "are you going to call me by my first name or
are you not?"

"Well, I'll try what I can do," replied Howgate lazily,
"but I'm not much good at these modern names, you
know."

In the event he called her Esmé when they were alone,
Mrs. Rowland when the others were there, which was not
quite what Esmé had intended. Or was it? Looking back
at it now Esmé was not quite sure. After those first chatty,
lively Sundays there came Sundays when they simply sat
side by side basking in the sunshine and saying absolutely
nothing. Perhaps they had exhausted all they had to say
at their meetings during the week. For Esmé now rather
often found herself in the neighbourhood of Bierley Green
between twelve and one o'clock, and as Alfred Howgate
always rode during that hour, naturally they quite often
met. Esmé drew up her car at some corner or other (usually

a different one from day to day) with a casual little smile, Howgate reined in his fine bay mare—who sometimes resented this and danced about on her dangerous-looking hoofs, frightening Esmé and causing Howgate to laugh at her fright—and they exchanged half a dozen sentences. They spoke about the weather, Rachel, Charles, Mrs. Deller, and the view ; Arnold, Rowland and Lena never entered the conversation. Esmé learned the name of the mare, but when she one day brought some sugar for her Howgate simply galloped away, laughing heartily. Esmé drove off in a fury, and it was several days before she went round by Bierley Green again. When she did, and encountered Howgate, he simply touched his hat with his whip and rode by. Next day, however, they met at West View, as Mrs. Deller was entertaining ; and Esmé, who had been thinking hard, managed delicately to indicate, when she got Howgate to herself, that everybody had one subject on which they could not bear either teasing or false sentiment : the Averys, she said, were Lena's ; her own was Arnold ; she skilfully hinted that it might perhaps be inferred that Howgate's was horses, and that was why he would not drive a car. Howgate did not take this up at the time, but later he mumbled : " So you're very fond of your brother ? Jealous of him perhaps ? Eh ? " Esmé's eyes flashed and her breast heaved ; Howgate looked shrewdly at her, and then remarked with a sigh : " Well, life's very odd sometimes."

" But you like it, Mr. Howgate, don't you ? " said Esmé, turning her beautiful eyes full upon him. " You like life ? "

" As well as most people, I daresay," replied Howgate shortly. " But what do you know about life, Mrs. Rowland ? " he went on in a tone of raillery. " You're a mere child ; you don't know any more than young Charles there. How old are you, eh ? " Esmé told him. " I'm nearly twice that," he said.

" Are you really ? " cried Esmé. She was genuinely surprised. " I don't believe it ! " she said.

" Well, you can knock four or five years off if you like,"
conceded Howgate. There was a pause ; Esmé was busy
with calculations. "You'd best do it on your fingers,"
suggested Howgate with an amused glance at her preoccupied face. " I reckon arithmetic isn't the Dellers' strong
point." Esmé blushed and laughed and hung her head.
Howgate stroked the corner of his eyebrow in the characteristic gesture which Esmé had noticed for the first time
that day on the steps of the Hudley Club. " You haven't
been up to Bierley Green much lately," he observed.

Somehow Esmé did not remind him that she had been
there the day before ; somehow, too, all the fine days which
followed in the next few weeks found her there. She regarded Howgate as a lonely man—how could a man be
anything but lonely who lived with Lena ?—and it was
quite a good deed to cheer him up by a few minutes' chat.
On her way back she was wont to call at the Grammar
School and pick up Rowland, who was very much touched
and pleased by this wifely attention. It made a great deal
of difference to his mere comfort, as well as to his happiness,
for he left school at half-past twelve and had to return by
half-past two ; West View was a good walk across Hudley
Moor, and he still said he could not afford to keep a car.
As Esmé was always in a good temper when she thus gave
him a lift, Rowland enjoyed this new custom very much
indeed, and Mrs. Deller encouraged it.

And then there came the day of the Howgates' garden-
party. When the invitation came, Rowland had charged
Esmé to accept for him, but explain to Lena verbally that
he could not arrive till somewhat late ; it was understood
that the Deller car should take Mrs. Deller and Esmé and
then return for Rowland and his father. In the morning
Esmé rather hesitated whether to go to Bierley Green or
not ; it seemed perhaps a little unnecessary, a little excessive.
But after some indecision she went, and met Howgate as
usual. As their few minutes' talk together drew near its
end, Howgate observed :

" Well, I suppose we shall be seeing you all this afternoon, then ? "

Esmé, remembering that she had omitted to give Rowland's message to Lena because she hated any close intercourse with Lena, pouted, and replied : " Rowland can't arrive till very late."

" But you won't wait for him, I don't suppose," said Howgate drily.

His emphasis on the pronouns was slight but unmistakable, and Esmé coloured. Why should he assume she would not wait for her husband ? In a natural reaction she dropped her hand to the gears, and said : " I must be going now."

" Why must you ? " enquired Howgate with some irritation. " You've a minute or two yet. Don't be in such a hurry."

Esmé at once took off the brake, let out the clutch and put the car in gear, but found that she simply dare not put in the clutch and drive away. A deep blush scalded her cheeks, her ears, her neck, her breast ; she hung her head, and sat beneath Howgate's eyes drenched in scarlet.

" What's the matter ? " he enquired in a tone of amusement. As she did not, could not, answer, he went on : " Vexed, eh ? " Esmé still was silent, and her vexation seemed to spread to her companion. " Oh, well ! " he exclaimed, touching his hat, " I won't keep you from your husband any longer. Good morning, Mrs. Rowland Avery." The mare's hoofs thudded on the grass, and he was gone.

Esmé, almost weeping with humiliation, at once drove rapidly off down Bierley Lane. It infuriated her to find that Howgate was right and she was too early ; as she sat outside the school gates waiting for her husband, a tumult raged in her heart. How dared any man assume that she—she, Esmé Deller (she never thought of herself as Esmé Avery)—would of course leave her husband behind to go to *his* entertainment ? How had Howgate obtained such an ascendancy over her that he dared suggest such a thing ? How had he gained such an ascendancy, such an almost physical ascendancy, over her, that she dared not drive her car away when he said nay ? She wanted Rowland or Arnold or Rachel, or somebody belonging to the old days, to reassure her quickly that all was well, nothing had happened, nothing had changed, everything was just as it used to be, Howgate was still merely Lena's father, an outsider scarcely on the fringe of their little family group, the only group which counted with Esmé. Why did not Rowland come quickly ? By the time he came, limping rapidly down the school yard amid a herd of boys, Esmé had worked herself into such a fever that she cried out fretfully : " Rowland, you *are* late ! "

Rowland's face at once clouded, but he replied mildly. " I don't think so," he said. " Am I ? "

" Why should I say you were if you weren't ? " demanded Esmé, driving away. " You *are* late ; I've been waiting ages for you. Rowland," she continued on a softer note as they turned off across Hudley Moor, " I do want you to come to the garden-party at the proper time this afternoon."

" My dear, I can't," began Rowland.

" I want you to come *with me*," continued Esmé, disregarding him. " Can't you get off for once ? "

" If you'd mentioned it sooner I might possibly have done so," said Rowland with a harassed air. " But now I can't. I can't really, Esmé. It would cause an amount of inconvenience totally unjustifiable for a garden-party. I'll leave the minute school's over," he added soothingly.

" Couldn't Mr. Avery stay away from the garden-party and do your work ? " suggested Esmé.

" More likely I should stay away and do his," said Rowland with a worried look. " I don't think he'll go to the Howgates' ; he isn't too well to-day."

" Rowland, I think you *might* come to please me ! " cried Esmé.

" But what *does* it matter ? " demanded Rowland, beginning to be irritated. " It isn't as though you were going to

strangers, or for the first time. In any case, you've your
mother to support you, and Arnold."

"Yes, that's true," agreed Esmé, feeling that she was
beginning to make a fool of herself by her insistence. And
for what, after all ? A mere chimæra ! She put it resolutely
from her as they turned into the West View gates, and kept
it at bay all through lunch. She then offered to run round
to Cambridge Place and take Mr. Avery down to school ;
Rowland's astonished delight at this piece of thoughtfulness
wounded her, but she carried it out punctually, and put
the two Averys, father and son, down together at the
Grammar School with a feeling of warm pleasure at her
own virtue. When she returned she found Mrs. Deller
already in the throes of her complicated garden-party
toilet. "Surely it's not time to dress yet, mother ! " she
exclaimed.

"We ought to start about three," replied Mrs. Deller
briskly. Three events—John Deller's death, Charles's birth,
and the return of Rowland and Esmé to Hudley—had
made Mrs. Deller a happy woman ; she joyfully allowed
herself to be dragged at the chariot-wheels of the next
generation and took pleasure in their doings alone.

Esmé went to her own room, took out her new frock and
hat and shoes—yes ! she had positively bought a new frock
for this detestable garden-party ; she had looked forward
to it immensely, had wanted to see Bierley Hall and shine
there. She began now to change, flinging her discarded
clothes sulkily about the room, but suddenly stopped, revolted. "You won't wait for *him*, I don't suppose," Howgate had said. Oh, it was insulting, insulting ! The blood
rushed to Esmé's face now at the mere thought of it ; she
felt that it was physically impossible for her to appear at
Bierley Hall that afternoon without Rowland by her side.
If she did so appear, she felt, it would be a complete victory
for Howgate, a complete surrender, defeat, humiliation
for her. But a surrender of what, a victory and a defeat in
what battle, she asked herself ; and sank down on the

window-seat to find the answer. Unfortunately the answer was only too clear ; and it was this which made the day of the garden-party such an unforgettable, horrible day, a day which necessarily inaugurated a new period in Esmé's life. For it seemed to her that somewhere, sometime, at some fatal point between Rachel's dinner-party and to-day, she had slipped over the boundary of what was natural and allowable in her conduct to Howgate into the land of the wrong and improper. She had not the vaguest notion how it had happened, but really anyone who had a nasty mind might easily say that she had been meeting Howgate clandestinely during the last few weeks ! The notion was absurd, of course, but still ! The fearful, terrible part of it was that Howgate evidently did not think the notion absurd ; " You won't wait for him, I don't suppose," he had said, implying that where *he* was concerned, in Esmé's estimation Rowland was nowhere. He expected her to put on a new frock (thought Esmé rather unjustly) and rush off to his garden-party early, leaving her husband to trail along later by himself. Well, she would not do it. Definitely she would not do it ; if Rowland had not the sense and the manners to come early with her, she would be a faithful, loyal wife at some cost to her courtesy, and go late with him. Was Alfred Howgate so presumptuous, so utterly misled by his own conceit, as to imagine that she—she, Esmé Deller—would forget her duty as a wife for his sake ? Esmé might be a little cross, a little tiresome, a little selfish and a little naughty, she might perhaps be a little unfortunate in her marriage, a little difficult in finding herself unable to love her husband just as much as she ought ; Esmé would admit that ; but if anyone imagined that she was of that false, heartless type which breaks up homes and trifles in men's hearts, if anyone imagined that Esmé Deller, Arnold's sister, was going to carry on an intrigue with a man behind her husband's back—well, they were wrong, hopelessly, ludicrously wrong. The notion was absurd, and the man who had such a notion was absurd. Esmé devoted

two or three minutes to regarding Alfred Howgate as
ludicrous and absurd. But alas ! she could not do it ; it
was useless for her to tell herself that he was old enough to
be her father, with all those characteristics of middle age
which she usually found so boring and ridiculous ; he was
not ludicrous, he was not absurd, in her eyes, and to account for this to her own satisfaction she was obliged to go
one step further in her painful argument. Let me be quite
frank, Esmé urged herself, let me be absolutely candid ;
I must face this absolutely honestly and probe it to its depths,
and so I may as well admit that Alfred Howgate has an
attraction for me, yes, a strong, one might almost call it a
physical, attraction. Some people, she admitted recklessly,
might even go so far as to say that I fell in love with him
the moment I met him in Rachel's drawing-room—but
that of course would be going too far. All that Esmé would
admit on that score was that at some point between Rachel's
dinner-party and to-day she had become more interested
in Alfred Howgate than as a good wife she ought to be. It
was a mere interest, a mere passing fancy, of course, thought
Esmé, becoming quite light-hearted and cynical about the
matter now that she had got to the bottom of it ; but it had
better stop, for it gave rise to mistaken notions, such notions for instance as the one which had caused Howgate
to say : " You won't wait for *him*, I don't suppose," that
morning. She coloured again at the memory of that moment ; she would remember it with humiliation for months,
thought Esmé angrily.

Mrs. Deller, coming into the room at this point in gala
attire, was astounded to find her daughter sitting by the
open window half-dressed, with an angry flush on her
cheeks ; she enquired in alarm what was the matter.

" It's no use getting ready yet," observed Esmé crossly.
" Rowland can't leave till half-past four."

Mrs. Deller exclaimed ; surely it was understood that
they were to leave alone at three.

" *You* can go without Rowland if you wish, mother,"

said Esmé in a dignified tone. " It's your car of course, and you must do as you wish ; but *I* shall wait for my husband."

Mrs. Deller, quite disconcerted, exclaimed again, argued and expostulated ; Esmé stubbornly repeated her decision ; the argument grew acrimonious ; Mrs. Deller said it would look so *odd*, and seeing that Esmé winced at this, pursued the theme ; Esmé at last consented to dress, and with her charming face contorted by scarcely repressed tears, slowly and reluctantly did so. It was a quarter to four by the time she was ready, and Esmé evolved a fiction that Rowland had said he might be able to leave by four ; she almost persuaded herself that it was true, so earnestly did she plead it, and the perplexed Mrs. Deller was quite overborne ; they therefore hastily mounted into the car, which had been standing at the front door since three o'clock, and rushed across to the Grammar School. They had not been there five minutes before it became obvious, by the quiet hum of classes within, that Esmé's fiction *was* a fiction, and their position, as they continued sitting there in the sun by the gate, became ridiculous. Esmé's cheeks quite burned with the ridicule of it, and when the school porter advanced to them and asked if he could do anything for them she wished the floor of the car would open and conceal her. Mrs. Deller suggested that they should send in a message to Rowland. Esmé cried : " No, no ! " but the porter had already gone off with alacrity. After a horrible pause, during which Esmé had time to reflect that Rowland would be furious, he returned to say that Mr. Avery senior had gone home, as he was not too well, and young Mr. Avery was sorry, but he could not leave till half-past four, and he would be glad if the ladies would proceed without him.

" There ! " said Mrs. Deller with justifiable vexation. " You were wrong, Esmé, I knew you were. We'll go straight to Bierley Hall at once."

" Oh, no, mother ! " pleaded Esmé piteously. " We can't turn up without Rowland at this time. We shall have to wait and take him now, to justify our being so late."

This was only too true, and Mrs. Deller admitted it by an embarrassed sigh. " Have we to sit here for another half-hour, then ? " she demanded. " In this sun ? "

" We can just drive round the Moor a little," suggested the hapless Esmé.

Mrs. Deller almost with a groan gave the order, and the chauffeur drove them solemnly twice round Hudley Moor, bringing them back to the school gates on the stroke of half-past four. Rowland came out promptly when the school bell sounded, and hurried towards the car ; he looked displeased, and when he perceived his wife and mother-in-law within, his face darkened still further. He said not one word to either of them, but climbed into the front seat and shut the door himself (a habit of his which Esmé detested). Esmé, her heart beating painfully, hoped that they would reach Bierley Hall without any further discussion about the time, but unfortunately Mrs. Deller plunged them all into one.

" Well, Rowland ! " she began, and went off into a long rigmarole about the exasperations of the afternoon.

" I'm sorry you've been inconvenienced, Mrs. Deller," said Rowland coldly. " Very. But it is not my fault ; I told Esmé definitely that I could not leave till half-past four."

He was obviously very angry indeed ; and Esmé, sick at heart, wondered how it was that whereas when Howgate was angry, as he had been that morning, she felt afraid in every limb, when Rowland was angry she merely felt provoked to say the most cutting things she could think of. She began to do this now in her fretfullest tone, accusing her husband of being thoughtless of her mother's comfort— " and after all it's her car." An unpleasing family wrangle occupied them as the car sped onwards, which changed into an attack by Esmé on the chauffeur when she saw that he was taking them the long way round by the tram route, instead of up Bierley Lane. The chauffeur did not like the surface and the gradient of Bierley Lane, and said so.

"It looks as though our car couldn't take the hill!" protested Esmé.

"It looks nothing of the sort," said Rowland hotly. "Besides, what does it matter how a thing looks if it isn't so? Don't be childish, Esmé."

At this Esmé burst into angry tears. Mrs. Deller followed suit; they had barely dried their eyes when the car drew up at the Hall. Lena, looking really rather handsome in a weird but graceful frock of her inevitable rose-colour— "Since Rachel took her in hand she dresses quite well," thought Esmé—advanced to meet them, and Esmé made the party's excuses for being late. She could see that this vexed Rowland more than ever, and she resented his vexation bitterly. "I'm doing it all for him," she thought, "and this is how he treats me!" But in spite of his ingratitude she would continue to be a good wife to him, she resolved virtuously; she was glad she had waited for him, in spite of the trials of the afternoon: she looked forward to seeing Howgate's expression as he greeted them standing side by side. Howgate was coming towards them now; his eyes were partly hidden by his heavy lids; his expression was cold and indifferent. And at once Esmé knew that she simply could not stand by Rowland's side and greet Howgate in a calm society tone; she could not, she could not, her throat contracted at the thought; looking wildly round she perceived Lena moving off in search of some tea for the late-comers; in a panic she flew after her. Howgate's glance, insolently quizzical, rested on her for a moment as she went; Esmé hastily in a loud voice said something about their being late—in her agitation she really hardly knew what— and quickened her step. Her heart was beating so unpleasantly fast that it was a real relief to find herself in the cool dining-room, and she was immensely glad when Lena took her hint about their having tea there together. After a moment or two she began to collect herself and look about; and then her heart sank still lower, into a kind of settled despair. For the room was so terribly expressive of Alfred

Howgate. The enormous gleaming mahogany furniture, the horse's hoof mounted in silver, the racing cups, all spoke of him ; the portrait over the mantelpiece which Lena said was Howgate's mother had the same full lids, the same insolent powerful air, as this man whom Esmé was growing to fear—it was like Lena too, and Esmé said so, but Lena did not receive this as the compliment it was meant to be. Yes, every detail of Bierley Hall breathed its owner ; Esmé felt suffocated, longed to escape into a freer air. She was glad when Lena suggested tennis, and accepted willingly, thinking that she would thus avoid speech with Howgate ; but he stood by the court talking to Mrs. Avery and Rowland, and her performance was ludicrously incompetent. When the set was over, another four players were urged upon the court by Lena ; Esmé, to show how little she cared about her abominable play, went about with great enthusiasm retrieving balls. On returning from one of her little excursions into the bushes she found Howgate standing in her path. He took the ball from her unresisting hand and threw it over the wire netting on to the court, then observed with a lazy smile :

" So we're having a quarrel ! "

" Now he's going to say he's sorry," thought Esmé gleefully, and her spirits soared : everything looked different, and she was once again thoroughly in command of her destiny, as she always had been. She thought she knew well the way to handle an incipient apology from a man so as to make him humble himself still further ; so she put on her haughtiest little air, and said coldly : " Are we ? "

" Nay, it's for you to say," replied Howgate with cheerful casualness. " If you say we aren't, we aren't. It's nothing to me either way." He turned away from her, cried " Good shot ! " to Rachel, who was playing with her usual serene vigour, and walked off.

The baffled and wounded Esmé was unfortunately obliged to go in the same direction, the path being only a

cul-de-sac. This appearance of following Howgate maddened her, and as soon as she had disentangled herself from
the bushes she went to her husband's side and said she was
tired and would like to go home. Rowland with a dark look
—" Really he's getting very bad-tempered lately ! "
thought poor Esmé—enquired if she were serious, and
being assured that she was, obediently hunted up the
Deller car from the long string which was beginning to form
in Bierley Lane, and collected Mrs. Deller and his mother.
The party made their farewells, Mrs. Deller with her face
quite puckered with disappointment at having to leave this
agreeable entertainment so early after coming so late, Mrs.
Avery quiet and sombre, as usual. (" Why does she always
have that unsatisfied brooding look ? " thought Esmé critic-
ally. " Rowland's beginning to look the same.") Esmé
managed to avoid shaking Howgate's hand by being very
affectionate with Lena, putting her hand within Lena's
arm and keeping her in earnest conversation until the two
elder ladies were seated and Rowland displayed slight signs
of impatience by the open door, so that Esmé had to break
away in a sudden pretty flutter. Howgate stood by watching all this, and Esmé was pleased with her little triumph in
not bidding him farewell ; she felt she had paid him back
for the incident of the path. " He's a bad man," thought
Esmé as the car rolled away, " and I detest him. Or at
least, if I don't perhaps detest him, he's dangerous for me
and I must keep away from him. I ought to be reconciled
to Rowland," she concluded with a sigh, and at once began
the good work. She smiled at her husband, became very
lively and chatty about the garden-party, asked his opinion
on many points of detail, and agreed with it when given,
pressed Mrs. Avery to come and have supper at West View,
and when she would not, because of Mr. Avery alone at
home, sent her love to Mr. Avery with great gusto. Finally
when they reached West View and were faced with a long
bright evening with nothing to do in it and an after-the-
party feeling to do it with, Esmé put her arm about her

husband's shoulders, picked a hair from his coat-collar caressingly, and suggested they should go for a walk.

" A walk ! " exclaimed Rowland. " I thought you were tired."

" I was tired of the party," explained Esmé hastily. " So much noise and glare."

" You're a capricious young female, aren't you ? " said Rowland.

He nevertheless took her out for a walk, but his manner was cold, weary and unresponsive. Esmé felt that he realised the essential falsity of her endearments, of which indeed she was herself ashamed. But she persisted in them with all the strength of purpose of which she was capable ; an abyss had yawned at her feet, and she had stepped definitely back from it : she was determined to be a decent woman and a good wife, determined to love Rowland. She even ventured that very night to propose a physical reconciliation.

" You don't really want it, Esmé," Rowland told her sadly. " You're only trying to be good."

Esmé pouted, and let him see that even in that case her impulse might surely be taken advantage of.

" You'd regret it again, and I couldn't stand that," said Rowland.

" Well," said Esmé, seeing that she could do nothing with him on this point as yet, " if we can't be lovers, Rowland, we can at least be friends."

As this was his own phrase Rowland perforce agreed. She offered him her cheek, he kissed it gravely and withdrew to the room Esmé had equipped as a study for him. He had work to do, he said ; but Esmé suspected that he sat up to all hours of the night, reading.

In spite of this rather discouraging beginning Esmé adhered to her resolution staunchly ; she avoided Bierley Green entirely and Oddy Hall whenever possible, and instead haunted Cambridge Place ; she kept her mother always at her side ; she tried at first even to refuse Rachel's invitations, but Rowland seemed so astounded and

unhappy at this that she could not persist in it without
arousing his suspicions. When she met Howgate at Oddy Hall
she determinedly avoided him—and to do him justice he
seemed to avoid her—though she was painfully conscious
that, the moment she saw him, life, from being drab, seemed
to flush to a rich deep hue. The strain she was putting on
herself made her irritable, so that in her treatment of her
husband she varied abruptly from the effusive to the snappish ; she knew this, tried to curb her tongue and sometimes
succeeded but more often failed, and sick at heart struggled
along the path of faithfulness as best she might. The end
of the term approached ; if she could but last out till the
holidays she and Rowland would go away, to Devonshire
perhaps, at any rate a long way away from Bierley Hall.
Unfortunately Rowland was always rather cross at the end
of the term ; he had a lot of work to do, was always to be seen
surrounded by stacks of silly papers, and looked white and
haggard. Esmé, who at the bottom of her heart disliked
the fact that her husband was a schoolmaster, and was
always uncomfortable in an academic atmosphere, found
it difficult to be suitably sympathetic.

Nevertheless she tried hard, and all might have been well
if Arnold had not driven rather forcibly into the gate-post
of the Oddy Hall garage, and put his car out of action for
a few weeks. He rang up Esmé one morning to ask rather
timidly if he might borrow hers for business purposes ;
Esmé bit back her first impulse to say crossly that she could
not possibly spare it, and replied instead with sisterly
sweetness : " Of course, Arnie," she added pleadingly,
" do let me drive you about in it."

" Oh, you can't," said Arnold flatly. " How can you ?
You'd have to sit about for hours in the mill yard."

" Sitting about is all I do at home," said Esmé wistfully.
" Rowland's so busy just now. I shall be rather lost without
my car, you know," she hinted.

" Well, bring it down now, anyway," said the harassed
Arnold, ringing off.

Esmé, overjoyed at having something to do—for the omission of the Bierley Green programme made her mornings very empty, and if she showed too much interest in the West View housekeeping her mother was hurt—gladly obeyed. Arnold came out of the mill to greet her ; he was getting rather fatter lately, and looked quite the responsible mill-owner and father. His smile, however, was rather sour.

" Do you think I can't drive your car ? " he demanded. " Is that why you won't trust me with her ? "

Why did people always impute these ungenerous motives to Esmé ! " Really, Arnold ! " she said, vexed. " Of course I trust you ; it's just that it's a nice day and I've nothing to do and was going to take the car out, and so I thought—— "

" Oh, all right," said Arnold, mollified. " Turn her round while I get a hat. We'll go to Bradford."

Esmé accordingly drove him to Bradford. It was delightful to have him all to herself again, talking to her alone as in days gone by. " Why *do* people grow up and marry ? " thought Esmé wistfully. " It's so much happier when you're children." When they returned to Adela Mills, Arnold proposed that she should come up to Oddy Hall and lunch there—she could telephone a message to West View—so that she could run him about again in the afternoon. Esmé accordingly waited for him and ran him up home ; Rachel was very pleasant in welcoming her and thanking her for being of service to Arnold ; after lunch there was an amusing interlude with Charles, who really was rather sweet ; altogether Esmé's heart felt soft and her nerves soothed— there were rewards in keeping one's resolutions and being good, after all.

It was therefore a horrible shock to her when Arnold, having climbed into the car beside her, in a business-like tone bade her drive to Bierley Bottom Mills. Esmé's heart stood still. " Bierley Bottom Mills ? " she repeated faintly. Surely the stars in their courses were fighting against her. " Do you often go there, Arnie ? " she asked, feeling that she must know just how much of a coincidence this was.

St

" Nearly every day," replied Arnold. " Howgate's always writing or telephoning or something."

He sounded a little cross, as though the subject were not a pleasing one, and Esmé did not pursue it. As she drove along she turned over in her mind the possibility of putting Arnold down at Howgate's mill door and then going away. Could she pretend to remember an engagement ? She tried wildly to evolve some story which would sound not too hopelessly improbable, but could think of nothing ; at length she murmured—in that tone of voice which, as Rowland sometimes said, expects the answer " no "— " Shall I wait for you, Arnold ? "

Arnold looked at her in surprise. " Yes," he answered. " It'll be an excuse for me to get away."

" Do you want to get away ? " demanded Esmé in the same tone as before.

" Yes," replied Arnold with conviction. He hesitated, then after a moment observed with a depressed and boyish air : " He's a difficult man to deal with, you know."

" Mr. Howgate ? " queried Esmé, her heart beating fast. Arnold nodded, and they reached the mill gate. " I shan't go into the yard," said Esmé, drawing up to one side of the archway.

" Shan't you ? " said Arnold. He sounded disappointed, but dutifully began to get out, and continued : " All right. I can tell him you're here."

Esmé gave a sharp sigh, and resigned herself to the inevitable. " Perhaps he won't come out," she thought, " then everything will be quite finished." Yes, he would not come out, and that would show that everything was finished : the stars were perhaps fighting for her after all. As she sat there in the sunshine she remembered the other occasion on which she had visited Bierley Bottom Mills ; that day Lena had referred to at the garden-party, when they all got wet and Lena took them to tea at Bierley Hall and then brought them down the hill by a short cut down some steps through the mill yard. It was just after Lena

had been re-introduced into the family circle, an event to
which Esmé mournfully traced all her own subsequent
disasters. She might never have married Rowland if it had
not been for that sudden swift pang of jealousy of Lena.
Yes, it was all due to Lena, thought Esmé ; how she wished
(she thought rather inconsistently) they were all back at
that far-off day, when Arnold and Rachel were only just
engaged, and she herself was flirting with Frank Annison—
not that she wished she had married him ; oh, no ! That
would have been as bad a mistake as Rowland. She
remembered how the others had stood that day admiring
the dray horses, and Howgate had come out and spoken to
them, and she had found it all so irritating and had gone
on. Why had she not looked at him then, alas ! She was at
liberty to fall in love with him then, and she had turned her
back on him and walked away. *Why* had she been such a
little fool ? *Why* had she thrown away her chance of happiness like that ? (For it was useless to deny, sitting here in
front of his big mill, with its slender soaring smoke-stack,
that her only happiness was lodged in Howgate.) Her conscience told her relentlessly that she had walked away from
Howgate because he was Lena's father, and she had kept
away from Bierley Hall because it was Lena's home ; and
Esmé could not endure anything to do with Lena, for
reasons which unfortunately did not bear investigation.
Well ! It was no use thinking of all that now, it was all over
and done with long ago ; she was Rowland's wife now, she
must not allow her thoughts to dwell upon any other man
now ; it was useless to want to be back at that other time
when she visited Howgate's mill. As though to wring her
heart still further by making the resemblance more complete, at that moment a dray drawn by two great horses
came crashing and thundering out of the yard. The glossy
brown beasts lifted up their enormous feet and planted them
vigorously down again with a kind of deliberate but fierce
inevitability, like fate ; their harness glittered dazzlingly in
the hot July sunshine ; they seemed to Esmé the incarnation

of strength and virility, like their master. They turned
towards Esmé and stamped past her in a long crashing roll ;
the driver, a man of about Howgate's age, sat sideways on
the dray, swinging his feet carelessly ; he had a flower in his
cap. Esmé turned and watched them till they reached the
corner of the road and passed out of sight ; a sick longing
was in her heart, tears in her eyes ; out of patience with
herself, she turned back, to find Howgate at her side. A
look passed between them ; Esmé's resistance broke, and
she was wax in his hands.

"You can't sit out here in the sun like this," said Howgate. His tone was light and careless as usual, but gentler
than Esmé had ever heard it. "I shall be a long time with
your brother," he went on. "You'd best come in." He
opened the car door ; without a word Esmé climbed out
and moved beside him through the archway. It was so
dark in the shaded mill yard after the brilliant sunshine
outside that Esmé was dazzled and stumbled up the office
steps ; Howgate took her by the elbow to guide her in.
"You shouldn't have left your sister out in the sun, Deller,"
he said to Arnold, who sat looking hot and uncomfortable
in a revolving chair, fidgeting with some papers. "The
heat's been too much for her. She looks quite pale." He
seated Esmé in a chair which she knew at once was his
own ; a solid enormous affair of mahogany and leather.
"You'll be all right there," he said. He turned to Arnold,
and his voice changed. "Well, shall we go along and look
at that, then ? " he commanded curtly, moving towards
the door. Arnold, looking young and miserable, silently
rose and followed him.

Esmé, thus left alone, sank back with a sigh, and to save
herself from thinking began to look about her. Alfred
Howgate's office was like Bierley Hall, solid and spacious,
with heavy, well-kept furniture. On a kind of dark network
across the two huge windows the words "JOHN HOWGATE"
could be read twice in reverse ; Esmé presumed that John
was the present Howgate's grandfather, and two or three

portraits about the room testified to the continuity of the firm. The large flat table of mahogany and American cloth was strewn with letters and papers, some with snippets of cloth attached, others with large figures scrawled untidily across them in coloured pencil. Esmé picked up one with a stamped heading " JOHN HOWGATE " in scrolled and twirly blue, and read on it, in Alfred Howgate's curt scrawl, that Messrs. John Deller had returned piece No. 384165 in a damaged condition, and he would be glad to see their Mr. Arnold about it. Attached to it by a pin was Arnold's neatly typed sheet rudely denying all responsibility for the damage of the piece in question. Esmé smiled ; how fierce men were with one another ! A man looked in from the outer office and withdrew with apologies; his opening of the door had brought to Esmé's ears the hum of machinery, to her nose the peculiar woolly, greasy West Riding smell. She remembered old days when John Deller had proudly shown his pretty, precocious little grand-daughter over Adela Mills ; she smiled again and somehow felt at peace. This was the atmosphere she understood and was happy in, whereas the mere thought of schools and lesson-books and blackboards made her sick. The door opened again and a typist entered with a cup of tea for her which she said Mr. Howgate had instructed her to prepare ; Esmé sat up and gave her a shrewd and jealous look, for this was a girl in whose society Alfred Howgate spent many hours each week, and Esmé was not going to pretend any longer that that was a matter of indifference to her. She was reassured to find that the girl had an expression like Lena's used to be, lively, but innocent of all desire to attract. Lena ! It seemed strange to reflect that Lena was Howgate's daughter, but stranger still that Esmé had once thought of Bierley Hall as *Lena's* home. Lena now seemed a mere child, an unimportant appendage ; she had faded into the background ; and Arnold and Rachel and Mrs. Deller and (alas !) Rowland, were fading into the background too. Esmé picked up Alfred Howgate's letter again, and after a quick glance about the room, put it passionately to her lips. Voices sounded in the outer office ; she hastily threw the letter down, then on reflection took it up and, holding it with a casual air, began to read it. The writing danced before her eyes ; before it had settled, Arnold and Howgate entered the room.

" Admiring my handwriting, eh ? " demanded Howgate at once, laughing.

" Not at all," replied Esmé with a demure look. " I'm trying to understand the mysteries of the woollen textile trade, that's all."

" Oh, if you want to do that, you'd better come through the mill and see it at first hand," said Howgate rather eagerly. " It's no good on paper."

" I'm afraid we shan't have time to-day," hastily said Arnold, who looked chidden and anxious to be gone. " Come, Esmé."

Esmé obediently rose, and thanking Howgate for the tea, moved towards the door ; the others followed her.

" Come some other day by yourself, Mrs. Rowland," suggested Howgate as they went down the stairs and out towards the car. " Then I'll explain the whole thing to you."

Perhaps it was his use of this name which made Esmé say primly : " I haven't my car just now, so I'm afraid I can't."

Howgate demanded : " Oh, how's that ? " and Arnold, colouring, explained the circumstances. " Well, it is an awkward turn out of your garage, certainly," commented Howgate in a soothing tone. " Joe and Lena say the same thing."

At this Arnold coloured more deeply, and threw out : " Of course I shan't want your car every day, Esmé," in a petulant tone. " I only want it to-morrow. After all, you have the big car, you know," he added reproachfully.

Esmé, perceiving that he was irritated by the slur which must necessarily fall either on his garage or his driving, observed : " Mother is taking Mrs. Avery to tea at Lady Annison's in it to-morrow." She was merely, as she thought,

making an easy social transition from an awkward subject
by introducing the names of people about whom Howgate
must necessarily enquire, but the moment she had spoken
she realised that Howgate might well take her remark as
an invitation, an intimation to him that she would be alone
the next afternoon. Well ! Let it be so, she thought, as
Howgate with his customary casual courtesy and dropped
lids hoped that Mrs. Deller was well ; let it be so. If he
understood it as an invitation, and came to West View
while Rowland was out, let it be so ; let the die be so
cast. Sooner or later, in one way or another, some such
test was bound to come ; let it be to-morrow : it would
be the sooner past. If Howgate did not choose to understand—well, in less than a week from now Rowland and
Esmé would be going away from Hudley for their holiday ;
Esmé's feelings would change, she would be reconciled to
Rowland, and Howgate's chance of her would be for
ever lost. Let it be so. She started the engine ; Howgate,
who was resting his hands on the side of the car, withdrew
them, and said shortly to Arnold :

" Well, you'll remember what we decided."

" Yes, I'll remember," muttered Arnold. " Good
afternoon."

" Good afternoon," said Howgate drily.

Esmé put in the clutch. " Thank you for the tea, Mr.
Howgate," she cried over her shoulder, moving off.

" You're welcome," replied Howgate in a Yorkshire
tone. As he had no hat to take off, he sketched a farewell
wave of the hand ; his eyes met Esmé's, and she was sure
that the morrow would bring him to West View.

" Drive a bit faster, do," urged Arnold peevishly as they
turned the corner. " I thought I was never going to get
away from Howgate in this world or the next."

" You don't like Mr. Howgate ? " enquired Esmé, for
the mere pleasure of continuing to talk about him.

" Like Howgate ? " cried Arnold in capitals. " Me ? No,
I don't like him, damn him."

" He's good at his job and you aren't," said Esmé ruth-lessly.

Arnold turned crimson. " Thank you, Esmé," he said. " That's kind of you. I make your dividends for you, any-way." He was so deeply offended that he could hardly articulate.

Esmé gave him a glance of compassion ; she was sorry for him because she cared so little for his feelings. If How-gate came to see her on the following afternoon the whole world might go hang itself for all she cared. She left her car at Adela Mills for Arnold's use, and walked slowly home through the perfect summer afternoon, dreaming. She felt a bodily sickness for Howgate's presence ; how she was going to live through the long hours without him until the next afternoon she could not tell. Rowland went round to Cambridge Place that evening to help his father with some work, so Esmé sat in the garden dreaming the hours away. She could not read, she could not sew, she could not listen to Mrs. Deller's aimless chatter ; she simply lounged in a chair with her head against a cushion, her eyes wide and her face wistful with expectation, waiting for the day to pass.

The next morning was rather grey, and seemed inclined to turn to rain ; Esmé tormented herself with the fear that if the day proved bad Mrs. Deller would not go to Lady Annison's. She skirmished round the subject with her mother, afraid to approach it too directly lest she should scare Mrs. Deller into saying that she would not go ; at length she extracted an emphatic statement from Mrs. Deller that she wanted to go, was anxious to go, would cer-tainly go ; besides, how could she disappoint poor Mrs. Avery, who had so few pleasures ? Esmé, secretly enrap-tured, pouted and said that *she* didn't want to deprive Mrs. Avery of any pleasure, she was sure.

At length it was afternoon ; Rowland went off to school, Mrs. Deller was at last comfortably packed into the car and driven away. The agony of wondering whether Howgate

would arrive before her mother went, whether he would
arrive after Rowland returned, whether he would not arrive at all, put bands of iron round Esmé's brows. She
trembled with emotion as she changed her frock, and seated
herself by the open window of the drawing-room with some
pretty embroidery on her knee. She hoped she was looking
cool and fresh as she drew out the soft-coloured silks, but she
felt haggard and worn. The hour, the fatal hour, between
three and four o'clock drew on ; he was not coming after
all, thought Esmé, and she felt abased to the earth. Ten
minutes later she was greeting him.

"I thought Lena was here," he said as the maid announced him. "I'm wrong, it seems."

"No, she hasn't been here to-day," said Esmé in an
artificial society tone. They sat down together by the
window ; Howgate was in light grey, with one of his old-
fashioned silk cravats ; he sat with one arm flung carelessly
over the back of his chair, and looked spruce, debonair and
worldly, as usual. The maid withdrew.

"Hot, isn't it ? " said Esmé.

"I shouldn't think you feel hot in that frock," replied
Howgate with a complimentary intonation.

"Do you like it ? " asked Esmé.

"It's well enough," said Howgate, glancing it over with
an experienced eye. Esmé, as usual with him, was left with
nothing to say, and there was a long pause.

"Well, I've come, you see," said Howgate at length in a
quiet casual tone. As the frightened Esmé merely smiled
nervously at this and made no reply, he went on : "That's
what you meant me to do, isn't it ? " He seemed to expect
an answer ; Esmé gave a terrified gasp but could not utter
a word, or indeed decide what she wanted to say. "It's
what you wanted me to do, isn't it, Esmé ? " repeated Howgate in his careless drawl. He caught Esmé's eye ; she felt
compelled to answer him.

"Really, Mr. Howgate ! " she panted weakly.

Howgate slightly laughed, and continued to look at her

with an amused and quizzing air. " Well, now you've got me here," he observed, " what are you going to do with me ? Eh ? " As she was still silent, being in truth afraid of what she had brought upon herself by getting him there, he laughed again heartily, flicked his eyebrow and said : " Eh, Esmé ? "

At this moment a piece of rose-coloured silk blew from Esmé's knee to the ground ; Howgate stooped to retrieve it. " Oh, thank you ! " cried Esmé nervously. " Thank you ! They're so light. They blow so easily. Thank you." Glad of any topic which was not herself or Howgate, and feeling obscurely that Lena's name was a protection to her, she went on : " This is Lena's favourite colour, isn't it ? "

" I believe so," said Howgate carelessly.

" Mr. Howgate," demanded Esmé in a sudden fatal rush of words, " is Lena really your daughter, as people say ? "

" Aye, she's mine," said Howgate calmly.

" Tell me about it," commanded Esmé.

Howgate laughed and coloured slightly. " Not I," he said. " Why should I ? Tell me that, Esmé."

Esmé, panic-stricken, perceived that her long preoccupation with the subject of Lena's birth had betrayed her ; she had thrown down her own defences ; she had admitted to an interest in Howgate's past—and what a past !—which no woman married to another man ought for a moment to have felt. She had exposed herself, given herself away ; she had practically thrown herself at Howgate's feet and told him that she loved him. In a desperate striving to retrieve the situation she cried distractedly : " These silks—they so easily blow—they don't weigh much—what do you think they weigh ? "

" Well, not as much as you, you know," said Howgate teasingly.

" Yes ! I must get back to that light joking tone," Esmé told herself. " It's the only thing to do. And pray how much do you think I weigh ? " she demanded aloud on a coquettish note.

" About seven stone four, I should think," said Howgate consideringly.

" How did you know ? " cried Esmé, startled and humiliated by the accuracy of his guess.

Howgate laughed. " Oh, I'm a good judge of weight," he said. " Used to it, you know."

" Are you ? " panted Esmé. " I'm not. I've no idea how much people weigh, or how old they are, or anything."

At this Howgate smiled, then with a steady look at her said coolly : " I don't think you're as bad a judge of men as you'd like to make out, you know."

Esmé felt that she was lost, and in a last expiring impulse of self-defence demanded faintly : " How much do you think Rowland weighs ? "

" Oh ! " said Howgate in his careless drawl. " Your husband carries a good deal less weight than I do, I should think, Mrs. Rowland Avery."

" Mr. Howgate ! " cried Esmé in an agony at this symbolic utterance. She sprang up, but could not force herself to move away, and stood there, trembling.

" Well, what do you want me to say ? " demanded Howgate, getting up slowly and looking down at her with a great air of reasonableness. " Now you've got me here, what do you want me to say to you, Esmé ? "

The wretched Esmé cast a last despairing glance around her gods to see if there was anything that would save her ; but there was nothing, nobody. Her mother, her brother, her husband, Rachel, her good name, none of them were of the slightest account beside this man who stood there smiling in genuine amusement at her profound distress ; they were mere names ; she would gladly give up everything, everything, to feel Howgate's arms about her and his kisses on her lips. She was lost, and glad to be lost.

" Alfred ! " she wailed, and gave herself to the caresses she so ardently desired.

When Rowland returned from school three-quarters of an hour later, Esmé, who was now alone, said coolly as

she handed him his tea : " Oh, Rollo, what do you think ?
Mr. Howgate came this afternoon. He said he thought Lena
was here."

" Lena ! " exclaimed Rowland. " What an idea ! West
View is the very last place where I should look for Lena."

With as much ease as though she had practised an intrigue for years, Esmé said : " Quite," indifferently, and
dropped the subject. She was sewing, and as she sat with
bent head no doubt made a pretty picture, for she could
feel that her husband was regarding her admiringly from
time to time. She looked up, and their eyes met.

" That's a pretty frock," observed Rowland, smiling.
" Is it new ? "

Esmé slightly shivered, and there was a moment when
she wished with all her heart and soul that the events of
the afternoon were a mere dream, so that she could sit and
talk to her husband with a light heart and a clean conscience. But she looked at Rowland again, and the moment
passed ; alas ! he was not her destiny.

" Yes," she said. " It's new. I'm glad you like it." To
herself she thought : " I'm being as false as hell, and I don't
care. How have I come to this ? " She answered herself
wistfully : " It's because I truly care for him," and her
thoughts flew out across the valley to Bierley Hall and
Howgate.

# CHAPTER XI

# TRIO

The summer holidays came, and then the autumn term ; Mr. and Mrs. Avery left Hudley, Susanna moved to Oddy Hall, and the Cambridge Place house stood empty. Though Lena and Rachel and Esmé all became conscious of a great gap when the Averys were gone, perhaps none of them was able to mourn their absence sincerely, as friends from whom they had nothing to conceal.

For several weeks after her garden-party Lena had gone about feeling very sick, sore and sorry. She went rather often to her mother's grave, and allowed her imagination to play morbidly about the old sordid story. She would have liked to know more details of it, so that she could exonerate her mother and throw the blame on Howgate, but she did not see herself asking either him or Mrs. Preston—who presumably knew them : a thought at which Lena winced—for them. Meanwhile there seemed a shadow over everything, and the world looked a gloomy place, full of baseness. Her holiday with Howgate—another sea trip, which had long been planned, and from which it was practically impossible to recede at the last moment— was a misery. On her return, however, Lena gradually, and chiefly by the aid of Baby Charles, who was now tottering about from chair to chair and clutching at Lena's knees with a smile just like Rachel's, recovered from the shock, to find that life was really the poorer by one item, for the relation between Howgate and herself was quite spoiled. The slight romantic tinge which had coloured it was gone, and had to be replaced at a moment's notice by something different which might have been much finer, but was not, because neither of them seemed in the mood to make it so. Lena was too heartsick and discouraged by this second blow to make the effort, and Howgate seemed cross and preoccupied. He spoke to Lena with more authority than ever before, and this fed the resentment into which his avowal had turned her previous gratitude. They lacked their old ease with each other, and did not find a new intimacy ; Howgate went out more than ever ; indeed Lena hardly ever saw him except at Rachel's, where they were invited together rather often. Owing to these invitations meetings between Lena and the Rowland Averys took place much oftener than Lena liked ; and from each of these meetings she returned with an added grief for Rowland, and an added fury against the soul-destroying pinpricks he had to suffer from his wife, of which Esmé never failed to make an exhibition which Lena found quite maddening. She noticed with a kind of scornful amusement that Howgate on the contrary seemed quite entertained by Esmé. " Yes," she thought bitterly, " Esmé is just the kind of girl my father *would* prefer," and she detested her more every day. Lena was not, therefore, very anxious to meet the Averys ; she would not have minded discussing her misery about her birth with such trusted friends, but she was afraid that if she began to explain how she had learned the fact she would betray to them her conviction that Rowland was not very happy in his wife. Rachel for her part, though ashamed of her own relief, was relieved not to have to deceive her father and mother for Arnold's sake, at close quarters, any longer ; while Esmé was quite heartily glad when Mr. and Mrs. Avery left the town, for she could now cross two people off her list of those from whom the secret of her intrigue must be kept at all costs. It opened another district of Hudley, too, for the little afternoon excursions which Howgate and she so often took in her car ; no longer need they look anxiously about them when they drove up Prince's Road. Not that Howgate ever looked anxiously about ; he was quite terribly and calmly reckless, seemed

indeed never to consider the chances of discovery ; he wrote
letters to Esmé on her summer holiday quite openly, so that
she had some very narrow escapes, indeed would not have
escaped at all but for Rowland's quite absurdly honourable
views about private letters, and when later Esmé suggested
that they might with advantage meet at the empty house
in Cambridge Place, he laughed uproariously, pinched her
cheek and told her she thought she was living in a French
play.

"Well . . ." said Esmé, colouring.

"That's the very way to be found out, as you call it,"
concluded Howgate. "Not that there's anything to find
out yet, as I can see."

Esmé pouted and blushed and laughed, for all through
the glowing weeks of this autumn she was extremely if pre-
cariously happy. She met Howgate often in public ; there
were dinners at Rachel's when she sat next to him, dances
at Rachel's when she had the exquisite pleasure of dancing
one dance with him—not more, for he said contemptuously
that he did not care for these new-fangled dances, and
Esmé agreed that they were silly, as she agreed with everything that he said. She also met him secretly, but not as
often as she wished, because though Rowland was out so
much now that school had begun again, Mrs. Deller was
always at Esmé's side, and Mrs. Deller—probably through
her experiences with Clement Deller, as Esmé reflected
with a pang—had a rather discerning eye for such affairs
as the one her daughter was carrying on. When Esmé
realised the obstacle which her mother provided, which she
did about the beginning of October, she set herself quietly
but ruthlessly to eject Mrs. Deller from her path by a skilful
alternation of fear and cajolery ; she painted the tours
which had marked Mrs. Deller's early widowhood in glowing colours, stressed the bleakness of the Hudley winter,
fussed over a cold which Mrs. Deller conveniently caught,
and frightened Arnold by looking grave and hinting at
specialists for their mother's chest ; finally she let drop a

very slight, extremely delicate, almost impalpable hint that perhaps she might get on better with Rowland if she could be alone with him for a little while again. At this Mrs. Deller in a fluster decided to go to the south of France at once ; Arnold and even more Rachel, to Esmé's irritation, urged her to stay at home till Christmas was over, but the poor lady seemed to feel that she was in the way, and must go at once ; she made arrangements to travel about the middle of November. When Howgate heard of this he remarked that it was rather a shame.

" How do you mean, rather a shame ? " demanded Esmé, concerned.

" To turn your mother out of her own house in winter like that," said Howgate.

" I did it for you," urged Esmé, disconcerted—she had thought he would be jubilant at the removal of this hindrance to their love.

" Oh ! Did you ? " said Howgate sarcastically. " Well, I'm not grateful."

" Don't be so unkind, Alfred," pouted Esmé, weeping a little.

" It's you that's unkind," observed Howgate. " Turning your own mother out of doors in winter like that. You haven't got a heart the size of a pea."

" I *have* ! *You've* no reason to complain of the size of my heart, anyway," cried Esmé, now frankly in tears. " It's you that's heartless—you're not fond of me a bit."

" Oh, yes, I am," returned Howgate grimly. " I'm fonder of you than you deserve, by a long chalk."

This kind of speech somehow repaid Esmé for the feeling of deceit, and the incessant watch upon her words and actions, which her present position entailed. That deceit and watchfulness were necessary was unfortunately made more certain every day, and even with Esmé's utmost care she sometimes made slips which brought anguished blushes to her cheek and made her heart stand still. There was, for instance, the matter of the spelling at the farewell party which

Rachel gave for Mrs. Deller. The Howgates were as usual invited, and as this made an awkward number for bridge, they played instead paper games of various sorts which caused a good deal of hilarity. During one period of the evening and some game or other they all wrote a word which had to be passed on to and used by their next-door neighbour. Arnold having been provided by Lena with a word difficult for his purpose, calmly altered the end of it to suit him, and when hotly challenged by Lena, pretended, as far as his laughter would allow him, that he had really read it so.

" Arnold, how could you ! " cried Lena.

" I always said that Lena's writing was a cross between a spider's web and a jig-saw puzzle," remarked Rowland solemnly, with intent to tease.

(Esmé thought : " That's just like Alfred's.")

" Rowland ! " cried Lena amid the general laughter. " You are too bad, you really are. Besides, I'd printed it."

Amid further howls of laughter Esmé, to keep up the joke and conceal her own thought, said : " Then you must have spelled it wrong."

" *I* spell it wrong ! " cried the indignant Lena. " I never spelled a word wrong in my life."

" Sorry, sorry ! " laughed Esmé. " I thought it was a habit——" She was going to add : " at Bierley Hall," but suddenly remembering herself, stopped, not quite in time. " Of yours," she substituted lamely.

Lena gave her a swift look, then said in a quieter tone : " Well, I vote that Arnold be utterly disqualified for this round."

" Hear, hear ! " boomed Rowland. " I agree. Voting will be by show of hands."

Arnold protested with assumed ferocity against having to suffer for Lena's (alleged) mistake, and it was a few minutes before the incident had quite passed over. Esmé felt wretchedly uncomfortable while it lasted ; what bad

Tt

luck that the subject of writing and spelling had come up, she reflected. But then, with a philosophy which she had only recently begun to acquire, she decided that if it was not writing or spelling, it was horses or the weather or the time which made an awkward subject—when one had a secret it was always in danger, if not from one detail, then from another ; just as, if it had not been silks and weight which had led up to her throwing herself into Howgate's arms, it would have been something else equally trivial ; great feelings used small details rather than were moulded by them. In any case, she thought, throwing the present incident off her mind, nobody had noticed.

But both Rachel and Lena had noticed. Lena, who knew Howgate's deficient spelling so well that it seemed fairly natural to her that other people should know it too, wondered a little, but merely thought that Esmé was making another of her awkward references to the fact that Howgate was Lena's real father, from whom she might be supposed to have inherited this trivial disability. With a passing scornful wonder that the subject should interest Esmé so much, she gave her credit for having faltered and changed her words from a (very unusual) desire not to wound, and passed off the incident as quietly and simply as she knew how. But Rachel's reaction was naturally different. That night as Rachel and Arnold were undressing she remarked with interest to her husband : " Is Mr. Howgate a bad speller, Arnold ? "

" Sometimes he is and sometimes he isn't," replied Arnold judicially. " He never makes a mistake in a textile term, you know."

" But how could Esmé know about that ? " wondered Rachel.

Arnold, having enquired why she wanted to know, thought a little, and then told her that Esmé had once driven him to Bierley Bottom Mills, and while waiting for him in the office had picked up a note of Howgate's to him, to which they had both been referring.

" And was there a spelling mistake in it ? " enquired Rachel dubiously.

" I shouldn't wonder," replied Arnold. " There usually is."

Rachel, conscious of an obscure relief, decided that it was just like Esmé to condemn a person's spelling from a single letter, and dismissed the incident from her mind.

It recurred, however, the following week, the occasion being Mrs. Deller's departure. Mrs. Deller had rather piteously rung up Arnold herself and begged him to take her to London and put her on the boat train ; she was older than she had been, she wept, and had not travelled alone for so long that she had forgotten the knack of it. Arnold of course agreed, went to West View the night before the journey to make the necessary arrangements, and on his return seemed rather unhappy, and said that Esmé was being beastly, as usual, and worrying his mother by contradictory advice about packing. Esmé was already furious with him because he had insisted that the large Deller car should be put down and the chauffeur dispensed with, during Mrs. Deller's absence ; and she now seemed hurt, he said, because Mrs. Deller had not asked Rowland to take her—as though a son-in-law were like a son ! Not of course that Rowland would not have gone with the greatest pleasure, but if Esmé were so keen to be alone with him, why should she want to turn him out so unnecessarily ?

" *Is* Esmé keen to be alone with Rowland ? " demanded Rachel with contempt.

Arnold, who of course was as well aware as his wife of the relations between Esmé and her husband, coloured and threw out jerkily : " Mother seems to think so."

" Arnold ! " cried Rachel in distress. " Is that why she's going ? Oh, I do hope not ! She could have come to us for a while."

" Well, it's too late to do anything now," reflected Arnold. " She's taken her rooms and packed and everything ; she can hardly decide not to go now."

" Then you must tell her she can come to us when she feels she's tired of being in France," urged Rachel.

Arnold promised that he would do so, and Rachel, feeling that she had perhaps not taken quite as much interest in Mrs. Deller's going as she ought to have done, went down to the station next morning to see them off. She thought that her mother-in-law looked unhappy and perplexed ; she wept at leaving Esmé, and seemed hopelessly vague about her luggage and her tickets ; how she would manage the long and not uncomplicated journey alone in this cold weather—there was a dank November fog overhead—Rachel did not know. Drawing her husband aside, she urged him to take his mother down to Dover and see her comfortably on the boat. Arnold nodded, and accordingly Rachel was not surprised to receive a telegram from him later in the day telling her not to expect him back until the morrow. Rachel rang up West View to tell Esmé this ; the maid said that Mrs. Rowland was on her way to Oddy Hall—indeed she was surprised that she was not there already. Rachel thereupon sat down and waited for Esmé, but she did not arrive.

When Arnold returned next day, tired and cross, with the beginning of a cold upon him, Rachel plied him with questions about Mrs. Deller's comfort and safety. He answered shortly and with irritation, and finally burst out :

" It's no use trying to make me say that I think mother will be all right, Rachel, because I don't think so. And I don't think she wanted to go, either ; it's all Esmé."

" Esmé ! " repeated Rachel.

" Yes, I think Esmé wants West View to herself," said Arnold in an angry tone. " That's what I think ; and you know what she's like when she's set her heart on anything. I don't believe mother ever wanted to go at all."

To Rachel, sitting beside him and plying him with food, his words seemed somehow to make another piece of a puzzle which was trying to put itself together in her mind.

Esmé wanting the house to herself, Esmé wanting Rowland
to be away, Esmé not turning up at Oddy Hall when she
had told the maid she was going there, Esmé looking so
much happier lately while Rowland looked as miserable as
ever—yes ! It was like a puzzle, like a *jig-saw*, thought
Rachel with a shudder, suddenly remembering Rowland's
joke, and Lena's writing, and Esmé's remark about spelling,
and the way she stopped and blushed and changed her
words. It all fitted so horribly that Rachel could not believe
it, would not believe it ; yet she lay awake pondering it all
night, and in the morning said to Arnold :

" I suppose that agreement with Mr. Howgate isn't
signed yet ? "

" Of course it isn't signed," said Arnold irritably,
sneezing. " Do you suppose I shouldn't rush home and tell
you if it were ? We'd put the flag up," he added with a sort
of melancholy humour.

Rachel went to him, took the lapels of his coat in her
hands, and putting one knee on the bed so as to bring her
face below the level of his, looked up at him and said very
earnestly : " Arnold ! "

" Well, what's the matter now ? " asked Arnold. He
showed a disposition to kiss her, but she resisted, and went
on seriously :

" *Do try to get that agreement signed soon.*"

" I am trying as hard as ever I can," cried Arnold
irritably. " Don't be unreasonable, Rachel."

" But try specially hard," urged Rachel. " Couldn't you
make some concession, so that Mr. Howgate would want to
sign it, so that it would be greatly to his advantage to sign
it ? "

" I daresay I might," grumbled Arnold. " But would it
be sensible ? Think of Charles."

" I *am* thinking of him ! " cried Rachel. " Oh, do get it
signed soon, Arnold ; somehow or other, by hook or crook,
get it signed *soon*."

Arnold, impressed, promised that he would renew his

efforts—" Though I don't see why you're so fearfully keen on it just now," he said.

Rachel, who did not want to know why she was so fearfully keen on it just now, hoped indeed that she was all wrong and making a complete fool of herself by being so fearfully keen on it just now, kissed him by way of answer. In a few days the weather brightened and a letter from Mrs. Deller relieved their keenest anxieties on her behalf, and Rachel tried to persuade herself—and at times succeeded—that her other anxiety was equally unnecessary.

But about a week later, one bright cold day, Lena arranged to take Rachel over to Bradford in her car that afternoon to buy Charles some new gaiters of a particularly warm kind. Rachel was dressing Charles to go when the telephone rang, and Mrs. Preston explained that Miss Lena had told her to tell Mrs. Deller that they could not have the car that afternoon, but she herself might come round later. Rachel, disappointed and a little perplexed that Lena had not rung up herself, took off Charles's coat again (at which he naturally wept), and sat down to await developments. Presently Lena came in, looking rather hot and very remorseful.

"I *am* so sorry, Rachel," she began breathlessly. "Father suddenly said at lunch-time that he wanted my car; he wouldn't take Joe and the big one, he said Joe was going to wash it down, though it seemed to be the first Joe had heard of it. So I had to drive him down to the mill. And then he made me *leave* the car there, though what use it is to him, seeing he can't drive, I cannot imagine. So my pet can't have his gaiters to-day," she concluded fondly, picking up Charles. "It's a shame, darling. Rachel," she went on, putting her cheek against the child's, "I suppose we couldn't have Arnold's car by any chance? Perhaps he wouldn't mind my driving her for once."

"I'm sorry," said Rachel, suddenly feeling an obscure dismay, "ours isn't running just now. Arnold," she added

with a kind of reluctance, " has got Esmé's for the day, and
gone to Leeds."

" What a pity. You've had bad luck with your car
lately," observed Lena, her voice somewhat muffled by
Charles, who was climbing over her face.

" We need a new one really, but we can't afford it," said
Rachel. She sighed ; but her sigh was not for her lack of a
new car ; somehow the conjunction of Esmé being without
her car and Alfred Howgate forcibly appropriating Lena's
struck a chill into her heart. "Well, we'd better go for a
walk," she said, rising.

" Come and have tea with me," urged Lena.

Rachel agreed ; they dressed Charles, which pleased him
very much, and settled him in his pram ; then pushed him
slowly up the hill from Oddy Hall, and turned along the
road towards Bierley Green. His beautiful clear eyes seemed
to gaze upon all the Bierley phenomena with calm content,
and Lena and Rachel were happy in his happiness. As
they walked along Lena observed idly : " There's a car
coming up Bierley Lane. Look, Charles." She pointed.
" Why ! " she exclaimed, and paused.

" What's the matter ? " enquired Rachel in alarm, her
heart beginning to beat hard in anticipation of the
answer.

" It's *my* car, Rachel ! " replied Lena in an astonished
tone.

They stood still, and watched the car winding up the
zigzags of Bierley Lane. They lost it for a moment as it
passed Bierley Hall, which was hidden from their view by
a bend in the road, then it appeared again on the curve to
the left. It was at a moderate distance, but the day was
clear, and its occupants, who were Alfred Howgate and
Esmé, were plainly visible. A horrible, an absolutely horrible, idea flashed through Lena's mind like lightning, and
left devastation in its train. " Why ! " she thought, " if it
were so—that would be how she knew about the spelling. Oh,
how horrible ! " She flung the idea from her, metaphorically

holding her nose as she did so, but she could not help seeing Joe's surprised face as he said : " Am I, Miss Lena ? " when she observed crossly that she supposed he was washing the big car down that afternoon. Esmé had no car to take her father out in, and therefore her father almost forcibly appropriated hers. Oh, it was horrible ! The car vanished, still moving rapidly, behind the houses of Bierley Green ; Lena and Rachel, as though released from a spell, moved on.

"Rachel ! Did you see who those two were ? " gasped Lena. " Esmé and my father ! " Rachel said nothing, and Lena struggled for her self-control. " Rachel," she went on soberly after a moment, " doesn't that strike you as rather strange ? Father, and Esmé ? "

" Oh, I don't know," threw out the unhappy Rachel. " Why should it ? There's nothing very wicked about taking a girl for a ride in your car, is there ? "

" Then why should father take such trouble to conceal it ? " demanded Lena.

This was unanswerable, and Rachel was silent.

" He wouldn't take Joe, you know," persisted Lena, unfortunately gaining conviction from her own arguments. " It seemed strange at the time, especially as it was so inconvenient for me. I don't like it, Rachel."

Rachel sighed, but said nothing, and they walked on a little way in silence. When they reached the turning into Bierley Lane, Lena laid her hand on the pram and said : " Don't let us go to Bierley Hall, Rachel."

" Why not ? " said Rachel, astonished.

" Because we can't discuss father there," replied Lena.

" Do we need to discuss him ? " enquired Rachel, nevertheless turning the pram.

" Well, I think we do," said Lena soberly.

" I think you're making a great fuss about a very small thing, Lena," lied Rachel. " There are a hundred perfectly natural explanations ; you shouldn't condemn—Esmé—without hearing them."

" I can't help remembering how they always seem to sit together," persisted Lena. " I've noticed before that Esmé and he seem to amuse each other ; I really have noticed it, Rachel. And then father was so strange about the car. And," she added, suddenly struck by this, " why has Mrs. Deller suddenly gone away ? "

" Oh, Lena ! " cried Rachel. She stopped abruptly, afraid to say more ; but she had already given herself away.

" I see you really think as I do," said Lena sadly. " Rachel, shall you tell Rowland ? "

" Tell Rowland ! " exclaimed Rachel in capital letters. " My dear child ! One doesn't tell things like that."

" Of course I don't mean that you should tell him what you've seen to-day," said Lena impatiently. " But you can give a hint, a warning."

The unhappy Rachel, seeing before her all the horrible consequences to Adela Mills if Rowland were to discover an intrigue between Howgate and his wife, murmured faintly : " I can't tell tales of Esmé, Lena. I can't interfere between husband and wife."

" If he were my brother *I* should interfere ! " cried Lena impetuously. " Surely you don't mean to let Rowland go on in the dark and be deceived by those two ? "

" But, Lena," expostulated Rachel, " you rush to conclusions so. There probably isn't anything in it at all."

" Then speak to Esmé, tell her you saw her, and see what she has to say," urged Lena. " Of course it must be done delicately ; I don't mean you must seem to be accusing her. You can do it skilfully."

" I'm no good at such things," murmured Rachel wretchedly.

Lena's brow suddenly cleared. " There's one thing you can do, Rachel, at least," she cried on a note of relief. " You can give up asking us so often to Oddy Hall. Then father and Esmé wouldn't meet so much—just in case there *is* something in it."

Rachel groaned. " I'll think about it, Lena," she promised.

She did think about it, at length, in detail, and from every angle. She knew that she could easily find out by the exercise of a little tact whether Esmé would admit frankly that she had been with Howgate that afternoon, and whether Rowland knew it or not. But Rachel loathed such small diplomacies, and could not—or at least that was the reason she gave herself—bring herself to do it. Whether there was some slight intrigue between Howgate and Esmé was therefore left obscure in Rachel's mind, and so she was not, as she told herself, justified in telling tales of her sister-in-law or seeming to accuse her. But that was not the real reason why she refrained from every course of action which Lena had tried to force upon her. Oh, no ! Rachel knew well enough why she did not let Esmé see that her actions were observed, why she gave no hint to Rowland that perhaps Howgate admired his wife more than he should, why she did not even cease to ask the Howgates to Oddy Hall. Rachel's real reasons were Arnold, Charles, Adela Mills, and that agreement which was yet unsigned. For suppose there *was* something between Esmé and Howgate, and Rachel thus showed that she had discovered it ; then Howgate, hating Rachel for the part she had played, would drop the Dellers utterly, cut them dead— not to mention that Arnold's wild resentment would cause him to do the same to Howgate. And then good-bye to Adela Mills, and Arnold's peace of mind and Charles's future. But if there were *nothing* between Esmé and Alfred Howgate, then there would be a great deal of family un- pleasantness if Rachel took any action ; Esmé would be furious, Rowland miserable, and Arnold vexed with his wife ; Howgate too might possibly come to hear what she suspected him of, and, hating Rachel, would in disgust drop the Dellers utterly, cut them dead. And then good-bye to Adela Mills, and Arnold's peace of mind and Charles's future. It came to this : if there were an intrigue, for

Rachel to speak would bring certain disaster, and she simply could not do it. If there were no intrigue, for Rachel to speak might mean disaster. But then if there were no intrigue, why speak ? So Rachel said nothing ; spoke no word to Rowland, to Esmé or to Arnold ; continued to ask the Howgates to Oddy Hall. Lena's reproachful eyes she avoided ; a reproachful speech or two she cut short by telling her that she, Rachel, was sure there was no need to worry or suspect. It was a lie ; she was far, very far, terribly far from being sure ; but then it was for Arnold and for Charles she lied. If the fates wanted her to be good and noble, then they should not have subjected her to that dreadful torment of her engagement, when the Dellers did not want to let her have Arnold, and she had fought them tooth and nail ; something of the old gentle Rachel had been killed then, and could not be revived now ; now all she cared about was Arnold and Charles, and she would lie and fight to save them.

At the beginning of December Howgate announced that as usual he and Lena were going away for Christmas, this time to a large hotel in Scarborough. Only Arnold and Rachel were present when he made this remark, and Rachel politely said : " How jolly ! "

" You'd better come too," suggested Howgate. " Eh, Arnold ? Why not ? Let's have a lively party."

It seemed such a good sign that he should want Arnold to be with him that Rachel, overjoyed, jumped at the idea. (It was not often that Howgate called Arnold by his first name, and Rachel was pleased at that too.) " Yes, let us go, Arnold ! " she cried.

" What about Charles ? " demanded Arnold, who, as Rachel had sad cause to know, always hung back when he should have come blithely forward, and vice versa. She explained that Susanna could surely look after Charles for three or four days. " Well, then, I should like to go," said Arnold rather wistfully. He loved dances and all such gaieties, and Rachel felt rather conscious that she did not indulge him in them as much as she perhaps ought to.

" Really I think we might," she said, thinking of this and of Howgate and of Lena.

" Then you'll have to write at once," said Howgate, flicking his eyebrow.

" Should I write now, Rachel ? This very minute ? " suggested Arnold with sparkling eyes. " It would be rather a joke. Should I ? "

Rachel solemnly nodded her head, and Arnold gleefully wrote the letter.

A day or two later, when they were having supper at West View, the subject of the Christmas holidays having been somehow introduced (was it by Esmé ?), Arnold naturally spoke of their plans. He had now a tariff of their hotel, with pictures ; and he displayed these with boyish pleasure.

" Oh, I wish we could go ! " cried Esmé. " Rowland, I do wish we could go too. Couldn't we go, Rowland ? It would do you such a lot of good." She smiled at him very sunnily, and added : " I shall treat you to it. There ! "

This allusion to their separate incomes very naturally caused Rowland to say at once that he needed no treating ; he could perfectly well afford it (Rachel knew this was not true), and they would go. He took the booklet from Arnold's hands.

" Of course," objected Arnold dubiously, " it's How-gate's party really, you know. I don't quite know—we should have to ask him."

" Yes, ask him," said Esmé, when the circumstances had been a little further elucidated to her. " I shouldn't think he'd mind."

Something artificial and insincere in the tone of these last words struck cold upon Rachel's heart, and for a horrible moment she wondered whether she and Arnold were being made the tools of a vile conspiracy. But it was too late to draw back now without hopelessly offending Howgate ;

and accordingly the party of six repaired to Scarborough. For when Rachel asked her husband what Howgate had said to Arnold's rather timid mention of the Averys' desire to join them, Arnold replied : " Oh, he just said he didn't mind. He didn't seem too pleased, I thought ; but it's difficult to tell with him." Rachel's heart had sunk low at what might be truth, but might as easily be a piece of acting ; and it sank lower still at Scarborough. When they were all under the same roof there were so many opportunities. " Opportunities for what ? " Rachel asked herself angrily, but she did not venture to answer her own question. The visit, apart from these qualms, was a great success ; Rowland at first said he did not dance nowadays, but that, as Esmé said, was *too* absurd ; and she obliged him to break this vow, if vow it was. Esmé was very charming throughout their stay ; she laughed and sparkled, and was very sweet to all three men and to Rachel ; occasionally she made little hits at Lena, but Lena nowadays, as Rachel reflected with some surprise, was very well able to take care of herself ; she usually managed to turn off Esmé's shafts with quiet composure.

Lena was, as a matter of fact, becoming hardened and tempered by the fires of suffering. Since Rachel seemed to make light of what they had seen that day in the fields, Lena was at first inclined to make light of it too ; but little incidents from the past and present kept combining to make this agreeable process impossible, and the torturing struggle to reconcile what she saw with what she wanted to see recurred almost daily. When Esmé, for instance, showed that she knew the names of both Howgate's animals, Lena could not help remembering that morning when Esmé, meeting Lena in Hudley about half-past twelve, had enquired : " How is your father, Lena ? " rather as though she meant it—and then when Lena returned to Bierley Hall she found Preston subdued and muttering ; the mare had strained a shoulder muscle, and Howgate had been unable to ride that morning. It was not Lena's habit, nor in her nature, to make detailed enquiry as to how her father spent his days, but she could not help noticing that he was rather often absent from the mill for an hour or so during the afternoon, because the mill office rang up Bierley Hall several times to see if he were at home. There were also trifling details about the car, and trifling details about meals and the weather and clothes, which pointed in the wrong direction ; all the minutiæ of daily family life together, in themselves so small, but adding up to so large a total, could not be made to look what they were not, and exposed Howgate's preoccupation to his daughter's eyes now that they were opened to its possibility. Lena could not help noticing, for example, that on one or two mornings when she came down to breakfast there was no post on the table, though she had seen the postman coming down the road. The letters might have been for the kitchen, of course ; Lena naturally did not enquire ; but for the Prestons or Mary, all of whose relations lived in Bierley Green, to have a letter was so unusual as to be almost unknown. At first Lena waited pantingly for some interference from Rachel, or at least some confidence from Rachel to show that she had tried and failed. But none came. Had Rachel disposed of her doubts, or of her conscience ? It was another pleasing problem. Lena could not and would not force a confidence from her friend ; her efforts to invite one were repulsed. At times the whole affair seemed to Lena such an absolute farce, so utterly ironical—especially considering her father's warning to her not to indulge in any " nonsense " with Rowland after his marriage—that she simply could not believe it to be true ; then she had some pleasant hours when she altogether discredited it and was able to be easy with Rachel ; but soon some chance word or look of Esmé's, some pause of Howgate's, some little discrepancy of time in his programme as he described it, would set her on the path of doubt again. And granted that her father and Esmé met privately, how serious was the intrigue ? A mere flirtation on Howgate's part, a mere piece of bad

temper towards Rowland on Esmé's ? Or something more
serious ? Lena did not know ; but she could not credit her
father with any very serious feeling about anything. One
Sunday morning as they were returning from Oddy Hall
together she said to him, with a level glance from beneath
her dark brows :

" You like Esmé, father, don't you ? "

" She's a silly little thing," replied Howgate with a laugh,
" but she knows how to make herself valued."

This did not help Lena much in solving her doubts ; and
all she continued to know was that to be in the society of
Rowland, Esmé and her father was a living death to her.
She had therefore been intensely relieved when, as Christmas approached, Howgate announced that they would
spend it at Scarborough. When a few days later it tran-
spired that the Dellers were going too, Lena shuddered and
metaphorically closed her eyes—she did not wish to see the
fiery abyss which yawned before them all. The next news
was that it had engulfed them : Esmé and Rowland were
also to be of the party. After their first afternoon at Scarborough, when Esmé said she was too tired for a walk, and
Howgate said he was going to have a nap, and nobody tried
to persuade them to change their minds, Lena ceased to
expect interference from Rachel or withdrawal from Esmé ;
and when they returned to Bierley Howgate's sudden passion for early morning riding confirmed all her fears.
Thenceforward Lena lived hourly in the flames and had
no one to whom she could utter one word of her torment ;
she questioned herself with anguish as to her duty, but
found no answer save the old one that she would not be
defeated, would not run away ; and so she waited on and
on for some moment when she could be of use to Rowland
—not that she saw any hope of that. She continued to sing,
to read, to attend meetings, to entertain, to live a sane and
normal life—outwardly, so as not to give Esmé and her
father the satisfaction of having distressed her ; within, all
the forces of her nature seemed to be gathering for some

fearful battle. She noticed herself that her manner was becoming very grave and quiet and her speech rather sardonic —" Rather like my father's, in fact," thought Lena, with a strong sense of life's little ironies. Her relations with Howgate, already uncomfortable, became cold to the verge of hostility ; and she avoided Rachel, for she feared that if they met there would be open warfare between them.

Rachel had returned from Scarborough to find Charles well and flourishing. Arnold too looked well after his holiday, and seemed more cheerful about affairs at the mill ; and one day he came home with the joyous news that Howgate had mentioned the agreement of his own accord, asked Arnold for the document and said it was about time they came to some decision ; Rachel, enraptured, lulled her doubts to sleep and tried to be happy, though she was uneasily conscious of Lena's withdrawal. The weeks passed on ; Howgate said nothing more about the agreement ; snow and ice came and went, tremendous winds followed ; at last a few crocuses, and a kind of purple haze over the Oddy Hall trees, announced that spring in its progress northwards was reluctantly approaching Hudley. Suddenly, in a night as it were, it arrived ; the trees grew thick with bud, and began to unfold delicious light green leaves ; daffodils danced in the garden and short tulips held up their gay heads stiffly ; the sun was quite hot, and Charles took off his gloves and threw them over the pram side. Preston was growing some seedlings under glass for Rachel, and one afternoon she made this an excuse for visiting Bierley Hall without being invited. (Invited ! What a word between herself and Lena !) She was received by Lena in her new manner, which Rachel found very uncomfortable ; they stood side by side for several minutes gazing solemnly at the glass which covered the green shoots without making much progress in the recovery of their former intimacy. When however Charles was taken from his pram and began to totter about with a ball, Lena seemed to unbend considerably, and they were just beginning tea with some cheerfulness when Esmé suddenly burst upon them.

" I've been to Oddy Hall to look for Rachel," she explained, " and they told me she was here. You don't mind my coming, Lena ? "

Lena, in a tone which Rachel thought extremely dry, assured her that she did not mind at all, and rang for an extra cup and saucer and some fresh tea. Esmé was looking charming in one of her exquisitely fresh and neat little frocks, of a blue to match her eyes. " You're looking very pretty to-day, Esmé," Lena told her grimly. " Of course you always do, but what a particularly charming frock ! "

" Thank you for these kind words," said Esmé, laughing. " It was about a frock that I came to see Rachel."

" Don't let me interrupt you," said Lena, as drily as before.

" Mother wants me to take one out to her," explained Esmé, colouring a little at Lena's tone.

" Mrs. Deller ! I didn't know you were going to her," exclaimed Rachel in surprise.

" Didn't Arnold tell you ? " queried Esmé. " What a head that boy has ! Oh, yes, I'm going out the week after next to fetch mother home. And she wants a frock."

She turned to Rachel and explained the matter, which to Rachel did not seem to concern her very much. She was very glad, however, that Mrs. Deller was to come home soon, and in her daughter's care. A thought struck her. " Is Rowland going ? " she asked.

" Oh, no ! " replied Esmé. " It wouldn't be much of a holiday for him, would it ? All that travelling. No, I'm going before the end of the term ; I shall have to begin to be busy with luggage and tickets."

A few moments later she thanked Lena for allowing her to intrude and giving her tea, and departed.

" I'm glad Esmé's going to fetch Mrs. Deller " said Rachel when she had gone, beginning to put on Charles's coat.

Ut

" So am I." said Lena.

" Why, Lena ? " demanded Rachel in surprise.

" Rachel," said Lena after a pause, " you didn't say any-thing to Rowland, or Arnold, or Esmé, after that day in the fields, did you ? You know when I mean ? You didn't say anything, did you ? "

Rachel, colouring, replied shortly : " No."

" I thought you hadn't," said Lena. She was silent for a moment, then went on : " How can you reconcile it with your conscience, Rachel, to aid and abet another man's secret courtship of your brother's wife ? "

" Lena ! " cried Rachel, appalled. " How can you be-lieve such a horrible thing ? Would Esmé have come here this afternoon if it were as you say ? "

" Don't be so simple, Rachel," said Lena sardonically. " Esmé came here this afternoon because she's been with my father, she's just left him ; she called at your house to make an alibi for herself with Rowland, and as you weren't there followed you here. I expect she's told Rowland so often that she called at Oddy Hall and you were out that the story's beginning to wear a little thin. I'm surprised they've been together in the afternoon," she went on mus-ingly. " The early morning is their favourite time now. I rather gather that Rowland sits up to the early hours read-ing, then sleeps rather late. Isn't that so, Rachel ? "

" Lena ! " muttered Rachel, too stricken to say more.

" Well, you wouldn't do anything to stop it," said Lena in a hard tone. " What did you expect ? " Rachel silently continued to dress Charles, and Lena went on drearily : " Perhaps it may all come right yet, as Esmé is going away. But I warn you, Rachel, if it goes on again when Esmé comes back from France, I shall tell her what I think of her and then leave Bierley."

" What right have you to interfere ? " cried Rachel in anguish, " What business is it of yours ? "

" What, indeed ! " said Lena drily. " The Averys are friends of mine, that's all."

Rachel picked up Charles and walked out of the room. The child's perambulator stood in the porch ; while Rachel was strapping him in Lena appeared, and watched her, looking very grave and pale. At length the last strap was buckled and the pram cover with the white rabbits which Lena had worked was in place ; Lena stooped down and kissed Charles, and Rachel wheeled him slowly away.

When she reached Oddy Hall, Susanna, who admitted her, informed her that Mr. Deller was already in. Sure enough Arnold came flying out of the drawing-room to greet her, his face flushed, his hair rumpled, an immense joy on his boyish face. He seized Charles and kissed him frantically, then putting him down took Rachel in his arms and shouted : " It's all right, Rachel, everything's all right. The agreement ! "

" What ? Not *signed* ? " cried Rachel loudly.

Arnold nodded so violently that it seemed as though his head must come off, and crushed his wife in his arms again. " This afternoon—just now—Howgate rang up to say come along at once—I dropped everything and flew," gasped Arnold triumphantly, as though this were a piece of mar-vellous wisdom on his part. " It's signed." He hugged Rachel to him and kissed her cheek in an ecstasy. " It's signed," he said, his voice breaking with joy.

" This is what I've sold Rowland's happiness for," thought Rachel, for she now in a flash perceived that from this time onward, if any family quarrels arose, Arnold and Arnold's wife would be obliged to take Howgate's side. " What have I done ? " thought Rachel in an agony of remorse, her head on Arnold's shoulder. " What have I done ? " Here Charles, very naturally considering himself neglected, set up a loud cry. Rachel looked down at him. His fair childish face was contorted into a mask of wounded pride, and he had squeezed out two or three real tears, which rolled pathetically down his round rosy cheeks. Rachel, freeing herself from Arnold's arms, picked up her son and held him to her breast. " There, there ! " she said, patting his back and swaying slightly on one foot to impart a soothing motion to the weeping child. " My darling ! Don't cry ! " To herself she thought : " I don't care. I'm glad I did it. Rowland must look out for himself." Aloud she said : " You didn't tell me Esmé was going out to fetch your mother home, Arnold."

" First I've heard of it," replied Arnold cheerfully—it was easy for him to be cheerful now.

Lena, who regarded their quarrel of the afternoon as a final breach with Rachel, was naturally rather silent and preoccupied that evening, and when she rose at last to go to bed her father called her back.

" What is it ? " demanded Lena in the cold reserved tone which was now habitual with her.

" Do you know you haven't spoken one word to me since eight o'clock ? " said Howgate roughly. " I'll tell you what it is, Lena ; we don't seem to get on as well together as we used to do, somehow."

He seemed to expect some reply to this, and Lena, controlling her contempt, said : " No ? " with as cool and indifferent an air as she could manage.

" So we'd best separate," continued her father. " I'll arrange some money for you, and you can go and stay with the Averys till you decide what to do."

" Oh," said Lena in the same non-committal tone.

" Doesn't that suit you, eh ? " demanded Howgate pleasantly. " You shan't lack for money, you know. Think it over, Lena, and let me know in a day or two what you decide. It's no good going on being uncomfortable like this. Think it over."

" Very well," said Lena composedly. " I will."

She went upstairs to her room quietly, but she raged within. So it had come to that ! He wanted to get rid of her so that he could have Bierley Hall free for his purposes with Rowland's wife ! Well, he should not have it, he should *not*, thought Lena furiously to herself, almost grinding her teeth in the intensity of her emotion. She thought of Rowland,

good, honest, decent Rowland, Rowland who used to have
such a jolly smile and be full of fun and laughter, and who
now looked so weary and old and sad, Rowland who was so
passionately fond of Esmé, Rowland who had never intentionally hurt anybody in his life. She thought of Mr. and
Mrs. Avery and their immense enduring kindness to her,
she thought of poor old Thomas Deller, whom she had hurt
as Esmé was hurting her husband now, she thought again
of Rowland, Rowland as he had looked that day she first
went to Cambridge Place, lively and jolly, with his deep
booming voice and his agreeable, young man's conceit,
Rowland who had told her that she ought to learn to sing.
No ! Lena would *not* go away and leave Alfred Howgate a
free hand with Rowland's wife ; she would not, she would
*not* ; she would stick on at Bierley Hall, she would contrive,
even more than she had hitherto contrived, to be constantly
in their way, to dog their footsteps, to cling to them like a
burr ; and, moreover, since some innate repulsion forbade
Lena to tell tales, as Rachel called it, of Esmé to her husband or her brother, she would tell Esmé herself, face to
face, what she thought of her, as she had warned Rachel
that she would. But she would not leave Bierley Hall at
Alfred Howgate's bidding. No ! Never ! Not even if he
told her plainly why he wanted her to leave. He would have
to invoke the aid of the law to get her out ; if he dared do
that, then let him. Lena looked at herself in the glass as she
brushed her hair, and saw the face of a powerful, determined and mature woman. " He won't easily get the better
of me now," she thought with a fierce satisfaction. " I've
been through too much these last two years to care for
anything he says. I won't go."

For a few days the subject of her departure was not
mentioned, but there came a moment when Howgate
looked up from his newspaper and observed amiably :
" I've been fixing up that money for you, Lena. Have you
decided when to go to the Averys ? "

Lena replied : " I'm not going."

" Not going ! " repeated Howgate in an angry tone.
" What do you mean ? "

" I mean I'm not going," said Lena quietly. " I don't
want to leave Bierley Hall."

" You'll find it best to do as you're told, I think," said
Howgate, ominously calm. " You can send a telegram to
Mrs. Avery, and go the day after to-morrow."

" I'm not going," said Lena. Howgate gave her a furious
look ; Lena met his eyes steadily. " I'm not going," she
repeated. " Stay, then ! " shouted her father. Immediately regaining his temper and dropping his voice, he
added in his usual nonchalant tones : " It's nothing to me
one way or the other." He laughed. " Stay if you like," he
said.

His tone was ironical, but Lena stayed ; and during the
next week accordingly spent some of the most wretched days
of her life. She did not see Esmé, and would not see Rachel,
who indeed at first made no attempt to see her, neither
calling nor writing nor ringing up. An atmosphere of
brooding suspense hung over Bierley Hall ; Lena felt
that things could not continue as they were, but did not see
from what quarter any change could come, unless it were
from Rowland's discovery of the intrigue. She saw no way
out from stormy misery for all of them, unless indeed Esmé
could change her mind and love Rowland again, which
did not seem very likely. Howgate went about during this
period with a satisfied and amused air which puzzled Lena,
for as far as she could make out he did not see Esmé at
all. He seemed very busy, and spent long hours at the
mill. Once he came home and said that Arnold had asked
them to go to Oddy Hall to dinner on a certain night. " I
shan't go," he said, " I'm too busy ; but you can if you
like."

" I'm afraid I can't," said Lena, hastily inventing an
engagement.

Her father looked as surprised at her refusal as she was
by his own. Was he perhaps beginning to tire of Esmé, she

wondered ? If so, and if only they could gradually move apart without discovery, what a tremendous blessing that would be for all the three families concerned. Again Howgate came home with an invitation to Oddy Hall ; this time it was for luncheon on the following day. " I told Arnold you would go," he said. " But I'm not sure about myself ; I'll drop in if I can. Tell them not to wait for me."

Lena, rather perplexed as to what she ought to do, said nothing, and allowed him to suppose that she would go. She had felt that her quarrel with Rachel was final, and their disagreement too profound ever to permit of recon-ciliation ; but she could see that if she took up that attitude an explanation with her father as to its motive was sooner or later inevitable, and she was not sure that she wanted to have to tell him what she thought about his behaviour with Esmé just yet. There was still hope ; Esmé would be going away in a few days now, perhaps had already gone ; perhaps her absence explained Howgate's indifference to Oddy Hall invitations, or perhaps they had determined to break off their relations and this was the first step towards doing so. Lena, troubled and uncertain, now began to understand the difficulties of Rachel's position more clearly, for she felt afraid to act decisively lest her action should provoke unnecessary evil. In this mood she decided to lunch at Oddy Hall, and having put on a light frock and coat, set out across the fields to do so. It was a glorious day, hot and bright ; all the neat little rows of houses on the opposite side of the valley stood out clear and distinct. " I ought to be enjoying this," thought Lena. " Alas ! " Her steps grew slower and slower, and at last ceased ; she felt more and more revolted by such a paltry compromise with her conscience, such a petty act of submission to everything she loathed, as was this accepting of the hos-pitality of Oddy Hall in the present situation. The luncheon might well be a kind of farewell party for Esmé ; Esmé would be there, Rowland would be there, Rachel would be there, Howgate would be there. Was she to sit at the same table with those four, and conceal what she knew, and so help Esmé and Howgate in their concealment ? Was she to abet Rachel in keeping her brother in the dark ? Hateful phrase ! Lena felt suddenly that she simply could not stomach it ; the thought of it induced a physical revolt. She turned round abruptly and retraced her steps to Bierley Hall.

The large car stood by the front door. Lena's heart rather sank, for this meant that her father was within the house. She crossed the road towards it in a preoccupied way, wondering what she ought to say to him, and it was not until she was barely two yards from the car that she saw Esmé crouching in the back seat, with the rug drawn up about her as if to conceal her face. The sight of her was a trumpet call to Lena ; this was the moment she had so long been waiting for ; without stopping to think she sprang vehemently forward, and grasping the frame of the open window with both hands, bent her head and looked fiercely in.

" Esmé," she said clearly, " I'm glad to see you ; I'm glad to have this opportunity of telling you how much I despise you." Esmé exclaimed and shrank back ; Lena bent towards her and went on inexorably : " If you really love my father, as I suppose you think you do, why don't you admit it openly and take the consequences, instead of hiding about in cars in this contemptible fashion ? "

" We *are* admitting it openly," cried the wretched Esmé in her high, shallow little tones. " We're going away openly together to-day."

" You're going away together ! " repeated Lena, astounded. She now perceived that several pieces of hand luggage were bestowed about the car, and the luggage carrier in the rear stood open.

" And after the divorce we shall be married," explained Esmé with a little air of triumph.

" Oh ! " cried Lena. " After the divorce you'll be

married ! I see ! And what about Rowland's heart that you've broken meanwhile ? " All the bitter griefs which Esmé had caused Lena, her cruelty as a child, her rough jeering at Lena's birth, her capture of Rowland's love and her trampling down of this that Lena valued more than life, suddenly flamed in Lena ; she remembered every biting, wounding little sentence she had ever heard Esmé say ; she remembered that day of the garden-party, and how she had vowed to hurt Esmé with words if ever she could, she remembered Rowland's sad look and weary voice : it all surged up in her in a fiery, angry flood, so that the blood swam before her eyes and her whole body trembled and her heart beat so fast that it nearly choked her. She clenched her hands, and gathered all her wits together and put them to the task of finding the bitterest, the most wounding thing she could possibly say. She found a verbal weapon ready to her hand, and she struck hard. " I can't think why my father should take the trouble to marry you," she said coolly. " Surely it isn't necessary ? Unless of course it's because one illegitimate child is enough for him, and he doesn't want another."

Esmé turned pale and burst into tears.

" Oh, Esmé ! " cried Lena, springing forward. " I'm so sorry, I'm so *sorry*. I do beg your pardon. Please forgive me for insulting you."

" How do you mean, insulting me ? " quavered Esmé, dabbing feverishly at her wet cheeks. " Don't be so *silly*, Lena ; it's true."

" True ! " cried Lena, bounding back. " True ! Oh, Esmé ! " Trembling with indignation, she threw out in a loud sardonic tone : " And I suppose you've left a note on the pincushion for Rowland ? Have you ? "

Esmé gulped, but answered : " Yes—at least, it was in the hall."

" To tell him *that* ? " cried Lena wildly. " Esmé ! "

" I didn't tell him quite everything," faltered Esmé. She gave a quick look towards the Hall. " Oh, Lena, if

Alfred comes out and finds you here he'll be so angry," she wailed. " He thinks you're at Rachel's ; he arranged for them to ask you there, on purpose. Do please go."

" Oh, I'll go ! " cried Lena. " Don't be afraid ; I'll go ! Which way are *you* going ? Down Bierley Lane ? "

" No," murmured Esmé plaintively. " We're going up the hill to avoid Hudley."

" Then I'll go *down* the hill," said Lena emphatically ; and away she flew. She had barely gone two hundred yards when the sound of the engine starting came to her ears ; she turned and shaded her eyes ; she could not at first see the car, for it was in the Bierley Hall bend, but in a few moments it appeared higher up ; Joe was driving ; Howgate and Esmé sat behind ; as she looked her father leaned forward to pull up the window.

" Well, they're gone ! " said Lena.

She retraced her steps to Bierley Hall, where Preston and his wife surveyed her with curious and pitying looks, got out her car and drove as fast as she could towards West View.

" Life's very odd," thought Lena as the car bounded down Bierley Lane : " Here am *I* rushing towards Rowland, *I* think his love is the most desirable thing in the world, and I detest and despise my father ; while Esmé detests Rowland so much that she can't bear to live with him, and she adores my father—I can see she does. *I* think she's the most detestable little thing who ever lived, and has behaved abominably throughout ; and I expect she makes out an excellent case for herself—thinks she's an absolute martyr and a noble soul. Rachel has her point of view too, I expect—poor Rachel—and in every one of those thousands of houses across the valley there are three or four people, each seeing things in his or her own particular little way, and not understanding how anybody else can possibly see things differently. And all their lives are interwoven with each other just as Esmé's and Rachel's and mine are. Yes, life is very complicated and very strange."

She crossed the bridge and turned up the hill, and presently passed the Grammar School. It was of course the
lunch hour, and all was quiet and still, except for two or
three belated masters and boys who were walking home-
wards; she stopped and asked one if Mr. Avery were there,
and was told that he had set off home some half-hour
before. Lena drove on again; a curious feeling of having
done all this before came over her, and as she passed the
corner where the Hudley Girls' College used to be, she remembered in detail the day when she ran away from school.
" What a morbid, miserable little thing I was then ! "
thought Lena. " Really Esmé has a good deal to answer
for." But even as she thought this she was suddenly glad,
immensely, overpoweringly glad that Esmé had been so
detestable to her, had made her suffer so much humiliation. Because Esmé had so deeply wounded her self-esteem,
Lena knew just how one felt when one's self-esteem was
deeply wounded; she knew how one suffered, what made
the suffering worse, and what soothed one's bruised feelings, revived one's courage, enabled one to hold up one's
head and carry on the fight. Oh, she knew it, she knew it
all; she was made to be a comforter, Esmé had made her
into a comforter; and she was glad, a thousand times glad,
for Rowland's sake. Rowland would be in the abyss, Rowland would be feeling that he must indeed be a poor creature, for his wife, on whom he had lavished all the treasures
of his love, had left him for a man nearly twice his age.
Rowland would be feeling as Lena had felt in the little bedroom with three beds and two jugs at the top of the Hudley
Girls' College; despised, unwanted, worthless, and alone.
What one wanted to be told when one felt like that was just
that one was not unwanted, not despised; and Lena could
tell Rowland that. She could explain to him that though
Esmé did not love him, she, Lena, loved him and had always loved him, admired him more than any man she had
ever seen, prized him above everything on earth. Oh, it was
all so easy, so easy, thought Lena; she laughed to think how

easy it was, found that she was laughing her " well-known "
laugh, which had not been heard since Rowland's marriage,
thought of Rowland and grew sober again. (" If only I can
catch him before he shoots himself or something," she reflected, pressing the accelerator.) But it could all be so
easy ; Rowland could leave Hudley, and get a job somewhere in the south of England, and Mr. and Mrs. Avery
could go and live near him, so that Mrs. Avery would not
after all lose both her children. Rachel, alas ! reflected Lena
sadly, Rachel was lost for always ; Arnold tied her to Esmé,
and Arnold's business seemed somehow to tie them both to
Howgate. The Dellers must be left to Alfred Howgate and
his wife, and Hudley and Lena's beloved West Riding hills
must be left to Alfred Howgate and his wife. But Lena
would go to the Averys at Bournemouth—Howgate had
himself suggested it, so he could not object—and Rowland
could find a new post in some agreeable warm place a long
way from Hudley ; and then when the divorce suit (un-
defended, of course) was over, Lena and Rowland could
marry, and the Averys could come and live beside them.
Lena was not in the least afraid of arranging Rowland's
future in this way ; as long as he was strong and happy she
would not have dared, would not have thought it right, to
thrust herself unasked upon him ; but now he was wretched,
weak, defeated, alone : he needed her, and she had not the
slightest compunction in joining his life to hers.

She reached West View, flew up the steps, rang the bell
and walked in. A flurried maid, with the scared look common to members of households upon which calamity has
fallen, came out of the dining-room and stammered that
Mr. Avery was in his study. Mrs. Avery, she added, was
not in ; she had left a note. . . . Her voice trailed off into a
horrified whisper. Lena brushed past her and entered the
room.

Rowland was huddled in an easy chair by the hearth,
gazing fixedly at Esmé's note, which he held between his
fingers. His face wore a leaden pallor ; his dark eyes seemed

to have sunk into his head ; as Lena came into the room he
turned on her a ghastly look of defeated love and pride.

Lena knelt down beside him and put her arm about his
shoulders.

" Rowland, my dear, my dear," she began.

THE END

# CEDRIC CHIVERS LTD.
## PORTWAY, BATH
### ENGLAND

## PORTWAY REPRINTS

### STOCK TITLES AVAILABLE FROM THE ABOVE

## Non-fiction

| | |
|---|---|
| p, W.A. | WINGED WARFARE |
| , William | HOME IS THE SAILOR |
| as, Neville | DAYS IN THE SUN |
| ett, William | COTTAGE ECONOMY |
| J. Wentworth | GHOSTS AND WITCHES |
| ett, Alastair M. | IT'S TOO LATE IN THE YEAR (originally published as "Quest by Canoe: Glasgow to Skye") |
| onds, Charles | A SUBALTERN'S WAR |
| s, A.J. | THE ESCAPING CLUB |
| Bernard | OLD Q.'S DAUGHTER |
| ly, Ida | A WILTSHIRE CHILDHOOD |
| ons, Floyd | RED KNIGHT OF GERMANY |
| s, Philip | REALITIES OF WAR |
| gh, General Sir Hubert | THE FIFTH ARMY |
| Sir Basil Liddell | A HISTORY OF THE WORLD WAR 1914-1918 |
| , Christina | HAUNTED ENGLAND |
| on, Allan | SUFFOLK YESTERDAYS |
| s, Jack | GIVE ME BACK MY HEART |
| s, Jack | UNFINISHED JOURNEY |
| s, Jack | ME AND MINE |
| e, George | BECAUSE IT IS THERE |
| efield, John | THE BATTLE OF THE SOMME |
| nann, Major Georg Paul | THE GERMAN AIR FORCE IN THE GREAT WAR (translated by J.E. Gurdon) |
| , Harry | THE MOST HANUTED HOUSE IN ENGLAND |
| e, Harry | THE END OF BORLEY RECTORY |
| per, Joseph | LESS THAN THE DUST |
| er, Bram | FAMOUS IMPOSTORS |
| es, Sewell | ISADORA DUNCAN |
| gye, Derek | TIME WAS MINE |
| gye, Derek | WENT THE DAY WELL |
| e, Lillian de la | ELIZABETH IS MISSING |
| lant | RICHTHOFEN - RED KNIGHT OF THE AIR |
| lant | GERMAN WAR BIRDS |
| ers, Alan | SONS OF SINDBAD |
| Richthofen | THE RED AIR FIGHTER |

# Fiction

| | |
|---|---|
| Ainsworth, W. Harrison | GUY FAWKES |
| Aldington, Richard | DEATH OF A HERO |
| Aldington, Richard | ALL MEN ARE ENEMIES |
| Anderson, Verily | SPAM TOMORROW |
| Anthony, Evelyn | CURSE NOT THE KING |
| Anthony, Evelyn | IMPERIAL HIGHNESS |
| Anthony, Evelyn | VICTORIA |
| Arlen, Michael | MEN DISLIKE WOMEN |
| Arnim, Von | ELIZABETH AND HER GERMAN GARDE |
| Ashton, Helen | DOCTOR SEROCOLD |
| Ashton, Helen | FOOTMAN IN POWDER |
| Ashton, Helen | SWAN OF USK |
| Ashton, Helen | FAMILY CRUISE |
| Barke, James | THE LAND OF THE LEAL |
| Barke, James | THE SONG OF THE GREEN THORN TRE |
| Barke, James | THE WELL OF THE SILENT HARP |
| Barke, James | THE WONDER OF ALL THE GAY WORL |
| Barke, James | BONNIE JEAN |
| Barke, James | THE GREEN HILLS FAR AWAY |
| Barke, James | MAJOR OPERATION |
| Benson, R.H. | LORD OF THE WORLD |
| Benson, R.H. | COME RACK COME ROPE |
| Bentley, Phyllis | A MODERN TRAGEDY |
| Bentley, Phyllis | THE PARTNERSHIP |
| Bentley, Phyllis | LOVE AND MONEY |
| Besant, Walter | DOROTHY FORSTER |
| Birmingham, George A. | THE INVIOLABLE SANCTUARY |
| Birmingham, George A. | GENERAL JOHN REGAN |
| Blackmore, R.D. | MARY ANERLEY |
| Blain, William | WITCH'S BLOOD |
| Blaker, Richard | MEDAL WITHOUT BAR |
| Bottome, Phyllis | MURDER IN THE BUD |
| Brophy, John | ROCKY ROAD |
| Brophy, John | GENTLEMAN OF STRATFORD |
| Brophy, John | WATERFRONT |
| Broster, D.K. | A FIRE OF DRIFTWOOD |
| Broster, D.K. | THE WOUNDED NAME |
| Broster, D.K. | SHIPS IN THE BAY |
| Broster, D.K. | SEA WITHOUT A HAVEN |
| Broster, D.K. | CHILD ROYAL |
| Broster, D.K. & Taylor, G.W. | CHANTEMERLE |
| Broster, D.K. & Forester, G. | WORLD UNDER SNOW |
| Buchan, John | GREY WEATHER |
| Buchan, John | WITCH WOOD |
| Buck, Pearl S. (trans.) | ALL MEN ARE BROTHERS (SHUI HU CHUAN) (in 2 volumes) |
| Buck, Pearl S. | FIGHTING ANGEL |

| | |
|---|---|
| Keyes, Frances Parkinson | ALL THAT GLITTERS |
| Keyes, Frances Parkinson | IF EVER I CEASE TO LOVE |
| Keyes, Frances Parkinson | CAME A CAVALIER |
| Keyes, Frances Parkinson | FIELDING'S FOLLY |
| Keyes, Frances Parkinson | LARRY VINCENT |
| Keyes, Frances Parkinson | HONOR BRIGHT |
| Keyes, Frances Parkinson | LADY BLANCHE FARM |
| Keyes, Frances Parkinson | CHRISTIAN MARLOWE'S DAUGHTER |
| Keyes, Frances Parkinson | THE GREAT TRADITION |
| Kirkham, Nellie | UNREST OF THEIR TIME |
| Knight, Eric | THIS ABOVE ALL |
| Knight, L.A. | CONQUEROR'S ROAD |
| Knight, L.A. | DEADMAN'S BAY |
| Knight, L.A. | JUDGMENT ROCK |
| Knight, L.A. | THE BRAZEN HEAD |
| Knight, L.A. | THE VIKING FEAST MYSTERY |
| Knight, L.A. | HIGH TREASON |
| Knight, L.A. | THE DANCING STONES |
| Kyle, Elizabeth | THE PLEASURE DOME |
| Lawrence, Margery | MADONNA OF THE SEVEN MOONS |
| Lawrence, Margery | NUMBER 7 QUEER STREET |
| Lewis, Hilda | PENNY LACE |
| Lewis, Hilda | BECAUSE I MUST |
| Lewis, Hilda | THE DAY IS OURS |
| Lewis, Hilda | STRANGE STORY |
| Lewis, Hilda | I, JACQUELINE |
| Lewis, Hilda | WIFE TO HENRY V |
| Lindsay, Philip | PUDDING LANE |
| Lindsay, Philip | THEY HAVE THEIR DREAMS |
| Lindsay, Philip | LOVE RIDES TO BUTTERMERE |
| Lindsay, Philip | HERE COMES THE KING |
| Lindsay, Philip | LONDON BRIDGE IS FALLING |
| Lofts, Norah | REQUIEM FOR IDOLS |
| MacDonnell, A.G. | HOW LIKE AN ANGEL |
| MacGill, Patrick | CHILDREN OF THE DEAD END |
| MacGill, Patrick | MOLESKIN JOE |
| MacGill, Patrick | THE RAT PIT |
| Mackenzie, Compton | POOR RELATIONS |
| Mackenzie, Compton | THE PASSIONATE ELOPEMENT |
| Mackenzie, Compton | EXTRAORDINARY WOMEN |
| Macpherson, Ian | SHEPHERD'S CALENDAR |
| Macpherson, Ian | LAND OF OUR FATHERS |
| Macpherson, Ian | PRIDE OF THE VALLEY |
| Macpherson, Ian | HAPPY HAWKERS |
| Macpherson, Ian | WILD HARBOUR |
| Marton, Francesca | ATTIC AND AREA |
| Masefield, Muriel | SEVEN AGAINST EDINBURGH |
| Maturin, Henri | MELMOTH THE WANDERER (3 volumes) |
| Meredith, George | DIANA OF THE CROSSWAYS |